"You're beautiful, Anna."

She felt a sudden fluttery panic. "Fancy talk," she said, attempting a laugh. "It comes cheap to an Irishman."

His lips touched her temple, her brow. "You promised," she said faintly. "We had an agreement."

"Did we?" He eased her back into the curve of his arm. She didn't resist. He was so careful, so slow, there was nothing to fight.

Stephen lifted her chin, and an expression came over his face that was so deep and hungry that it went straight to Anna's heart. She felt a sudden shift of feeling, a light breathlessness, a swift tug of yearning . . .

FROM THE ACCLAIMED AUTHOR OF
***SEA OF DREAMS* COMES A DAZZLING STORY**
OF LOVE IN A WORLD OF
DREAMERS AND FIGHTERS . . .

Touch of Lace

Praise for *Sea of Dreams*
by Elizabeth DeLancey:

"*SEA OF DREAMS* IS A DREAM COME TRUE . . . FRESH AND ENTERTAINING . . . EXCELLENT."

—*Romantic Times*

"A COMPELLING STORY, TOUCHING EVERY HUMAN EMOTION—PASSION, JEALOUSY, HATE, SUSPICION, DECEIT, AND INTRIGUE. THIS BOOK IS MORE THAN A MOVING LOVE STORY . . . I HIGHLY RECOMMEND *SEA OF DREAMS*."

—*Rendezvous*

Diamond Books by Elizabeth DeLancey

SEA OF DREAMS
TOUCH OF LACE

Touch of Lace

Elizabeth DeLancey

D

DIAMOND BOOKS, NEW YORK

This book is a Diamond original edition,
and has never been previously published.

TOUCH OF LACE

A Diamond Book / published by arrangement with
the author

PRINTING HISTORY
Diamond edition/June 1993

ISBN: 1-55773-851-3

Diamond Books are published by The Berkley Publishing Group,
200 Madison Avenue, New York, NY 10016.
The name "DIAMOND" and its logo
are trademarks belonging to Charter Communications, Inc.

PRINTED IN THE UNITED STATES OF AMERICA

10 9 8 7 6 5 4 3 2 1

To my parents, Mildred and Al,
for the lives they led
and the tales they told.

And, as always, for Jimmy.

Prologue

Guardian Island, New York
September 1857

The mob, more than a thousand strong, gathered shortly before
noon. They spilled ashore from a flotilla of paddle steamers
out of New York's Catherine Dock and swarmed onto the
sun-filled meadow just below Fisher's Hill. For the most part,
they were city men: flash sportsmen, sleek-haired politicians,
shirt-sleeved workingmen, uptown gents indulging their taste
for violent amusement. Among the dark coats and checked
suits, a scattering of gaily plumed women stood out like the
last petals of summer.

The fight had been called for one o'clock. By half past two
the impatient crowd, sweating in the Indian summer heat, had
trampled the island's field to a muddy ruin. Dying cigars and
half-eaten sandwiches littered the ground. Careless bootheels
crushed whiskey bottles to shards of glass. Having made their
wagers and drunk their whiskey, the men fingered their bank-
rolls and complained about the delay.

At the far side of the meadow, where the ground lay flat as
a drawing room floor, a gang of bare-armed toughs spaded
twenty-four square feet of earth into soft, comfortable turf.
With cudgels, they pounded eight pine billets into the ground
and connected them with two lines of rope. A second ring,

about fifty feet across, was erected around the first. When the last stake was driven and the last rope tied, a sweating roustabout approached two young men, garbed in hot broadcloth and wilting stock.

"It's done, then," the roustabout said. "Tell the lads it's time."

The young men hurried off in different directions to deliver the message. One of them ran down the hill, away from the mob, his black coattails flapping. At the bottom of the slope, he raced toward a rock-strewn point where a broad-backed, muscular man paced a patch of sand.

"Stephen! Stephen! It's time."

Stephen Flynn glanced in the direction of the shout. The sight of Emmet Cavanagh running across the grass brought on a heavy feeling of dread. It was time. Stephen looked back at the sunny blue water of Long Island Sound and thought how peaceful it was on this breezy point of land. He could stand here all day, watching the white-capped waves, listening to the gulls. The point was far from the mob's commotion, a good spot for a man to think about his future.

But Stephen knew he'd have no such thoughts until he finished the business at hand. He had to climb the hill and fight a match he didn't want, for money he didn't need, for acclaim he no longer sought. He'd fought nineteen prize battles in his time, each one a victory. Today he doubted the outcome.

"Stephen!"

Stephen ran his hands over his closely shorn hair and turned to his friend. "So, Emmet, you've come for me at last."

Sweat dampened the dark hair at Emmet Cavanagh's temples and brow, and his breath came hard. "They took the devil's own time, but it's a fine ring," Emmet said. "A soft base and not too wet."

Stephen gave him an approving cuff on the shoulder. "Then it's worth the wait."

He fell into step beside the young man who normally spent his days behind the bar at Stephen's Bowery saloon. Today Emmet would serve as his second. In honor of the occasion, the barman had changed from shirt-sleeves and starched white apron into a new silk-lined dress coat and white stock. Stephen looked at Emmet's face, flushed with pride, his dark eyes sharp with anticipation, and wished he shared his friend's excitement.

They crossed the grass toward a weathered fisherman's shack. Stephen glanced up the slope toward the meadow, teeming with dark figures—the mob, waiting for him and Billy Maguire to square off and beat each other bloody.

Emmet followed his gaze. "There are hundreds, Stephen, so drunk they don't know if they're standing on their head or their heels, and that's a blessed fact."

"If they're drunk, they must be Maguire's crowd," Stephen said. "Our side attracts the finer element."

Emmet grinned at the jest. "Aye, Stephen, the finer element."

Stephen ducked through the doorway of the fisherman's shack. In the dim light, he saw Hammer Moran dozing on a dusty bench against the wall. Two canes rested on his knees. Stephen looked at Hammer's face, etched with old pain, and thought how quickly it could happen. Just one brutal fight could leave a man crippled for life.

He sat down on the bench and pulled off his boots. "Emmet, if things go bad, throw in the sponge."

Emmet, unpacking the bag that held Stephen's fighting gear, looked up in surprise. "Why, Stephen, you never dodged a fight."

Stephen glanced at Hammer. At thirty-eight, he was a bent, bewildered figure, a testament to too many brutal encounters. "I'm not forfeiting the match," Stephen said. "I only want it stopped if it goes too bad for me."

Hammer stirred, his gnarled hands trembled. "Don't speak so, laddie," he said, his words slurring. "It won't go bad. You can win any scrap."

Stephen stood up and stripped off his shirt. "I'm thirty years old. When all's said and done, I'm not as quick as I used to be."

Hammer's childlike eyes blinked at him. "Why, laddie, I fought Yankee Sullivan when I was your age. 'Twas back in 'fifty, before the Hyer fight. . . ." Hammer's voice trailed off. "Could do it again," he said softly, "save for the knees. They've gone bad on me, the knees."

"Never mind the knees," Stephen said, teasing Hammer out of his reverie. "I may need you to stand in for me today."

Hammer's ruddy cheeks creased into a smile. "You won't be needing me, laddie."

"What I need is a bit of luck," Stephen said. "Irish luck and my grand right hand." He cocked his fist at Hammer's chin, and the contours of his arm sprang into hard ridges.

"A grand right hand, laddie," Hammer agreed. "Grand indeed."

Stephen kicked off his trousers. He stood naked in the shack's dusty light, six feet two in his bare feet, every inch of him armored with long, supple muscle. He ran a hand over his chest and felt the slow, steady beat of his heart. For the past two months he had pushed himself hard, running and sparring, pounding the heavy bag, swinging a forty-pound hammer. He'd always thrived on training. He'd never smoked, which took away a man's breath, and hadn't developed a taste for spirits. The only thing he'd missed was the lovely warmth of a woman.

Stephen pulled on his buff-colored fighting drawers. Around his waist, he tied a sash of emerald green. Then he dressed himself in a fresh shirt, black broadcloth trousers and coat, a four-in-hand tie. A fighter always entered the ring looking dignified. Not until the rituals were completed did he strip for battle.

Once he'd laced on his boots, Stephen handed Emmet a battered cap of green felt, a cap tossed into many a boxing ring over the years. "You do the honors today, my friend."

Emmet took the cap and turned it in his hands, his face anxious. "Sure, you don't mean it, about stopping the match. Why, the fight is your life, Stephen. You're a grand battler."

Stephen glanced away. "I've a son to think of now, Emmet."

From Emmet's unhappy expression, Stephen knew that his young friend didn't understand his misgivings. Emmet would forever think him young and strong, forever the champion. "Don't worry, then," he said with a reassuring smile. "We'll see it through."

They left the shack and headed up the path toward the meadow, walking slowly so as not to hurry Hammer's painful pace. As Stephen watched the windmills turning in the sunny breeze, the letter came to his mind, the carefully printed letter he'd received from Ireland barely a week ago.

"Dear Mr. Flynn," the letter said. "Gran is dead. I am living with Uncle Padraic. I wish I could go to America and live with you. Uncle Padraic says it is time. Your son, Rory Flynn."

Stephen had stared at the letter, trying to envision this Rory Flynn, his son, ten years old and in need of a father. In an instant, he'd known that the time had come to claim his son. After ten years, it was time to lay the past to rest.

But first he had to teach a lesson to Billy Maguire, the swaggering darling of New York's Fourth Ward gangs. Maguire fought aging opponents for swift, cruel victories, then boasted about the ease of it. After his last fight, he'd claimed the title of America's champion, a boast Stephen could not leave unchallenged.

They crested the hill. The mob surged and broke about them. Men pushed close, shouting insults and praise, reaching out to touch and shove. The heavy aromas of cheap liquor and hair oil overwhelmed the fresh smell of salt water and damp, newly turned earth.

A gang of Bowery men fell in around Stephen, shouldering a path through the multitude that roared its excitement. "Mind Hammer," Stephen called out.

"Aye, Stephen, we have him."

The violence of the fight crowd had once emboldened Stephen. Now his palms were damp, and there was a tightness his chest. He tried to focus on the fight, tried to rouse some of the old anger, but his thoughts kept slipping back to Rory: "I wish I could go to America and live with you."

When he reached the outer ring, Stephen ducked through the ropes. He surveyed the lay of the inner ring, the demarcations of the corners, the line dividing the center. He glanced at the men with cudgels posted as guards in the outer ring. When he nodded his approval, Emmet tossed Stephen's cap over the ropes, and the crowd roared out his name.

Stephen barely heard. He slipped through the ropes of the inner ring and went to his corner. He looked out at the Sound, the broad blue water speckled with white. He stared hard into the distance, as if he could see Ireland and the boy who waited there. There would be no more prize matches, no more blood and pain and rage. Tonight he would pack away his fighting gear forever—his green felt hat, his boots and drawers. Tomorrow he would hand Emmet the keys to the saloon's storeroom and board a ship for Ireland.

He was going to fetch his son.

PART I

The Arrangement

Chapter 1

May 1858

Anna Massie tapped her toe and swayed to the lively strains of a jig. The fiddler's tune sang to her west country heart, stirring up memories of village fairs, of tables laden with apples and sweet cakes, of horse auctions and tales told over pints of porter. It brought back thoughts of green fields and fuchsia hedges, of drifting mists and the sharp tang of burning peat. More than twelve years and an ocean of heartache separated Anna's girlhood in Kerry from the deck of the *Mary Drew*, bound for America. But time and distance meant nothing when she was hearing a familiar tune.

Suddenly she felt a gentle shove from behind. "Go to it, girl," urged a masculine voice. "You'll be a pretty picture. Give the lads a show."

The lure of the fiddle was too strong for caution. Caught up in the moment, Anna moved toward the fiddler. There was nothing wrong in a bit of a dance, she thought. She was a woman alone, with a face and form that made men stare, but what harm could come to her on a stout ship packed with emigrants? Let any man step out of line and she'd knock today clear out of him. Oh, yes, she would.

The fiddler gave Anna a wink of encouragement, and she was beside him, hands on hips, pounding the deck with her worn leather boots. The crowd of men pressed closer. Sun-browned faces beneath rough cloth caps creased into smiles. Coarse hands clapped and feet stomped amid shouts of approval. Sunlight poured down from a blazing blue sky, and Anna's feet skipped and hopped and beat out their rhythm.

"You're a cure for sore eyes, you are," a man called.

Anna's brow grew damp and her breath short, but she kept up the rhythm as the *Mary Drew* surged and dipped with the roll of the sea.

"Mother o' God, did I ever see the likes of you in all me life!"

Anna raised her skirts above her ankles. Her legs, free of their long woolen stockings, flashed bare beneath her red flannel underskirt. The men cheered louder. Anna tilted her head back and laughed. Pins slipped from her hair, and her thick red-brown curls spilled into the breeze. The music carried away the troubles of her twenty-four years, and for the moment there were no thoughts for poor dead souls and times best forgotten, for faithless husbands and dead dreams. Anna recalled her mam and her da, the handsomest couple in the valley, dancing on the long line, while she and her little brothers watched with pride. Then she thought of her new home, America, where bellies were full and there were no masters. America, where a woman could keep herself with no need of a husband. Oh, it was worth a dance.

Anna swayed and hummed and stamped her boots until she could dance no more. With one last flourish of her skirts, with a final skip of her feet, she dropped a curtsy to the fiddler and pushed her way through the crowd of smiling emigrants.

"Give us another, love."

"Faith, you're a fine shapely one."

A skinny red-haired youth in a battered cloth cap seized her arm. "I think I'm in love. Marry me and spare me what I'm thinking."

Anna gave him a good-natured shove. "You'd be better off with a bit of sense. I think God forgot to put the brains in you."

She pulled her arm away from the young man and made her way across the deck, over cordage and crates, around shallow tubs of potatoes, through mobs of children who rushed and shrieked. A group of men bent over a three-card trick, another man toodled on a tin whistle and gave her a wink. Humming to herself, Anna picked her way around clothing spread to dry on the deck boards and beneath shirts and petticoats that hung from the mainstay.

A cluster of boys huddled at the chicken coop, teasing the hens that would be served in the first-class dining saloon. The cook ran out of the galley brandishing a spoon. "Git," he shouted at the children, "or I'll have you in the pot!" The boys fled and Anna laughed.

She turned to continue on her way and bumped into a figure that gave off a musty, unwashed odor.

"In a hurry, Irish gal?" A thin, chinless face leered at her. Yellow hair stuck out from beneath the seaman's cap, and a growth of whiskers sprouted on his receding jaw.

Anna drew back, feeling her cheeks flush. "I've nothing to say to you."

Since the start of the voyage, she had ignored the sailor's stupid gaze, his obscene mutterings as she passed. Now she stepped to one side to go around him. But the man moved with her, matching her step for step. Anna turned to find another avenue of escape, only to encounter three more men. They moved closer, eyeing her with slack, insolent smiles. Anna's cheeks grew hotter. She turned back to the first man. "Let me pass!"

"There now," the sailor drawled. "Ain't you on yer high horse." A long dirty finger scratched at his pale-stubbled neck. "Figure you'll be needing a bit of companionship before we reach New York. The name's Tom Spinner, at yer service." He touched his filthy cap. "This here's Fallows and Cockburn." He nudged his hawk-nosed companion. "And Nosy Gibbs."

The men shuffled their feet. Anna glimpsed their wet grins and fixed her eyes straight ahead. "I'm needing no companionship," she said curtly, "so let me pass."

The men made no move to step aside. "We'll let you pass, all right," Spinner said. With his dingy red sleeve, he wiped a bright drop from the end his nose. "Just wanted to make yer acquaintance. Anna," he added with a purposeful leer.

A hand fumbled low on Anna's belly. She jumped back only to bump into a second man who gave her a hard pinch on the backside. She yelped and thrashed out with her arm, striking at the hand. The sailors drew away in mock fear. Anna stood with fists clenched, panting with fury.

"There's fire in that one," Spinner chortled.

"And you're the one to put it out, Tom," said the hawk-nosed Gibbs. "A handful, she is, a fine handful."

Anna backed away, her head ringing with curses. "You touch me again," she warned, "and there'll be the taste of blood on your teeth." She turned and plunged into the crowd.

When she reached the dim sloping space behind the cow shed, Anna sank onto a coil of rope, her body trembling with rage and self-reproach. Hadn't she just brought this on herself with her dancing? she thought. For a few careless moments, she'd forgotten that she was a woman alone and that wherever she went, trouble followed. From now on, there would be no more frolics; no more foolish enjoyments would imperil her future.

Anna rubbed her neck, easing herself out of the tense grip of anger. She reached back to pin up her tumbled curls and glanced around her hideaway. The first day at sea, she had staked out the shady nook for herself. It smelled like a barn-yard and the tarry ropes stained her dress, but it was a comfort having her own place. Here she could think and work in peace, away from the noise and crush of people on deck.

Reaching into a small opening in the bulwark, Anna drew out a white bundle. She laid the bundle on her lap, wiped her hands on her skirt, and unfolded the cloth. Within lay a steel hook, a ball of white cotton thread, and a half dozen pieces of white cotton crochet. Anna set the finished pieces on her knees, inspecting the pinwheels, the flowers, the perfect little leaves. Her stitches were uniform and compact, flawless.

Anna picked up her hook and thread and bent over her work, humming softly. She worked a rose motif, tightening the foundation cord to ensure the curve of the blossom. As her hook moved swiftly through the stitches, the encounter with Spinner and his mates faded. Anna imagined herself in New York, in a shop of her own, making lace for the fine ladies of the city.

A timid voice interrupted her thoughts. "Will you be wanting a drink, then?"

Anna glanced up. A dark-haired boy stood before her, holding a dipper of water. His pointed face was small and pale, and his eyes shone with admiration.

He gave her a shy, appealing smile and extended the dipper.

Anna couldn't help but smile back. "Would that be for me, now?"

The boy's cheeks bloomed crimson. "I thought you'd be wanting a sip after your dancing."

"Bless you," Anna said, taking the dipper from his hand. "I'm parched, that's for sure."

Mercy, she thought, here's a gallant little lad, a pleasant change from the usual lot of males. Anna took in his bony frame. Beneath his box jacket and crisp shirt, the boy looked as thin as a spoke. Her own brother Sean, gone these twelve years, had been about the size and color of this one, probably not a day over ten.

Anna lifted the dipper to her lips and filled her mouth. The water had been none too fresh when they'd started out, and in the days since it had turned warm and brackish, palatable only when mixed with peppermint or boiled with tea. But to please the boy, Anna drank deeply, as if it were as cool and sweet as Kerry springwater.

When she handed back the dipper, the boy made no move to leave. He shuffled his boots and stared at her as if trying to think of some way to prolong his stay. Anna patted the deck beside her and the boy sat down, his cheeks aflame with pleasure.

"So who are you?" Anna asked.

He lifted his eyes to hers. His brows were charcoal strokes upon his pale face. His overgrown thatch of black hair was sorely in need of a brush. "Rory," he said. "Rory Flynn."

"Rory, is it?" Anna leaned back against the bulkhead, crossed her ankles, and laced her fingers together in her lap. "A fine, noble name. The last high king of Ireland was Rory O'Connor."

Rory Flynn's eyes brightened and his reserve fell away. "I know of Rory O'Connor. My gran told me the tales of the high kings of Tara and the great chiefs. And she told me of Grainne de Mhaille, the warrior queen. None in her court could do a finer dance than you."

Anna laughed, which brought a deeper flush to the boy's cheeks. "Why, that's a pretty compliment," she said. "And your gran, is she traveling with you to America?"

Rory shook his head. "My gran's dead, and so's my ma. I'm with my da." His small face burst into a proud smile. "He's a prizefighter. He's taking me to New York. I never saw him before he came to Kilkenny to fetch me."

Anna glanced down at the crochet work in her lap and fingered it absently. She'd heard talk of Stephen Flynn. The ship had buzzed with excitement when the sailors reported his presence aboard the *Mary Drew*. Stephen Flynn of Kilkenny, Stephen Flynn of the 'forty-eight rising, Stephen Flynn, the prizefighter.

"So he's your da," she said.

"He's the champion of America." Rory's voice was hushed with reverence.

"Well, then. Aren't you in luck."

"He says he won't be fighting again. He says he's too old and sore." Rory's eyes dimmed wistfully. "But I know my da's not old. He's stronger than any man. I wish I could see him fight, just once."

"It's just as well he's quitting," Anna said. "It's a brutal business, fighting. You wouldn't want your da hurt, now, would you?"

Rory regarded Anna with disbelief. "He wouldn't be hurt."

Anna rolled a strand of crochet cotton between her fingers and studied Rory more closely. She'd heard that the man and the boy were traveling with no woman, yet except for his rumpled hair, Rory Flynn looked well cared for. Did Flynn himself see to it?

"Would you like to see his book?"

Before Anna could respond, Rory pulled from his pocket a wrinkled sheaf of paper and thrust it at her. Anna took the book and smoothed it flat on her lap. A solemn, wide-browed man wearing a stiff collar and dark bow stock stared from beneath the title, *The Life and Battles of Stephen Flynn, The Emerald Flame*. A banner beneath the portrait read, "Champion of America!"

Rory leaned close to Anna, his thin shoulder brushing her arm. "That's my da," he said proudly.

Anna browsed through the text with distaste: "Poole caught a smacking cut on the cheek which brought him to the ground. . . . Platt down on his knees, up again, knocked down by Flynn. . . . A terrible right-hand blow on McClusky's ribs, which were dreadfully swollen from Flynn's repeated hittings. . . ."

Anna closed the book and handed it back to Rory. He tucked it tenderly into his pocket and said, "You'd like him."

Anna sighed. How well she knew Flynn's sort, men who strutted and swaggered and gave a girl smiles powerful enough to crush stone. They begged like children to have their way, and when they'd had it, they hurried off to their crude and noisy mates. "You leave your da to himself, Rory Flynn. Now go along and let me do my work."

Anna didn't look at Rory's face, but from his hurt silence she knew her words had stung.

"All right, then," she said. "You can visit me, but don't be dragging your da up here. I've no wish to meet with him."

Rory scrambled to his feet, grinning. "Next time I'll bring you an orange. We have lots of oranges in the cabin."

"And don't be getting yourself in trouble taking oranges," Anna scolded. But her mouth watered at the thought of the sweet fruit. In her chest of provisions she had only oatmeal and eggs and a small slab of salt pork. The ship stores provided nothing as tasty as an orange.

"I'll be back!" Rory cried, and with a slipping of boots, he spun off around the cow shed and disappeared.

The sun moved down the sky. The bell at the foremast rang eight times. Four o'clock. The emigrant women would already be standing in line with their pans and kettles as they waited for a turn at the grates. The grills closed at seven, and more than once Anna had arrived too late. If she wanted to cook her supper, she had best get going.

She emerged from her shelter into the confusion of the deck. A group of women worked around the large wooden cases lined with brick, which served as the emigrants' stoves. Anna hurried toward the hatch that led below. As she passed the foremast a voice sang out, "Anna! Oh, Annaa!"

Spinner stood at the galley, one shoulder braced against the doorframe, his hands behind him. Anna started away, anxious to be gone, but Spinner's hand darted out before she'd taken two steps. Her head shawl dangled from his tar-stained fingers. He grinned. "It fell off while you were doing yer Irish dance."

Anna paused. The shawl wasn't so precious, but the thought of Spinner having it disgusted her. She held out her hand. "I'll thank you to give it to me, then." She kept her voice flat, her tone deliberate.

Spinner laughed. "And what'll you give in return, pretty girl?"

Anna stared into his small, pale eyes and made no response. Spinner's tongue dampened his thin lips. "I seen you dance. I bet you can do it just as good laying down."

Anna curled her hands into fists to keep them from trembling. "Give me my shawl or I'll report you to the mate."

"Mr. Kincaid don't much care for emigrants, especially you Irish ones. As for you, girl, he thinks you're showing yerself off. Asking for it, he says. Whatever happens to you, Mr. Kincaid'd say you deserve it."

Two more sailors lounged against the rail, smirking and nudging each other. Anna turned abruptly away from Spinner. "Keep the shawl," she said over her shoulder. "I'll not touch what you've soiled with your filthy hands."

Spinner flung the shawl to the deck. It lay there, a sad dark rag on the bleached deck boards. "Pick it up, girl," he said. "It's yourn, and I've no need of it."

Anna hesitated, then bent to retrieve the cloth. As soon as she reached out, Spinner was beside her, his fingers clamped on her wrist. "You'll be needing me, Irish girl. Real soon, you'll be wanting me to do you favors." He spoke quickly, his voice low. "You might be getting hungry or be needing an extra ration of water to wash that pretty face o' yourn, or you just might need some company back of the cow shed where you hide yerself."

"Never!" Anna hissed. "I'd never ask you for a thing!" She tried to pull away, but he held her wrist fast, his rough fingers tight as a vise.

"Don't be so sure, beauty. We drawed straws for you the first day out, me and my mates. I got the long straw. You're mine whether you want me or not. I have three weeks of you, and one's near gone. I don't want to waste more time."

Anna's body turned hot with revulsion, her throat tightened with rage. She yanked her arm away with such force that Spinner's ragged nails dragged across her forearm, leaving a trail of scratches. "I'll spit on you before I give you the time of day!" she cried. "Don't think I can't take care of myself and anyone else who gets in my way." Snatching up her shawl, she scrambled to her feet and hurried past a group of gaping women to the hatch.

Anna climbed down the ladder to the steerage deck. The humid tunnel was lit only through the open hatchway, and the air stank of slop jars and sickness. She groped her way down the aisle, stumbling against emigrants' chests and boxes toward the women's quarters and the bunk she shared with a widow and her two daughters. Oh, the curse of being a woman, she thought. Defenseless, to blame for every man's lustful thoughts. She'd heard of outrages against women on emigrant vessels, but they occurred on slow sailing ships. Twenty-five pounds of her precious resources had gone to purchase passage on a steamer with a reputation for safety and speed—not on one with a crew that played a lottery with her as the prize.

Anna sat down on the straw mattress of her bunk and tried to calm her thumping heart. Surely Spinner and his mates could not harm her in the midst of so many people, she told herself. At night she lay in a hold full of women, and on deck she was never more than a few feet away from another person. Captain Blodgett, who had spoken to the emigrants on deck the first day out, seemed like a decent man. He would never permit his passengers to be abused.

Anna reached for her supply chest. Like all of the emigrants, she locked her provision box with a padlock. But as she fumbled for it, she found the lock hanging loose. For a moment she thought she'd forgotten to secure the box, but with sudden alarm she knew she wouldn't have been so careless.

Anna sank to her knees and flung back the top of the small chest. The sight inside made her cry out. Her fresh eggs were smashed, her hard-cooked ones were broken and squashed. Bags of oatmeal and tea had been torn open and mixed with the salt in which she had packed the eggs. And her supply of salt pork was gone!

Anna dug frantically through the mess. Eggshells scratched her skin, yolks and whites covered her fingers and stuck to clumps of meal. There was nothing to save.

A shiver of panic raced through her. No food! Nothing but meager ship stores—moldy biscuit, a bit of flour and tea.

Suddenly she was back in Kerry, scratching among the thistles while the stench of the potato blight filled her nostrils and the little ones chewed on grass and wailed.

Stop! Anna commanded herself. You'll not starve.

She sat back on her heels and stared at her hands, filled with lumps of ruined oatmeal and tea. This was Spinner's doing. He had spoiled her food so she would turn to him, so he could use her as he chose. A sick feeling rose in her stomach. Guilty memories, long buried, seeped into her mind—memories of a shop's storeroom, sacks of corn against her back, the smell of molasses, a man's groping hands. Anna bowed her head. Tears slid down her cheeks and across lips clenched tight against sobs. Once, she had traded her body for food. She had not meant it to happen—never would she have done such a thing—but she'd wanted to save her family, and it seemed to be the only way.

Anna wiped her cheeks with her arm. That would not happen again, she told herself fiercely. Not on this ship, not in New York. Never again would she be beholden to a man for her survival.

Chapter 2

❧

"Her hair's red, Da, not bright red but dark red with lots of curls, and when she was dancing it all fell down. The wind blew it around like . . . like flames." Rory leaned on the dressing stand, his chin on his palm, his dark eyes aglow. Words tumbled out in an excited rush. "She looked beautiful, Da. Watching her made me feel . . ." Rory twisted his mouth, searching for the right word.

"Warm?" Stephen suggested. He raised his chin and adjusted his collar.

Rory thought for a minute. "Not warm. Light. Like flying on a cloud."

Stephen rumpled the boy's hair. "Wash up, lad. You're hungry. Or have you forgotten?"

Since arriving back in the cabin, Rory had spoken of nothing but the red-haired dancing girl. Stephen knew little about boys, but he was certain that at Rory's age he'd paid scant attention to women. Since they'd left Kilkenny, however, Rory had pointed out several pretty girls, praising their hair or their smile or their rosy cheeks. None had caught the boy's fancy, though, like the girl he'd met today.

Padraic had warned Stephen that the lad might try to make a match. The night before he and Rory departed for Liverpool, Stephen had sat in the McCarthys' tidy parlor, furnished with plump horsehair and polished oak, and talked with his brother-in-law into the small hours of the morning.

"He's got a father now, Stephen," Padraic had said, "but he misses his gran. Don't be surprised if he's looking to find himself a mother in America."

"He had a mother," Stephen replied, his voice sharper than he'd intended. "And there's no woman in the world good enough to take her place. You know it as well as I do, Paddy."

Padraic had removed the pipe from his mouth. "You're right about that," he'd said with a wry smile. "Saints are hard to come by."

Stephen thought of her now as he looked at his son's dark eyes and pointed chin, so like his ma's. Pious, obedient, beautiful Rose. She'd been too good for this world, that was sure. And too good for him.

"Will you, Da?"

"Will I what?"

Rory rubbed his face with one of the steamship company's thick towels. "Will you talk to her? To Anna?"

Stephen took his coat from its peg. "There's good women, Rory, and there's bad. Your ma, God rest her, was a good woman, a pure woman. She lived and died by the faith. Why, your ma would no more show herself to a deck full of men than she'd leave the church. Your dancing girl, now, she's got an easy way about her that's not decent. It'll get her in trouble, sure as I'm looking at you."

"But, Da—"

Stephen tossed the boy his jacket. "As your gran used to say, 'If a girl walks with God, the Devil will never follow.' Now give your hair a brush and let's get some dinner."

The passageway to the dining saloon was filled with rainbows of silk, ballooning crinolines, and stern black morning coats. Stephen kept a hand on Rory's shoulder as the two of them made their way through the crush of chattering passengers, who smiled and waved in their direction.

Stephen acknowledged the greetings with some amusement. Earlier in the voyage, the other travelers had kept their distance, behaving as if he were a threat to life, limb, and virtue. Stephen hadn't minded being ignored, since he'd never been one to mix with the gentry. But Rory bragged so much about his da that the passengers' curiosity had overcome their apprehensions. Now men recruited him for hands of cards and asked his opinions on politics and sporting events. Ladies who had once paled when they found themselves in his presence, smiled and blushed and vied to sit at his side during dinner. Stephen could no longer stroll the deck or wander about the saloons without a group of ladies crying out, "Oh, Mr. Flynn, there you are," as if he'd somehow been mislaid along with their knitting.

Being sought after by ladies of quality was not new to Stephen. Years back, when he lived on the road and fought bouts from Boston to New Orleans to San Francisco, respectable females had regularly appeared at his hotel room, eager for his company. More often than not, they wanted passion that was rough, abrupt, and out of the ordinary. Stephen, being young and full of himself, had been happy to oblige. In time, however, he'd tired of playing to ladies' fantasies. Now, aboard the *Mary Drew*, he could manage to be no more than the polite ruffian.

"Mr. Flynn, your son is simply the loveliest boy. We had such a pleasant chat on deck this morning."

It was young Miss Camberwell, shapely and glowing in pink silk and velvet ribbons. Translucent blue eyes looked into Stephen's, far deeper, he thought, than her mother would have considered proper.

"His gran taught him good manners, Miss Camberwell," Stephen said, giving Rory's shoulder a playful punch. "I expect one day he'll teach me."

"I doubt you need improving, Mr. Flynn," Miss Camberwell said and promptly blushed. Her pale lashes fluttered as she hurried on. "Rory told me you have traveled in the American West. I would adore hearing about some of your adventures."

Stephen imagined removing Miss Camberwell's pink silk gown and the contraptions she wore underneath. No doubt she would decide at the last minute that her virginity was sacred. "My stories are hardly suitable for a young lady's ears," he said and gave her a wink.

Miss Camberwell's color deepened. She filled her lovely chest with a breath to continue, but was interrupted by the tall, beribboned Mrs. Charles, whose cheeks bore bright circles of rouge. "Oh, Mr. Flynn, there you are. We were wondering, do you sing?"

"Sing? I'm afraid—"

"The ladies are organizing a concert. Mr. Cookworthy and Miss Russell have agreed to sing a duet, and Mrs. Smith-Hampton will do 'Autumn Fruits' and 'The Spirit Song,' but we need a gentleman with a strong baritone for 'Lo Squarto, Sargo al Factotum.' "

Stephen glanced around for an avenue of escape, but the passageway was hopelessly clogged. "Unfortunately, Mrs. Charles, singing isn't one of my accomplishments."

"Really, Mr. Flynn," Mrs. Charles said, her tone sharp with displeasure. "We're all in this together, and you might at least try—"

"Mrs. Charles, the man is quite opposed to the idea."

Stephen cast a look of gratitude at yellow-haired Mrs. Smith-Hampton, who he'd decided was the most sensible of the ladies, but Mrs. Charles barreled ahead. "The Irish sing," she proclaimed, fixing Stephen with a bullying stare. "Irish men in particular. It's a characteristic of your race."

Stephen began to feel annoyed. "Especially when we're drunk," he said.

"I daresay that's the truth—"

"Mrs. Charles, *really*!" Mrs. Smith-Hampton looked appalled. "I must apologize, Mr. Flynn—"

"Mr. Flynn, you mustn't disappoint us," Miss Camberwell said, laying white-gloved fingers on Stephen's arm.

Stephen was close to exasperation; already, his hands had curled into fists. Fortunately a steward in green and gold livery appeared at his side.

"The captain would like a word, sir," the steward said. "A brief word in his cabin."

"Thank God," Stephen muttered. "You saved me, man." With a nod to the ladies, he drew Rory aside. "Stay away from Miss Camberwell, sport. She's got designs on us both."

He left Rory amid the billowing skirts. As he took off down the passageway, Mrs. Charles called after him. "I'll speak to you later, Mr. Flynn. Things are far from settled."

Stephen muttered a curse. "Goddamn ladies."

He followed the steward to a winding staircase that took them to the upper saloon level. The climb brought on a deep ache in Stephen's hip. Maguire had thrown him hard to the ground last September, and now the pain came and went, causing him to favor his right side. It was a habit that he had best overcome if he didn't want to turn into a cripple. Stephen wished he had a place to get some exercise. A good sparring match would improve his state of mind; he'd never been so restless in his life as he was on this floating palace with its horde of interfering females.

The steward knocked at the captain's door. At a bellowed command, he opened it, and Stephen stepped inside.

"Mr. Flynn." The ruddy-skinned captain, going to fat beneath his braid and dark wool, rose from behind his heavy mahogany desk and extended his hand. "Sorry to take you away just now. A small matter, a small matter indeed."

Stephen eyed Blodgett narrowly. He'd kept his distance from the captain since the voyage began. He had no desire to be included among the rich and eminent passengers whom the man gathered around him at dinner. "What can I do for you, Captain?"

Blodgett tugged at his abundant ginger-colored side-whiskers. "It's your boy I'm concerned about."

"Rory?" Stephen asked, surprised. "Surely there's no trouble."

"Nothing serious," Blodgett said with a wave of his hand. "But I hear from my chief mate that he's been mixing with the emigrants. I'm concerned about the boy's safety."

Stephen stiffened with annoyance. He was sick of hearing about the bad manners, dirty habits, and low morals of the emigrants, as if they were some inferior form of humanity rather than poor travelers making do under wretched conditions.

"Rory'll come to no harm."

The captain frowned. "Certainly it's not my place to choose your son's companions. But the steerage boys are a rough lot."

Suddenly Stephen had an idea far more interesting than Rory's playmates. "I've something on my mind, Captain," he said. "I need a place to spar and some worthy partners. If you don't object, I'll set up some matches on the forward deck with the steerage men."

The captain looked taken aback for a moment; then he brightened. "A fine idea, Flynn. Yes, indeed. It would entertain the emigrants and no doubt some of our first-class gentlemen as well."

"Good," Stephen said, anxious to conclude the interview. "If the weather's fair, I'll arrange a session tomorrow."

"Speaking of matches," Blodgett said, clapping Stephen on the shoulder. "I'm reminded of your bout with Maguire last September. I'm normally not a wagering man, but I was persuaded to put down a few dollars on you. To a most favorable result, I might add."

Stephen managed to look pleased. "Glad to help you out."

"I was in New Orleans at the time," Blodgett went on as he guided Stephen toward the door. "Never saw such interest in a prize match. The telegraph office was full of planters and merchants and seafaring men like myself. One chap wagered half his crop on you." The captain gave Stephen a confidential look. "I hope to have the opportunity to wager a more substantial sum in the future."

Stephen shook his head. "From now on, the only ring I plan to step into is the sparring ring in my own saloon. And that for no other reason than to keep myself fit. Maguire left some marks on me. I was lucky to get out of that fight alive."

"Lucky!" the captain cried. "There was no luck about it. You wore Maguire out and hung him over the ropes like a laundry shirt." He gave Stephen a good-natured nudge. "We'll see just how permanent your retirement is."

Stephen didn't argue, but as he followed Blodgett down to the dining saloon, he knew the captain was wrong. He was finished with fighting. He wanted nothing in life but to settle down in the spacious flat above his saloon, tend his business, and raise his boy.

The following afternoon was cool and misty. Despite her wool stockings and warmest shawl, Anna couldn't stop shivering. She was cold and hungry, and her trembling fingers fumbled with the hook and thread that she normally handled with ease. She glanced up at the fat black funnel spewing cinders over the deck and decided it was no use trying to work. She could wash the dirt from the crochet pieces, but her hands were too unsteady to make her best lace.

Anna closed her eyes and leaned back against the bulkhead, savoring the galley smells of cooking meat and coffee. The odors brought an ache to her head and made her mouth water. Last night she'd made a dinner of stirabout from the bit of oatmeal she'd salvaged from her box. The lumpy mess had barely covered the bottom of her pot. Since then she'd eaten nothing. She had considered spending a few of her precious coins on food, but she feared depleting her reserves before she reached New York. It was said that emigrants with no means of support were put on the next boat back to Ireland.

She would wait. In two days Mr. Kincaid would distribute another weekly ration of ship biscuit, molasses, potatoes, and tea. Until then she would make do with the handful of biscuits that had survived Spinner's mischief. Anna reminded herself that she had suffered worse than the teasing smell of meat and coffee. She'd seen her own mother, unable to feed her children, slip into madness. Anna had held the little ones, silent bundles of rags and bones, as they sighed their last breath. What was a spell of hunger, Anna asked herself, compared to helping her da dig four graves?

She fingered the biscuit that she was saving for the dinnertime bell and thought of Spinner. Even without a crumb in her pocket, she would survive. Spinner could wait a lifetime for her to give in, and then he could burn in hell.

"Anna?"

The boy Rory stood beside her, his wool jacket and cap beaded with mist, his face flushed with health and shyness. He extended his hand. "I brought you an orange."

Anna reached for the fruit. It was round and bright and weighed heavily in her hand. She turned the orange slowly, looking at it, smelling the rind. "Oh, Rory. Aren't you a grand, good-hearted boy."

With his penknife, Rory carved off the skin. When the orange was stripped bare, Anna pulled it apart. Each bite filled her mouth with a torrent of sensation; its sweetness was almost unbearable. Juice ran down her chin. She caught the nectar with her fingers, dark with soot, and sucked them dry. Not until she saw Rory's amazed stare did Anna realize how desperately she was eating.

He hunkered down beside her, hugging his knees. "Why are you so hungry?"

Anna attempted a laugh. "They don't give us much to eat on this ship. In fact they're giving us a right good starving."

The corners of Rory's eyes pinched with concern. "We have lots to eat in the cabin."

"Of course you do. Your da paid a good deal of money for your passage. I paid only a few pounds."

Rory considered her words. "I can get you more food. I can take meat and bread from the table and bring it to you every day."

"You'll get us both in trouble doing that," Anna said sharply. Then she looked at his anxious face and spoke more gently. "You're not to worry about me, Rory Flynn. I've got my money." She patted her waist where the little cloth pouch hung secure beneath her dress. "If I get hungry enough, I'll buy some salt pork and potatoes and sugar and tea and have myself a fine dinner. For now I'll save my coins for New York."

She gave him a grin and Rory's worried eyes brightened. "You can see my da tomorrow," he said. "If the weather's fair and the deck's not slippery, he'll be sparring with some of the men."

"So he's sparring, is he?"

"He wants to keep in practice. His arms and legs go stiff when he doesn't use them every day."

"Oh, we wouldn't want that to happen," Anna said. To herself, she thought, Stephen Flynn could spar all he wanted, but he'd do it without her looking at him. There was nothing to interest her in two men whaling away at each other.

After Rory headed aft for tea, Anna made her way below. It was too cold to remain on deck, and she felt too weak to do more than lie on her bunk. As she munched on her biscuit, she imagined the sweet taste of potatoes fresh from the ground, succulent cabbage boiled with tangy onions, the crisp crust of wheaten bread, a cup of thick buttermilk.

She dozed restlessly until the rank below-deck air drove her back up top. Behind the cow shed, she took out her crocheting, but could do no more than stare at it. Her head buzzed and her arms felt too weak to lift.

A shadow fell across her. She looked up into Spinner's face, freshly shaved and nicked with blood. His pale eyes, normally empty and stupid, were bright with purpose.

"You're looking a mite peaked. I'd say you're hungry."

Anna was too weary to argue. "I have nothing to say to you."

Spinner took a strand of her hair in his fingers. "I'm wondering if your curls is as pretty alow as aloft."

Anna jerked away from him and scrambled to her feet. "Leave me!" she cried, brandishing her crochet hook. "Leave me or I swear I'll kill you!"

Spinner's lips twisted into a smile of scorn. "That bitty thing won't protect you, girl." He snatched the hook from her hand and before she could react, snapped it in two. Bending down, he retrieved from the deck her crochet flowerette. He pulled at the thread, unraveling it.

Anna flew at him with a cry of rage. Spinner grasped her wrists and threw her back against the cow shed. His body pressed hard, his lips moved on her face, seeking her mouth. Anna twisted her head, hearing the panicky sounds in her throat, feeling the wild pounding of her heart. She struggled against him, but her strength was gone. Then, as suddenly as he'd begun, Spinner stopped. Releasing her, he stepped back and mocked her with his leer.

"I can take what I want, girl. Don't think I can't. And I'll be taking you soon enough."

Chapter 3

"You have captured everyone's interest, Mr. Flynn. You're a curiosity." Gerald Shaw crossed his legs, steepled his fingers beneath his goatee, and fixed Stephen with an amused look. "But I suppose you're accustomed to such attention."

Stephen pulled his unlit cigar from his mouth and stuffed it into his pocket. He disliked the gentlemen's smoking room, stifling with cigar smoke and gossip, but it was his only escape from the ladies who continued to hound him about their blasted concert. "I don't care a rat's ass for attention. Especially from the confounded women. They won't leave me alone."

Shaw chuckled. "A pity, Mr. Flynn, that you should be so abused."

Stephen glanced around the gentlemen's retreat, paneled in black walnut and furnished with scarlet leather. He thought of his New York saloon. Even on the hottest nights he could open the swinging doors for a breeze to clear out the smoke. The men who filled his place were neighbors and friends out for a game of cards or a round of billiards or a turn in the back-room sparring ring. They were men he could talk to, men he felt easy with.

"I understand you'll be sparring on the forward deck."

Stephen's attention wandered back to Shaw. He was a prim man in his forties with glossy dark hair and a clipped accent, a professor of some sort at Dublin's Trinity College. Stephen thought it odd that a queer fish like Shaw would seek him out for conversation, and it made him wary. "Tomorrow, if the weather clears."

"I'm sure your compatriots will find your appearance heartening. You're renowned in Ireland for your pugilistic efforts. Your visit to Kilkenny was thoroughly covered in the Dublin papers."

Stephen settled back in his red leather chair and stifled a yawn. "You follow prizefighting, Shaw?"

"Alas, no. My interest in you, Mr. Flynn, evolves from my interest in the 'forty-eight rising. From the accounts I've read, you're related to Padraic McCarthy."

Stephen's eyes narrowed. "What of it?"

Shaw smiled at Stephen's defensive tone. "Simple curiosity, Mr. Flynn, nothing more. It was McCarthy's notion that provoking the government into repressive action would stimulate the peasants to rise."

"Seems he was wrong on that," Stephen said coldly. "He spent seven years in Tasmania for his trouble."

"Ah, but he could have been hanged for his trouble." Shaw stroked his goatee, studying Stephen through keen eyes. "I hear there are plans afoot to stir up something again, this time with the rebels better armed."

Stephen's muscles tensed. He looked away from Shaw's curious gaze and stared hard at the fire burning in the grate. Politics, he thought. By God, he was sick of it.

"Better armed this time, and better led, I would think," Shaw continued. "The failure at Ballingarry in 'forty-eight was due to Smith O'Brien's indecisiveness. I'm sure you would agree, Mr. Flynn, as one who was there."

Stephen thought back ten years to the pathetic little rising. A small force of men had marched around for a week waiting for their leaders to decide what to do. "Smith O'Brien chose failure over a massacre."

"By all means, a wise choice."

Shaw's condescending tone grated on Stephen's nerves. "I suppose you're doing a bit of spying for the British."

Shaw appeared startled. "Good heavens, Flynn. You attribute quite sinister intentions to me. I'm simply a professor of political economy furthering my research in America."

"Research on the 'forty-eight exiles, no doubt," Stephen countered. "With a report due back to Dublin Castle."

Shaw's eyebrows rose, but he ignored Stephen's accusation. "My interest, in fact, is the institution of slavery in America. It might surprise you to know that slavery has become a field of academic inquiry."

"Has it? I suppose you academics favor the enslavement of the black man as enthusiastically as you do that of the Irish peasant."

"Ah, there you're wrong, Mr. Flynn. The union of England and Ireland has its economic advantages, whether or not one agrees with the politics. American slavery, on the other hand, will prove in the long run to be unprofitable."

Stephen stared at Shaw, amazed that the man could so easily reduce moral judgments to a simple question of money.

"Cheap Indian cotton," Shaw went on. "England's cotton resources in India will bring about the extinction of America's slavery more efficaciously than any sort of social or political agitation."

"So the abolitionists might as well give up the fight."

Shaw nodded. "You see my point exactly, Mr. Flynn. The course of history is determined by economic forces. In the long run, your abolitionists' ravings are irrelevant. The results, however, will be the same: slavery will simply fade away."

The soft gong of the supper bell sounded. Stephen glanced around the room, relieved at the interruption. He watched the men drink off their whiskey, brush cigar ashes from their chests, and struggle to their feet.

"So, Mr. Flynn," Shaw said, rising. He tugged briskly at the points of his waistcoat. "Are you going in to supper?"

Stephen got up from his chair, wincing as pain gripped his hip. His head throbbed from breathing cigar smoke. "I'll be going on deck. I could use a breath."

"I've made a study of Irish land reform, which should be of interest to an old rebel like yourself."

"Another time, Shaw." Stephen moved toward the door, anxious to be gone.

As he mounted the winding staircase to the deck, he speculated about his new acquaintance. Just possibly, Shaw had been put on his trail to sniff out a plot. Stephen had been out of politics for years; he had little to do with John O'Mahony and the other New York exiles. But he was Padraic McCarthy's brother-in-law, and that alone was enough to arouse the suspicions of British authorities.

Stephen stepped out on deck and filled his lungs. The damp foggy air was a balm to his smoke-laden senses. As he leaned on the rail, he thought of the rumors of rebellion that Shaw had mentioned. And he thought of the request Paddy had made of him—that he collect money from the 'forty-eight exiles in New York and find a trustworthy courier to take the cash across the Atlantic to England. In Birmingham, a contact would purchase guns and see them shipped to Cork. Paddy's men would meet the ship and have the crates sent on to Kilkenny.

"We have to prepare," Padraic had said. "In another few years the whole lot of 'forty-eighters will be old and lazy, the patriotism burned out of us. We'll never be able to shake off the unjust yoke."

Stephen had wanted no part of the plan. "There's no organization, save for the lads in New York, and they're too eager for a fight," he'd argued. "You'll have another disaster, Paddy."

In the end, however, Stephen had agreed to Padraic's request. He'd agreed out of loyalty to his dead wife's brother, the man who had looked after his son for ten years. But he knew he would have to be careful. One loose Irish tongue, one spy out for English coin, and Padraic's circle would end up in Dublin's Kilmainham prison.

Stephen stared into the mist, feeling a great weariness settle in his bones. He hated the treacherous game of Irish politics. He'd gone to Ireland to find his boy and to find his peace. He had the lad, and he loved him. But peace was yet to come.

The next afternoon, the sails were hoisted to help speed the *Mary Drew* on to New York, adding the thunder of canvas to the rumble of the ship's propeller and the emigrants' chatter. Anna stood at the rail behind the cow shed, her face turned into the sunny breeze, hoping for a wash of salt spray. Her meager ration of water was nowhere near enough to keep ahead of the dirt; she felt as if soot were ground into her every pore. During last night's hard rain, she'd longed to creep up on deck with her block of soap and give herself a good scrubbing, but she'd been too weak from hunger to stir from her bunk.

Anna no longer felt the hunger in her stomach. It now sat in her head as a dull dizziness and in her mouth as a taste of cinders. Tomorrow Mr. Kincaid would open the supply door and she would again have food. Unwholesome food, to be sure, and not plentiful, either. But she would make do for two weeks. When she stepped ashore in New York, she would have survived Spinner's mischief and saved her fifteen pounds.

As she clung to the rail in the warm sunlight, Anna was aware of a shift of sound beneath the steady rattle of canvas and the throbbing propeller. The drone of deck voices quieted, followed by a rising commotion. Anna looked around the cow shed. Men rose to their feet and gazed aft. Pipes came out of mouths, cards were abandoned.

"Why, it's himself," she heard someone say, followed by murmurs of approval and wonder. Men straightened their caps, women smoothed their aprons, children stopped their games and stared.

"It's himself. It's Flynn the fighter."

Anna intended to pay no attention. It didn't matter to her that Rory's da had come to spar with the men. She hated the murderous sport of boxing and the sort of men who practiced it; she had good reason, God knew. And yet she couldn't help feeling a prickle of curiosity. The famous Mr. Flynn was a veteran of 'forty-eight and the champion of America. It wouldn't hurt to have a look at him.

Anna found a block of wood beneath a pile of rope and dragged it close to the cow shed wall. She mounted the little step, rested her elbows on the shed roof, and discovered she had as fair a view as anyone.

From a distance, Stephen Flynn looked like a strapping farmer come to town on market day. He wore a plain dark jacket and a shirt with no collar. A cloth workingman's cap was pulled low on his forehead. As he made his way through the crowd toward the center foredeck, Anna saw that he didn't carry himself with the pugilist's cocky strut. Nor did he affect the bragging tilt of the chin typical of men of his kind. As he drew closer, Anna glimpsed bronzed cheeks, a strong jaw, and when he turned, she saw the firm, jutting lines of his profile. She raised herself onto her toes for a better view. His height alone drew the eye, not to mention those shoulders, his easy grace.

Swiftly the voice of her own good sense took over, reminding Anna that Flynn was a fighter. His gifts were physical—looks, strength, and skill. Like all fighters, his brain was as thick as his body, and his heart was only for battle. He was spoiled rotten by women and accustomed to getting his way with men.

Anna knew all that. And yet she couldn't look away.

Flynn stopped several yards from the cow shed. He spoke a few words and waved his arm. The men fell back to give him space. Flynn paced out the ring, then pulled off his cap and tossed it into the center of the cleared space, bringing cheers and laughter from the emigrants. As the breeze caught at his coarse golden brown hair, Flynn hoisted a pair of sparring gloves and shouted, "I need a strong man to give me a match."

"Aye," responded a male voice, "and who's strong enough to knock the smoke out of you, Flynn?"

Flynn turned to the emigrant, his face frank and open, humor softening his angular features. "I'm soon to see the other side of thirty, my friend. Even a noble horse can't run well forever. With a bit of faith, you might be the man to take me down." Flynn's voice was deep and friendly, an Irish voice with an accent no doubt of America. "You've got the size and build for the game, Jack," he went on. "And no doubt the hard head."

The crowd of men guffawed, and the young challenger's mates pushed him into the circle. Anna recognized the raw-boned redheaded young man named Davy Ryan. Flynn said something to the boy that Anna couldn't hear, and the two of them shed their jackets.

Anna shaded her eyes from the sun's low rays. Stephen Flynn tossed his coat into the crowd and pulled off his shirt. In the honeyed light of late afternoon, he appeared to be carved from some sort of golden wood, lean and narrow at the belt line, broadening gracefully to powerful, well-turned shoulders. His upper arms, thick with rolling muscles, gathered and relaxed as he flexed his shoulders and jabbed the air.

Anna held him in her gaze, mesmerized by the dangerous beauty of his form. There was no sin in admiring a man, she thought, then immediately reminded herself that a fighter's body was a weapon—to dominate, to injure and kill. She remembered the night when one deadly blow had changed the course of her life.

Nonsense, she argued back. There would be no violence today. This encounter was a sparring match, not a fight. No blood would be spilled. Yet as she watched the pale-chested Irish boy with his devil-red hair struggle into his gloves, Anna's heart beat quickly and her stomach tightened with apprehension.

Flynn waited in the breezy sunshine, dancing from one foot to the other. He glanced about, assessing the crowd of spectators, exchanging comments with the men nearby. He looked up to the ropes where sailors and emigrant boys hung like spiders in a web. He appeared to be searching for someone, and when he grinned, Anna saw Rory there, crouched low on the rung of a rope ladder, peering between his arms.

Then Flynn's gaze moved to the roof of the cow shed. He looked directly at Anna, and his smile broadened as if he knew her. Before she could react, before she could look away, he returned his attention to his opponent.

Anna touched her hair, a tangle of wild and dirty curls, and felt a flush rise in her cheeks. She wondered if the glance had been real or imagined, if perhaps Rory had spoken of her to his da.

No matter, she told herself. She had no business watching half-naked men play their brutal game. She should leave her place, slip back to her nook behind the cow shed, and save her strength for the hours of hunger ahead. Yet she remained where she was, held by a curious fascination beyond her control.

The fighters touched gloves and squared off. They moved about their space, eyeing each other, gloves raised to their chins. The spectators stood shoulder to shoulder, a solid mass of dark clothing and cloth caps. Their cheering all but drowned out the rattle of the rigging and the rumble of the propeller.

Anna saw the concentration on Flynn's face. Davy Ryan licked his lips. When he lunged forward, Flynn was ready. His gloved fist shot out so swiftly that Anna jumped with fright. Again and again, Flynn jabbed at the boy. Anna covered her mouth in horror. Davy backed into the crowd, gloves raised to his head, his forearms shielding his face.

"You're about as dangerous as a chicken, lad," someone called out. "Must be you're an Ulsterman." The spectators laughed good-naturedly and pushed Davy back into the ring.

When she heard the laughter, Anna realized there had been no smack of glove on flesh. Flynn had only tapped his opponent; he intended no harm. Anna let out her breath.

"Strike a blow, Davy," came a shout. "Or are you afeard of hurting the old man?"

Davy swung wildly, his teeth bared. Flynn slid away as quick as a snake and responded. His fists grazed the boy's chest, his chin, his belly and shoulders. Davy's face grew red and feverish as the spectators laughed and teased him.

"Why, Davy, you'll plague him to death with that left hand of yours."

As the sparring went on, Anna found herself smiling. There was a rhythm to their dance—one partner graceful, the other clumsy, shooting and circling in an elaborate, harmless pantomime.

Davy Ryan became bolder. He landed a few glancing blows to great acclaim, but soon his arms seemed to grow heavy, and Flynn breached his defenses at will. The boy's chest heaved. Sweat glinted on his back, and Anna could hear his labored grunts.

Flynn showed little strain and no malice. Anna wondered what it must be like to inhabit a body like his, to feel strong and invincible, to feel unthreatened by any man. She searched the rigging for Spinner and saw him there, very still, his eyes upon her. Anna looked away, feeling a quick, sick fear.

Davy held his arms before him in surrender. Flynn batted him lightly on the shoulder, acknowledging his gallantry, and the emigrant men gave a cheer. Grinning, his shoulders slumping with fatigue, the boy retreated among his mates.

Another man took his place, an older man with sinewy arms and a narrow chest. A group of children, no doubt his own, shrieked with delight from their perch in the rigging. The man lasted less time than Davy, but he appeared to enjoy himself more. When he quit, he laughed and shrugged.

One after another the emigrants took their turns against Flynn, then stumbled back into the obscurity of the crowd. The sun dipped behind a cloud, and Flynn called time. Sweat dampened his hair and gleamed on his muscles. His chest rose and fell with quick breaths. Men gathered around, and Flynn talked to them, a look of satisfaction on his face. Then he pulled on his shirt and retrieved his jacket. Someone tossed him his cap and he tugged it on.

Anna stepped down from her perch and settled on the coil of rope behind the cow shed. She thought of Stephen Flynn returning to his cabin to soak in a bath, enjoy a fine dinner, and lie down on a clean, comfortable bed. Her own hunger was back, grinding, dizzying hunger. And she'd stood too long in the sun without her head shawl. Anna drew up her knees and rested her forehead there. One more day, she thought. Tomorrow she would have food.

"Anna?"

It was Rory. She blinked at him, fighting the mist in her head, and managed a smile. She looked above him and saw Flynn.

At first Anna could only think what a peculiar pair they were. She looked from Flynn's massive fair presence to Rory's small face, his mop of hair, his dark eyes. Then she remembered her manners and tried to stand up. She'd managed only the barest movement upward when her head began to swirl. She struggled to keep herself upright, but her vision blurred and she groped wildly, her legs wobbling. The rumble of the propeller seemed to grow louder and Rory was crying out, "Da! Da!"

Suddenly firm hands gripped her upper arms, steadying her, and Anna felt herself being lowered onto the seat of coiled rope.

"Take a breath, now, a deep one."

Anna took a long breath and released it. She took another and blinked. Flynn's face came slowly into focus. He crouched before her, holding her arms, his brown eyes intent. Little half moons of scars pocked his forehead and chin; the skin of his bronzed, bony cheeks was coarse and braided with creases. A glaring white scar, testament to some brutal blow, snaked through his eyebrow.

" 'Tis only a touch of the sun, that's all," Anna said faintly.

"Hunger is what it is. My son says you're starving." Flynn leaned her against the bulkhead and sat back on his heels.

"I have money to buy my food," Anna said in a determined voice. She felt foolish, appearing helpless when she was as strong a girl as was ever made.

A smile tipped the corner of Flynn's mouth. "I hear you're miserly with that money of yours."

"A body can't arrive in New York with an empty purse," Anna said. "They'll send me back."

"A starved, sickly body won't be of much use in New York either." Flynn took a dipper of water from Rory and said to his son, "Ask the steward for some food, sport. Tell him to make up a small bundle."

Rory scampered off. Flynn held the dipper to Anna's lips, and she sipped greedily. Water trickled down her chin and dripped on the bodice of her dress.

When she'd drunk her fill, Anna wiped her mouth with her hand. "You mustn't get me food from the cabin. It will only bring trouble."

Flynn draped an arm over his bent knee. His face was narrow and high-boned. When he smiled, his sharp features softened and the scars seemed less harsh. "Trouble is my business," he said, a tease in his eyes. "Seems you'd have noticed that, watching the match as close as you did."

Anna stiffened. So he was going to flirt, she thought, now that the boy had left. "If it's trouble you're bringing, I have no need of it," she said with a warning frown. "Nor do I have need of a man, if you're thinking of that."

Flynn cocked his head and looked her over with a frank, sizing-up stare. "Aye, lass, from the lovely look of you, I'd guess that men bring you no end of trouble. But then, the best men are made up of their faults, aren't they? 'Twould be a sorry fellow who wasn't a little bad."

The expression in his eyes was lively and challenging. Anna saw no threat there, not even disrespect. Had she felt stronger, she might have returned the banter, but as it was, she just smoothed the stained and wrinkled fabric of her skirt and wished she wasn't so dirty.

"The poor lass's barely eaten a bite in days, Mr. Flynn."

Anna glanced up and saw a black-shawled woman looking down at her. Other faces were clustered about, looking over and around the cow shed, curious emigrants poking their noses into the scene before them.

" 'Twas one of the sailors who spoiled her food," the woman went on, her voice scolding. "He has his eyes on her, that one."

Flynn glanced around at the woman. "I'll see that she eats, Mother," he said. To the others he added sternly, "Get along with you now and leave the girl in peace."

Reluctantly the emigrants disappeared, leaving Anna alone with him in the confined space between the cow shed and the ship's bulkhead. Flynn sat with his back against the shed, his knees bent up, hands hanging loose between them. Anna risked a glance at his face and caught his eyes on her. The silence made her uncomfortable, but she didn't know how to break it.

At last he spoke. "Anna. What's the rest of your name, and where are you from?"

She was grateful to fill the silence. "Anna Catherine Massie. My people were from the west of Kerry near the coast, but I've been working in Dublin. In a doctor's home on Mountjoy Street and later in a hotel as maid of all work."

Flynn pushed his cap to the back of his head. "Dublin, is it? So you're hardly a country lass, not with those Dublin men giving you trouble."

His implication brought an angry flush to Anna's cheeks. "Think what you will about the Dublin men," she snapped. "It's none of your concern. I've been taking care of myself for half my twenty-four years and I'll be doing the same for plenty more."

Flynn laughed. "I've no doubt you will, especially with that sharp tongue of yours. You'll be needing it to lash the New York lads."

Anna was surprised at his admiring tone. Most men were annoyed by her impertinence.

"And how will you be supporting yourself once you reach our land of plenty?" he asked.

"Lace," Anna replied. "I'll sell my crocheted designs in the New York shops."

"And make enough to keep yourself?" Flynn looked doubtful. "You'll need a domestic position. In New York, a clever Irish girl can live safely and earn well in a rich man's home."

"Not me," Anna said firmly. "I'll not be tending and hauling and scrubbing again, even for a rich man. I've got my plans, and it's lace I'll be making to earn my living."

Flynn smiled. "So it is, then. But first you've got to reach New York. You'll be needing food for the rest of the voyage."

"Tomorrow the stores are given out. I can manage with biscuit and oatmeal."

"For two more weeks?" Flynn shook his head. "You'll eat from the cook's pots and get back your strength or else you'll be looking like a stray cat when they inspect you at Castle Garden. You think they won't turn you back if you're sick?"

Anna felt a jolt of alarm. She knew America wouldn't accept her if she was penniless, but no one had told her that she'd be examined for sickness. "The ship's food is too dear," she said. "I've got but fifteen pounds to my name."

Flynn waved her quiet. "Never mind that. A few pounds is no trouble to me."

"You would pay for my food?" Anna stared at him, aghast. "Why, I can't take your charity!"

"Of course you can. You'd be doing me a favor, accepting it."

"A favor?"

"I assume you're Catholic."

"Yes, but—"

"Then it's my duty." Flynn spoke solemnly, but a smile lurked in his eyes. "You see, I'm not a faithful communicant, nor am I one to confess my sins. I never did have much use for the priests. Feeding Anna Catherine Massie just might get me to heaven."

Anna tried to look disapproving, but instead she almost laughed. "You're wicked to speak so," she said, thinking how easily his battered face was softened by a smile. "All right, then. I'll take your food, but I'll pay you back every penny with the money I earn for my lace."

Just then Rory returned with a small bundle of food. He knelt beside Anna and unfolded the linen cloth, revealing the flaky crusts of two meat pies, a tart oozing apple glaze, and a generous handful of almonds and raisins.

Rory sat back on his heels and surveyed the meal. "The steward said there's more, if you like."

"He'd better say so," Stephen muttered, thinking how he'd tipped the man well enough to earn a few favors.

Anna glanced up from the delicacies, looking first to Rory, then to Stephen, her eyes brimming with gratitude.

Stephen gave her a nod. "Slowly, now, and best don't eat it all at once."

She ate with great concentration. Stephen saw her blinking away tears, and the sight angered him. This Kerry girl had likely lived through the famine, and now a sailor had spoiled her food. No doubt the bastard expected to get under her skirt in exchange for a bowl of watery stew. It gave Stephen some satisfaction to think that with just a few dollars he could foil the seaman's plans; in fact, he wouldn't mind busting the bloody tar in the face for his intentions.

Not that his own thoughts were so pure. Despite her dirty cheeks, her soiled gown, and her tangled heap of red-brown curls, Anna Massie stirred a man's imagination. Her eyes, a deep thundercloud blue, were direct and knowing, and she had a plump and saucy mouth. From the look of her, she wore beneath her dress nothing more than a shift and drawers and the thin red petticoat that showed beneath her hem. Stephen narrowed his eyes at her bosom, lovely and full, and at the outline of her legs along her skirt. He watched the way she ate, daintily, savoring every morsel. She sucked the tips of her fingers deliberately, one by one. By Christ, Stephen thought, this girl would start a fire in any man's cellar. And she was no innocent, not by the look of her.

Anna glanced at him, her expression weary and grateful, and Stephen felt a sudden sting of shame. The girl had chosen to starve rather than compromise herself with the sailor. She didn't need another man lusting after her.

"Come along, young Flynn," he said, getting to his feet. "We'll leave your Anna to herself. It's time to fill your own small belly." To Anna he said, "I'll be speaking to the mate. Tomorrow morning get in line at the cookhouse door." He nodded at the remaining meat pie. "That'll be enough for today. Stuff yourself and you'll be sick for sure."

Anna stood up, easily this time, and brushed crumbs from her lap. Stephen could see a bit of color on her cheeks and in her eyes the softness of relief. She touched Rory's shoulder. "You're a blessing to me, Rory Flynn, you and your da." She turned to Stephen and gave him a huge, shining smile that lit her dark blue eyes and brought deep creases to her cheeks.

"I'm obliged to you, Mr. Flynn. I'll find you in New York and repay you for your kindness."

Looking at her, tall and lovely and covered with soot, Stephen felt strangely hesitant, almost tongue-tied. He felt something deeper, too, a sense that the sight of her pleased him greatly, that he wanted to keep her safe. He reached out and took Anna's wrist in his fingers. It was cool and slim, nothing to it but bone.

"There's no need to repay, Anna Catherine, but you'll honor young Flynn and me if you come for a visit in New York. You'll find us at the Emerald Flame Saloon on Brace Street in the Bowery."

Anna looked startled at his words, and Rory did as well. The boy stared at Stephen and at the hand holding Anna, his two eyes big as bowls. Then his face burst into a smile. "You'll come, Anna, won't you?"

"Of course I'll come," Anna said. She pulled her wrist from Stephen's grasp and clasped her hands behind her back. "If I'm not too busy."

She didn't look at Stephen again, and he was glad of it. His face was hot with embarrassment. He hadn't spoken an honest word to a woman in years. Now a shabby girl had given him a smile and he'd started feeling weak-kneed and sentimental. "We'll be going, then," he said and, with a hand on Rory's collar, hurried the boy around the cow shed, leaving Anna once more to herself.

Anna sat back down on the coil of rope. She opened the napkin and bit into the second ham pie. As she chewed, she hummed to herself and thought of Stephen Flynn. Beneath his fighter's brawn and careless charm, he seemed a decent man. He liked to play with women, but a woman needn't fear him. If she were free, if she weren't tied till the grave to another man, she might well have found her way to Brace Street in the Bowery. But as it was, when she earned the dollars to repay Stephen Flynn, she would send the money around to his saloon. There was no point in tempting fate by paying calls on a strapping, smiling man who had a cherub for a son.

Anna folded her hands on her full belly and gazed up at the silk-blue sky. She would keep to her solitary path in life. Sure enough, that would suit her just fine.

Chapter 4

✦

By evening the hot odor of cooking meat was too tempting
to resist. Anna carried her tin bowl to the cookhouse door
and had it filled with fat pork and potatoes and greasy broth.
She took the precious stew back to the cow shed, where she
hunched over it, treasuring each bite. She was so engrossed in
her supper that she didn't notice Spinner until he jogged her
elbow, spilling broth on her skirt.

Anna glared up at him. "I'll thank you to be on your way.
I've nothing to say to you."

Spinner's lopsided face twisted in anger. "You think you're
free of me because a rich man likes yer looks and buys yer
dinner. Well, think again, girl. You got two more weeks of
Tom Spinner."

Anna resisted the urge to fling the bowl into Spinner's ugly
face. "The devil sweep you to hell," she hissed. "And take your
evil mates with you!"

Spinner's dull eyes lit with anger. "Curse me, will you?"
He reached out and grabbed a fistful of Anna's hair, giving
her head a painful jerk. Anna winced and bit her lip, holding
back a mouthful of curses that she knew would only provoke
him further.

"You eat up good," Spinner said bitterly. "I like a woman
with flesh on her." He released her with a rough shove and
stomped away.

Anna rubbed her sore scalp and tried to quiet her sudden fear. Now that Spinner's scheme to starve her had been foiled, he would surely think up some other mischief. Anna returned to her bowl of stew, but it was no longer appetizing. Her mouth tasted sour, and her stomach felt decidedly unsettled. She forced down the remainder of her supper, unable to bear the thought of wasting it.

When she finished eating, Anna made her way to the barrel of seawater by the galley, where she rinsed out her bowl. Then she crept down into the hold and collapsed on the rough straw mattress of her bed.

She slept fitfully. When she awoke, it was night, and the other emigrants had settled down to sleep. Anna's head ached in the close below-deck air, and her stomach pitched with the motion of the ship. Beside her in the bunk, the widow from Cork began her wheezing snore.

Anna longed for a breath of fresh air. She crawled over the sleeping forms of her bunkmates and groped her way down the passageway, stumbling against the emigrants' cargo.

When she reached the pale lamplight at the hatchway, someone touched her arm. "Don't be lingering up top, now."

It was Davy Ryan, the red-haired boy who had sparred with Flynn. Davy was taking his turn as watchman, regulating the ventilation and keeping an eye out for prowlers up to no good.

He gave her a grin. "You want me going up with you, darlin'?"

"Oh, Davy, I'm feeling sick."

His smile vanished. "I'm sorry, then."

He gave Anna a boost up the ladder, and she climbed onto the deck. The night was black and windless. A sudden flash of lightning outlined the masts and spars, the cookhouse and privies.

Anna felt the sickness rise; her stomach heaved. She clapped her hands over her mouth and ran across the deck to the rail.

She hung there, trembling and sick, then sank to her knees, gulping deep, sobbing breaths. She rested her head against the bulkhead until a measure of strength returned to her limbs.

After a moment she got to her feet and rinsed her mouth with brackish water from the barrel. She returned to the rail and leaned into the silent darkness, her face to the breeze, savoring its freshness. She felt empty again, but her desire for food had vanished. Now she yearned for a tub of hot water, a block of fragrant soap, and a board on which to scrub her dress. In New York she would have all those things. In New York everything would be fresh and new, the past put aside, the future full of promise.

Anna heard a thump and a muttered curse. She whirled around. In the darkness she made out a stumbling form. A jolt of fear caught in her chest. Dear God, it was Spinner.

"What do you want?" she demanded.

"I got you now, girl." He came closer, moving unsteadily.

Anna's body went weak with terror. With a cry, she pushed off from the rail, aiming to dash around him to the hatch.

Spinner lunged and caught her wrist, clamping hard. Anna took a breath to scream, but before she could make a sound, he struck her face. Her head snapped back, spinning with pain. He had hold of her hair and was pulling downward. Pain tore at her scalp; it throbbed in her jaw. Anna fought to stay on her feet, but suddenly Spinner kicked her legs out from beneath her and she was down on the deck, gasping for breath, hearing her own pleas.

"Help me!" Was it a scream or a whisper? Or merely a thought? "Dear Lord, help me!"

He banged her head on the planks, and banged it again. His mouth, foul with onions and whiskey, covered hers. His hand pawed at her dress, ripping the buttons, the cloth. He grasped her breast, pinching hard. Anna's fingers dug at his face and eyes. She writhed against him with all her strength.

Suddenly she felt something cold and smooth against the bare skin of her neck. A knife. Anna ceased her struggle. Terror stopped her breath. Slowly Spinner dragged the knife across her throat, the tip biting her skin. Anna made a small pleading sound.

Spinner raised himself from her and looked down. "I'll cut yer tit and yer throat if you keep fightin' me. Now, let's see what you got under here."

He was drunk. He couldn't find his way to the hem of her dress. Then he was there, his hand on her calf, groping his way upward. Anna heard her sobs of rage and fear. She hadn't come all this way to be so violated. Not for this disgrace had she suffered and saved and tried to forget her troubles. Not for this end had she dreamed of her life in America.

With a cry of fury and some inner strength, she pushed at his chest and brought her knees up hard. Spinner tumbled away, snarling in angry surprise. The knife clattered to the deck. Anna scrambled for it, feeling around like a blind woman. Spinner mumbled and staggered on hands and knees. Anna's hand knocked against the knife, then closed on the smooth wooden handle. Spinner reached for her, and Anna rolled away. Her thoughts came with crystal clarity. He was drunk, slow; she was faster, more agile and alert. If only she could keep out of his grasp.

Spinner was up, stumbling and swearing. Anna found her feet, but as she straightened, she stepped on her hem and tumbled forward onto her knees. Dear God! He was behind her. Some instinct made her roll over on her back, raising the knife to ward him off.

He kept coming.

"Stop!" Anna screamed.

He couldn't see in the dark. Perhaps he was too drunk, too stupid, too enraged.

"Stop!"

He threw himself on her, thrusting himself onto the raised knife, driving the handle, clutched in Anna's hand, back against her chest. The blade went into him, hard at first, through bone, and then easily, deep.

Strange sounds came from his throat as the life seeped out of him. Anna lay still beneath his weight and thought how odd it was that he would get heavier the more he bled.

Only gradually did another part of her stir awake, the part that understood what she had done. She had killed him. For an instant Anna was both within herself and without. She was victim and murderer, feeling relief and horror. Then she began to cry, and the sobs in her chest gathered into a scream that scraped her throat and hurt her ears. She screamed into the quiet night as Spinner's warm blood flowed over her.

She wasn't aware of throwing him off, but she found herself on her feet, staring down at the dark shape sprawled on the deck. For a long moment she stood still, her heart wild in her chest, her body limp. Then she heard pounding feet, male voices. She ran to the little shelter behind the cow shed and crouched there, her fists pressed to her chest. She was wet, drenched with sweat and blood, Spinner's blood. The truth of what she had done broke over her in waves, each one stronger than the last, burying her in horror. She had murdered a man. Her deed was disastrous, irreversible. She could never make it right.

And she would die for it. Surely she would hang.

Voices rose in anger and wonder. "Holy Christ, the bloody bitch killed 'im."

"Dead?"

"Best call Kincaid."

"What in bloody hell . . ." The mate's voice.

Anna pressed her cheek against the side of the shed. Murderer. Dear God. She hadn't meant to do it. No, never would she have wished it.

"It's the Irish gal, Mr. Kincaid. The red-haired one. She's killed Spinner. Threatened him the other day, he said. Threatened him with a knife."

"I'd say hang 'er, Mr. Kincaid. Strip 'er and hang 'er."

A numbness closed over Anna. She lay down on the deck and awaited her fate.

"Damn it to hell, where is she?"

She could see the glow of a lantern. The light moved closer. Anna's heart pounded. Doomed. Doomed and all but dead.

"There you are, you Irish whore!"

The light blinded her. Rough hands grabbed at her arms, dragging her. She couldn't get her feet beneath her. Her knees scraped along the planking. The full glare of the lantern fell on her eyes, and she turned her face away. Her teeth chattered. Someone pushed her, and she fell to the deck. Something hard, a boot toe, slammed into her side with stunning pain. She tried to crawl away. The boot stamped down on her dress, pinning her.

"Might as well finish what Spinner started, Mr. Kincaid." The voice was hopeful. "We could teach 'er a lesson."

"What the devil?" It was Davy's voice

"Keep them emigrants below. I don't want a damn one of 'em on deck. Cockburn, get the captain."

"Aye, sir."

"My God, you bastards . . ." It was Davy again.

Anna heard the sounds of a scuffle, of fists hitting and shouted curses. She kept her eyes closed tight, her cheek pressed to the deck, and whispered a prayer: "Jesus, Mary, Joseph, help me, save me, forgive me."

"Mr. Kincaid!"

Anna flinched at the roaring voice.

"Goddammit, man, what is this I hear? A killing?"

Anna was dragged to her feet. Her hair fell in her face. Her gown gaped open in front where Spinner had torn it. Someone clamped her arms to her back, twisting them painfully.

The captain stomped across the deck, flooded now with the light of many lanterns. His white shirttail flew out. "I'm trying to get a bloody wink of sleep on this bloody slaver, and I'm wakened to find that one of my men's been murdered!"

He jammed his shirttail into his trousers. His belly drooped over his belt. The first day aboard he'd addressed the emigrants. Then he'd appeared formidable in his gold buttons and braid. Now he was all sleepy, rumpled anger.

The captain stopped before her. His eyes were narrow and squinty. Side-whiskers puffed from his cheeks. He looked her over from head to toe. His gaze lingered at the gap in her dress that left her bosom nearly bare. No one said a word. The screw propeller rumbled. One of the crewmen coughed.

The captain reached out to clear the hair from Anna's face. Clamping her head between his palms, he studied her. He took her chin in his fingers and turned it roughly from side to side. His fingers plucked at the gap of her dress. He glanced inside. Anna closed her eyes and fought the urge to scream.

"What's your name, woman?" he demanded.

Anna licked her lips.

"Answer me!"

She flinched. "Anna Ma . . . Ma—"

"Good Christ, she stinks of blood! Where's this man Spinner?"

The captain strode away to where the body lay in a dark pool. Spinner was sprawled on his back, arms outstretched. The captain walked around the dead seaman, staring down. A lantern-toting sailor followed. The captain looked at Anna again, his eyes narrow and shrewd. He said, "Take her below to the prison deck. Put a man to watch her. I'll decide what to do with her in the morning."

The man named Cockburn, Spinner's friend, stepped forward and grasped one of Anna's arms. The hawk-faced Nosy Gibbs grasped the other.

Anna looked wildly from one to the other. "No!" she cried.

"Quiet!" Kincaid shouted. "Take her below."

"Wait!" The captain looked at Anna and the two seamen at her side, then addressed the mate. "I don't want her abused, Mr. Kincaid. No man will lay a hand on her. Put a trustworthy lad to guard her or do it yourself. I'll hold you responsible for any ill consequences."

"Aye, sir," the mate said.

The captain cast a lingering look at Anna and headed aft.

Kincaid put his hands on his hips and addressed the men. "All right, you bloody sods. You heard the captain. The man who touches this girl will be flogged within an inch."

Cockburn scowled at Anna. She heard him mutter, "Seems the old man wants her for himself."

"Flanagan!" Kincaid shouted.

A wide-eyed young sailor stepped forward. Kincaid pulled a pistol from his belt and tossed it to the youth. "Guard her like she was one of those flaming saints you pray to. Any man has a mind to touch her gets a bullet in the ear. Hear that, lad?"

The young man gulped and nodded.

Kincaid stared hard at the assembled seamen. "I'll pay this boy a dollar for every one of you he kills."

The crewmen, silent and hostile, shifted their feet. Kincaid nodded at Anna's keeper. "All right, then, take her below."

She should have felt relief, but she felt only empty and numb, drained of both hope and fear. She followed the young sailor down endless ladders to a black, stinking hold. A faint blue mist outlined the lamp, dulling the light. She could see only shadows, but she felt the dampness and smelled the stench of bilge water and musty cargo. She heard the scurrying sound of rats.

Flanagan stood close to her and stared at her gaping bodice. Anna pulled at the torn cloth to cover herself. The blood, which had hardened to a stiff crust, flaked off on her hand. The sailor gave her a blanket that smelled of mold and rot, and Anna wrapped herself in it. Then he fastened irons around her ankles. They were heavy and cold. The thick chains that held them to the wall clanked and echoed in the vast darkness.

"You needn't be worrying," the young man said in a soft Irish voice. "The captain will keep your head out of the noose. He'll clean you up and feed you and keep you for his own."

Anna said nothing. She had no need for false comfort, no urge to speak. She had done murder and would die for it. And after she died, she would suffer eternal damnation.

She closed her eyes and prayed.

Stephen brandished his open razor and glanced at the bright morning light pouring in through the scuttle. He leaned toward the mirror and maneuvered the blade between lip and nose, scraping up the last bits of lather and whiskers with small, deft strokes. He rinsed the razor and wiped his face. Running a hand over his chin, he studied himself, considering the scars and smashed bones of past battles, the lines chiseled deep in his skin. What, he wondered, had Rory's dancing girl thought of him? Not handsome, perhaps, but pleasing enough, a man who had experienced all that life had to offer. Virile, with a son, and rich enough to be generous to a pretty steerage girl. Stephen recalled Anna's blush, the bright beauty of her smile, and felt a measure of satisfaction. Like every woman who'd cast an eye over him, she'd not found him lacking.

The thought of her approval pleased Stephen, for Anna had been on his mind all night. He'd thought of her lips, her long-limbed grace, those thundercloud eyes. He'd imagined the rest of her, ripe, sweet, afire. By God, she was a handsome woman, and he'd been a long time sleeping alone. Not even after the Maguire fight had he sought out a woman's company, so absorbed had he been with plans for Rory and memories of Rose. . . .

Stephen forced thoughts of his dead wife back into the dark closet of his mind, quickly, before guilt could claim him. He'd learned to separate Rose from any notion of lust—out of respect for her memory and to preserve his own peace of mind.

Stephen grabbed up his shirt and returned his thoughts to Anna. Now, there was a woman made for sinful imaginings, for sin itself. Stained and smudged as she was, Anna Massie was more bedable than any fine lady in the cabin, even the saucy Miss Camberwell.

But he had the boy, and that posed a problem. A man couldn't make arrangements with ladies under the nose of a curious lad.

At that moment the cabin door flew open, banging hard against the wall, bringing an end to Stephen's speculations.

"Da . . . Da!"

Stephen whirled away from the shaving mirror. Rory stood before him, his body trembling, his face collapsed in grief. Stephen bent down and grasped the boy by the shoulders. There was no blood, no sign of broken bones. . . . "What is it?" he demanded. "Did you get yourself hurt?"

Rory shook his head. Choking and snuffling, he wiped at his wet cheeks. He tried to get words out, but each attempt brought on a fresh storm of tears.

Stephen had never seen his son cry, and he didn't know how to stop it. He gave the boy a gentle shake. "There now, sport. It can't be that bad. Tell me what's happened."

"Anna . . . Anna . . ."

"Anna!" Stephen's hands tightened on Rory's arms. "What about her? Speak up, now."

Rory found his voice. "She . . ." The bony shoulders shook. "That sailor . . . the one that spoiled her food. He tried to . . . to hurt her, and she *killed* him."

"Killed—"

"Stabbed him . . . with a knife! Oh, Da, they'll hang her!"

Stephen stared at Rory's face in shocked silence. Killed him! She *killed* the rotter? By God, he thought, I should have known that bastard would come after her. One look at that girl and I should have known. "Where is she now?"

"In the prison hold. Chained up."

"Christ!" Stephen got to his feet and swung his fist hard into his palm. They'd likely been at her all night. The lot of them. He ran a hand through his hair, thinking fast. Then he reached for his shirt and pulled it over his head. Forgoing a tie, he grabbed his coat.

Rory blinked at him. "You'll help her, Da? You won't let her die?"

Stephen cupped the boy's chin in his hand. "Don't cost yourself another thought, young Flynn. I'm right off to see the captain. Now, how about a smile for your old da?"

Rory's lips quivered, and Stephen thought, Anna Massie, if you hang, my boy will never forgive me. As for myself . . . He recalled her grateful smile, the dreams she'd never realize, and his heart began to pound in an odd broken rhythm. He gave Rory's chin a gentle jab and slammed out of the cabin.

Captain Blodgett sat at his sumptuous desk, his tunic unbuttoned, attacking a plate of eggs and ham. He took a long draft of coffee and motioned Stephen to a chair. "Mr. Flynn. What might I do for you on this fine morning?"

Stephen felt as tense as a cocked whip, but he'd be damned if he'd let it show. He took his chair and stretched his long legs out before him. "I understand there's a woman in the hold."

"How news does travel." The captain flourished a napkin and wiped his chin. A soft burp rolled from his mouth. He glanced down at his half-eaten meal.

"Please," Stephen said. "Don't let me interrupt your breakfast."

"Ah, you're too kind." Blodgett dug at his plate and thrust a fork dripping with egg into his mouth. "She killed a crewman," he said through the mouthful. "Stabbed him. A bloody mess. Took the crew half the night to scrub the deck clean."

"Self-defense, of course."

Blodgett applied the napkin to his lips and chuckled. "I'm no lawyer, Mr. Flynn. The facts speak for themselves. A man is dead and the woman stabbed him. Looks like murder to me. Pure and simple."

Stephen abandoned his cordial tone. "Dammit, Blodgett, you know very well that a woman traveling alone in steerage isn't safe. You're carrying a crew of riffraff and convicts. Nothing but Liverpool dive sweepings, the lot of them."

The captain scowled. "True enough. Never did see a worse lot of sailors than in the Liverpool–New York trade." He mopped at a pool of egg yolk with a piece of toast and stuffed it into his mouth.

"The man spoiled her food," Stephen said. "He wanted to get into her in exchange for something to eat. She wouldn't let him, so he decided to rape her."

Blodgett gave a short laugh. "Rape, hell. From what my chief officer tells me, she asked for it."

Stephen fought the urge to smash the captain's fat, muttonchopped face. Easy, he told himself. You'll win this one with words, not muscle. He flexed his fingers and drummed them on the brown leather arm of his chair. "A woman has a right to defend herself. Even an emigrant woman."

Blodgett pushed away his tray. He folded his hands on his paunch and gave Stephen a shrewd glance. Yellow traces of egg clung to his sandy mustache. "All right, Flynn. I'll concede the act was self-defense. I don't intend to hang the girl, don't even intend to turn her over to the New York authorities."

Stephen relaxed with a deep, silent sigh. Then he noticed Blodgett's smug smile, and relief gave way to suspicion. "What will become of her?"

Blodgett pursed his lips, making a show of annoyance. "Your interest is commendable, but you needn't concern yourself with this matter. The girl will come to no harm."

"You'll release her back to steerage?"

The captain emitted a noisy snort. "My dear man, that would be quite a waste of woman. Beneath the grime and malodorous clothing, she's a magnificent shapely thing. Bold as brass, from what I hear. No doubt a hellion in bed."

You bloody street dog, Stephen thought. No better than the one she killed.

"I plan to bring her into my cabin," Blodgett went on. "As a . . . stewardess, you might say." He smirked and smoothed his mustache with his thumb and first finger. "Thoroughly washed, she might brighten things up around here."

"There are laws that forbid a ship's crew from abusing female passengers," Stephen said, his voice threateningly low. "That includes masters. What would your employer think if the authorities got wind of your activities?"

The captain's eyes met Stephen's. He shifted nervously in his chair. "She'll be perfectly safe."

"Safe in your bunk."

Blodgett's cheeks reddened. "There are quarters for the cabin staff. Unpleasant, perhaps, and cramped, but nevertheless a good deal better than steerage."

"Do you deny your intentions, Captain?"

Blodgett slammed his fist on the desk. "Goddammit, don't push me, Flynn—"

"I'll pay for her passage. First class."

The captain stared, dumbfounded. Then he raised his brows and gave a bark of laughter. "Indeed. So it's your berth you want her to warm."

Stephen gritted his teeth. "I'll pay for her passage in her own bunk in her own cabin, and expect nothing in return, save for you to leave her alone."

"Admirable gallantry," Blodgett said with a sneer. "There's only one problem. I have one hundred and twenty-four passengers, and every cabin is occupied. I'll not inconvenience my passengers by having that woman sleep in the ladies' boudoir or in the public saloons."

"There are ladies' cabins with empty berths. Ladies often share."

Blodgett snorted. "Do you think Mrs. Pennington of Philadelphia or Miss Camberwell of Fifth Avenue would tolerate an Irish murderess lately of steerage as a cabin mate? Come now, Flynn, where is your good sense?"

Stephen faltered. Blodgett was right; that plan would never work. He racked his brain for another solution, but could only come up with one, an idea that made his heart race. "She'll stay in my cabin. As . . . nursemaid to my son."

The captain gave a shout of laughter. "Oh, come now, Mr. Flynn. Your son is too old for a nursemaid. Or could it be you who needs the attention?"

Stephen's face went hot. "I want that woman safe, Blodgett, and I'll pay well for her safety."

At the mention of payment, the captain's expression changed from scorn to interest. "Oh?"

"I'll pay the full fare of one hundred and forty dollars, despite the fact she's already paid for steerage."

Blodgett looked thoughtful. "I would expect a further consideration for myself. One hundred dollars more sounds fair enough."

"Fifty," Stephen snapped. Greedy bastard, he thought. No doubt Blodgett would pocket every cent of Anna's first-class fare, knowing the shipping company would be none the wiser.

The captain cocked his head. "Fine breasts. Had a glimpse myself. Long legs, Flynn. A snug harbor between. Let's say two hundred even for the whole transaction."

Stephen got to his feet. "I'll see you have your money when she's delivered to my cabin. I expect you to keep your part of the bargain all the way to New York."

"Of course." Blodgett rose and extended his hand. "Gentleman's word." He winked. "Enjoy her."

Chapter 5

Anna stumbled along the starlit deck toward the stern of the ship. She was free of the hold and free of her chains, but after so many hours in the clasp of iron cuffs, her legs felt numb and she had to struggle to keep up with Mr. Kincaid's long strides.

"Come along, girl. I should think you'd be eager for your freedom."

Anna knew neither the hour nor the day. Since it was night, she assumed she'd spent all day belowdecks, crouched under her filthy blanket. Her guard had sat beneath the swinging lamp, watching her, his pistol at the ready. Once, as he dozed, a rat had scrambled over Anna's leg. She'd screamed. The sailor jerked awake and aimed his pistol—at her. After that, Anna pulled the blanket over her head and kept quiet. Then Kincaid was kicking her awake, and she realized that she'd slept.

"The fighter's bought you," Kincaid had said. "I'm taking you up top."

He had offered no further explanation, and Anna had asked for none. Her mind was confused and her body weary. She'd been at the mercy of men since her first day at sea. She'd been attacked by one and imprisoned by another. Now she apparently belonged to a third.

As she trudged along the deck behind the mate, everything seemed distorted and distant, beyond her control. Anna looked up at the night sky frosted with stars. A slice of moon shone brilliantly, but the sight of it offered no comfort.

They passed the massive funnel and entered unfamiliar territory. Midships, the deck was spacious and orderly, clear of steerage clutter.

Kincaid stopped before a small deckhouse. "She's all yours, Flynn."

Flynn stepped from the shadows into the moonlight, a looming dark-clad figure. He didn't acknowledge Kincaid but looked only at her. Anna saw his anger as he took in her matted hair and torn, filthy clothing. She lowered her head.

"Did they harm you?" His voice was harsh and commanding.

Anna looked at him dumbly.

"Anna! Did they harm you?" He took her face in the fingers of one hand and squeezed her cheeks till she winced. "Don't be dreaming, now. Kincaid's gone. Tell me what they did to you."

"Nothing," she whispered, twisting away from his pinching grasp. "They did nothing."

He looked hard at her as if to make sure of the truth. "Did they force you?"

Anna shook her head. "They did nothing."

He seemed satisfied with her response. His deep-set eyes no longer looked dangerous, and it came to her that he was angry not with her but with the others.

"I wanted to get you earlier," he said. "In fact, I made a bloody row about it. But the captain claimed it would disturb the passengers, seeing you in such a state, so I had to wait till night." Stephen's smile was scornful. "Mustn't frighten the gentry."

Anna made no response.

"You must wash yourself."

Anna looked around. She saw no barrels, no buckets, no water at all. Stephen took her arm and led her to the deckhouse. "Take off every bit of clothing and scrub yourself. No one will bother you. I'll be waiting here." He opened the door and gave her a gentle push. "In with you, now."

Anna stepped into a small bare room. The walls and floor were covered with tiles that gleamed in the lamplight. The floor sloped to a little hole at the base of the wall. Anna put her fingers into a cistern filled with hot water. On a bench she found thick towels and soap that smelled like roses. Neatly folded beside the towels were her own white nightdress trimmed with lace, her linen drawers, her camisole, and her best wool shawl. They were her finest things; she'd made the lace with her own hands. Anna wondered how they had gotten here from the bottom of her box. Had Stephen Flynn gone through her possessions? Then she remembered— she belonged to him. He could do as he pleased with her box and with her.

Anna dropped her blanket and stripped off her torn and bloodied clothes. Her hipbones protruded pitifully. Her belly, once pleasantly rounded, had sunk with hunger. She filled the scoop with water and poured it over her head. Again and again she poured hot water over herself. She lathered her hair and her body, scrubbing away the blood and grime.

At first she didn't notice the tears that ran down her face, mingling with the soap and water. Then as her frozen emotions thawed, the tears came harder, dragging her from the warm retreat of numbness. The truth of what had happened swamped her with misery. Sobs shook her body, making her insides ache. Anna clenched her arms around her, but she couldn't hold back the sounds of despair. Her plans were destroyed, her dreams smashed. She had killed a man, and his death would soil her beyond salvation.

Anna wept through a second soaping. She wept as she rinsed herself clean. Then the sobs ceased, leaving her weak but free of the worst of the pain and blessedly empty. She wrapped a towel around her hair, and with another she rubbed herself hard. She thought of Stephen Flynn and felt a vague, formless hope. Surely he meant her no harm. He'd been kind to her once; perhaps he only meant to help her.

But reason hastily dismissed such wishful thinking. That day behind the cow shed, he had looked at her with the expression men wore when they were thinking their thoughts. Anna knew those looks and what went on behind them. Stephen Flynn was no different from any other man; he had bought her a reprieve from the noose so he could have her in his bed.

Anna pulled on her underthings, her nightdress and shawl. She combed her wet hair with her fingers and thought of her blackened soul. During the famine, she had traded her innocence for a sack of meal. Now she'd committed murder. What did it matter if she gave herself to Flynn?

But as she slid her feet into a pair of straw slippers, Anna knew that she must find another way to repay him. She had promised herself a new life in America, a life of virtue. She would refuse Flynn when he moved to claim his due, and pray that he wouldn't force himself upon her.

After gathering up the bundle of dirty garments and wet towels, Anna opened the bathhouse door. Stephen leaned against the rail, waiting. He came to her and took the filthy bundle. "We'll leave this here," he said. "The stewardess will take it away."

"Will they hang me for what I did?"

He studied her in the silver moonlight. "No. I have the captain's word on it. You're in my care."

In my care. Anna met his gaze and thought of muscular arms, of hard, seeking lips. The idea of his passion brought on a deep weariness.

"Are you hungry, then?" he asked. "You'd be better with some food in you."

Anna shook her head. She was empty, but her stomach felt tight and jumpy. "I'm only tired."

Stephen looked sympathetic. "You should be so." He took her arm and steered her across the deck.

"Kincaid said you bought me."

"Bought you!" Stephen stopped and stared at her. "I didn't buy you, Anna. I bought you passage to New York."

To her, it was the same. "What was the price of it?"

"It doesn't matter."

"Please. I have to know."

He smiled faintly and rubbed the flat plane of his jaw. "One hundred and forty dollars."

Anna's heart sank. It was nearly fifty pounds, an amount she could never repay. "I thank you for your trouble."

Stephen said nothing, but his hand tightened on her arm. They descended a stairway to the next level, a vast empty deck extending back toward the stern of the ship. Save for the rumble of the propeller and the glow from a few low lamps, the deck was dark and still.

"This is the first-class promenade," Stephen said as they proceeded along the deck's squeaking floorboards. "When the weather's bad up top, the passengers walk here. Back and forth. Mighty dull exercise." He gestured to the doors that lined either side of the promenade. "Passengers' cabins. They're all tucked up, snug and tight."

The walls and doors were painted blue and white and trimmed with gold. A center trail of white columns with gilded tops held up the low ceiling. Anna thought of the ladies and gentlemen promenading along this gleaming floor in their fine clothing, bowing to one another as they did in Dublin's Phoenix Park. Then she thought of herself among them, a woman from steerage, a woman who had murdered a seaman, and suddenly her insides went cold. She would never be permitted here. The ladies in silks and crinolines would never stand for her company. Not here on the promenade, not in the dining saloon, and certainly not in Stephen Flynn's cabin. They would send her back to steerage, to Spinner's friends, Gibbs and Cockburn and Fallows.

Anna stumbled. Stephen grasped her by the waist and said, "Ah, you are tired."

She glanced up at him. What could he have been thinking, taking her into his cabin under the noses of respectable people, and with his son there as well? Even if she remained hidden in his stateroom until New York, word would spread about Flynn's Irish mistress, the emigrant murderess.

Stephen opened a door. "Here we are, then."

Anna stepped inside the cabin.

"The lad's asleep." He gestured to a curtained berth that Anna could hardly see in the low lamplight. "He wanted to stay up to see you."

Anna twined her fingers together. "They'll never let me stay here."

Stephen glanced at Rory's berth. "Wake him, and we'll be up all night."

"They won't let me stay," Anna repeated in a soft but urgent whisper. "They'll send me back."

He patted her shoulder. There was a kind look in his eyes. "The captain gave me his word. You'll not go back there. Now get into bed."

He steered her to the empty lower berth. "If you need me, I'll be here, not a flea's jump away."

Anna stepped out of her slippers and dropped her shawl. She lay down between sheets that smelled sweet and clean. The pillow felt soft beneath her head. She turned away from Stephen, hoping he wouldn't lie down with her. She was relieved when he drew the covers about her shoulders, then pulled the bed-curtains, enclosing her in darkness.

Anna heard vague, distant voices, one high and questioning, the other deep. Rory, she thought. And Stephen. She opened her eyes. A crack of light showed through the place where the bed-curtains joined. She closed her eyes, and what seemed like a moment later she was waking for a second time. The light was brighter and the voices had ceased.

Anna sat up and lifted the edge of the curtain. She saw creamy walls and crimson-striped draperies. There were four bunks, two upper and two lower, each with cheerful red and white striped bed-curtains. Beneath a small round window stood an upholstered sofa of deep red plush. A rocking chair moved gently to the motion of the ship. Anna lifted the bed-curtain higher and looked around. Shirts and jackets hung from pegs on the wall. On the floor, boots sized for a man and a boy lay in tumbled disarray. Anna saw a huge trunk pushed against the wall opposite the sofa. Beside it stood her own small boxes.

It was a spacious, friendly room. A cozy home.

Anna pushed open the curtains fully and swung her feet to the floor. She looked for a chamber pot, but there was none to be seen. Surely, she thought, in first class there were proper conveniences.

Pulling on slippers and shawl, she shuffled to the door and opened it. The corridor was empty. Skylights illuminated the blue and yellow walls and doors. The only sound came from the rumble of the propeller.

Anna stepped into the hallway, then closed the door behind her. She had taken a few timid steps when another door opened. Startled, Anna clutched her shawl. A tall woman, draped in flounced silk flowing with ribbons and lace, stepped into the corridor. Her skirt was so wide she had to tilt it sideways to get through the doorway. The woman looked up and met Anna's gaze. Anna smiled and touched her hair, wishing she'd given it a bit of attention before venturing out.

The woman's face paled beneath her rouged cheeks.

"Forgive me," Anna said, trying not to sound too Irish, "but could you direct me to the ladies'—"

The flounced woman let out a shriek and maneuvered her skirt back inside her cabin. The door slammed shut.

Anna stared at the pretty blue door and felt her stomach knot with dread. No matter what Stephen Flynn might think, she would be packed off to steerage by dinnertime. There was no hope for her, no hope at all.

"Madam? Are you unwell?" A dark-skinned woman in a black dress and white apron touched Anna's arm.

"The . . . the ladies' convenience, if you please," Anna said, recovering herself. "I'm staying in Mr. Flynn's cabin. You see, I'm . . ." She paused, wondering how to explain her presence.

The stewardess didn't seem to need any explanation. She directed Anna to a doorway at the end of the hall, and when Anna emerged, the woman was waiting to accompany her back to the cabin. She showed Anna a bellpull that would summon her or a steward. Then she hurried away to fetch breakfast and water for washing.

While she waited, Anna sorted through her box. She handled each item with care, wondering when she would next have the luxury of puttering among her belongings. She took out a new toothbrush, her silver hairbrush, a packet of hairpins, a neatly pressed blue ribbon. She ran her fingers over the green silk dressing gown that her mistress had tired of and passed on to her. It was frayed but to Anna's eyes luxurious. Then came her best skirt of blue and white flowered cotton and a hip-length fitted jacket. Anna laid the clothes on the bunk and smoothed out the creases.

A steward brought water that was hot and plentiful, and the stewardess followed with a tray of rolls and jam, hot coffee, and stewed peaches. As Anna ate, she looked at the pretty blue and white skirt spread on the bunk and thought, why not wear it? It would boost her spirits to dress in her finery.

After she finished her coffee, Anna put on clean linen and all four of her petticoats, which filled out her skirt to something approaching fashionable fullness. She fastened herself into her best snowy white chemisette, tied the blue neck ribbon over the lace trim, and laced up her best gray cloth boots. Then she brushed out her hair, shining clean after last night's washing, and secured it in a loose knot at the back of her head.

Slipping on her jacket, Anna assessed herself in the mirror. Her face looked pale and thin; her clothing hung loose. There was a dark bruise on her jaw from Spinner's fist and red scratches on her neck from his knife. Anna smiled at her reflection, hoping to strike a spark of courage in her heart. But the smile did not reach her eyes. It was plain to see that the robust young woman who had set off for America with such high hopes had all but disappeared.

Stephen sensed trouble the moment he entered the dining saloon. The hum of voices chatting over breakfast dwindled, and a score of passengers twisted in their chairs to stare. Mrs. Smith-Hampton looked at Stephen with wide eyes while her rotund husband smirked behind his mustache and nudged the gentleman at his side. Mrs. Charles glared. The lovely Miss Camberwell didn't even glance up from her bowl of stewed fruit.

Stephen ignored them all. He sat alone, ate little, gulped his coffee, and departed. Instead of returning to the cabin, he went up top and paced the weather deck. He thought of Anna's fear that she wouldn't be allowed to stay in his cabin. Last night he'd dismissed her concern. After all, money had changed hands and Blodgett had given his word. But now the careful plan to keep her safe was in jeopardy. No doubt a delegation of outraged passengers had already called on Blodgett to complain about her presence.

Stephen leaned on the rail and stared out at the smooth ocean swells, wondering what to do. He remembered how Anna had looked when Kincaid brought her to him, her clothing torn and filthy, the life gone from her eyes. He thought of the bruises on her face and the scratches on her throat, and something fierce and protective rose in him. If he allowed Blodgett to send Anna back to steerage, how could he live with himself? If he saw her turned over to the crew, how could he call himself a man?

"Mr. Flynn, the captain wishes to see you in his cabin."

It was the steward. Stephen went below, prepared for a fight.

Blodgett, buttoned up to his officious best, stared out the stern window at the gray sea. He glanced at Stephen. "It ain't going to work, Flynn."

Stephen listened as the captain explained that he was sorry, but the situation was beyond his control. The way the passengers saw it, a murderess was being kept for immoral purposes in a prizefighter's stateroom. Not only were the two principals cohabiting in sin, but they were exposing a young boy to depravity.

Blodgett looked sympathetic. "To hear them tell it, your cabin is Sodom, a fight ring, and a child's brothel rolled into one. Boggles the mind, the sort of thing respectable people can come up with when they put their minds to it."

The ache had started again in Stephen's hip. He paced, working out the stitch as he tried to think of a way to save Anna.

Blodgett said, "She'll have to go back this afternoon."

A prickle of dampness started on Stephen's back. "No."

"Now, listen, Flynn. I'll agree the murder was self-defense. I'll testify as much to the authorities in New York. And I'll return all your money. Fair is fair. But the girl has got to go back."

Stephen thrust his hands into the waist of his trousers and glared at the captain. "She can't go back there. You know what'll happen to her."

"Goddammit, that woman will be removed this afternoon from your cabin. Forcibly, if necessary. If she ain't, the passengers say they'll file a report with the shipping office in New York, and I'm going to be an accessory to immoral behavior. D'you know where that'll get me? Beached, that's what. And maybe a spell in prison."

Stephen rubbed his hair. There had to be a way. . . .

The solution came swiftly, a solution so simple, so obvious, that Stephen wondered why it had taken him so long to see it. "I'll marry her."

Blodgett's jaw dropped. For a moment there wasn't a sound in the cabin, just the distant squeak of wood against iron.

"Marry her!" Blodgett's eyes looked ready to pop. "You'd marry the girl?"

Stephen's mind was racing. Married to him, Anna would be safe from the crew. If they were married, no one could object to her sharing his cabin. "Why not? You have the authority to perform the ceremony."

"Certainly I do, but—"

"Then it's done!" Stephen thought how relieved Anna would be. Relieved and grateful.

Blodgett let out a guffaw. "By God, Flynn. I believe you're serious."

Stephen was at the door. "Round up some witnesses, Blodgett. We'll have it straight by dinnertime."

When Stephen entered the cabin, Anna was sitting on the sofa, laying out on the table what appeared to be pieces of lace. He opened his mouth to speak, but no words came. He could only stand in the doorway, his hand on the latch, staring.

The tattered young woman had been replaced by a tidy beauty, brushed and scrubbed and prettily dressed in blue. Her abundant red-brown curls, loosely pinned up, shone in the light pouring through the scuttle. A touch of lace at her throat made her look sweetly reserved, almost virginal; yet on her bruised and weary face Stephen saw the sultry allure that had first drawn him, a powerful blend of propriety and worldly wisdom that left him unsteady on his feet.

Anna watched him warily. To cover his confusion, Stephen gestured at the lace. "What's this?"

"I'm making an opera bag." Her hands, coarse from work yet gracefully slim, lit on the delicate pieces.

Stephen sat down beside her, hardly daring to look at her for the effect she had. He studied the crochet fans and flowers, the buds and leaves spread out on the table. "What will you do then, sew them together?"

Anna explained. "First I'll tack all the pieces onto a cambric tracing, and then I'll make the network ground, which connects all the pieces. Once it's all put together, I'll line the bag with silk and make little pockets in the lining."

"Pockets?"

"For an opera glass, a handkerchief, that sort of thing."

"I see," Stephen said, although he wasn't sure he did.

A moment's silence followed as Anna fingered the crochet. "In Dublin, opera bags go for a fabulous amount."

"How much?"

"Five pounds."

"Ah." Stephen met her eyes, deep blue and unwavering, and felt a rising warmth. For the next few weeks, until New York, she would belong entirely to him. He would take his time with her, start out slowly, make sure he pleased her. "You're bound to be a rich lady one day."

Anna looked at him gravely. "Then I'll repay you for your trouble."

"Anna, I have something to say to you."

Her face went white as parchment. "They're sending me back."

"Listen to me—"

"I knew they wouldn't let me stay." Her chin quivered, and a blush of fear reddened her cheeks. Stephen wanted to take her hand, but she was busy collecting her crochet pieces.

"There's a way of keeping you here."

Anna paused and gave him a swift, desperate look. "How?"

"We'll be married."

She sat very still, her face drawn in disbelief.

"If we're married, they can't send you back," he said.

"Married?"

Her lips were lovely forming the word. Stephen imagined the softness of her mouth and felt a flash of impatience. "The captain can marry us today. Then you can sit in the ladies' boudoir and do your crochet work. You can go on deck as you please, take your meals in the saloon, enjoy the concerts and plays the ladies put on—"

"*Marry* you?" Anna seemed to find her voice, strong now with amazement.

Stephen shrugged. "Would it be so bad?"

"You would do that?"

"You'd be safe then."

"But . . . but I can't." She could never marry him not even out of this urgent necessity.

"It won't be forever," Stephen said. "Only until we reach New York. The captain's not a priest. The marriage can be dissolved."

Anna opened her mouth to explain that she was already married, that she'd been married for six years, although her husband had left her after a scant ten months. Then she thought of Cockburn and Gibbs and the other crewmen. She thought of Spinner's hands on her body, his foul mouth covering her own. A simple ceremony, she thought. A simple lie. It was but a few weeks till New York, and there would be no priest.

Anna looked at Stephen, grim-jawed and handsome, and saw the desire in his eyes. She knew what would happen if she agreed to his proposition. But she had no choice, no choice at all.

"Yes," she heard herself say. "Yes, I'll do it."

She saw the faintest smile on his face. "We'd best get ready, then," he said. "The captain wants it finished before the dinner hour."

The ceremony was brief. Mr. Kincaid acted as witness, and Rory, his small face rapt with delight, stood beside the bride. As Anna promised herself to Stephen, her cheeks burned with her guilty secret, and she offered a brief silent prayer for forgiveness.

Captain Blodgett gave them his best wishes, and Stephen kissed her on the cheek, a kiss so light she barely felt it. Anna glanced around at the company. So now she was Mrs. Stephen Flynn, entitled to enjoy the ladies' boudoir, the grand saloon, the afterdeck, the courtesy of the stewards, the goodwill of the passengers. Just a few words had made her a full citizen of the *Mary Drew*.

But instead of relief she felt only the heavy burden of guilt. She was now married to two men—one gone from her life yet tied to her forever, the other bound to her for a scant two weeks. She only hoped Stephen Flynn was as good as his word.

Chapter 6

After the ceremony they went to dinner. For Anna, entering the vast dining saloon was like walking into a dream. All about her, tasseled silk shimmered, gold-framed mirrors sparkled, chandeliers dripped beads of crystal. The black walnut paneling, embellished with carvings, gleamed like dark satin, and the ceiling was high and arched like a cathedral's. Anna gazed at the bronzed dolphins swimming across the walls and the potted palms basking beneath skylights. "God bless us," she murmured. Not even in her imagination had she encountered such a lavish display.

She followed Stephen across the thick carpet to one of three long, linen-draped tables, crowded with crystal and china and bowls of geraniums. The blue and white tableware was decorated with a banner that bore an inscription: SS *Mary Drew* Saloon. Anna sat down on a chair of petal-soft leather and noted with approval the bright shine of the crystal and the orderly arrangement of the silverware. A glance at the pieces satisfied her that she knew the purpose of each.

Stephen handed her the bill of fare, acknowledging her wonderment with a smile. "You're sure to find something you like."

Anna took the card and studied the list of mouth-watering roasts and fowls and stewed steaks. "I can have any of it?" she asked.

"All of it, if you wish."

She read her way through the assorted omelets, macaronis, and vegetables, the puddings, custards, and tarts. When she finished the list, Anna laid the card down and looked around with hungry impatience. The other diners—well over a hundred of them—sparkled in their silks and jewels and starched white shirtfronts. The ladies wore gowns of every color, shining gowns of cherry and smoke gray, daffodil and violet, topaz and sky blue, gowns overdraped with roses and ribbons and lace. There were buxom figures and figures as slim as sticks, plump necks and swanlike necks. Anna gazed at them in admiration. She had observed Dublin's gentry at close quarters during her years in service, but never had she seen such a gathering of elegance in one place. And never had she sat among them as an equal.

But not a true equal. There was a generous space of unoccupied seats on either side of her and Stephen. Anna fingered the ribbon at her throat and gave Stephen a wan smile. "The others don't seem to favor us."

Stephen scanned the room, noisy with the rumble of men's voices and the high, light laughter of women. "They stuck up their noses at me at first, but they soon recovered their manners. They'll come around in time."

Anna stared at the ladies, bright as parrots, looking so careless and assured. "They'll never have anything to do with the likes of me."

Stephen shook out his linen napkin. "We'll have to see about that, won't we?"

"Oh, but they'll never," Anna insisted. "And I would never expect it."

"They're no better than you."

"But they're quality." She didn't state the obvious—that although Stephen looked dignified in his formal attire, his starched and snowy linen as bright as any gentleman's, he was a prizefighter and not a gentleman, any more than she, with her work-coarsened hands and her soiled past, was a lady.

"One thing's sure, you're prettier than the whole lot," Stephen said, frowning at the menu. "Champagne would be in order, don't you think? It's not every day you and I are married."

"Oh, but it's not really a marriage," Anna said hastily, "so there's no need to be celebrating. You yourself said it was only until New York."

Stephen lowered the card, his eyes teasing. "Did I, then?"

"It's an agreement we have," Anna persisted. "A marriage of convenience, nothing more."

"Nothing more?" His gaze rested on her, warm and admiring.

Anna's heart thumped anxiously. "I'm obliged to you for saving my life, for saving me from the captain. Sure, I owe you a great deal—"

Stephen waved her quiet. "Never mind what you owe me. Now it's time to enjoy your dinner."

"But you must understand—"

"Hush, now," he said. "Don't be worrying."

Anna stared at her plate. Her uncertainty about Stephen's intentions made her feel desperately ill at ease. She thought of the honorable life she'd planned for herself, a life of virtuous solitude after years of mistakes. Then she thought of being at Stephen Flynn's mercy for the next two weeks and how completely he could ruin her.

Before Anna could dwell further on such thoughts, a plate of soup appeared, followed by a succession of courses of roast veal and bacon, boiled mutton and caper sauce, French beans and mashed potatoes. Anna ate sparingly, savoring each luscious bite, mindful of the disaster that might befall her should she again gorge her half-starved body. When the batter pudding and jam tarts arrived, she was too full to do anything more than gaze at the confections in appreciation.

Once coffee was served, Stephen glanced around the saloon. "You might find some customers for your lace among the ladies."

Anna set down her coffee cup with a clatter. "These ladies?"

"Why not?"

"Faith, but they despise me!"

"It doesn't matter what they think of you as long as they like your lace."

"Why, they'd never even look at me after what's happened." It astonished her how unmindful Stephen was of his place—and hers—when it came to his betters. "Why, decent ladies like them—"

"Decent!" Stephen looked scornful. "They wouldn't know decent if it jumped up and bit them on the backside. They're not shocked by us; they're enjoying it, lapping it up like cream. A bit of scandal excites them, relieves the boredom. Look how they're staring."

Indeed, Anna saw curious glances shift in her direction, then quickly away, even as the commotion of conversation and laughter seemed to grow louder.

"Take your lacework to the ladies' saloon," Stephen said. "After a few days I'll wager more than one of them will be asking for your services."

"But they have lady's maids."

Stephen shrugged. "Who knows what might catch their fancy? Maybe your opera bag, maybe some other lacy thing."

Anna looked more closely at the ladies. On nearly every one she saw lace at the neck, the wrist, decorating a flounce, trimming a shawl. There was a spark of sense in what Stephen said. "Do you think so, then?"

"Sure. And their husbands have plenty of money."

Money. If she began earning money now, she could start to repay Stephen the price of her fare. The sooner she repaid him, the sooner their arrangement would be over. Anna's stomach gathered into a nervous knot at the prospect of facing the first-class ladies. But wouldn't it be worth risking humiliation if Stephen was right? She looked back at him. "Show me where it is, then, the ladies' saloon."

Stephen smiled. "Finish your coffee and we'll be on our way."

The ladies' boudoir had a cozy elegance that Anna found less intimidating than the grand saloon. Brocaded blue silk lined the walls, and the floor was heavily carpeted. The low ceiling appeared to be covered with shiny brown leather. A profusion of geraniums bloomed before the stern windows that looked out on the *Mary Drew*'s wake. Another plant, thick with green blossoms, filled the air with a delicious fragrance.

Anna was grateful that the plump upholstered sofas and chairs were unoccupied. The ladies, Stephen had said before he left her, rested in their staterooms after dinner, so she would have a chance to settle herself before they arrived for their socializing. If she didn't have to make an entrance, there would be less chance of an embarrassing scene.

After some indecision about where to station herself, Anna sat on the blue plush sofa in the stern windows' plentiful light. There the ladies would notice her, but not immediately. And the black lacquered tea table would show her finished pieces to good advantage. Anna opened her workbag, took out the white crochet blossoms and pinwheels and snowflakes, and arranged them on the table. Once she was organized, she felt surprisingly composed. What terrors could she encounter in a room so sweetly scented, its appointments so tasteful and calm? At worst, the ladies would simply ignore her. Lulled by the monotonous rumble of the screw propeller, Anna took up her spare hook—Spinner had broken her favorite—and began work on a medallion.

She had finished the medallion and two pinwheels and was beginning a rose blossom when the door opened and a half-dozen ladies rustled in. Anna watched from the corner of her eye as the room bloomed with bright silks, rouged cheeks, and laughing voices.

"I'll admit she's attractive, Mrs. Smith-Hampton, but in an ever so *common* way."

A second voice spoke with an audible sniff. "Speaking of common, I should say the very same about *him*."

"Why, Miss Camberwell," chimed in a third, "I do believe you're jealous. Only yesterday you were quite agog over him. Now, don't deny it."

"I was not agog!" cried Miss Camberwell. "I was only being kind to his child."

"I've heard that the Irish have unusually strong appetites," interrupted a voice laden with authority. "And an Irishman like him, a prizefighter and heaven knows what else—why, his needs must be quite extraordinary."

A gasp went up and a chorus cried, "Mrs. Charles, *really!*"

"Why else would he take that woman into his cabin? He married her for no other reason, and we may as well admit it."

Anna slid down on the sofa, her face on fire. The luxurious, fragrant boudoir had abruptly turned ugly and sour, and Anna's insides filled with shame. Oh, why had she listened to Stephen? She had no business here, intruding on ladies who despised her. Anna glanced around, looking for an escape, but before she could make a move, she heard, "Oh, it's *she*," followed by a deathly stillness.

Anna stared at the lace blossom in her frozen hands, not daring to lift her head. She felt trapped and humiliated, like a freak at a fair. Moments passed, silent, agonizing moments that only increased her embarrassment. Then she recalled Stephen's words at dinner: "They're no better than you." She thought of his careless shrug as he dismissed the other passengers' disapproval. "Decent!" he'd said. "They wouldn't know decent if it jumped up and bit them on the backside."

Anna knew he was right. The ladies had no business making her feel small. Why, they had no pity, no hearts at all. Anna straightened, lifted her eyes, and glared at the giggling cluster of females, daring them to utter one more insult.

But the ladies' attention had turned elsewhere. They were busy settling themselves, accompanied by low murmurs and the rustling of expensive fabric. Only one woman met Anna's gaze, a thin, rather ordinary woman wearing a vivid green gown. Her face, free of rouge and as pale as marble, was framed by fair, fragile curls. Anna returned the woman's gaze with bold hostility, feeling some satisfaction when the pale cheeks colored and the woman turned away.

Anna crocheted furiously, her mind ablaze with indignation. How dare they judge her, these women of wealth who had no more to worry about than what ribbons to wear with their gowns? What did they know of terror and hunger and hard choices? She was fighting for her life and her honor; she was doing her best to follow a virtuous path while they sat cloaked in comfortable smugness and considered her lower than dirt.

By the time tea arrived, Anna had completed three more rose blossoms, and the tide of her anger was ebbing. She put aside her work when the steward set a small tea tray before her. For the benefit of the ladies across the room, who continued to cast her an occasional glance, Anna took elaborate care in sipping from the wide china cup. She held the twiglike handle with exquisite delicacy, fully extending her little finger, and nibbled her sandwich as daintily as a mouse.

And she eavesdropped with a vengeance. From what Anna gathered, the ladies were organizing a concert for the following week. They discussed performers and musical pieces, gowns to be worn, refreshments to be served, introductions to be made. When there was a disagreement, the overbearing Mrs. Charles, the expert on Stephen's appetites, bullied the others into accepting her point of view. The pale woman, who was addressed as Mrs. Smith-Hampton, said virtually nothing.

When Anna finished her tea, she popped a sugared fruit candy into her mouth, dipped her fingers in a bowl of scented water, wiped them dry, and took up a lace collar she'd begun in Dublin. She was ornamenting the edge with little scallops when she glanced up and again met Mrs. Smith-Hampton's eyes. This time the woman smiled. Anna, who had been preparing a scowl, could do no more than stare in response.

As the afternoon progressed, gathering clouds dimmed the shine on the brocaded walls, and the steward came in to light the gas lamps. The motion of the ship grew more vigorous, sending the ladies scurrying for the safety of their staterooms. Anna had begun to pack her belongings when suddenly the stern lifted high out of the water, causing the propeller to scream in the open air. It was a piercing sound that made Anna wince and cover her ears. Then the ship gave a hard lurch that nearly threw her to the floor.

The steward, grasping a handle on the wall to steady himself, said, "The captain's shut down the engines and gone to the sails. It's only because of the rough sea, missus. There's no cause to be frightened."

"I'm not frightened in the least, thank you, steward," Anna said. She gathered up her lacework and stuffed it into her pull-tie bag. After all she'd been through, she thought, nothing so ordinary as a rough sea could frighten her.

She made her way to the door that led to the main saloon. No sooner had she stepped into the vast unlit dining room than she heard a feminine voice say, "Mrs. Flynn?"

Mrs. Flynn? Good heavens, Anna thought, *she* was Mrs. Flynn! She peered into the dimness, looking for the speaker.

The voice belonged to Mrs. Smith-Hampton. She sat in one of the dining chairs not six feet away, her gloved hands clasped in her green silk lap. "Forgive me for approaching you so directly," Mrs. Smith-Hampton said, "but I noticed your lacework, and I need some mending done. My girl could never do it properly."

"Mending?" Anna asked dumbly.

Mrs. Smith-Hampton's delicate cloud of curls and her pale face made her appear ghostlike in the dimness, but her smile was decidedly human. "Do sit down, Mrs. Flynn. This beastly sea makes standing and walking quite impossible."

Anna pulled out a chair and sat, clutching her workbag.

"How much do you charge for mending a length of lace? It doesn't matter at all to me, but my husband insists on an accounting."

Anna thought quickly. She had no idea of what to charge a New York lady. "I . . . I don't rightly know, madam. It depends on the piece."

Mrs. Smith-Hampton touched her forehead with her fingers and laughed. "How silly of me. Of course, you must first see the piece. I can bring it to the boudoir tomorrow." She opened her reticule and began rummaging. "The New York shops charge four dollars for even the smallest piece."

"Gracious," Anna said in amazement. Four dollars seemed a vast amount for a small bit of work.

"Astonishing, isn't it? My husband calls it robbery. Let me give you my visiting card." Mrs. Smith-Hampton drew from a small gold case a piece of white pasteboard, which she extended to Anna. Anna took the card and ran her fingers over the raised print.

"I must go along," Mrs. Smith-Hampton said, rising. "I expect my husband is wondering where I am. Perhaps we could meet in the ladies' saloon after breakfast tomorrow?"

Anna could only nod her assent as Mrs. Smith-Hampton staggered toward the doorway. "Oh, this weather is such a nuisance," she cried, "making us stumble about as if intoxicated. Good-bye, Mrs. Flynn. I shall see you anon."

Anna looked down at the card in her hand. In the faint light from the skylights she read the address:

> Mrs. Horace Smith-Hampton
> No. 9 East 21st Street
> Gramercy Park
> New York City

Gramercy Park. The sound of it was graceful, bringing to mind ancient trees and elegant mansions and the clip-clop of horses' hooves on cobbled stones. Gramercy Park was probably one of the finest neighborhoods in New York City, Anna thought, a neighborhood of wealthy ladies like Mrs. Smith-Hampton, who would prefer doing business with a lace maker like her rather than with the expensive New York shops. The idea of it brought on a fever of anticipation.

Anna jumped to her feet and hurried through the dining saloon, bumping against tables and stumbling into chairs as the *Mary Drew* pitched and rolled. She raced up the winding staircase to the promenade deck, cleared of strollers by the rough sea, and flew down the blue and yellow hallway to Stephen's cabin. Tomorrow in the boudoir, in full view of all the other ladies, she would examine Mrs. Smith-Hampton's lace and decide on a price. Together they would do business. Oh, what sweet revenge that would be, Anna thought gleefully, to be acknowledged by a fine New York lady in front of the others. How Mrs. Charles would gasp in surprise. How the haughty Miss Camberwell's scorn would change to amazement!

Anna threw open the cabin door. "Stephen!" she cried, her excitement soaring. "Oh, Stephen, you'll never guess . . ." She looked around expectantly, but the room was empty.

Without stopping to fetch hat or shawl, Anna ran back through the hallway to the stair leading to the deck. She took two steps at a time, gripping the rail as the motion of the ship knocked her against the wall. Outside, beneath the leaden sky, the salt-scented wind whipped her hair and pasted her blue-flowered skirt to her legs. Sea spray showered her with freezing drops. "Stephen!" she cried into the wind as she made her way across the deck to the rail and looked along the length of the ship. Two figures, one large and one small, stood at the stern rail.

Anna made her way toward them, bracing herself against the wind. When she reached the stern, she saw that Stephen had hold of Rory's coat. The boy was peering and pointing down at the sea.

"Stephen!" Anna touched his arm.

He turned to her, his face damp with spray.

"I have work!" Anna shouted. "Mrs. Smith-Hampton!"

Stephen shook his head, indicating that he couldn't hear over the noise of the wind-pounded sails.

Anna held up Mrs. Smith-Hampton's visiting card. Stephen's fingers closed around her own to steady them. He read the card and nodded, forming the word "good."

He tugged Rory away from the rail, took Anna by the arm, and bowing into the wind, headed them down the spray-soaked deck toward the companionway.

Inside, where they could hear each other, Anna said, "Where's Gramercy Park? Is it very grand?" In her mind she saw summer flowers and a carousel with music.

"Not so grand," Stephen said. "It's a private park between Twentieth and Twenty-first streets, little more than a plot of grass and some trees."

Anna's disappointment must have shown, for Stephen quickly added, "But it's pretty enough. And only the richest people live there."

Rory tugged at her sleeve. "Did you hear the propeller, Anna? Did you hear it when it came out of the water? Da and I were looking at it over the stern rail."

"Yes, I heard it, and it hurt my ears."

"It didn't hurt mine." Rory jumped down the winding stair-case with both feet. "It went *reeeeek*! and everything shook. I thought we were going to sink!"

Stephen grabbed at his collar. "Easy, sport. One slip and you'll go headfirst." He turned to Anna. "What does Mrs. Smith-Hampton want with you?"

"She wants me to mend her lace," Anna said proudly. "She says the New York shops charge four dollars for even the smallest piece."

"Then you should ask for three."

"Three dollars," Anna said in wonderment. Rory bounded ahead of them down the promenade deck, whirling one-handed around each column. "Three dollars for a bit of mending."

"In a day or so the other ladies will be giving you work."

"Oh, the others will have nothing to do with me. They said . . ." Anna stopped, remembering their words about her and Stephen.

"They'll follow Mrs. Smith-Hampton's lead," Stephen said. "And once they see your opera bag—then you'll keep busy."

"They would follow Mrs. Smith-Hampton's lead? But Mrs. Charles is the bossy one."

Stephen kept his eyes on Rory, who was taking a long slide down the promenade's polished floor. "Mrs. Smith-Hampton is one of the Albany Smiths, an old family, land-rich colonial stock. She's about as high as they come in America."

"She's a lady," Anna said admiringly. "With a ring on her finger and a watch in her pocket. But she's not proud, not like the others. Her husband must be grand as well."

"Her husband's as common as clay."

"Oh, isn't that a pity." Anna felt disappointed.

"But he's rich. Turned a livery stable business into an omnibus company. From what I hear in the smoking room, his friends at City Hall gave him a franchise to lay rails for the city's new West Side line."

"I'm glad for her, then." If any woman deserved to be rich, Anna thought, it was Mrs. Smith-Hampton. "She must have a sweet clutch of children."

Stephen glanced after Rory, who had disappeared into the cabin. "No children. And no wonder. Her husband keeps a mistress in the St. Nicholas Hotel. They say she's a grand shapely piece. When he finishes with her, he probably hasn't a thing left for his wife."

Stephen's crude remark brought Anna abruptly back to earth. She shot him a fierce look. "What a thing to say! What a thing to say about the husband of a lady like Mrs. Smith-Hampton."

Stephen's eyes were bright with mischief. "That's what they say. I swear on my honor."

"It's not right for you to speak so. And I'll not be listening to it. Whatever you'll be thinking, I'm a decent girl, not one of the men in the smoking room."

"I know that, darling. Forgive me, then." Stephen sounded apologetic, but he continued to look amused.

Anna swept past him and entered the cabin. She wasn't going to permit bawdy jokes at the expense of Mrs. Smith-Hampton. In fact, she wasn't going to permit bawdy jokes at all, especially on her wedding night, when she intended to keep Stephen Flynn at arm's length. The thought of what lay ahead all but spoiled her excitement over Mrs. Smith-Hampton's lace.

Rory stood in the middle of the cabin stripping off his wet coat and shirt. His skinny shoulders shivered and his teeth chattered. Anna grabbed up a towel and rubbed his hair, which drooped like seaweed. "Mercy, you're as cold as frog's blood. You've no business going on deck in such a blow. You'll catch your death, and then where will we be?"

"I wanted to see the propeller. My da says it's turned by a giant screw."

Anna rubbed his body vigorously, rocking him back and forth. "You wait for a sunny day to see it, not when it's blowing a gale. Your da shouldn't be taking you out in this weather."

"But it only comes out of the water when the sea's rough," Rory said impatiently, "not on fair days."

Anna chafed his spindly arms. "Get out of those trousers and put on your nightshirt. And bundle yourself up in your robe. We'll call the steward for a cup of chocolate."

She turned away to give the boy privacy and found Stephen watching her with interest. "Bossy as Mrs. Charles."

"Oh, you think so?" Anna said, giving him a look. "Well, Mr. Flynn, you'd best be a little bossy yourself or the boy will grow up to be as spoiled as you."

A light leaped in Stephen's eyes. "We'd both gladly be spoiled, darling, if it's at your lovely hands."

Rory chortled and Anna flushed, angry at herself for being drawn into Stephen's teasing. "You'd best hush before he hears something he shouldn't."

Stephen acknowledged her admonition with a smile. "And you'd best get out of that wet dress and into your own warm nightclothes. We'll have a small supper here by ourselves, the three of us, and turn into our bunks early."

The expression in his eyes reminded Anna of her apprehensions. "If you're thinking—"

"Go along, then." He pulled closed the candy-striped curtain that separated the cabin into two sections and gave her a nudge.

Anna stepped behind the curtain into her own half of the cabin. As she removed her jacket and skirt, she wondered how she would go about rebuffing a man as strong and determined as Stephen Flynn.

After a supper of pea soup and boiled potatoes, brought by the steward, Anna curled up on the red plush sofa with her lacework. Stephen lit the lamps, and then he and Rory stretched out on the floor with pencil and paper to discuss the mysterious machinery that drove the *Mary Drew*.

Anna worked at the trim on her collar and listened to father and son discuss cylinders and horsepower and steam pressure. Now and then she glanced at them. Stephen rested on his elbow, one leg bent up, his coarse hands moving in explanation. With his coat and collar off and the broad outline of his torso visible beneath his shirt, he looked like a rough and amiable giant beside his small raven-haired son. Rory, clad in his long white nightshirt, crouched on elbows and knees, his curious eyes moving from his father's face to the paper, dense with lines and circles.

Stephen would marry again, Anna thought. He'd find a New York girl to spoil him and the boy, to warm his bed and give him more handsome children. Anna's eyes drifted over Stephen's lean face, his grand frame. He'd have no trouble finding a wife, not a fine specimen like him. He'd be easy for a woman to go soft on, that was sure.

Anna pulled her attention back to her handwork, alarmed at the direction of her thoughts. Just because she was warm and clean, with a full stomach and a decent bed, she mustn't be wandering off on a fancy. Stephen Flynn had intentions, there was no question of that, and she was beholden to him. If she didn't take care, she would find herself sprawled on his bunk, defiled like a common whore.

Anna put thoughts of the Flynns firmly aside and focused on her loops and stitches.

"Anna."

She looked up at the soft sound of her name. Stephen gestured at Rory, lying flat on his belly, his cheek on the carpet, his bony legs splayed wide, fast asleep.

"Mercy," she whispered. "It's a surprise to see him quiet and still."

Stephen turned the boy over and scooped him up in his arms. "Open his bed and I'll toss him up."

Anna rose and crossed to the bunks, then climbed onto the edge of the lower one so she could pull down the striped silk coverlet on the upper. Stephen lifted the boy and placed him on the bed. Rory opened his eyes and struggled against the covers. "I'm not tired, Da," he mumbled. "It's too early to go to bed."

Stephen smoothed his hair. "Close your eyes, sport, and it'll be morning."

"I wanted to show Anna about the propeller."

"Anna will be here when you wake up."

In an instant Rory's lashes dropped, his lips parted, and he slipped into sleep.

Stephen turned to Anna, pride in his eyes. "He's a fine lad, isn't he?"

"Bright as paint," Anna said, stepping back down to the floor. "And he thinks the world of you."

Stephen looked back at Rory, his face thoughtful. "It's his mam he takes after, dark and small, with her sweet temper."

Anna tried to imagine Stephen's wife—a feminine version of Rory, a face with delicate angles and soft, innocent eyes, a woman cherished and protected by her strong young husband. "She was pretty, then, your wife?"

"Pretty?" Stephen gave a short laugh. "Rose was beautiful, her face, her soul . . ." He braced his elbow on the bunk frame, his fist clenched tight. "Rose had a way about her. Graceful. Pure." He rubbed his fist across his mouth. "She was perfect."

"Perfect," Anna repeated with a sigh, feeling a twinge of envy. "Imagine that, being perfect. You were a lucky man to have her."

Stephen didn't respond. He stood still for another moment, then pushed himself away from the bunk. "I'll be going on deck. I run there at night when there's no one about and it's not too rough. The sea seems to have calmed."

"Run?" It was a strange thing for a grown man to do.

Stephen shrugged. "It keeps the legs strong."

"But the deck will be wet from spray," Anna said. "You'd be daft running on that."

"I'll manage." Stephen pulled on his old frieze jacket and took down his cap from the shelf. "I'd be obliged if you called for hot water."

"When will you be back?" Anna asked. She planned to be washed and asleep when he returned.

Stephen opened the cabin door and paused. His eyes skimmed over her, quickly, thoughtfully, from brow to toes. "Soon," he said.

Chapter 7

"Do my eyes deceive me, or is the bridegroom pacing the deck on his wedding night, brooding alone in the darkness?"

Stephen cursed under his breath as Gerald Shaw approached through the mist, swathed to his goatee in coat and muffler, his bowler hat pulled low.

"Does this circumstance bode ill for the honeymoon?"

"It bodes nothing. I came up for a run. As it turns out, the deck's too slippery." Just as Anna predicted, he thought with annoyance.

"So it is," Shaw said cheerfully, falling into step beside him.

Stephen lengthened his stride. He'd planned to take two or three turns around the deck. With the professor bothering him, he'd leave it at one.

"You have admirable forbearance, my good man, taking the night air while such a delectable bride awaits."

"Stow it, Shaw," Stephen said, quickening his step.

The smaller man kept up. "If I many be so bold, what is the fortunate girl's name?"

"Anna," Stephen said. "Anna Massie."

"Massie." Shaw sounded thoughtful.

Stephen stopped abruptly. "Why the interest?"

Shaw threw up a hand in a gesture of innocence. "Simple curiosity, Mr. Flynn. Simple curiosity." He leaned on his walking stick and regarded Stephen through the gloom. "Surely you realize that many in the ship's company are enthralled with this story. The beautiful emigrant commits murder to defend her honor and is rewarded with the hero—the hero being yourself. Justice triumphs, the two lovers find perfect happiness. And that boy of yours has a mother."

Stephen pushed off again at a furious pace. "It's not permanent."

"I beg your pardon?" Shaw scurried to keep up.

"I said it's not a permanent arrangement," Stephen shouted. He didn't like hearing that the passengers were turning his business with Anna into some sort of melodrama.

"You don't mean to tell me you've married the girl under false pretenses." Shaw sounded genuinely shocked.

Stephen stopped again. "By hell, man, mind your own affairs. You and the rest of them."

"I would have thought better of you than to use an innocent girl for your own purposes and then discard her once you reach New York."

"Innocent in a pig's eye. She's been passed around like snuff at a wake."

Stephen regretted his words the moment he'd said them. Not that they weren't true, but they didn't sound right. And they made him feel mean-spirited.

"Rather harsh with your judgments, don't you think?" Shaw stroked his goatee with gloved fingers.

Damn the man, Stephen thought. He'd been looking forward to a night of pleasure with a beautiful woman, and now Shaw was implying that he was some sort of scoundrel. "My judgments are no concern of yours, Shaw. She's my wife for as long as I choose to keep her."

"Indeed." Shaw regarded Stephen thoughtfully. "On that note, Mr. Flynn, I shall bid you good night."

He swung off without a backward glance and disappeared into the misty night.

Stephen pulled off his cap, ran a hand through his hair, then tugged the cap on again. He felt deflated and annoyed. Damn Shaw for putting him in a bad light, he thought. He had a perfect right to Anna. He'd saved her from the captain. He'd paid her passage. He'd married her, for Christ's sake. Once they got started, she'd be as happy as a bird in May about their arrangement. When they reached New York, he'd give her some money and see her settled as a maid somewhere. Maybe Smith-Hampton would take her in.

Stephen headed toward the companionway. By God, there wasn't a man alive who would have behaved any differently.

By the time he reached the promenade deck, Stephen was feeling better about himself. He whistled a snatch of "Napper Tandy" and snapped his fingers. When he arrived at the cabin, he was cheerful with anticipation. He opened the door quietly to make sure he didn't wake Rory.

Anna stood before the washbasin, her back to him, her camisole open, one arm bent up, washing herself. Her hair hung down, a curly mass of dark reds and browns, thick as molasses.

Stephen stepped inside and gently closed the door, savoring the sight of her. A pale strip of skin showed between her camisole and the lace-trimmed drawers that bloomed about her slender hips. She bent forward to rinse out her wash-cloth. Stephen stared at her bottom, lovely and round beneath spanking white linen. His gaze traveled down her shapely legs, and he felt a sudden hot impatience. He wanted to see her shoulders, her breasts; he wanted to see her naked.

"Anna."

She turned, startled, groping to close her camisole. Stephen glimpsed a plump, creamy breast, a dark nipple.

"Oh!" She crossed her arms on her chest, her eyes huge with surprise.

Stephen touched a finger to his lips. He went to Rory's berth and closed the bed-curtains.

"You said you'd be running," Anna whispered accusingly. "I didn't expect you back so soon."

"The deck was slippery." Stephen pulled off his cap and tossed it on the shelf above the clothes pegs. He unbuttoned his jacket and flung it on the sofa.

Anna backed up against the washstand, hugging herself. The light of the gas lamp cast a soft warmth on her skin and made her linen glow.

Stephen stepped toward her, taking in her tumbled hair, her scarlet cheeks, the gentle curve of her bare white arm. Every nerve in his body was alert, hungry for her.

"Please," she whispered. "Please don't." She thrust out an arm to ward him off. Her other hand closed protectively over her breast.

"We're married," he said.

"We're not. Not really."

"We're as married as we'll ever be, darling."

Anna bowed her head, and her hair fell forward. Stephen pushed it back, clearing her face. Her curls were soft and springy to the touch. "Anna, come on, now." He pulled her toward him and bent to kiss her, searching for her averted mouth. Her cheek beneath his lips was smooth and warm. She smelled fresh, like soap and apple blossoms. He forgot everything but how much he wanted her. "God, darling, you're lovely."

"No," she whispered. "Oh, please . . ."

"Kiss me."

He forced her chin up and kissed her mouth, a gentle, coaxing kiss. He wanted her to welcome him. By God, he would make it so. Stephen tightened his grip on her shoulders and kissed her closed lips with greater urgency, trying to strike the spark that would make her respond. He grasped her hands, pressed against his chest, and forced her arms down. He was aware of her struggles, he heard her panting, but it meant nothing. Taking her by the waist, he dragged her into his arms, crushing her with all his strength, his mouth hard and open. Anna sagged against him, no livelier than an empty sack. Stephen tried to mold her lips to his, tried with his tongue to find a response. His hands slid beneath her camisole, up her back, stroking. Her skin felt like warm satin. He heard her moan. But it was not a sound of desire, but of despair. He drew back in frustration. "Dammit, Anna."

She pushed at his chest. "By all that's holy, you're no better than the others." She spat out the words in a furious whisper.

There was hatred in her eyes, but it didn't stop him. He held on to her, trying to subdue her. "Don't fight me, for Christ's sake. I won't hurt you."

"Is that a fact? I'd say you're a right beast, mauling me so."

"Calm down," Stephen said harshly. "I'm damned good with women—"

"Good with women!" Anna stopped her struggle, her face livid. "Oh, don't you just think so! You all think the same, you men, that a girl likes to be handled roughly, that she thinks being laid on and shoved at is just the grandest thing in the world!"

"Keep your voice down," Stephen snapped, shocked that she should speak so crudely. "Do you want Rory to hear?"

"Rory?" Anna gave him a crucifying glare. "You might think once of setting your son a decent example." She gave him a mighty shove, and Stephen released her. She pushed past him to her side of the cabin and flung closed the curtain behind her.

Stephen rubbed his face. "Laid on and shoved at." He'd never heard a woman speak so, and certainly not about him. He stared at the striped curtain that separated him from Anna. Christ, she was a bitch from hell if there ever was one.

He pulled the curtain aside. "You've got a crude way of talking for a woman."

Anna had put on her nightdress. It covered her from neck to toes. She gathered in her mass of hair and pulled it over her shoulder, then separated it into three thick bunches. "And you've got a crude way of forcing yourself on a girl."

"Forcing myself! We're married! I'd think you owe me something."

Anna stopped her braiding. "Don't you be worrying, Mr. Flynn. I'll be paying you back everything I owe. With money. Every last cent."

"I'll not be taking your money. And don't tell me about setting an example. Didn't you set a fine example, dancing in front of a ship full of men."

Stephen thrust his hands into the waist of his trousers and stomped back to his side of the cabin. He felt bruised and shaken, as if he'd lost a fight. Worse, he felt unmanned. Never in his life had a woman turned him down. Anna had not only turned him down, she'd insulted him. Christ Almighty, he must have been barking mad, taking her in as he had.

He sat down on the sofa, seething with frustration. He could beat the tar out of a man. But a woman? Until now, he'd never even exchanged harsh words with a woman.

"Stephen."

He looked up. "What now, for the love of God?"

Anna stood before him, stroking the thick braid that hung over one shoulder. In the lamplight, her nightdress glowed white and her hair burned with red-brown flames. Her expression had softened; she looked almost sorry.

"I know I owe you a great deal. I don't want you thinking I'm not grateful to you."

"Now, why would I think you're not grateful?" Stephen said, making no attempt to hide his sarcasm. "I'd say you're the most grateful girl on this bloody ship, seeing how I saved you first from the noose and then from the captain's bed. Why, sure you're grateful, denying your husband what's rightfully his."

Anna dropped her hands to her sides in exasperation. "Oh, for pity's sake, let's not be quarreling."

Stephen jumped to his feet, pointing a finger at her. "You're lucky I don't just take what I want from you. I could do it, you know. I know how to play rough with a woman."

"Won't *that* earn you a throne in heaven!"

"You're lucky I don't take a strap to you."

Anna thrust her fists into her waist. "I'm lucky tonight at every turn, then, aren't I?"

Stephen hands itched to grab her. To throttle her. Or kiss her. Hard. "By God, you're enough to drive a man stone mad—"

"Da?" Rory's head popped out through his bed-curtains, his eyes screwed up tight against the light.

Stephen ran a hand over his face, trying to calm himself. He'd forgotten about the lad. "Sorry, sport. Go back to sleep." He glared at Anna, muttering, "Now see what you've done"

"Why are you quarreling?" Rory sounded frightened.

"A wee bit of a misunderstanding is all," Anna answered soothingly. "It's all settled now, thanks be to God. Go to sleep."

Rory retreated behind the curtains. Stephen grabbed up his jacket. He longed to be home in his own place. In New York, he would have sparred a round or two or knocked a few billiard balls around the felt. On this bloody ship he had to search hard to find a decent man he could talk to.

"I'm going out for a breath of air."

Anna folded her arms beneath her bosom. She looked infuriatingly calm. "I'll be going to sleep right now. You should, too."

"I'm not in the mood for sleeping alone."

"Sure, there are ladies on this ship who'd fancy a night with the great Stephen Flynn—"

He took her by both shoulders and dragged her to him, thrusting his face close to hers.

Anna's heart leaped at his sudden roughness. She winced, expecting him to strike her.

"Enough, Anna." His huge hands grasped her shoulders so tight she feared they'd break. Fury and frustration turned his eyes the color of hard-packed earth. "There's only so much a man can take."

She knew she'd gone too far. Men had always been her enemy, and words her weapon. Vicious words, scalding words. Words that Stephen Flynn, who had saved her, really didn't deserve.

"I . . . I'm sorry," Anna said.

He released her and headed for the door.

"You're not the worst sort of man," she said to his back, "if that's a comfort to you."

He turned and laughed, but the sound was bitter. "Coming from you, darling, that's fair praise."

Stephen climbed down the ladder into the steerage hold, which smelled of mildew and slop pots and rotting onions. It was dark, except for the safety lantern at the hatch and a yellow candle blinking toward the stern. From the tunnellike depths came snores and groans and the dreary cries of emigrant children.

A man emerged from the darkness, a worn and whiskered man with a toothless grin. "By the saints," he said, peering at Stephen, " 'tis Mr. Flynn, come to honor us."

"A good evening to you, Hughie," Stephen said. "You're the watchman tonight?"

"Aye, that's so."

"Where might young Davy Ryan be keeping himself?"

The watchman motioned toward the distant flicker of light. "He's having a game of cards with the other lads. They go on all night, those lads with no wives. Got nothing to go to bed for."

"I'd be obliged if you'd ask him to come up top. I've something to discuss with him."

Hughie bobbed his head. "Aye, Mr. Flynn. I'd be honored to deliver the message."

Stephen had started back up the ladder when the watchman said, "We hear you married the girl who killed the sailor. She's a fine strap altogether. Danced to my fiddle like none I've seen."

Something must have shown in Stephen's face, for the watchman gave him a sympathetic look. "She's got a proud way about her, but you'll put her to rights, Mr. Flynn. If any man can do it, tis you."

Stephen climbed back on deck, feeling a fresh wave of irritation. He should be lying in Anna's arms right now, content as a pig in clover. Instead he was passing half the night outside, wet and cold. Stephen turned up his collar against the mist and shoved his fists into his jacket pockets. By hell, he'd have her in his bed before they reached New York. He'd have her even if he had to bow and scrape like some bloody fool lord and kiss her hand while doing it.

"You were asking for me, Mr. Flynn?"

In the greenish light of the forecastle lantern, Davy Ryan's face was barely recognizable. His jaw was swollen, one eye looked puffed and dark, and his nose was strangely askew. "You took a fair beating, lad," Stephen said.

Davy stared at the deck. "There was too many of them, coming all at once. They knocked me around and tossed me down the hold. Before I could get up again, they'd clapped on the hatch cover."

"You did a fine job, Davy. I'm obliged to you, and so is Anna."

Davy's face brightened, and it occurred to Stephen that the lad thought he'd come to criticize his poor performance. "How is she, then?" Davy asked.

"Well enough."

"They say you married her."

"It was the only way. The passengers made a fuss, and the captain would have sent her back."

"He wanted her for himself," Davy said indignantly. "He wanted to keep her in his own cabin, that's what I hear."

"She's safe enough now." Safe as a fortress, Stephen thought to himself.

"You're a lucky man," Davy said. "All the lads say so. But I'd say she's lucky herself—"

"What are your plans for New York?" Stephen interrupted. He was tired of thinking of Anna.

Davy straightened up proudly. "Once I'm a rich man in America, I'll be sending for my da and my mam and the rest of them that's stayed back in Mayo."

"Well then," Stephen said. "That sounds fine. But before you get to be king, you might be wanting a job. Would you mind working around a saloon?"

Davy's eyes widened. "Work for you?"

"If you're inclined."

"Why—why, sure," Davy stammered. "That would be grand."

"It's settled, then," Stephen said, digging in his pocket for his card. "Stop around at the Emerald Flame, Brace Street, the Bowery. I'll find something for you."

As Davy stared at the card, Stephen studied him, wondering if he was the sort of lad who could carry out Padraic's mission to Birmingham. In his knitted gansey and corduroy trousers bagging around his boots, Davy Ryan looked like a Paddylander all right, but he had courage. He'd faced down a pack of rough seamen, trying to defend a girl.

No, Stephen thought. Davy's head was too full of his own ambitions. The flame that burned in his heart was not for Ireland but for all that America had to offer.

Davy looked up from the card. "You tell Anna I'll be seeing her, then. Tell her I'll be seeing her in New York, on Brace Street, the Bowery."

Stephen started to speak and decided against it. He decided not to say that Anna was with him only for the voyage, that when they reached New York, they would go their separate ways.

When Stephen got up the next morning, he was still in a foul mood. He had tossed all night and slept only when dawn was breaking. Now his eyes felt raw and his head groggy.

Rory's berth was empty and neatly made. Stephen was surprised; Rory never made his bunk. The red and white striped drape that divided the stateroom was drawn. Stephen pulled on his fighting drawers and took a look behind the curtain.

Anna's bed-curtains were still closed.

Blast the woman, he thought. Brooding about her had kept him awake half the night. Stephen banged the ewer and washbasin and pounded the floor with his heaviest walk. He cocked his head, listening for sounds of Anna stirring. He heard nothing save for the squeak and thump of the sea against wood. The engines were silent. *Damn!* They were shut down again. At this rate, it would take an extra week to get to New York.

Exasperated, Stephen threw back the curtain. "By the power, woman! Get off your lazy back and rise up to face the day!"

Just then the cabin door opened. He turned to see Anna coming in. "I'm not the lazy one, Stephen Flynn. I've been up since six. It's near nine o'clock."

At the sight of her, rosy and rested, Stephen's frustration boiled over. "Hell's fire! You took a start out of me, sneaking in like that."

"You're in a beast of a mood," Anna said, closing the door behind her. "And after such a long sleep, too."

"I barely slept a minute, thanks to you."

"Don't pass the blame to me. I didn't make a peep all night."

She was annoyingly chipper. Her springy hair was bundled high on her head, but already curls had worked loose and were falling about her neck and ears. Her pale green dress, faded almost to silver from too many washings, was clean and pressed and snug on her figure. Stephen thought of her damp, clinging camisole, the shape of her through her drawers. He sat down on the sofa and ran his hands over his weary face.

"Prut, Mr. Flynn, you need some food to soothe your mood. I'll ring for the steward. And put on your shirt. It's not decent, showing yourself so."

Anna reached across him for the bellpull and farther still to open the scuttle for a fresh breeze. Her nearness stirred his senses. Stephen closed his eyes and groaned.

Anna made an impatient sound. "A wee bit tired and you're moaning like you're tied to the rack. Get dressed, then. The steward will come with some coffee and you'll feel better."

Stephen clapped his hands on his thighs and stood up. He pulled himself into a mighty stretch, filling his lungs, flexing his muscles.

Anna glanced at him, a flush rising on her creamy cheeks. Stephen laughed and reached for his shirt. He pulled it on, pleased that he'd made her blush. "Where's Rory?"

Anna was on her knees, poking about in one of her boxes. "He's with the steerage boys, those Curran twins. A gang of them organized a game of running through the holds."

Stephen fastened his shirt cuff and yawned again. "See that he has a bath when he comes back."

Anna sat back on her heels. "So I'm in charge of Rory's baths?"

Stephen's fingers stilled on his buttons. He looked at her, kneeling with her pale skirts gathered around her, and thought of the way she'd peeled the boy out of his clothes yesterday. She'd given him a cuddle and a tickle, the sort of thing a father didn't do with a son. And when the chocolate had arrived, she'd scolded the steward because it wasn't hot enough and sent him back for a fresh pot. It seemed natural that she'd look after the boy.

"You're good with him, that's all."

Anna turned back to her box and pawed among linens until she pulled out a little drawstring bag. "I don't mind doing it." She closed the trunk and got to her feet.

"No, I'm his da," Stephen said. He'd best not start counting on Anna to look after Rory. She and the boy might grow too fond of each other, and that would mean trouble when she left them in New York.

"It's up to you," Anna said with a shrug. She brushed past him to the table, where she emptied the bag of crochet pieces and began sorting them. "I want to be working on my opera bag when I see Mrs. Smith-Hampton. If she buys one, all the other ladies will want one, too." Anna glanced up at Stephen. "That's what you said."

"That's what I said. They'll all want one, sure as eyes blink."

"I saw her this morning, passing in the corridor. She'll be bringing her mending by the ladies' saloon at ten." Anna's hands on the crochet pieces trembled slightly, and Stephen realized that she was nervous.

"They'll all want one bag, maybe two," he said. "And you'll be doing their mending as well."

Anna sighed. "I hope my fingers stay still enough to work. Oh, they shake so, just thinking of those ladies."

"Those ladies have nothing on you."

She admonished him with a glance. "How you talk."

"It's true. I swear it. How many of them put their husbands in their place last night?"

Anna's smile widened and her color rose. That smile did something to Stephen. He stood looking at her, lost in the pleasure of her beauty, then brought himself up fast. He was going soft on her. It just went to show how long he'd been sleeping alone.

The steward arrived with a tray of breakfast. Stephen munched on bread and bacon while Anna sat across the table, stitching through several thicknesses of fabric. Stephen watched the needle in her hands, the concentration on her face. She was damned capable, for a woman. And determined, too. No doubt about that.

Stephen refilled his coffee cup from the pot. She could go about her business in New York and make a success of herself, he thought, as long as there was no man to bother her. But likely as not, there would always be some blackguard sniffing around. Anna was so tempting that any number of characters would be wanting to take advantage of her. Stephen pushed away his coffee cup. The idea of any other man putting his hands on her roused his temper.

Anna glanced up at the little gold clock that hung on the cabin wall. She folded her bundle of fabric. "It's time for me to meet my ladies. Wish me luck, then."

"When will you be back?"

"Oh, by dinnertime, for sure." Anna stepped before the mirror to tuck her curls in place. Her ears were pretty, Stephen thought, delicately edged with pink. "This dress is a sin," she said, "so old and faded, but I can't wear my blue jacket and skirt every day." She twisted before her reflection, showing herself to lovely advantage.

Stephen couldn't take his eyes off her. "You look all right."

"Well, then," she said briskly, gathering up her bundle and her workbag. "I'll be gone."

Stephen got to his feet and held the door for her. He leaned against the doorframe and watched her hurry down the passageway. At the turn to the promenade deck, she turned and smiled. He raised his hand in a salute. "Good luck, darling," he said, even though she was too far away to hear him.

Chapter 8

❧

Anna arrived at the ladies' boudoir well before her appointment with Mrs. Smith-Hampton. Glancing inside, she saw that the room was empty, save for three elderly ladies in black faille and pearls seated on stout high-backed chairs. Two of the ladies conversed loudly while the third dozed.

Anna touched her hair to be sure her tortoiseshell combs were in place, squared her shoulders, and entered the saloon. To her relief, none of the ladies noticed her.

She took her seat on the blue sofa by the stern windows. The morning sun poured into her lap and shone on the black lacquered tea table. Anna unfolded her bundle, placed the crochet motifs on the table, and began to work a chain of stitches for the opera bag's border.

As her crochet hook spun out a delicate chain of white, her eyes traveled frequently to the boudoir doorway. At any moment Mrs. Smith-Hampton and the other ladies would bustle in, shrill-voiced and confident. Anna moistened her lips. Mercy, she was nervous, and for what reason? For all she'd been through, there was nothing to fear from a few ladies armed only with sharp words and lofty glances. Even if these women didn't want her opera bag, the New York shops would surely be interested—not just in her bag but in her yokes and cuffs and her lovely tea cloths as well. Hadn't Stephen himself said she would find customers? Sure as eyes blink, he'd said.

Anna smiled to herself. Wasn't he a character? So different from the cocksure man she'd first taken him to be. For a few moments of kissing and grabbing last night, she'd been afraid he would overpower her. But she'd tamed him quickly enough, put him right in his place. Now he was a bit sulky, but hardly dangerous.

A gentle throat-clearing interrupted Anna's thoughts. She looked up to see Mrs. Smith-Hampton standing before her, her slim figure and delicate coloring overwhelmed by a voluminous gown of too-bright yellow. In her gloved fingers she clasped a frothy bundle of lace.

"Good morning again, Mrs. Flynn. I hope I haven't kept you waiting."

Anna eyed the lace, her nervousness pushed aside by the prospect of work. "I haven't been waiting a moment, Mrs. Smith-Hampton." She patted the fuzzy velvet sofa cushion beside her. "Please sit yourself."

Once seated, Mrs. Smith-Hampton unfolded a sheer length of lace. "I hope you don't think me forward to approach you as I did. About the mending, I mean."

"Not at all," Anna said, studying the delicate work. She saw both appliqué and guipure techniques. "I'm flattered that you would trust me with such a lovely piece."

"It's one panel of an overskirt. Mr. Smith-Hampton stepped on it as I was climbing down from a carriage." She laughed. "My husband is not the lightest man on his feet."

Anna glanced at Mrs. Smith-Hampton's face, flushed and merry. *She loves him,* Anna thought, *that wicked man with a mistress.*

She bent closer to examine the rent. She would fill the torn places with wheels, stitches, and buttonhole bars. "It will take a few days."

"Oh, heavens, there's no hurry. I don't need the gown till the concert next Monday. My girl only needs some time to sew the panel back onto the skirt."

"Very well, then." Anna folded the lace carefully. "I'll give it to you on Friday."

Mrs. Smith-Hampton turned her attention to the crochet motifs on the tea table. "Aren't these lovely!" She picked up a pinwheel. "What fine work you do, Mrs. Flynn. Where did you learn?"

Anna felt a moment of embarrassment at the stigma of poverty attached to lace making. "Relief lace" it had been called during the famine and after, when ragged girls and poor women took to crocheting lace as a means of earning a wage.

"I learned as a girl from the landlord's wife. When I went to Dublin, my mistress sent me to a real school, where teachers from England and Belgium taught appliqué and point."

Mrs. Smith-Hampton picked up a small leaf and traced the curve of the spine. "I do embroidery myself, but it's very poor, I'm afraid."

"I like crochet best," Anna said, pleased at Mrs. Smith-Hampton's interest. "It's sturdier, and all the time I can think up new stitches."

While Mrs. Smith-Hampton examined a pinwheel, Anna explained further. "Making crochet designs is like drawing a picture," she said. "Some people make a commonplace picture, while others make a picture that's special, artistic. It all depends on how you hold the cord, how you make a curve, where you add a little sprig."

"You, Mrs. Flynn, are obviously an artist."

"Oh," Anna said, flushing. "I didn't mean to brag."

A commotion at the door announced the arrival of the other ladies. Mrs. Smith-Hampton gathered her skirts. "I must join them," she said. "We're rehearsing for the concert."

Anna retrieved her crocheting and resumed work on the chain border. As she worked, she kept an eye on the ladies. Miss Camberwell, her hair trailing lavender ribbons, sat at the polished walnut piano, running through scales and chords. The other ladies clustered around Mrs. Charles, who passed out leather-covered songbooks and decided the order of the program. Then the ladies, except for Miss Camberwell and Mrs. Smith-Hampton, withdrew to chairs and sofas. Miss Camberwell struck the opening chords of a song, and Mrs. Smith-Hampton took her place at the curve of the piano, her hands loosely clasped before her. She closed her eyes and her voice rose sweetly. Anna's hands stilled in her lap.

It was a sad song, a ballad of love and lost happiness. Mrs. Smith-Hampton sang with assurance and feeling, her voice flawless and clear.

When I close mine aching eyes,
Sweet dreams my senses fill;
And from sleep when I arise,
His bright smile haunts me still.

Anna glanced around. The elderly ladies leaned forward on their canes, intent on every note, and a stewardess listened at the door. Gracious, Anna thought, Mrs. Smith-Hampton was an artist herself, a musical artist.

The other ladies were apparently familiar with her talents, for when the last few notes died away, they didn't applaud, but fell to chattering and arguing about who should appear next on the program.

Another lady took her turn, but her voice was shrill and warbling, and Anna winced at the high notes. Then Mrs. Smith-Hampton sang again, a livelier tune, delivered with a style and verve that made Anna smile.

She listened to the rehearsal long enough to finish crocheting the opera bag border. Then she gathered up her work and Mrs. Smith-Hampton's skirt panel and departed.

She hummed to herself as she strode down the promenade deck, her head high, her stride brisk. Passengers stared as she passed, but Anna paid them no attention. What did she care what they thought? She had Mrs. Smith-Hampton's lace in her workbag, she'd soon be earning money, and Stephen wouldn't be bothering her. She felt as free as the air.

As Anna turned off the promenade deck and headed toward the cabin, she saw a small figure skulking about outside the cabin door. It looked like Rory. Anna quickened her pace.

By the time she reached him, Anna was running. She dropped her bag and crouched down before him. With his chin on his chest, all she could see was a tangled thatch of black hair. Then she noticed blood on his shirt, and her heart jumped. "Show me your face," she said. "Look at me, now."

She nudged Rory's chin upward. Blood crusted his nostrils, and his lip was cut and swollen. A bruise darkened his left eye.

Anna winced. "Oh, my, will you look at that. Took the worst of it, did you?"

Rory's face was screwed up against tears, and there were wet tracks on his cheeks. "Open your mouth," Anna said. He bared his teeth, which all seemed to be in place.

Anna got to her feet and pushed him into the cabin. "Why are you lurking about out here? Why not go inside?"

"My da," Rory said. He threw his arm across his face and began to sob. "He won't like it."

"Oh, whisht now," Anna said. "What's he going to say? That you shouldn't fight? Who is he to talk?" She helped Rory off with his jacket and unbuttoned his shirt.

Rory licked his lips, grimacing in pain, and scrubbed at his cheeks with his palms, trying to rid them of tears.

"We'll fix you up before he comes back," Anna said. "He'll never know the worst of it."

Anna had just eased Rory's shirt over his head when the door opened and Stephen walked in. Rory's face again disappeared behind his arms.

Anna got to her feet. "Now, Stephen," she began, hoping to head off an explosion.

"What the devil?" Stephen stood in the doorway, staring at Rory.

"It was a wee bit of a scrap," Anna said. "Nothing to bother about—"

"Christ Almighty!" Stephen grabbed Rory's arms away from his face. The boy shrank back with fright.

"Stephen, now calm yourself."

"Who did this!" Stephen bellowed, glaring at Anna. "Who did this to him? I'll have his sacred life."

"For pity's sake, Stephen, boys fight all the time." Anna went to the door and closed it. "There's no harm in it."

"No harm in it! He's too small!"

"Stephen, he's a boy—"

"He's my son!"

"Oh, is that it? The son of a prizefighter should get the best of it, not the worst. Is that what you're saying?"

Stephen's face turned thunderous. He pointed a finger at Anna. "Understand one thing," he said in a voice low with anger. "This boy is a blessing to me. I don't want him fighting because I don't want him hurt."

Anna felt the blood rush to her face. Hadn't she just spoken without thinking? "That's as it should be, then," she said. "But you're still making a mountain out of a molehill."

Stephen inspected Rory's wounds. "It was the Curran twins, wasn't it?"

Rory nodded, staring at Stephen as if surprised that his father found him worthy of attention after his miserable beating.

"Those Currans are too old for you to play with. I've seen them, a couple of dirty, smirky-faced boys. Trouble written all over them."

"They're only ten years old," Anna said.

"I don't want him running around with steerage lads."

"Good heavens, Stephen—"

"He'll be picking up their habits. And when he gets to New York he'll take up with street gypsies, stealing from stores and docks, picking pockets. Next thing I know, he'll be working for a gang—the Water Rats or worse, the Dead Rabbits . . ." Stephen's face darkened. "What's so damned funny?"

Anna covered her mouth. It had been a long time since anything had struck her so funny as Stephen Flynn's wild leap of imagination. "He's a good boy, Stephen, not a criminal."

"You don't know—"

"I *do* know," Anna said, smiling. "I know little boys. Now, sit down and rest yourself. Your temper's frayed, Mr. Flynn, that's for sure."

"Thanks to you," Stephen muttered. But he did as he was told. Anna watched from the corner of her eye as he slumped down on the sofa and rubbed his big hands on his knees.

Anna turned her attention to Rory's bruises and clucked her tongue. The child was not a natural fighter, she thought. Surely he'd been provoked beyond patience. "What was it, then, Rory? Did they say something?"

Rory swallowed hard and kept silent.

Anna picked up his bloodstained shirt. "Now isn't this a mess," she said. "A whole evening's mending for me, not to mention scrubbing out those spots. What I need is some lemon juice, a pinch of salt—"

"Don't bother with it. He's got plenty more."

Stephen sat with shoulders hunched forward, his hands clasped loosely between his knees. Anna met his eyes and saw that his anger was gone, replaced by something softer. She looked away. "I won't be throwing out a perfectly good shirt."

"I didn't think you would."

The guarded admiration in his voice made Anna flush. For a minute she felt as if the three of them belonged together, as if they were a family.

She drew Rory to the washbasin and poured fresh water from the pitcher. She wet the cloth and pressed it to his nose and dabbed at his lip. Rory winced, but made no sound.

"Did those Currans say something about me?" Anna asked.

Rory started to speak, but tears filled his eyes. He pressed his lips together and nodded.

Anna smiled. "I knew you were a gallant little lad from the moment I laid eyes on you. But you needn't fight for me, Rory Flynn."

"They said bad things."

"Oh, I'm sure they did. I've been called plenty of names in my life, but I've lived to laugh at all of it." Anna pinched his nose. "Even so, I thank you."

Rory's bruised eye was darkening by the minute, but his gaze was rapt. Anna could have crushed him in a hug. Instead, she rumpled his hair. "Folks will be confusing you with your da when they see that eye."

"The devil they will," Stephen said gruffly. "I've never taken such a blow."

Rory looked at his father. "You have, Da. You've been hit worse."

"Come here, young Flynn." Stephen drew Rory between his knees. Curling the boy's fingers into fists, he covered them with his own big hands. "I think you'll be needing some lessons. Not to make you a fighter, mind you, but to keep you from getting hurt. There's boys in New York who've been fighting in the streets since they could walk, boys your age who are bigger and plenty mean."

Rory nodded solemnly.

"Tomorrow we'll start. You and the other boys, too, if they want. Even the Currans. I'll teach them to fight fair and you to fight dirty."

Anna smiled. It was a relief that Stephen wasn't going to make the boy a mollycoddle.

Rory squirmed away and ran to his trunk. He dug out a fresh shirt. "I'll tell Eddie and Mike that we'll be getting boxing lessons. Real lessons."

"Oh, so you're friends again, you and the Currans," Anna said.

Rory pulled on his shirt impatiently. "They're not so bad."

Anna glanced at Stephen. " 'Twould be a sorry fellow that wasn't a little bad," she said, reminding him of the words he'd spoken the day they met.

She saw that he didn't need reminding. He gave her a small, private smile. "Doesn't hurt a woman to be a little bad herself."

Rory dashed for the door. "Don't forget your dinner," Anna said. "I want to see you in the dining saloon, Currans or no Currans."

The cabin fell silent. Anna picked up the torn shirt and took it to the washbasin. With the block of soap, she rubbed the blood spots, trying to concentrate on her work and not on Stephen, who she knew was watching her. As the silence lengthened, Anna felt a rising tension in the room that was lovely and disturbing at the same time.

At last Stephen spoke. "How do you know so much about boys?"

Anna shrugged. "I had brothers."

"How many, then?"

"Three." Anna said. "Sean was just ten, and the babies . . ." She stopped, her voice cracking "The babies were just two."

He was silent for a moment. "They died in the famine?"

Anna nodded. She continued to scrub at the shirt, though it was now clean of spots. She didn't want to stop; she didn't want to look at Stephen with her eyes full of tears.

"That's in the past now," Stephen said. "You've got a new life ahead."

Anna wiped her eyes with the back of her arm, careful to keep her head averted.

"What about your mam and your da?"

"When the babies died, my mam went off her head." Anna spoke softly, not trusting her voice. "That was the end of her, God rest her soul."

"And your father?"

Anna wrung out the shirt and slapped it on the wash-stand. "I'll thank you not to be prying where you've got no business."

She emptied the basin, splattering water on the floor. Tears blurred her vision.

Then Stephen was beside her, taking the basin away. "You had a bad time, darling." He put his hands on her arms.

She tried to push him away. "So hasn't everyone?"

He held her fast. "I'm sorry for your trouble."

"There's plenty who fared worse than me." But she stopped struggling. She felt a longing for comfort, and Stephen was easy to rest against, big and solid as he was.

"Anna," he said. "Look at me, now."

She kept her forehead against his shoulder, not daring to lift her face. He held her innocently enough, but she knew his intentions. If she looked up, his mouth would be on hers, and she wouldn't have the will to fight him.

Stephen's hands moved on her back, rubbing away her distress, easing her closer.

Anna closed her eyes and leaned more heavily. It was good to be held so. Her hands slipped around Stephen's waist. Her head fit snugly between his shoulder and neck.

He nuzzled her hair. "Sweet Nan. Aren't you a lovely armful."

"Don't be forgetting yourself," she warned.

She felt the laughter in his chest. "As if you'd let me."

Anna smiled. Her fingers splayed on his back. Stephen's arms tightened, pressing her breasts against his chest. Anna tensed, and he loosened his grip. "You don't like hugs?" he asked. "You give such nice ones to Rory."

"You're too big for that."

"Ah, darling. It's a sorry man who's too big for hugs from a loving woman."

"I'll not be your loving woman, Stephen Flynn," Anna said. She pulled away, careful not to look at him.

She refilled the washbasin and rinsed Rory's shirt one more time. She twisted the water from the cloth and draped it over the corner of the washstand, thinking all the while how strong Stephen's arms had felt, how comforting.

Anna devoted the rest of the day to Mrs. Smith-Hampton's lace. The next morning she presented the mended skirt panel.

"So quickly!" Mrs. Smith-Hampton exclaimed as she examined the lace. "And so lovely. Why, Mrs. Flynn, I declare, you're a wonder."

The other ladies observed from across the room. Anna hoped they would be impressed enough by her prompt and flawless work to give her their business once they got to New York.

"I'll speak to my husband about settling the bill," Mrs. Smith-Hampton said. "I believe you said four dollars would be adequate payment."

Anna hadn't indicated anything of the sort, but four dollars seemed more than generous. "Fair enough," she said, concealing her excitement.

"I'll have my girl deliver an envelope to your cabin after dinner."

Anna worked on her opera bag for the rest of the morning. While the ladies sang, declaimed, and labored over piano pieces, Anna sewed her crochet motifs to the cambric foundation, making sure each one was secure enough not to pull out of shape when she worked the background. She looked up occasionally to observe the activity, but mostly she kept her mind on her work, on Mrs. Smith-Hampton's four dollars, and on the hundred and forty dollars she owed Stephen.

At four dollars each, it would take thirty-five mending jobs to pay Stephen the price of her passage, Anna figured. Or seven opera bags, if she charged twenty dollars a piece. Or some combination of opera bags and mending jobs. She might also interest the ladies in her supply of lace collars and bonnet trim. . . . Oh, bother! Trying to figure the mathematics of it made her dizzy. And there was no use counting her money or her debts, since she hadn't yet sold an inch of lace.

Anna remained in the ladies' saloon until dinnertime. During the meal she didn't mention the four dollars to Stephen. In fact, she said little to him. She had been much too free with him, digging up memories best left to the ages and then giving in to his embrace. If she knew what was good for her, she would keep her distance.

That afternoon she waited impatiently for Mrs. Smith-Hampton's payment. At three o'clock the girl arrived at the cabin with an envelope and a curtsy.

Anna stared at the envelope. Written across the front in a flowing script was her name: Mrs. Flynn. Anna eased open the flap. Inside was a bank draft and another of Mrs. Smith-Hampton's cards. Across it she had written, "Thank you. I am very pleased."

Anna held the draft in her palm, savoring the feel of it. Then she replaced it in the envelope and laid it on Stephen's bunk.

He came in an hour later, damp from a session of sparring with the steerage men. He shed his jacket, grabbed his towel and soap, and prepared to go for a bath. Then he noticed the envelope on his berth.

"What's this?" He leaned down and picked it up. "Mrs. Flynn," he read. "It's yours, Anna."

Anna bent over her work. "It's for you."

Stephen tossed his towel over his shoulder and opened the envelope. "Four dollars," he said. "It's payment from Mrs. Smith-Hampton."

"I owe it to you. Part payment for my fare." Anna kept sewing, her cheeks warm, waiting for his response.

"You owe me nothing."

"I owe you one hundred and forty dollars."

"I'm not taking your money."

Anna looked up from her work. "You'd rather have something else as payment, wouldn't you? Well, I won't be doing that, so you may as well take my money."

Stephen swore softly. "Listen to yourself one time, Anna," he said. "Listen to the things you say."

Anna stared at him defiantly. "I'm speaking the truth, and you know it."

But before she'd finished her words, he'd left, slamming the cabin door behind him.

When Stephen ran along the starlit deck that night, he thought about Rory needing a mother. He had fought the idea since first hearing from the lad; recently, however, he'd decided that he wasn't up to raising his son by himself. He needed a woman to see that the boy made his bed in the morning and kept things tidy. A woman would make sure that Rory didn't suck on candy day and night or swing from the curtain rods or neglect his prayers.

It was the issue of prayers that had started him thinking. Anna had brought up the subject one evening, and Rory had complained loudly, "But my da doesn't make me say prayers."

Anna had given Stephen a sharp look. "Oh, he doesn't, does he?"

Stephen had had no defense. He'd forgotten all about prayers. But he'd been pleased to see Rory on his knees, his small hands clasped, his eyes closed tight, blessing everyone he could think of, living and dead.

Stephen jogged to a stop by the bathhouse, then jabbed the air a few times before stepping inside. As he stripped off his clothes, he thought about Rory's fight with the Curran twins. Anna had handled it, smooth as silk. If it hadn't been for her, he'd have gone off to steerage and given those boys a good smack. Probably had a row with their father. Instead, he'd started giving boxing lessons to a whole pack of scruffy little devils, showing them there was more to fighting than shouting and punching. Giving the lessons had been his idea, but he would never have thought of it had it not been for Anna's good sense.

Stephen poured cold water over himself, sputtering and shivering, and scrubbed himself with soap. Rose had been the best wife in the world; a more selfless and saintly girl he couldn't imagine. But wouldn't Rose want him to marry for Rory's sake? To see that the boy was decently raised, that he didn't fall in with the wrong crowd?

He would find the sort of girl that Rose would approve of, Stephen thought. A good, God-fearing Irish girl, trained to cook and clean, who was cheerful and sensible. And she wouldn't have Anna's sharp tongue. He'd make sure of that. He'd choose a girl with a sweet disposition who wouldn't talk back.

When Stephen returned to the cabin, Anna and Rory were sleeping. He was too restless to turn in, so he pulled on a clean pair of fighting drawers and sprawled on the sofa with an old issue of *Harper's Weekly*. As he leafed through the pages, he glanced at the pictures—the Crystal Palace exhibition hall, the Fifth Avenue Hotel, Barnum's Museum—and remembered Anna's excitement over Gramercy Park. She would love the city, strolling along Broadway, looking at the handsome shops fitted up with plate-glass fronts. He imagined taking her for a meal at Delmonico's. Maybe a moonlight steamboat excursion on the Hudson. Afterward he'd take her up to his flat and show her the improvements he'd made.

Stephen tossed aside the magazine and sat up, surprised at his thoughts. He reminded himself that all he wanted from Anna was a few nights in bed. And he would have her, too, with a small change in tactics. He'd discovered that she liked things sweet and easy. She liked to be stroked and nuzzled and hugged. That was fine with him; he'd do whatever it took.

"Da?"

Stephen looked up to see Rory's shaggy head poking out of the bed-curtains.

"What are you doing awake so late, sport?"

"I want to ask you something." Rory pulled aside the curtains and dropped lightly to the floor.

"Make it quick, then," Stephen said as Rory bounced down beside him.

"I was thinking . . . will Anna be my ma?"

The question took Stephen aback. "You know who your ma was."

"But she's dead. And you're married to Anna."

Stephen hunched forward on the sofa. "I married Anna to save her from going back to steerage. You know that. It's just to get her safely to New York, not to be your ma."

Rory stared at him, awaiting further explanation. "The priest didn't marry us," Stephen continued, "so we're only part married." He rubbed his palms together. The devil, he thought. "It's hard to explain."

Rory thrust out his legs and studied his bare toes. "Do you sleep with her?"

Stephen glanced at the curtain dividing the cabin. "Of course I don't sleep with her," he said, lowering his voice to a whisper. "I have my own bunk."

"I know what the sailor tried to do to her. The one she killed."

Stephen felt his stomach clench. "Well, forget about it. Put it out of your mind."

"Do you do that to her?"

Stephen jumped to his feet. "Good God, Rory! You're too young to know of that."

Rory slumped farther down on the sofa, looking glum. "I already know."

Stephen glanced desperately at the curtain. If Anna was awake, she'd know how to deal with the boy's questions. Then again, he wouldn't want her to hear this sort of talk.

"Eddie and Mike said you—"

"Never mind what Eddie and Mike say. They don't know anything."

"They said all people who are married—"

"Don't talk about it!" Stephen's muscles were tense with alarm. He glanced at Rory, whose chin rested on his chest, and wondered what he should do. "It's time you went back to bed."

"I wish I could go down to the engine room."

Stephen sat down gingerly on the sofa, grateful for a new topic of conversation. "You can't go down there."

"Why not?"

"It's hot," Stephen said. "And dangerous."

"I wish I could see it."

"I'll tell you about it and you can imagine it. There are long shafts moving up and down turning the screws, and it smells like oil. The stokers keep throwing coal into the furnace. You can see the flames eating up the coal. It's so hot it makes your eyes burn in their sockets, and your mouth feels full of ashes."

"You've seen it, then?"

Stephen nodded. "When I left Ireland years ago, I worked as a stoker for my passage."

"You did?" Rory asked, his voice soft with awe.

"Aye, I did. And I hope never to set foot in an engine room again." Stephen smiled at Rory, thinking how good it was to be worshiped by his son. He reached out to rub the lad's hair. Rory moved beneath his hand like a grateful pup.

"Do you think I'll be a good fighter, Da?"

Stephen laughed. "No, and I don't want you to be. Uncle Padraic says you're clever at school."

"Anna's da was a schoolmaster."

"Was he?" So that explained why a girl from the west country could read and write and speak proper English.

"He kept school in his house when he wasn't working in the field. He taught Anna and her brothers Irish and English, and he wrote letters for the people who couldn't write. Anna has five of his books in her box. One of them is about the history of America."

"Well, then, our Anna is a scholar."

Rory worked his way into the circle of Stephen's arm. "Da?"

"What is it?"

"You said there were two kinds of women. The good ones, like my ma, and the other ones, like Anna."

Stephen stiffened. Wouldn't you know the lad would divert his attention and then bring the conversation back to her. "Listen to me, Rory," he said, losing patience. "Your ma, God rest her, was more than good. She was a saint. That's all I'm going to say. You go to bed, now, and this time I mean it."

Chapter 9

Anna spent the following day in the cabin, working on her opera bag. Not until late afternoon did she go down to the ladies' saloon. As she made her way to her customary seat on the sofa by the stern windows, the buzz of conversation dropped off and the clink of teatime silverware and china ceased. All attention, it seemed, turned to her. Anna lifted her chin, prepared to return the ladies' haughty stares, but to her surprise, the glances were more curious than hostile. A few ladies wore expressions that were almost friendly.

Anna hurried to the sofa and busied herself with her work-bag. She took out the cambric foundation, around which she had sewn a chain of crochet, and laid out the motifs. Being the object of curiosity made her stomach jittery and her mouth dry. It was easier being ignored, Anna thought, as she licked the end of her thread and thrust it through the needle's eye. But if she wanted wealthy ladies as customers, she would have to learn to hold her own.

Anna had finished sewing a star flower in place when a voice interrupted her. "Pray, what are you working on, Mrs. Flynn? You have us all curious."

Anna looked up into the horsey face of Mrs. Charles and felt a start of fright. "It's . . . an opera bag."

"Indeed." Mrs. Charles stared down her nose at Anna. Or perhaps it only seemed so, since she was so tall and Anna was seated. Mrs. Charles held out her hand. "I'd like to inspect it, if you please."

Anna was about to comply, when she caught herself. She patted the seat beside her. "Please sit yourself, Mrs. Charles," she said. "I'll show it to you."

Mrs. Charles hesitated. Then, tilting her voluminous crinolines, she sat.

Anna spread the cambric on her lap. "It's a bag to carry an opera glass and handkerchief and anything else you might want. The bag will be lined with silk, and there will be pockets inside and a frill at the top—"

"I know what an opera bag is," Mrs. Charles said impatiently.

"I can make any size—"

"I like a bag that is heavily decorated."

Anna moistened her lips. She wasn't ready for selling, especially to a woman who wouldn't let her finish a sentence. "I can do pendants and flowers and balls on the sides."

"I want cord for the drawstring, not ribbon. And I want decorative knots in the cord and pendants, too."

"Yes'm."

"When can you have it finished?"

Anna's thoughts flew. "This . . . this very bag?"

Mrs. Charles pursed her lips. "That, Mrs. Flynn, is what I'm asking."

"Two days."

"Very well." Mrs. Charles prepared to rise. "The price, I assume, will be reasonable. Surely not more than ten dollars."

Anna opened her mouth to agree, then quickly closed it. She looked at Mrs. Charles's rouged cheeks, the sleek pomaded hair, the expensive silk roses that decorated her lavender gown. Mr. Charles, whoever he was, had to be rich. "The price is twenty dollars."

Mrs. Charles sank back on the sofa, her eyes wide. "You are not serious."

Anna's gaze didn't waver. "I am quite serious," she said. "This is a fine bag."

"Have you any idea what this sort of thing goes for in the New York shops?"

"I'm afraid I don't," Anna said, copying Mrs. Charles's tone. "But I would be most interested."

Mrs. Charles made no further comment, but she moved her shoulders indignantly, a signal that Anna had won. Digging in her reticule, she took out a card similar to Mrs. Smith-Hampton's and dropped it on the table. "I shall inspect your work periodically over the next two days."

"That won't be necessary, Mrs. Charles. I understand what you want."

"My dear Mrs. Flynn, if I am to pay the outrageous price of twenty dollars for an opera bag, I expect to monitor its creation."

On this point Anna would not give in. "I'll be making it with your wants in mind," she said, "but I won't be changing it as I go along. When it's finished, you'll have no obligation. If you don't like it, I'll sell it to someone else."

Mrs. Charles drew in her chin and fixed Anna with a glacial stare. "Well! Aren't you the cheeky one. Irish to the bone."

Anna flushed. "I mean no disrespect. It's only that I have to do my work as I see fit."

Mrs. Charles sniffed. "Very well, then. I'll expect to see the bag in two days' time." And with a rustle of silk she rose and hurried out of the saloon.

Anna sank back on the sofa. She had done it. She had sold her first bag entirely on her own terms.

Only then did Anna notice that the saloon was silent. Every woman present had watched the exchange. They had overheard every word. From across the room, Mrs. Smith-Hampton caught Anna's eye and smiled.

During the next hour several ladies consulted Anna on lace-mending projects. They complimented her on the work she'd done for Mrs. Smith-Hampton, and each left a visiting card. Anna peeked at the addresses and felt a dip of disappointment. Fifth Avenue, Broadway, and Fifteenth Street didn't sound nearly as lovely as Gramercy Park.

By six o'clock the ladies were drifting out the door in chattering clusters. Anna sat quietly, feeling happiness of the purest sort, happiness that came from one's own accomplishments and not simply from luck.

She hummed a tune as she gathered her belongings together. She hoped Stephen would be in the cabin. He would be pleased at her success; she knew he would.

Moments later when Anna stepped into the cabin, the lamps had not been lit. Stephen was sprawled on the sofa, his collar off, his shirt rumpled and open. At first Anna thought he was asleep, but then he lifted his hand in a dispirited greeting. "Good evening, Mrs. Flynn."

Anna put down her bundle. "What are you doing, sitting in the dark?"

"Being bloody bored, that's what. There's not a damned thing worth doing on this ship."

Anna thought of showing off her newly acquired cards, but Stephen didn't seem to be in a mood for seeing them or for hearing the news of Mrs. Charles and the opera bag.

"You should be busy enough," she said, "what with giving lessons to the boys and sparring with the men. And the gentlemen in the saloon enjoy your company."

Stephen stood up and stretched, displaying a generous expanse of bare chest. He went to light the lamps. "How are things with the ladies?"

"Good enough," Anna said.

There was a little puff of sound as the gas caught the flame. Light flared, striking Stephen's hair with gold. His shirt sleeves were peeled back, revealing muscular forearms, brown from the sun. The sharp angles of his profile appeared carved from granite. Anna felt a disturbing surge of warmth, followed by a feeling of real affection. She'd felt differently about Stephen since he'd held her so gently. She was going soft on him, that was sure—she, who wasn't free so much as to kiss him, let alone to be married to him.

When he turned to look at her, Anna rushed into words. "Mrs. Charles wants the opera bag."

Stephen shook out the taper and grinned. "What did I tell you?"

"She agreed to pay twenty dollars, would you believe."

Stephen whistled. "Twenty! How the devil did you manage that?"

Anna held out the cards. "And more ladies have mending for me."

Stephen turned up the lamp and took the cards. "You'll need your own cards in New York."

Anna stood close to him, admiring the cards in his hand. She reached out and ran a finger over the engraved letters.

"If I had some now, I could give them to the ladies."

Stephen looked thoughtful, then tapped the side of his head. "Wait one moment, madam."

He reached above the pegs on the wall to a caged shelf and pulled down a writing box. Setting it on the small table before the sofa, he opened it and took out a pen, a point, an inkwell.

"Sit down, Anna."

Anna sat on the sofa and watched him expectantly. Stephen went to his coat, which hung on a peg, and rummaged through the pockets. Finding what he wanted, he sat next to Anna and tossed a handful of cards on the table.

She picked one up. "Mr. Stephen Flynn," it said. "Pugilist and Sparring Master." In the lower corner it read, "No. 59 Brace Street, the Bowery, New York City."

Anna looked at him. "I should use your cards?"

Stephen uncapped the inkwell, affixed the point to the pen, wet it, and began to write. Anna leaned close, watching. He changed "Mr." to "Mrs.," crossed out "Pugilist and Sparring Master," and wrote "Lace Making and Lace Mending."

"There," he said, handing her the pen. "You write the rest of them. Your hand is prettier than mine."

"But this is your address," Anna said.

"I can tell any inquiring ladies where to find you."

"But I don't know where I'll be."

"I'll know where you are, darling. I'll make it my business to know."

Anna's cheeks warmed. "I won't be Mrs. Flynn in New York."

"We'll worry about that when we get there."

Anna picked up the pen to write the next card, but her fingers were shaking and she blotted the ink. "Look at that, now. Oh, I'm not too bright." She tried to laugh, but her voice sounded frail.

Stephen took the pen from her fingers and folded her hand into his.

Anna looked at his purposeful face, his searching eyes, and knew what was coming. Her throat seemed to close up. "Please don't," she whispered.

"You're beautiful, Nan."

She felt a sudden fluttery panic. "Fancy talk," she said, attempting another laugh. "It comes cheap to an Irishman." She put her palm on his chest to push him away. But she didn't push and her hand stayed still.

His lips touched her temple, her brow. A chill raced down Anna's spine. "You promised," she said faintly. "We had an agreement."

"Did we?" He eased her back into the curve of his arm. She didn't resist. He was so careful, so slow, there was nothing to fight.

Stephen lifted her chin, and an expression came over his face that was so deep and hungry that it went straight to Anna's heart. She felt a sudden shift of feeling, a light breathlessness, a swift tug of yearning.

His lips touched hers, then pressed harder. Anna could scarcely breathe for the feelings he aroused. He smelled of the outdoors; he tasted like a man. His fingers touched the back of her neck and slipped into her hair. His thumb caressed her cheek. He coaxed her lips and she parted them. She opened farther still, allowing him to take her mouth. Her fingers grasped the fabric of his shirt, clutching tight.

She pulled away abruptly. "I don't want to be with you. I can't."

Stephen said nothing. He sat beside her, stroking her hair. Anna didn't dare look at him, fearful of what she would see. She knew that she should tell him the truth. She should push him away and tell him why they could never be truly married.

But when her lips moved, they moved against his. His hands took her face, shaping, smoothing; his mouth was relentless. Anna felt him tremble, as if holding back, and his restraint inflamed her. She leaned toward him, pressing into his kiss, lifting her arms to his neck. He dragged her closer. His hand slipped away from her face and closed on her breast.

Anna stiffened and drew back, pulling her lips from his. But he wouldn't let her go. "Nan, don't." His mouth and his hands were on her again, and she whimpered with fear and excitement, not knowing what to do, afraid of where it would end. He was getting stirred up, she knew it; she was letting him do too much. But, oh, it felt lovely, his hands on her, making her feel warm and yielding. His stroking grew bolder, his open palm rubbed, his fingers gently teased. Pleasure burned in her body like a fever. A man's touch had never been like this, never such sensations. Anna's breath came quickly in gasps; her fingers dug into his arm. "Stephen," she whispered. His hand moved to her lap, stroking downward. Even through folds of fabric, she felt his fingers seeking, following the arch of her hips, arousing in her something both wicked and dangerous.

A pounding started up in her head, a pounding that wouldn't stop. Stephen pulled away from her, cursing. He was on his feet, looking wild, disheveled, tucking in his shirt all around.

Someone was banging at the door. "Mr. Flynn. Sir!"

"Stephen!" Anna saw how she had aroused him. She jumped to her feet and grabbed his arm. "I'll see to it."

He stared at her as if in a daze. His arm slid around her waist, pulling her close. Anna pushed him away. "A moment!" she cried, straightening her dress, fastening up her hair. She pressed cool palms to her cheeks, burning with excitement, then hurried to the door.

It was Mr. Kincaid. He held Rory roughly by the collar.

When the mate saw Anna, he looked embarrassed. "Beg your pardon, ma'am."

Rory was covered with soot, his rosy cheeks shone with grease. Anna's hand went to her mouth. "Dear heaven."

"Found him exploring the engine room," the mate said grimly. "Don't have to tell you the danger down there."

Stephen was behind her, recovered, his hand on the doorframe. "I'll see to him, Kincaid."

The mate released Rory, who slunk close to Anna. She put her arm around his small shoulders and pulled him close.

"The brats with him got a beating," Kincaid said. "This one was mine, I'd take a strap to him."

"Did you touch my son?"

The tone of Stephen's voice made Anna shiver. It seemed to have the same effect on Kincaid. "Naw, sir," the mate said uncomfortably. "Thought you'd take care of him."

"Sorry for the trouble, then. It won't happen again." Stephen closed the door. He turned to Rory, who leaned against Anna, his head hanging. "Let him stand on his own."

"Stephen . . ." Anna began, but the look on his face told her she'd best hold her tongue. She stepped away, leaving Rory alone before his father.

"I told you not to go down there."

Rory aimed his face at the floor. Anna heard him snuffle.

"What did you say?" Stephen snapped. "I didn't hear you."

"I . . . I'm sorry, Da."

There was a drumming in Anna's head. She pressed her fingers to her lips, staring at Stephen, terrified of what he might do.

"Tell me why you went to the engine room when I forbade it." Stephen's voice was sharp with anger. "And look at me when I'm talking to you."

Rory raised his head. Anna saw his beautiful face smudged with soot and tears, and her eyes stung. Her hands closed into fists. By all that was holy, she would protect him. No matter what.

"I . . . I couldn't help it, Da."

"You couldn't help it?"

"I told Eddie and Mike what you said last night about the fires and the furnaces and how the flames ate up the coal. Eddie said it sounded like . . . hell, and maybe the Devil was down there. So . . . we went down to see the Devil." Rory wiped his cheek on his sleeve.

Stephen's eyes moved from Rory to Anna. She saw a gleam there, the beginnings of a smile, and her heart slipped back into place.

"You know what my father did to me when I misbehaved?" Stephen said.

Rory gulped and shook his head, his eyes round with fear, and Anna saw that Stephen wasn't finished.

"He took a strap to me, just as Mr. Kincaid said."

Rory licked his lips. Anna took a step forward and put her hands on his shoulders. "Stephen, you wouldn't."

He ignored her. "Did your gran ever hit you? Or Uncle Paddy?"

Rory pressed hard against Anna and shook his head.

"What did your gran do when you were bad?"

"She made me think about what I did wrong." The words came out in a frightened whisper.

Stephen scratched his head. "Is that all she did?" He looked at Anna quizzically, and it occurred to her that he knew all about scaring a child, but nothing about choosing a fitting punishment.

"I'd say spending a day in the cabin will do Rory just fine," she said hastily. "He won't be forgetting it soon."

Stephen seemed satisfied. "Hear that, young Flynn? You'll spend the day here tomorrow."

"All day?" Rory looked dismayed.

"That's right, sport," Stephen said. "All day."

"But I'll miss my boxing lesson."

Stephen caught Anna's eye and smiled. "That's the price you pay for looking for the Devil."

After he'd gotten Rory to sleep, Stephen thought about pulling Anna down on the sofa and continuing what Kincaid had interrupted. But she was all closed up again, absorbed in her opera bag, barely speaking to him. Stephen decided to keep quiet and let her make the first move. If he behaved himself, she'd lose her wariness. Before the hour was out, she would be talking again.

He picked up one of Anna's books, propped it open on his thigh, and pretended to read about the history of America.

As he turned the pages, Stephen glanced at her, bent over her work, her red-brown curls shining like polished chestnuts, her fingers nimble and sure. In his arms that afternoon she'd been all he had hoped for: warm, willing, sweet as heaven. Now she was shy again, like a bruised bud that had to be coaxed into bloom.

Somewhere along the line, Stephen decided, Anna had been roughly used. Some bloody bastard had succeeded in accomplishing what Spinner had tried, and it had put her off men. Stephen could come up with no other explanation of why a spirited girl like Anna didn't fancy a good wrestle in bed with a fine-looking man like him.

Stephen yawned and turned another page, scanning the dry account of the American Revolution. He'd been talking to Shaw about that very subject earlier in the day, why the Americans had succeeded with their rebellion when the Irish risings always failed. Stephen blamed the priests and the lack of guns. The peasants always listened to the priests, never thought for themselves. And even if they found a leader, a people couldn't rise up armed only with hoes and pikes.

Shaw had argued that the deciding factor was distance. The British army couldn't put down a rebellion an ocean away. And the Irish, he'd added without apology, were simply too ignorant to get themselves organized.

There was really no point in talking to Shaw, Stephen thought. The man was most likely a spy. Yet he was the most interesting of all the men in first class. Even if he didn't agree with Stephen's views, Shaw at least had the brains to understand.

Stephen shifted on the sofa. He felt as restless as a flea tonight. Anna was wearing her silver-green dress with the snug bodice that molded her figure so nicely. When she walked, she carried herself proudly, her shoulders squared like a soldier's, and she had a swing to her hips, too. By God, when she passed by, men snapped to attention. No wonder they gave her trouble.

Stephen thought of the weight of her breasts in his hands and felt a hot pulse beat through him. He studied her, imagining her naked. Then he saw that she had caught him staring. He gave her an embarrassed smile and returned to his book, trying to appear absorbed.

"Stephen?"

He looked up again, wearing an expression of innocence.

"I'll be going to sleep now." She was folding her work and placing it in her bag.

Stephen jumped to his feet. "But it's early, Nan," he protested. She couldn't end their evening; he'd not even started with her.

"It's not so early." She smiled, but it was a wary smile, and he saw that she was still tense.

"Stay up awhile and talk."

"Oh, Stephen . . ."

"Nan, come on, now." Disappointment cut deep. He'd planned to draw her out by bedtime, to wear her down a bit more. He took her by the arms. Anna pulled back at his touch, as if she expected force, and Stephen released her.

"I won't hurt you," he said, putting up his hands in surrender. "You know that."

Her fear offended him. And it made him feel helpless; he couldn't get anywhere if she wouldn't let him touch her.

Anna looked at her workbag in her hands and fiddled with the drawstring. "We shouldn't have done what we did this afternoon," she said.

Stephen's mouth felt dry. "I wouldn't have missed it for the world." He tried to sound tender, but his words came out husky and broken.

"It's my fault for letting you."

"Jesus, Anna—"

"It always happens that way with men."

Her voice was soft and sorrowful. Stephen had to lean close to hear her. He had a vague idea of what she was talking about, but it was hard to concentrate on her words when she looked so ripe and womanly. Every bit of her seemed to be ready to burst into bloom like some lush, bright flower that needed just a bit more sun.

He moved closer, resting his palm against the paneling. "You're so pretty, a man gets ideas without you helping him along." Behind Anna was the striped curtain. Stephen wondered if he could maneuver her back against the wall. He longed to press himself against her, to feel her softness along the length of him. Already he was stiff, and he'd not yet touched her.

"I sometimes wish I was plain."

"Ah, darling, you don't wish that at all." Stephen moved his hand toward her, hoping she wouldn't notice.

She noticed. "Don't your hands hurt you? They look terrible."

Stephen splayed his fingers. His hand was as broad and flat as a board, the fingers twisted and smashed. He took his other hand away from the wall and held it up for her inspection, pleased at her interest.

"That one's even worse," she said.

"The tools of my trade. Not very pretty, are they?"

Anna hesitated, then reached out to touch. Stephen maneuvered his hand so it lay open across her palm. Her fingers pressed his calluses. Stephen didn't feel much, but he liked her handling him, and he didn't want her to stop.

Anna looked at him. "Sure they must hurt."

Stephen gave her his left hand and returned his right to the paneling. "Sometimes they hurt. When the weather's damp." He looked into her eyes and saw that her wariness was gone.

"Fighters don't feel pain the way most people do. After the first couple of hits, you don't feel much at all."

Anna smiled, that glorious smile that never failed to make him weak in the knees. "I don't believe that," she said.

"Upon my word and honor, it's the truth."

"Blather, that's what it is."

"All right, then, it hurts like the devil. A man has to be stupid or stone mad to step into a prize ring."

Anna tipped her head to one side. "And which were you?"

Stephen watched her fingers lying still on his hand. "I was both, once. I liked matching my strength against that of other men. I liked feeling anger." He shrugged. "I've lost my stomach for it."

A little worried line formed between Anna's brows. "It seems a shame, breaking your hands like that."

"Fists break easier than heads." He smiled at her. "It sounds worse than it is, darling."

She ran her fingertips across his palm, and Stephen could no longer restrain himself. He grabbed her fingers in a tangle and spun her up against the wall.

Anna shrank back. "Stephen—"

"Just one kiss before bed."

Her cheeks flushed crimson. Her eyes didn't leave his; they held his gaze with near desperation. She was struggling, but he didn't know if it was with him or within herself.

"Only a kiss. I won't do anything more, I swear it."

Her lips trembled, uncertain, and then she closed her eyes.

He kissed her, willing himself to go easy, to do nothing hasty or crude. Her mouth grew warm and open with no coaxing at all. She put her hands on his back and allowed him to press against her. She moved, just a ripple of movement, a faint arch of her body, that made his need so intense he didn't think he could contain it. Still, he didn't rub or thrust himself against her. He didn't put his hands on her breasts. He kept his body under control, just as he'd promised; but in his imagination he possessed her. In his mind he parted her thighs with kisses, explored her most secret places, and made her shudder with rapture.

When she turned her face away, Stephen didn't fight for more. But he continued to rest against her and breathe in the scent of her hair.

"What can I do, Anna?" He knew she would understand what he meant—that he wanted more, that he wanted everything. He didn't know how he could stand it, not having her, not being able to do the things he'd imagined.

"Don't kiss me again," she whispered. "Not ever."

He drew back and looked at her face, soft with passion. He traced her lips with his knuckles. "Can water run uphill?"

She smiled, but her eyes were anxious. "Please."

She slipped away from him, and he let her go. She disappeared behind the curtain without a backward glance.

Stephen bent down and retrieved her workbag from the floor. He turned it in his hands, wondering if he was hungry for Anna only because he'd gone so long without a woman. He'd been as pure as a parish priest these past months in Ireland and before that, while training for the Maguire fight.

But he didn't think that was the reason, at least not the whole reason. He had a feeling that it would be all new with Anna, like with no other woman. With her, it would be as if there'd been no other woman at all.

Chapter 10

Rory spent the morning of his confinement sprawled on his bunk, browsing through his paper-covered books about prizefighters. While Anna worked on the frill of Mrs. Charles's opera bag, he offered to read aloud an account of the fight between an Irishman from Cork named Yankee Sullivan and Hammer Moran, who, Rory said, was a special friend of Stephen's.

Anna declined. "You shouldn't be filling your head with stories of fighting when you could be reading that book on America. It won't hurt to learn a bit about your new country."

Rory flopped onto his stomach and groaned.

"And you should be thinking about what you did yesterday, disobeying your da. It was foolish and dangerous, going down to the engine room. And the dirt! It took me near an hour to scrub your things clean."

Rory appeared unmoved. "You could have given my shirt to the stewardess to clean. That's what my da said."

Anna gave him a stern look. "I can do for myself when it comes to caring for you. There's no need to be making work for others just because you got yourself covered with soot and grease."

Rory rested his chin on his fist and watched Anna work. "I wish you'd live with us in New York."

Anna picked up the pace of her crocheting. She didn't dare think of that possibility. Already she had slipped close to ruin, feeling things she'd never felt in her life, doing of her own will what had once been forced upon her.

"Well, I won't be living with you, and that's that," she said. "I have better things to do than to take care of your mending and washing."

Rory was in the midst of a protest when a tap sounded at the door. Anna looked up, surprised. Stephen was sparring with the steerage men, and he never thought to knock before barging in.

The knock came again, and Anna put down her work. Rory scooted to the corner of his bunk. "It's Mr. Kincaid. He's come back for me."

"Nonsense," Anna said.

She opened the door to find Mrs. Smith-Hampton's maid bobbing a curtsy. The girl handed Anna a note and said, "I'll be waiting for an answer."

"Come in, then," Anna said. She waved the maid inside and unfolded the note. "Dear Mrs. Flynn," it read. "Could you possibly find time to trim the flounces of my concert gown? If so, I shall come by at 11:00. Mrs. H. Smith-Hampton."

Anna glanced at the clock. It had just turned ten. Dear heavens, she was up to her ears in work, and Mrs. Charles's opera bag was due tomorrow.

She folded the note. "Tell your mistress I'll be pleased to see her at eleven."

"Yes'm." The maid jounced politely and departed.

Anna gave the cabin a quick appraisal. Rory's books on building strength and muscle were scattered on the floor along with his dumbbells and Indian clubs and boxing gloves.

"I want you picking up your things."

Rory sat up. "But I'm using them."

"You'll be picking them up *now*," Anna ordered. "And line up those boots nice and straight, and smooth your bunk. Mrs. Smith-Hampton isn't used to boys, especially boys with necks dirty enough to plant a row of potatoes and hair that needs a good trimming."

"She's not coming to see me."

Anna poured water into the washbasin. "You'll be washed and tidy and in a clean shirt, Rory Flynn, and this cabin will be as neat as a pin. Get moving now."

In fifteen minutes both Rory and the cabin were in order. Anna brushed her hair, pinned it up, and changed into her blue skirt and her best gray cloth boots.

Rory slumped in the rocker, unhappy that Anna had forbidden him to lie in his bunk when company was visiting. His boots scuffed the carpet as he rocked. "Can I sleep in steerage one night? Eddie and Mike want me to."

"What a time to be asking!" Anna said. She was trying to finish the frill before Mrs. Smith-Hampton's appointment. "Those wicked boys. Tinker's children, both of them."

"They're not so bad," Rory said. "And Mrs. Curran is a kind one. I give her oranges for her baby."

"So you're still giving out oranges, are you?" Anna thought of Rory's kindness to her when she was half starved. If it hadn't been for him, heaven knew where she'd be now. "You've got a good heart, Rory."

"So I can sleep there once?"

"You ask your da. I don't think one night in steerage will do you much harm, but he might have other ideas."

Rory rocked faster, pleased at the prospect of an adventure. Anna concentrated on her work, trying not to think of how hard it would be to give this child up.

Mrs. Smith-Hampton was apologetic. "Of course, if you haven't time, I'll certainly understand."

"I have plenty of time," Anna said. She took the concert gown from Mrs. Smith-Hampton's arms and spread it on the sofa. The gown was made of satin, striped in shades of pink and mauve. In addition to the lace skirt panel, it was decorated with two short bodice flounces. A narrow edging of guipure on each flounce, Anna decided, would be suitable.

"I have just the thing." She went to her box and sorted through her lace until she found a scalloped length with a delicate pattern of star flowers.

"Oh, how lovely," Mrs. Smith-Hampton said. "Yes indeed, that will be perfect. I hope it's not asking too much on such short notice."

"It's no trouble at all," Anna said. "I can attach the trim in less than an hour. Send your girl around in the morning to collect it."

She picked up the gown and laid it on the top berth above her own. When she turned back, she expected to find Mrs. Smith-Hampton preparing to leave. Instead, her guest was glancing around the cabin with interest.

"I see evidence of your husband's profession." She nodded at the gloves and dumbbells stacked neatly in a corner.

"Oh, they're not Stephen's," Anna said. "They belong to Rory."

Mrs. Smith-Hampton smiled at Rory, who stood on one foot and then the other, knowing he mustn't sit in a standing lady's presence. "So, young man, you would like to follow in your father's footsteps."

Rory answered proudly. "Yes, ma'am."

"We'll see about that," Anna said, giving him a sharp look.

The cabin fell silent. Mrs. Smith-Hampton made no move to leave, and it occurred to Anna that she might want to visit.

"Oh, please do sit yourself," Anna said hastily, embarrassed that she had appeared rude. "Would you be wanting some coffee?"

"Why, that would be lovely. If I'm not keeping you."

Anna turned to Rory. "See if you can find a steward on the promenade deck and ask for coffee for two."

"But I'm not supposed to leave the cabin—"

"Rory!"

He ran for the door.

Mrs. Smith-Hampton arranged herself in the rocker, and Anna sat down on the sofa, wondering what they would talk about until the coffee arrived. She picked up the bowl of sugared candy. "Please, have a candy."

Mrs. Smith Hampton selected a tiny cherry drop. "He's a charming child," she said. "All the ladies adore him."

Anna warmed at the compliment. "Oh, he's a devil. His eye is black-and-blue from fighting. And just yesterday he and some steerage boys got down to the engine room."

Mrs. Smith-Hampton sucked on her candy. "I pray for a child of my own. Somehow it doesn't seem to happen."

Anna froze at Mrs. Smith-Hampton's intimate confession. Ladies didn't discuss such matters, especially with their social inferiors. Her mistress in Dublin, the doctor's wife, had never once spoken to her confidentially.

"Surely you'll be blessed in time," Anna said through her embarrassment. She gave a sharp thought to Mr. Smith-Hampton, wasting himself on his mistress in the St. Nicholas Hotel.

Mrs. Smith-Hampton picked at the pearl buttons on her gloves. "So my husband says." She sighed. "He's a fine man."

Anna's lips tightened. "Oh, I'm sure he is."

Another silence followed. Mrs. Smith-Hampton eyed Anna speculatively. "Have you a gown for the concert, Mrs. Flynn?"

Anna shook her head, too startled to speak. The question was preposterous.

"Stand up for a moment."

Mrs. Smith-Hampton came to stand beside her. Their shoulders touched. "You have a much prettier figure than I, but our height is the same. With a bit of adjustment, you could wear one of my gowns." Her face brightened. "I have just the thing for you, Mrs. Flynn. A sapphire blue. It would suit your coloring perfectly."

Anna was speechless. She was perfectly content with her few plain dresses. No one expected her to be fashionable. Then it crossed her mind that perhaps she was being insulted, that the woman was having a joke with her. "I'm not a grand lady, Mrs. Smith-Hampton. I needn't be putting on airs."

"You're too lovely to dress so plainly. Just think how pleased your husband will be, seeing you in sapphire silk. It would be a special surprise for him."

Anna thought of Stephen and the other gentlemen attired in their formal evening wear, and of the ladies in their elaborate gowns. Then she thought of herself; she didn't own even a simple evening bodice. The fanciest thing she possessed was her mistress's hand-me-down silk dressing gown with its fur-trimmed sleeves.

"He would be so proud of you," Mrs. Smith-Hampton said.

Anna wove her fingers together in her lap, wondering if Stephen would be ashamed of her in her simple skirt and jacket. The prospect of embarrassing him put the offer in a different light. "Do you think it would matter to him?" she asked.

"He would be pleased to have you in a proper gown. Any man would."

Anna made her decision swiftly. "All right, then. Just for the concert."

Mrs. Smith-Hampton clasped her hands with excitement. "It will be such fun. My girl will do your hair—"

"No," Anna interrupted. "We'll leave my hair well enough alone, and there'll be no rouge, thank you, and no scent—"

"Perhaps some lovely pearls."

"And no jewels, either. I'll be presentable, nothing more."

Mrs. Smith-Hampton's eyes were full of mischief, as if she knew a secret that Anna didn't share. "I assure you, my dear Mrs. Flynn, that you will be presentable indeed."

The next day in the ladies' boudoir, Anna gave Mrs. Charles the completed opera bag. Everyone gathered around for a close inspection. The bag was passed from hand to hand, each lady exclaiming over the lovely workmanship, the perfection of the detail, the artistry of the motifs. Anna kept to the background, allowing Mrs. Charles to accept the compliments as if she had done the work herself.

Once they had thoroughly examined the bag, the ladies turned to Anna, drowning her in questions. They wanted to know where in New York she planned to set up her business, if she could possibly see her way to call on ladies in their homes, if she did shawls and berthas, and could she trim cuffs, and was that lovely collar she'd been working on the other day for sale?

Anna answered yes to the questions and handed out Stephen's cards. The ladies seemed to find the cards a delightful novelty, and there was great laughter all around. A bit too much laughter, Anna thought.

She remained in the boudoir for the afternoon, working on her mending projects. Toward teatime, she was interrupted by the haughty Miss Camberwell, carrying an exquisite fan of Italian lace that was badly torn.

As Anna examined the damage, Miss Camberwell said, "I'm rather disappointed in your husband, Mrs. Flynn. I thought he would reside in a better neighborhood than the Bowery."

Anna didn't like Miss Camberwell. She didn't like the way the young woman seemed to size people up with her eyes. And she especially disliked the narrow, speculative way she looked at Stephen in the dining saloon.

"He lives upstairs over his business," Anna said. "It's a perfectly respectable neighborhood."

Miss Camberwell smiled, as if amused by Anna's ignorance. "Anything below Bleecker is impossible, Mrs. Flynn. It was gauche of you to hand out that card, as if any one of us would call at a Bowery saloon."

Anna felt a spurt of annoyance. Whatever "gauche" meant, it wasn't a compliment. She glared at Miss Camberwell's sugary smile. "You needn't call at the saloon, then. And I needn't be mending your fan, either."

"Oh, Mrs. Flynn," Miss Camberwell said, her voice ringing with laughter. "I had no intention of offending you. I was only trying to help. If you want to succeed, you must learn the ways of New York."

"It will cost you five dollars to have the fan mended," Anna said rudely.

She felt cross for the rest of the afternoon, both at Miss Camberwell for her superior ways and at herself for giving the ladies a card bearing the address of a saloon in a bad neighborhood.

Later, in the cabin, she complained to Stephen. "They laughed at the cards. Miss Camberwell told me none of them would ever call at a saloon in the Bowery."

Stephen seemed vastly amused, which annoyed Anna even more. "It was your idea, my using your cards," she reminded him. "You should have known they'd never come."

"And it's just as well they won't," he said, grinning. "A trail of uptown ladies would ruin my business. The lads would think they were Temperance."

Anna sank onto the sofa and pulled from her workbag a length of lace for mending. "I don't know what Mrs. Smith-Hampton is thinking. She's too familiar, speaking of having babies."

"I think she admires you," Stephen said.

"Why should she admire me?" Anna asked suspiciously.

"She leads a sheltered life, like all of her rank."

Anna made a sound of disgust. "A pity for her, such hardship."

"She once had dreams of singing on the stage."

Anna looked up. "Such a lady, singing on the stage? How do you know it?"

"I heard it in the smoking room."

Anna sat back in amazement. "Don't you men gossip so! Why, you gossip worse than the ladies themselves." She returned to her mending. "Singing on the stage. Who would have thought it?"

Stephen sat down on the rocker and watched Anna work. Her red-tinged curls were atumble, as usual, her wide forehead furrowed with thought. It occurred to him that she had no idea of her own appeal. No idea at all. "I'll tell you what's to admire about you, Nan. You're clever at lace, you're earning your own money, you're living with a couple of fine fellows like me and Rory. Why, you even killed a man with your bare hands."

Anna made a face. "There's nothing to admire in doing murder."

"Maybe not, but you were brave to fight back so. To a woman like Mrs. Smith-Hampton, what you did is beyond imagining."

Stephen leaned back in the rocker. He was due on deck to spar with the boys, but he didn't feel like moving. Lately the best part of his day was spent here with Anna, talking to her, watching her hands, her face, undressing her in his mind.

He thought of Mrs. Smith-Hampton wanting to befriend her. "Let me tell you, Nan. It does her credit, admiring you."

Anna dreamed of Spinner. He was coming at her, stumbling in the dark, muttering. She lay on her back, paralyzed with terror, trying to scream, but no sound came. She gripped the knife, prepared to plunge it into him.

Then it was no longer Spinner looming over her, but Stephen, coming to her with love.

"Stop, Stephen!" she cried. But he bent closer, smiling at her, and she knew that he would fall on the knife just as Spinner had, and she would drive it into his heart.

She woke, gasping, her body clenched with horror, her cheeks wet with tears. Then she realized where she was—in her bunk. She heard the engines rumble, felt the ship rise and fall with the sea. Her muscles slackened. She was safe. Stephen was safe, alive, sleeping not two feet away.

Stephen. She wanted to go to him, to crawl into his arms and lie against his strong, warm body. She wanted to feel his heart beat, feel his need for her. She wanted to take him inside her.

Anna pressed her hands to her cheeks. Dear God, what was happening to her? Their marriage was a temporary arrangement, a simple deception. She had never expected Stephen to want anything from her but the crudest sort of loving. And she'd never thought of wanting him at all.

But she did. With a fever of longing.

He had shown her kindness; he'd given her comfort. He aroused in her passions she'd never imagined. He'd awakened the deepest yearnings of her heart—to share her burdens, to love without fear, to be loved in return.

But Anna knew that a woman's happiness was beyond her. She could take no husband, bear no children. Even if she were free, she wouldn't stay with Stephen Flynn, for she dragged trouble behind her like a curse. In time she would bring harm to him, just as she'd dreamed.

She had no choice but to live her life alone.

The next morning Stephen gave Rory permission to sleep in the steerage hold on the night of the concert.

"We'll be late, most likely," he said to Anna after Rory had run off to tell his friends. "It won't be finished before eleven."

He cradled a coffee cup in his big hands. He looked rumpled and sleepy but blessedly alive, for which Anna was grateful after the terror of her dream. As for herself, she had a headache from too little sleep and too many tears, but she felt better for having cried her heart out.

"I hope he'll be all right down there in the hold."

"He thinks it's a lark," Stephen said. "Young Davy Ryan will keep an eye out."

Anna finished pinning up her hair and turned away from the mirror. "I worry about Rory getting into trouble."

"Do you, now?" Stephen grinned. "It's you who said he'd not turn criminal."

Anna thought of Rory's mischief in the engine room and hesitated, uncertain how to proceed. "Oh, Stephen, it's not him I worry about; it's you. I'm afraid you'll lose patience and take the strap to him."

Stephen's smile vanished. "Is that what you think? That a man my size would beat a small lad, my own son?"

The hurt in his eyes made Anna wish she hadn't spoken. "You threatened as much," she said, "telling him how your own da beat you."

Stephen got up from his chair and began organizing his shaving things, his face hard and closed. After a moment he glanced at her. "You needn't worry about me beating my own son. I'll threaten him, put the fear in him, but I won't be laying a hand on him in anger. I thought you knew me better than that."

Anna folded a pile of lace and tucked it into her work-bag. She was due in the ladies' boudoir to deliver Miss Camberwell's fan and Mrs. Otis's mended shawl, but she didn't want to go just yet, not with Stephen's feelings so hurt.

"I knew you wouldn't," she said. "But I wanted to hear you say it."

Stephen shaved in silence. Anna looked at his broad bare back, the sleek outline of his shoulders, his lean-hipped stance. She watched the play of muscles in the sunlight and thought of last night and how she'd longed to have him. Oh, it was madness to crave a man so, to imagine the feel of his hands on her body, the fullness of him inside her, when all she'd ever gotten from men was grief and pain.

"I guess you were a wicked boy, then, for your da to beat you so."

Stephen rinsed his razor, dried it on a towel, then mopped the soap from his face. "I wasn't so bad to start with. The beatings made me worse."

"And your mam let him do it?"

He gave her an impatient look. "What is this, Anna, all these questions?"

"Whisht, now, don't be touchy," she said, making a face. "I'm curious is all. Tell me what became of your family and how you got your boy."

He was still annoyed, Anna could tell, but after a moment's silence, he began to speak. "My da was a blacksmith, a big man, rough-spoken. I got my size from him, and he taught me the trade. My ma was sickly from the time I was a babe. When I was fifteen, maybe sixteen, the blacksmith shop caught fire and burned. The house went, too. They both burned with it."

Anna gasped. "Dear heaven."

"It was a long time ago."

"You were saved," Anna said.

"I was out. Up to the usual mischief, drinking poteen with the lads, fighting, full of the devil." He glanced at her. "There was a widow outside of town, a pretty woman. She taught me a thing or two. I slept that night with her."

Anna fixed her mouth in a disapproving line. "And you just a boy."

Stephen gave her a smile. "I'll go to hell when I die, so there's no use to worry."

"What a thing to say," Anna scolded, but she did it gently.

He sat down at the table, poured coffee from the pot, and stirred in some milk. "The McCarthys took me in, got me on the straight and narrow, got me back to smithing. It was Paddy who did it, the oldest son." Stephen looked thoughtful. "I thought the world of him—still do. He was a schoolmaster, a thinker and writer. Serious as a church. Paddy'd gone up to Dublin to university and caught the fever. He filled me with ideas of revolution. Paddy and I were as close as a dog and its shadow."

He drank his coffee, lost in his memories. Anna held her tongue, waiting for him to speak of Rose.

"When I married Paddy's sister, it made me a McCarthy more than it made her a Flynn." Stephen looked off into the distance. "Rose was the finest girl who ever lived. She hated politics, hated me mixed up in it, but I was too much afire to care. I went off after guns for the rising, and when I came home, Rose was dead of childbirth and Paddy was locked up in prison. The rising failed. I took off for America. There was nothing left for me in Ireland."

"You had your son," Anna said.

Stephen shrugged. "I knew nothing of babies. The lad was better off with his gran."

Anna wondered how a man could leave his own child, but she kept silent.

"I never understood why Rose had a fondness for me," Stephen said. "A boy so wild."

Anna felt a twinge of irritation. "Don't be dense, Stephen. A handsome, wild boy can stir the heart of even a saint from heaven."

He didn't seem to hear. "Rose wanted to make me good. As good as she was . . ." His voice trailed off and his face took on an embarrassed hue. "Ah, you've got me babbling."

Stephen clapped his hands on his thighs and got to his feet. "I don't like to think back," he said roughly. "What's past is past, and thinking of it only brings trouble." He glanced at Anna's workbag and then at the clock. "Off with you, now. Your ladies are waiting."

The next afternoon, Mrs. Smith-Hampton took Anna to her cabin. It was no grander than Stephen's, but there were more feminine touches—rouge pots and ribbons, fashion magazines and fringed parasols, jewel boxes and folded fans. Mrs. Smith-Hampton had a great hanging wardrobe from which she pulled a gown of shimmering blue silk.

"It's bound to be snug on you," she said, spreading the gown on the sofa. "We'll have to lace you up tight."

It was beautifully plain. The neckline, cut straight across from shoulder to shoulder, was trimmed with a ruffle at the chest, and a flounce covered the bosom. The skirt was a series of three flounces, each trimmed with lace dyed blue.

Anna had never imagined wearing anything so lovely. Not in four years at Mountjoy Street had she dared try on one of her mistress's gowns.

"Lilly will help you off with your dress."

When Anna was down to her underthings, the maid got her into a corset and tugged at the strings until Anna could barely breathe.

"You'd best not eat dinner tomorrow," Mrs. Smith-Hampton said with a smile. She handed Anna the first petticoat.

"I won't wear a cage," Anna said. She could never manage one of the tremendous skirt supports that could tip up at the wrong moment, revealing an entire length of leg.

Mrs. Smith-Hampton exchanged looks with Lilly and said, "We'll have to baste up the hem."

Once the petticoats were in place, Lilly slipped the gown over Anna's head and tugged at the back fastenings. It felt strange to be bare-armed. The bodice flounce didn't even reach her elbows.

"La, madam, it'll never close."

Mrs. Smith-Hampton, who had been studying Anna from the front, joined Lilly at the back, jerking and pulling until Anna felt thoroughly mashed.

"It fits at the waist," Mrs. Smith-Hampton said, "but the bust and those broad shoulders are a bit too much. I'm afraid, Anna, we'll have to cover you with a shawl."

Lilly found a shawl in the storage drawer under one of the berths, a paisley silk in hues of blue and pale gold with a silken fringe that exactly matched the dress. Mrs. Smith-Hampton arranged it over Anna's shoulders. "We'll baste the gown at the back and cover you with the shawl," she said. "Come look, Lilly."

The two of them studied Anna, who squirmed self-consciously.

Lilly was the first to speak. "She's lovely, madam, don't you think?"

Mrs. Smith-Hampton took Anna by the shoulders and turned her toward the full-length mirror that hung on the back of the door.

Anna glanced at her reflection and quickly lowered her eyes. She felt a queer shiver in her stomach, and a flock of goose bumps sprang up along her arms.

"What do you think?" Mrs. Smith-Hampton asked.

Anna kept her eyes on the floor. It was a sin to be vain, she thought, to stare at oneself and think, How lovely!

"I look well enough," she said. "I won't shame Mr. Flynn."

Mrs. Smith-Hampton's squeezed her shoulders. "No, my dear," she said in a voice that was soft with laughter. "The last thing Mr. Flynn will feel is shame."

Chapter 11

She wore a shawl with blue and gold swirls. It was draped over her shoulders, leaving bare her throat and chest, showing the rise of her breasts. The rest of her floated in yards of deep blue silk and ruffles, nipped in at her slender waist. Stephen was too dumbstruck to speak.

When he found his voice, he could manage to say no more than "What's this?"

Anna's long, fine lashes swept down with the shyness of a young girl. "Mrs. Smith-Hampton said I should dress properly for the concert. It's her gown, you see, and her shawl."

Her red-tinged hair, brushed tight, was already bursting from its pins, giving her a look of magnificent disarray, as if she had been handled by a man, as if he himself had taken her in his arms and only with great restraint heeded her protests.

Anna touched her cheeks with white-gloved fingers. "She wanted to rouge me and put pomade on my hair. She even offered me pearls for my ears and a necklace, too. But I didn't want to seem too fancy." Anna looked at him anxiously. "You don't think it's foolish, do you, to dress up so?"

Stephen couldn't take his eyes off her—the curve of her cheek, her lips, the brightness of her eyes. No jewel or flower or false bit of color could compete with her powerful beauty. Then he noticed her uncertain expression and realized that he'd neglected to answer.

"You look beautiful." The words came out in a husky whisper. "Lovely as sin."

Anna seemed relieved. "I didn't want to embarrass you, looking as if I'd just crawled out of a bog."

"You'd never embarrass me, darling," Stephen said, beginning to recover himself. "You should know that."

"I have to wear the shawl because I'm bigger around than Mrs. Smith-Hampton. Her maid had to sew me up the back."

She drew aside the shawl to show him. Stephen looked at the part of her that was bigger around than Mrs. Smith-Hampton and was glad that Rory would not be sleeping in the cabin tonight. Tonight he'd have Anna all to himself.

The gleam and polish of the grand saloon was magnified by candlelight reflecting off wood and mirrors. Beneath two ponderous crystal chandeliers, the first-class passengers mingled, champagne glasses in hand, while Miss Camberwell played a lively march on the piano. The air was filled with laughter and music and the scent of flowers and perfume. The fragrance and the vivid colors of the ladies' gowns made Anna think of some enormous bouquet continually being rearranged.

She held tight to Stephen's arm, trying to quell her nervousness and questioning her good sense in allowing Mrs. Smith-Hampton to dress her so. If she'd worn her flowered cotton skirt and her smart little jacket, she wouldn't have felt so self-conscious. In this gown she was trying to be someone other than herself. As she looked around the saloon, Anna felt as if she didn't know who she was.

"Oh, Stephen," she whispered. "I feel all skittery inside."

He pressed her arm to his side. "Don't be worrying, darling. They're all just a skin away from being common, and none is as lovely as you."

Anna glanced at him gratefully, thinking how grand he looked. The stark black and white of his formal clothes made his features seem sharper, his lines chiseled deeper. With his cheeks clean-shaven and his rough golden brown hair more or less at rest, he looked handsome and powerful and, in a formidable sort of way, dignified.

"And you," she said. "You're more a man than any of them."

His deep-set eyes sparkled. "Well then, we're a pair, aren't we?"

The buzz of voices grew louder. Heads turned. It seemed the entire company was staring at them. Anna lowered her eyes and waited for the laughter.

Stephen covered her hand that lay on his arm. "Come, Mrs. Flynn," he said. "Don't be bashful."

They made their way through the crowd. Anna focused on the stewards, who passed big trays of sandwiches and pulled champagne bottles from silver ice buckets. She tried to ignore the ladies holding fluted glasses in their fingers, craning their necks to get a better view. Some faces were friendly; others looked right through her. Their husbands rocked on their heels and stared.

"Oh, Anna, Mr. Flynn. There you are."

Mrs. Smith-Hampton, flushed and rouged, appeared at Anna's side. Her fair hair, puffed at the forehead and pulled away from her face, was threaded with tiny silk flowers that matched the vivid pink and mauve of her gown.

"Mr. Flynn, may I borrow your wife for a moment?"

Stephen squeezed Anna's hand. "Only if you return her."

Mrs. Smith-Hampton's color deepened, and it occurred to Anna that she found Stephen attractive.

"I'll keep her for only a moment. There's someone she must meet."

Anna looked around anxiously. She didn't want to meet anyone. She wanted to stay with Stephen.

He disentangled their arms. "Introduce her to anyone you want, just so long as he's not a gentleman."

Mrs. Smith-Hampton laughed. "Oh, but I'm afraid he *is* a gentleman, Mr. Flynn, and a very fine gentleman indeed."

She seized Anna's hand and pulled her through the crowd, ignoring her protests.

The size of the ladies' skirts made maneuvering difficult, so it took several minutes to reach Mrs. Smith-Hampton's goal—two gentlemen, one of whom Anna recognized as her husband.

Mr. Smith-Hampton took Anna's hand in greeting. "How charming you look tonight, Mrs. Flynn."

He was a short, broad chunk of a man with a merry gleam in his eye and cheeks red and puffed from good eating. A cherry diamond sparkled on his shirtfront.

Anna managed a smile. "I have your wife to thank for it."

Mrs. Smith-Hampton turned to the other man. "This is the mystery gentleman."

The man was slender and elegant and wore a mustache and goatee. He watched Anna expectantly, a smile quivering at the corners of his mouth. "I don't suppose you remember me," he said.

Anna looked him over from his dark hair, sleek with pomade, to the soft white hand that held his glass. There was something familiar about his face. And the voice. Staring at him, Anna felt both bewildered and alarmed.

"The goatee is a recent addition," he said, winking at Mrs. Smith-Hampton.

Suddenly Anna knew. Her heart tumbled. "Mr. Shaw," she said faintly. "Mr. Gerald Shaw of Dublin."

Mr. Shaw shouted out a laugh. "There you have it, Smith-Hampton, I bested you on that one."

"You had to give her a pretty broad hint," Mr. Smith-Hampton complained.

"In time she'd have managed even without the hint," Mr. Shaw said. "Anna always was a clever girl. 'There's spirit in that maid of yours,' I said to her mistress on more than one occasion. 'And brains as well.'"

Anna stared at him, stunned and terrified. She tried to see from his face how much he remembered, which of her secrets he knew.

"I still call around at Mountjoy Street on Tuesday evenings," he said. "The musicales, you recall."

Anna managed to form words. "You sang lovely, Mr. Shaw."

He gave her a modest bow. "And you made beautiful lace. Mrs. Wyndham showed it off with great pride."

Oh, surely he knows, Anna thought in despair. He would remember the row over her leaving Mountjoy Street. He'd wonder what on earth she was doing on this ship, dressed up in Mrs. Smith-Hampton's gown and married to Stephen Flynn. Suddenly the corset was crushing her, and she felt near to fainting.

"How . . . how are Dr. Wyndham and my mistress?" she asked, struggling to appear calm, to keep the panic out of her voice.

"In excellent health, I'm pleased to report. The little girls are growing into quite the ladies."

"I'm glad to hear."

Mr. Shaw gave the Smith-Hamptons a jolly account of the Wyndhams' daughters, then turned back to Anna.

"I quite admire your husband, Mrs. Flynn."

"My husband?" Anna blurted. "You know where he is?"

Mr. Shaw laughed heartily. "Indeed I do. He's staring at me this very moment, looking most displeased."

Anna followed Mr. Shaw's gaze and saw Stephen several yards away, scowling.

"Your husband and I have had many a discussion about the 'forty-eight rising," Mr. Shaw said. "His brother-in-law is Padraic McCarthy, transported for sedition. McCarthy's case interested me a great deal."

"Oh," said Anna. Please don't let him remember, she prayed silently. Please don't let Stephen find out.

"Mr. Shaw is going to America to study the institution of slavery," Mrs. Smith-Hampton told Anna. "He will be giving a series of lectures at Columbia College."

Anna remembered that Mr. Shaw lectured in political economy at Trinity College. She searched her scrambled mind for something to say.

Mr. Shaw was motioning for Stephen to join them. "I'm afraid I was forced to exclude your husband from this little joke, my dear. I was afraid he'd let the bird out of the cage, so to speak. From the expression on his face, I don't believe he is amused."

Stephen joined them, looking decidedly displeased. His size and scowl made the other two gentlemen appear small and defenseless. Anna listened with dread as Mrs. Smith-Hampton explain to Stephen that the two men had wagered that Anna wouldn't remember Mr. Shaw.

"He has a new goatee," Mrs. Smith-Hampton said. "But it only took Anna a few moments to recognize him."

"I knew her the moment I laid eyes on her," Mr. Shaw said merrily. "I thought to myself, so that's the girl who took a knife to that luckless seaman. Well, I wasn't surprised. Anna always did have a mind of her own and a brave heart. Ready to plunge off into the unknown, and woe to anyone who stood in the way." He winked at Anna. "Quick thinking to marry the girl, Flynn. If I'd thought of it, I'd have done so myself."

"You didn't think of it, then, did you?" Stephen said coldly. He didn't like Shaw withholding his past association with Anna. And he didn't like Shaw and Smith-Hampton wagering over her.

"Come, come, Flynn," Mr. Smith-Hampton said. "It's all in good humor."

Stephen glanced at Anna's flustered expression and put his hand on her waist. "You embarrassed my wife, Shaw. It's not right."

The tone of his voice and the look in his eye alarmed Anna. She cast a pleading look at Mrs. Smith-Hampton, who hurried to the rescue. "Oh, Mr. Flynn, you mustn't be angry. Truly, the gentlemen meant no harm."

"No harm at all," Mr. Shaw said, appearing undismayed. "But please accept my apologies for any discomfort I may have caused."

At that moment Miss Camberwell played a fanfare of chords on the piano.

"We must take our seats," Mrs. Smith-Hampton said with evident relief.

Mr. Shaw and Mrs. Smith-Hampton hurried off to join the other performers, calling out promises to meet after the concert. Mr. Smith-Hampton looked about furtively and slipped away to smoke a cigar. Stephen took Anna by the arm and led her through the crowd. He found seats midway down the length of the saloon. Once Anna's skirt was arranged, he rested his arm on the back of her chair and cast a threatening look around to warn off any men who might be tempted to stare.

"Shaw's a bloody bounder, playing that trick," he said.

"And what about you?" Anna said sternly. "You frightened Mrs. Smith-Hampton. She probably thought you were going to fight with Mr. Shaw."

"I wouldn't have minded. Playing a trick like that and wagering on top of it, he deserved to be taken down."

Anna rapped his knee with her program. "Don't tell me a man like you has never wagered over a woman."

Stephen looked at her lovely face, intent and scolding, and had the urge to tip up her chin and kiss her mouth. "That's different. A man doesn't allow certain things done to his wife."

"But, Stephen, I'm not really your wife."

He squeezed her shoulder. "Hush, now. They're starting."

The rustle and laughter were dying down. The lights dimmed in the chandeliers, leaving the room bathed in an intimate candlelit glow. Mrs. Charles stepped forward and made a speech praising the artists' hard work and generous spirit in sharing their talent with the assembled guests. Then Miss Camberwell, dressed in a gown the color of skin, a huge silk rose nodding from her shoulder, played a complicated piece full of runs and trills.

Anna tried to concentrate, but her thoughts kept returning to the exchange with Mr. Shaw. Each time he'd opened his mouth, she had expected him to ask, "What became of that chap you married, the one Mrs. Wyndham was so set against?" But he'd said nothing. Either he was being kind or he'd forgotten. The more Anna thought about it, the more she believed that Mr. Shaw was purposely keeping her secret. He had always been good to her, greeting her cordially, asking after her health, slipping her a coin on special occasions. He probably saw no reason to complicate her life. But even if he did say something, it hardly mattered now. In just a few days they would reach New York, and she would be on her own, free of Mr. Shaw. And free of Stephen, as well.

She glanced at him and found him watching her. He leaned close. "Are you enjoying this?"

"It's lovely," Anna whispered. "Don't you think?"

His hand tightened on her shoulder. "It's lovely looking at you."

Mrs. Smith-Hampton's song came next. She hit each note with soaring assurance, but Anna heard a melancholy strain that added to the tender emotion of the song. Anna listened to the words, which reminded her of her own journey through life, and tears filled her eyes.

> 'Tis sad to leave familiar things
> For objects new and strange,
> The heart must rest where first it clings,
> It never sighs for change;

The meadow and the winding stream
Where first we gather'd flowers,
Ah! never was so bright a dream
As that sweet dream of ours:
Turn where we may, roam where we will,
For rest the spirit yearns,
The home-love is the strongest still,
To that the heart returns.

Stephen's hand slipped beneath her shawl and stroked her bare arm. His touch made Anna feel warm and shivery and brought to mind her carnal thoughts. She would miss him, she thought, this rough man with his gentle core who tempted her to forget her past and all its lessons. But their parting would be for the best. Stephen knew nothing of her life, nor could he ever understand it. He was a jealous man, a proud and possessive one, who had loved his wife for her virtue. To tell him about her own life and the shame of it would sicken him, and he would hate her.

Mrs. Smith-Hampton finished her song and bowed to the applause. Mr. Shaw's song was next, a lively tune, followed by Mrs. Otis's dreary recitation. Miss Camberwell played again, and four ladies and gentlemen sang together in a foreign language. Anna tried to pay attention. She smiled and applauded with the others. But her heart felt as heavy as stone.

When the concert concluded, the chandelier lights went up, along with voices and laughter. People moved toward the buffet tables for more food and champagne.

Stephen stood and stretched. "I could use a breath of air."

"Maybe we can find Rory up on the forward deck," Anna said, thinking it would be a blessing to get away from the crowd and clear her head of melancholy thoughts.

"The lad's not awake at this hour," Stephen said.

"Oh, he'll be awake all night. From just the adventure of it, let alone all the racket."

Stephen looked doubtful. "I know my boy. He likes his sleep."

"He'll sleep tomorrow when he's back with us."

They exchanged glances. Stephen was thinking the same thoughts, Anna was sure of it. He was thinking how complete it felt to share this child, how much a family they had become.

"Leaving so soon, Flynn? Not even stopping for a glass or two?"

It was Captain Blodgett, resplendent in brass and braid, his paunch straining at his buttons, his face florid from drink.

"We'll be taking a breath of air up top," Stephen replied.

Blodgett seemed unsteady on his feet. He stared at Anna. "Can't say as I blame you, Flynn," he said, smoothing his ginger mustache. "Best-looking woman in the room, no doubt about it. Came close to taking her for a stroll myself, didn't I?" He leered drunkenly. "Come to think of it, I probably sold her too cheap."

Stephen laid his hand on Anna's back and pushed her firmly ahead of him. "Go to hell, Blodgett," he muttered, his voice flat with disgust.

Anna said nothing as they mounted the winding stair. They stepped out on deck into a cool breeze and a flood of moonlight. Stephen strode to the rail. Anna, shivering beneath her paisley wrap, followed. She leaned on the rail beside him and gazed out at the sea, splashed with silver, while the engines chugged and the ship dipped and surged.

"You paid for more than my fare, didn't you?" she asked.

Stephen's face was stony, his mouth tight with anger. "I should have busted the bastard. I should have laid him out right there for all the others to see."

"And been thrown in the hold for your trouble? Don't be foolish. It's nothing new for men to speak of me so. They always have."

"You deserve some respect for once," Stephen said bitterly.

Anna felt no anger or outrage, only resignation. And the certainty that she could never repay Stephen for what he'd done. "You're as gallant as your son," she said. "How much did you pay to keep me out of the captain's bunk?"

"I'd have paid my last dollar, and then I'd have fought him to the death."

He looked at her, his outward strength betrayed by his eyes. Anna saw gentleness there and some deeper emotion that she dared not contemplate. "You didn't answer my question," she said.

He studied her for a moment, and the hard set of his mouth softened. "Who can say what you're worth, Nan?"

Anna rubbed her hands up and down her shivering arms. "Don't speak in riddles."

Stephen pulled off his jacket and draped it over her shawl. The white of his shirt shone like the moon. "It's hard for a woman alone, isn't it? Always at the mercy of men."

"Mercy?" Anna made an impatient sound. "Few have mercy. Very few."

"I'll teach you how to defend yourself against those others."

"Defend myself! Oh, now I know you're daft."

He took her by her shoulders and turned her toward him. "There are two tender parts of a man."

"If you think I can fight, Stephen, you're mad."

"You fought Spinner, didn't you? You fought him before you went to the knife."

"All I did was tire myself out."

"Tonight you'll learn another way." He gave her a little shake. "Are you listening?"

He looked so earnest that Anna couldn't help but smile. "I'm listening."

"You kick him hard between the legs."

Anna gasped. "Stephen!"

"Hard and swift, with your knee or your foot, before he knows what you're about."

"And then he'll kill me."

"No, darling, he'll be on the ground screaming."

"He never will!"

"He will if you kick him hard enough. Believe me, Nan."

Anna shivered beneath the jacket. "And the other place?"

"The eyes. Gouge them good. With your thumb or the tips of your fingers."

Anna laughed. The idea of her doing such a thing was absurd.

"I mean it, Anna."

"All right, then, I'll remember your lesson."

Stephen's hands left her shoulders and lightly cupped her cheeks. Anna looked at his eyes, serious and searching, and the blood warmed in her veins. He was starting again, she thought. He'd softened her up and now he would reward himself. But when he tipped up her chin, Anna gazed back at him heedlessly, knowing she would do nothing to stop him.

"There, now," he said, slipping his fingers into her hair. "Look at me like that and I'll go to heaven for sure." He bent toward her and his lips touched hers. He kissed her gently until her lips slackened, until the heat rose through her, until her shivers were no longer from the cold.

"You're a wicked one," she whispered.

"I never said otherwise."

"I told you not to kiss me anymore."

"I never agreed."

He took her in his arms, kissing her with patient ardor. Anna thought briefly of all she had learned of men, and a warning passed through her mind, a warning of the perils of opening up to Stephen Flynn. But the warning melted in the heat of his kisses. Her body felt weak with pleasure, her mind misty with desire. Her arms slipped around him, and she yielded her mouth to his.

Stephen lifted his head and looked at her, reading something in her eyes that seemed to give him satisfaction. "Anna," he said, his voice rough and soft at the same time. "My darling Nan."

He kissed her again, deeply, until she was consumed by the force of his passion, until she could no longer distinguish between will and desire, peril and salvation. She thought of the past that she could never change, and a wave of emotion shuddered through her. She clung to him, helpless before memory and desire, powerless to express the dilemma of her heart.

He nuzzled her hair and kissed the little hollow beneath her ear. "Come with me, darling. Let me love you like a husband."

Anna sagged against him. She felt dizzy and directionless. Her life's path, so recently clear, was now strewn with distractions and contradictions. Not two weeks ago she'd nearly starved in steerage; she now wore a rich woman's gown. Mr. Gerald Shaw, to whom she'd curtsied for years, now bowed over her hand and called her "dear lady." The man who embraced her believed himself to be her husband, while her true husband lived a life unknown to her.

And she, who had barely endured a man's touch, now craved Stephen Flynn with the last fiber of her being.

"I don't know," Anna whispered. "Oh, Stephen, I don't know any longer."

"Yes, you do, darling. You do indeed."

Anna looked at his firm, virile features, at the face so dear to her. He smiled, his expression kind and knowing, and she responded the only way she could.

"Stephen," she said, "I have another husband."

Chapter 12

❧

Once she began explaining, she couldn't stop. "I was married in St. Brigid's in Dublin six years ago this June. I didn't tell you, because I thought you'd send me back to steerage. Oh, you'd have sent me back for sure. I couldn't have borne it, Stephen, not with those sailors coming after me."

Stephen had let her go and stepped back, staring at her in stunned silence.

Anna was barely aware of his expression, so intent was she on purging herself of her terrible secret. "Then later I couldn't tell you. I couldn't, not when we were . . . I thought we'd each go our own way in New York and leave it at that. I thought it wouldn't matter if you knew or not."

Stephen's heart was pounding in his chest. He felt it in his ears and brain, and the rushing blood made him light-headed. Somehow he found his voice. "He's in America, then, your . . . husband. You're going to meet him in New York."

"Oh, no, he's not in New York. He left me five years ago, and I've seen neither sign nor light of him from that day to this."

She clutched his coat around her. A piece of paisley shawl fluttered beneath it. She looked desperate and confused, but all that mattered to Stephen was that his Anna, his beautiful Anna, had deceived him. He could hardly believe it. Never had he felt so betrayed.

"You say you don't know where he is?" Stephen spoke with mounting bitterness. "I don't believe you."

Anna brushed at her curls, wild and loose, flying about in the wind. "For the love of God, it's the truth."

The truth. It was sinking in slowly. She belonged to someone else. Stephen now understood all the coy maneuvering, the protests that they weren't really married, the claim that she had to be on her own. He'd been used. She'd used him for a free ticket and safe passage to America so she could be with another man.

"Married. Well, doesn't that beat the devil."

"He was never dear to me, not like you."

"Oh, so I'm dear to you, am I?" Stephen asked, mocking her. He looked into Anna's stricken face and felt only his own pain. He wanted to hurt her to the core, the same as she'd hurt him. "Well, you're not dear to me, never were."

"Stephen," she said softly. The tears shining in her eyes made her lovelier than any woman had a right to be. "You don't mean that, surely you don't."

"Didn't I play the fool. Your *husband*, your protector. Why, I didn't even have you in bed, so careful was I of your honor." His anger was boiling now. Never, never had he taken such a jolt, never had he allowed such a blow to slip by his defenses.

Anna's face filled with despair. "Don't speak so. Oh, where is your heart?"

"My heart?" he shouted. "It's here." He grabbed the front of his trousers. "Here's my heart and all the feelings I had for you. All I wanted from you was this, right here, and I was well on my way to getting it, wasn't I?"

Anna was losing her struggle against tears, and Stephen was glad of it. Her throat looked white and tender in the moonlight as she worked to swallow her sobs, but the sight didn't move him; his own pain was too raw. He turned away, adopting a careless stance against the rail. His mind grasped at defenses until he found the only one that could serve as a barrier against his feelings for Anna.

Rose. By God, wasn't that the shame of it, that he'd forgotten her? He'd allowed himself to be tangled up with a woman like Anna, allowed himself to be duped and trapped, a prisoner of his basest desires, when he had Rose's son to look after.

Christ, she had deceived Rory, too. A ten-year-old boy.

"You can stay with us for the rest of the voyage," he said coldly. "I don't want Rory crying when you leave, so don't be fussing over him like you do, making him love you more. And don't be talking about your . . . husband in front of him."

Anna gasped. "I'd never! How could you even think it?"

"I don't want you making the lad cry."

"And you think I would?" Anna burst out. She pulled Stephen's coat from her shoulders and flung it at him. It whipped his face, stinging his cheek. "You're not thinking about Rory. You're thinking of your own self, your own pride. I know you, Stephen Flynn. I know that when it comes down to the nub of it, you're not thinking about Rory or me or what the truth might be, but about yourself! All that worries you is looking like a great thick fool for marrying me."

"Now just you wait—"

"And didn't you tell me this marriage was just for the voyage? 'It won't be forever,' you said. Didn't you say it that day in the cabin?"

"Don't be putting the blame on me, goddammit."

"I'm sorry to the heart for not telling you the truth, but you've no cause to speak so hatefully. You haven't enough mercy to overflow a pinhole—you, who I thought was the kindest of men. . . ." She faltered and wiped angrily at her eyes. "And kill me if I don't pay you back every cent, including the price of buying me from the captain!"

She turned and ran away from him in a flash of moon-drenched silk and tangled red curls.

Stephen slammed his fist on the rail. Damn her to hell's flames! Wasn't that just like a woman—deceiving a man and then twisting it all around to make it his fault? "You're thinking of your own self," she'd said, but he wasn't thinking of himself; he was thinking of Rory. He was thinking of Anna's treachery. He had every cause to feel betrayed.

He tried to whip up his fury again but could muster only a sour misery. Instead of feeling outrage, he was lapsing into gloom. If he weren't on this ship, he'd never see her again. As it was, he had to endure three or four more days watching her brush her hair and listening to her hum as she did her work. He'd have to speak civilly for the boy's sake, and for his own he'd have to stop remembering how she'd felt in his arms.

Stephen shook out his coat and slung it over his shoulder. A husband. What had she said? "He left me five years ago." Ah, how could it be? The husband must be waiting in New York. No man with a brain, a heart, and male parts that worked would leave that girl.

Or maybe she'd left him, run away. By God, maybe the bastard had abused her.

Stephen quickly dismissed that notion. He was no longer Anna's protector. She had lied to him straight on. She'd lied and used him and made him behave like a fool. A husband awaited her in New York, he'd bet on it.

A veil of clouds covered the moon. Stephen felt the cold down to his bones. He couldn't stand there all night freezing himself, and he damn well wasn't going to hide in one of the saloons because he didn't want to face Anna.

Stephen folded his coat over his arm. Casting a last grimace at the fading moon, he headed below.

Anna rose from the sofa when Stephen entered the cabin. "I've no mind to be bothering you," she said, avoiding his eyes, "but I can't get out of this gown. Mrs. Smith-Hampton's girl sewed it closed."

Stephen tossed his coat on a peg. Anna thought to tell him to hang it up properly, that it was his best evening coat, but she held her tongue. What he did with his coat was not her affair. He could throw it into the sea, for all she cared.

Stephen pulled at the studs on his cuffs and dropped them into a dish. "What shall I do, then?" he asked acidly, glaring at the gown. "Tear it off you?"

Anna was forming a sharp retort when she glanced at his face. He looked beaten, exhausted. A shadow of beard showed on his cheeks and chin, and his eyes were weary.

"Just cut the threads, that's all." She handed him her little scissors and turned her back.

The threads broke easily. Anna held the bodice close so it wouldn't slip down.

"Good night, then," she said.

"Anna."

She turned around.

"We'll be civil," Stephen said. "For Rory's sake."

His face was hard with resentment, but Anna could hear sadness in his voice, and just for an instant, she felt herself going soft. Then she remembered the cruelty of his words. "*I* would never be otherwise," she said accusingly, and stepped behind the drawn curtain.

Stephen lay awake, his hands folded behind his head, listening to the regular, hypnotic beat of the engines. He thought of Rose, who had never spoken against him, who'd never given him a moment's defiance, and told himself he'd been mad to involve himself with a woman like Anna. He should have used his head instead of letting his male appetites get the better of him. That was all he felt for her—carnal desire, pure and simple. He'd be better off keeping his mind on his main task, which was doing right by his son. Once they got settled in New York, he would find a chaste, obedient girl and marry her. That would take care of his problem and Rory's, too.

He rose at dawn, pulled on his fighting drawers and a shirt, and went up on deck to run. Last night's clouds had stacked up, obliterating the sky. A stiff wind, pungent with the smell of the sea, blew cold in his face. The *Mary Drew* dipped and rolled, making him stagger as he ran.

Stephen began his three laps around the deck. Sailors, accustomed to his daily routine, saluted as he passed, and the few early morning strollers stepped out of his way.

It was rough going. Stephen felt a heaviness that came from more than lack of sleep. It felt like grief, a dull, crushing sadness. Running seemed to make it worse, and the wind caused his eyes to tear. He wiped at his cheeks, bristly and unshaven, and thought how much he'd like to see Rory. He missed the little fellow gazing at him with wide-eyed admiration, as if his da could do no wrong.

It was just the two of them now, Stephen thought, father and son, the two Flynns. No Anna, just a hole in his life where there had once been a lovely woman.

Married. She'd been married all along. Christ, it was enough to make a man crazy.

The pain in Stephen's hip started as he rounded the forecastle for the second time, and he slowed to a walk when he reached the funnel. He was heading for a canvas deck chair when he saw a lone little figure leaning against the door of the men's bathhouse. It was Rory, his chin resting sleepily on the bundle of clothes in his arms. Stephen looked at the child, his own boy, and his chest tightened with emotion. One night away, and it seemed as if Rory had been gone a week.

He approached the boy, savoring the sight of him, and thought back to the morning last fall when he'd first laid eyes on the lad in Padraic's parlor. From that first moment he'd felt a passion of tenderness for his son. Rory had looked at him with eyes brimful of adoration, and Stephen had felt a part of him open up that he never knew existed.

"Morning, sport," he said.

Rory looked up, his face pale from lack of sleep, and gave Stephen the smile he needed. "Hello, Da."

Stephen laid a hand on the spiky hair that Anna had cut. The weight of despair began to lift. "You look as if you could use some sleep."

"Anna says I have to wash before I can get into bed. She said to find you and we can bathe together."

"She's awake, then?"

Rory nodded. "She looked me over for nits."

"She find any?"

Rory shook his head and gave a big yawn. "I didn't sleep all night, it was so noisy."

"You'll feel better after a bath and a nap."

The bathhouse was steamy and warm, the cistern filled with hot water. Stephen stripped and watched Rory do the same. They assessed each other and exchanged grins, then began scrubbing and sluicing.

"I've got a shower bath in New York," Stephen said, lathering up for the second time. "I rigged it up in the sparring room. You stand under it and the water pours all over you."

"You made it?" Rory's eyes grew big, a balm to Stephen's battered soul. "Can I use it, too?"

"Sure you can."

Rory puffed out his chest, throwing his small ribs into relief. "Do a lot of fighters come to your place, Da?"

"It's busy enough, not only with fighters but with gentlemen who want to keep themselves strong."

Stephen watched from the corner of his eye as the boy grasped his own thin arm, testing its strength.

"Will Anna stay with us?" Rory asked.

Stephen stopped soaping. "I don't think so, sport. I think she'll be leaving us."

Rory looked anxious. "But didn't you tell her we want her? She'll listen to you, Da. I know she will."

Stephen knew he had to put an end to Rory's hope. The boy had best start learning that his da couldn't work miracles every time. "She won't be with us; she said so. But we'll be fine, just you and me."

"But what about her? She'll be all alone, and where will she live? What if a man comes along like Spinner?"

Stephen had a vision of Anna wandering the streets of New York, looking for lodging, her boxes in tow, a perfect target for any masher. Then he thought of her husband and pushed all pity aside. "Anna can take care of herself. Now dry yourself off and climb into your nightshirt. You're long past due for some sleep."

Anna rose shortly after Stephen left to run. She'd barely slept a wink, for all the crying she'd done, crying and scolding herself for her tears. There was no earthly reason, she'd told herself, to feel sorry over a man who spoke with such pitiless scorn. He wore two faces, Stephen Flynn did, one when he got his way and another when he was denied. She'd felt guilty at first, telling him the truth, but when he wouldn't listen, when he lashed back at her so cruelly, she knew she need regret nothing.

And the sight that greeted her when she stepped out from behind her curtain further hardened her heart. Evidence of Stephen's anger was strewn all over the cabin. Normally he was reasonably tidy; in fact, it was he who'd first lectured Rory on the need to put away his things. But this morning Stephen's trousers and underthings, stockings and boots, even his best white stock lay on the floor right where he'd left them last night. He'd even pulled his coat off the peg and thrown it down in a final childish gesture of anger.

Anna set to work straightening up. If it hadn't been for Rory, whose eyes popped at the unholy mess when he came back from steerage, she would have left everything where it lay. She'd have given Stephen a piece of her mind and made him pick up after himself. But she didn't want any scenes in front of the boy.

Anna took up a length of lace and sat down on the sofa. She was well into mending Mrs. Otis's bonnet trim when Rory returned from his bath.

"Don't forget to clean your teeth," she said. "And say your prayers."

Rory's face, already glum, fell further. "Prayers? But it's morning."

"God listens all day long, Rory. Besides, I doubt you said them last night, not with those Currans."

Stephen came in, wet-haired and unshaven, looking like some ruffian just fished out of the river. Anna ignored him. She checked to see that Rory had hung up his clothes and his wet towel, and returned to her lace.

"I'm hungry," Rory announced.

"It's too early for breakfast," Anna said. "You'll have to make do with fruit." She nodded at a cut-glass dish of apples.

Rory grabbed an apple and climbed into his bunk.

"Sleep well, sport," Stephen said, pulling the bed-curtains closed.

"Prayers," Anna reminded him.

Rory rustled around, settling himself under the covers. There was a brief whisper of prayers and the cabin fell silent.

Anna was glad she had something to occupy her hands so she didn't have to look at Stephen. He stood by Rory's bunk for a while, then pulled off his shirt and crossed to the wash-stand, where he filled the basin with water. He sharpened his razor, dropped it with a clatter, and muttered an unnecessarily long stream of curses. Anna focused hard on her lace, taking tiny, careful stitches. Stephen shaved. The silence grew more strained.

Stephen mopped his face, then pulled out a storage drawer under his bunk and took some clean clothes. Anna watched discreetly. He began unfastening his fighting drawers. Her eyes jumped back to her lace. God's mercy, he was taking off everything, right there in front of her. Stephen took his time undressing and then dressing, all the while roaming around in front of her. Anna kept her eyes on her work and fumed silently, thinking how lacking in manners he was, how vulgar and crude.

When he was dressed, he broke the silence. "I'm going to breakfast. Come along if you like."

Anna looked at the clock. It was nearly eight. She set aside her lacework and took her warm wool shawl. Without a word she preceded him out the door.

The dining saloon was only half full, due to the late hour of the previous night's concert. Anna followed Stephen to a vacant section of a long table and sat down. Taking up the menu card, she risked a glance at him. A shave and a clean shirt had improved his appearance, but no amount of tidying up could change what he was—a bad-mannered, ill-bred dock-side brawler with a heart as hard as Satan's heel. Anna thought of Mr. Shaw and Dr. Wyndham and even the faithless Mr. Smith-Hampton. They were well-bred gentlemen, all of them. They would never speak crudely to a woman or throw their clothing on the floor or parade around stark naked before their wives.

Anna laid down the menu and arranged her napkin in her lap. "I have a crow to pluck with you, Mr. Flynn."

"And what crow is that?" Stephen asked with a smirk.

"We made an agreement to be civil, didn't we?"

Stephen watched her expectantly. When he made no response, Anna snapped, "A grown man, throwing a tantrum that would put his own son to shame."

Stephen's bland expression vanished. "What the devil are you talking about?"

"You know perfectly well what I'm talking about. You purposely threw your clothes on the floor and expected me to pick them up."

Stephen shrugged and looked back at the menu card. "You needn't have bothered yourself. I'd have picked them up in time."

"Oh?" Anna said, her anger flaring brighter. "And when would that have been, pray tell?"

A mutinous look crossed Stephen's face. He picked up a spoon and wagged it at her. "Don't be nagging me. If I have a mind to toss a few things on the floor, I'll do it."

"Without a thought to anyone else?"

He cast his eyes upward. "By God, I've heard enough of your tongue to last a lifetime."

The steward arrived with bowls of stewed fruit. When he left, Anna glared across the table. "And aren't you full of brass, stripping yourself naked right in front of me?"

Stephen's eyes gleamed, and Anna realized she was reacting with the indignation he'd hoped for.

"I thought you'd like to see what you missed."

"I didn't take a blind bit of notice, I'll have you know."

"A pity. I've got a fair size on me. I thought you'd want to compare me to your husband."

"Isn't that a fine way to talk!" Anna hissed. "Oh, you are a gentleman, Mr. Flynn, so refined!"

Stephen leaned forward and gave her a grin that all but bared his teeth. "And your husband waiting in New York, is he so refined? I'll bet he's a real gentleman, your husband. Does he beg your pardon each time he lays you on your back?"

Anna burned to slap the words right out of his mouth. But when she reached for him, Stephen was ready—he grabbed her wrist in midair. "Calm yourself, darling. You're making a scene. They'll all be saying you're Irish trash."

She felt all choked up, as if a rock had lodged in her chest. She pulled her wrist from Stephen's grasp. "You're no better, for all your swagger. A broken-down fighter, a failed rebel. You think it's so fine, you owning a saloon. Aren't you high up in the world . . ."

She could manage no more. She sat back, glaring at him with brimming eyes, and pressed her hand to her trembling mouth.

Stephen grimaced and shifted in his seat. "By God, you don't have to cry. Christ Almighty, what the devil did I say that was so bad?"

Anna was struggling against sobs. She hated Stephen, she despised him. She wanted to shake him, slap him. She wanted to unburden herself to him, and have him hold her while she wept. Anna pressed her fingers to her eyes and tried to control her huge, erratic gulps.

"Here, eat this." Stephen leaned across the table with a spoonful of fruit compote, his face tense and unhappy. Juice dripped off the spoon, staining the linen tablecloth. "You're hungry, that's all."

The fruit tasted sweet. Anna sniffed and wiped her nose.

"Are you better?" Stephen asked.

Anna shook her head. She felt so bad her heart hurt. "Excuse me," she whispered. She folded her napkin and got to her feet. With as much dignity as she could muster, she walked out of the dining saloon.

Stephen didn't enjoy his breakfast. Anna's tears had made him feel like the worst sort of louse, as if he were to blame for everything. She was the one who had deceived him, he told the judge in his soul, not the other way around. Anna had led him down the garden path, there was no way around it. So why did he feel so guilty?

He went on deck to walk off his aggravation. He paced the weather side, allowing himself to be buffeted by the cold, damp wind. It was the sort of day he used to enjoy spending in the cabin, talking to Anna, watching her work, letting his imagination roam.

Hellfire, she was a hard one to let go of, husband or no husband. And that sharp tongue of hers, the way she defied him at will . . . The truth was, when she got on her high horse, she aroused a lot more than his anger. And when she kissed him, it was like magic. With Anna's arms around him, he felt like a young god, not a battered and aging pug.

Stephen thrust his hands deeper into his coat pockets. When it came to women, nothing made much sense, that was sure.

He decided to go forward to have a chat with the steerage men and see what young Davy Ryan was up to. He'd only reached the mainmast when he was hailed by Gerald Shaw, shaved, pomaded, and attired in a well-tailored tweed coat.

Shaw hurried toward Stephen, swinging his walking stick. "I say, Flynn, there's something I'd like to speak to you about."

Stephen pulled up his coat collar against the wind and waited.

"I understand that in addition to your pugilistic encounters, you operate a gymnasium," Shaw said.

"I have a ring at my saloon and some equipment, but I don't teach fencing or gymnastics, only the art of self-defense."

"Self-defense is what I had in mind," Shaw said, leaning on his cane. "From what I hear about your city, self-defense is one of life's necessities. A few sparring lessons might come in handy if a gang of toughs decides to toss me into the gutter."

"They might, at that," Stephen said, fishing in his pocket for a card. "Stop by and have a look around."

"Much obliged," Shaw said as he studied the card and tucked it in his waistcoat pocket. "And how is Mrs. Flynn feeling this morning?"

Stephen eyed Shaw warily, wondering if he had witnessed the breakfast tears. "She's resting at the moment."

"Ah," Shaw said, stroking his goatee with gloved fingers. "Forgive me again for my little joke last evening. Anna is a lovely girl, lovely indeed. You are fortunate."

Stephen studied Shaw more closely. He saw something in the man's face that aroused his suspicion, a slight twitch of the mustache, a self-conscious shift of the eyes. With a sudden flash, Stephen realized Shaw might know some interesting facts. "Tell me, Shaw, what do you know of her past?"

Shaw's face became guarded. He spun his cane around and inspected the tip. "Very little, I'm afraid."

Stephen felt a bolt of anger. He knew what the man was hiding. "Out with it, blast you."

Shaw looked startled. "My dear fellow, you needn't bully a man."

"I'll bully whoever I want. You knew, didn't you? Blast you to hell, Shaw, you knew all this time and never said a word."

Shaw sighed heavily. "You're speaking of her marriage, I assume."

"That's exactly what I'm speaking of."

"Sorry I didn't mention it, old man, but I thought it best to let sleeping dogs lie."

Stephen all but ground his teeth in frustration. "Then wake them up, Shaw, and get them barking. Who the devil is this husband of hers?"

Shaw's fingers worked nervously at his goatee. "A foundry worker of some sort, I recall. A rough sort of chap. There was a great deal of upset when Anna went off with him. Dr. Wyndham and his family were quite taken with her, you see. I remember Josephine Wyndham in tears one evening telling me about it, how Anna was throwing her life away, that sort of thing. I thought it remarkable to carry on so about a servant, but Josie had grown fond of her, and the girl made extraordinary lace. It was the envy of all the ladies."

A foundry worker . . . a rough chap. Stephen hated to think of it. "Go on, then," he said impatiently. "What happened to him?"

Shaw was chewing on his mustache. "No idea where he got himself off to. It was about a year later, maybe two, that she came back."

"Came back? Anna came back?"

"To the Wyndhams. She wanted her position again. Seems the chap had left her. Josie wouldn't even receive her. Said Anna had made her own bed, that sort of thing. I felt rather sorry for the child. Then I'm afraid I quite forgot her."

Stephen ran a hand down his face. There was no husband waiting in New York. The smoldering anger that had plagued him these past hours seemed to dissipate in the breeze, formless as smoke. He tried to hold on to it, reminding himself that Anna had lied to him, that somewhere she had a husband. But all he felt was relief.

"Sorry I can't be of more help, old man," Shaw said. "If there's anything I can do . . ."

Stephen waved his hand. "Never mind, Shaw. Thanks for your trouble."

After Shaw left, Stephen stood alone by the rail, looking at the bulging clouds. He allowed Anna's husband to take shape in his mind. A rough young fellow, lusty and strong. Anna had lain in his arms more times than Stephen could bear to imagine. And there had been other men. There had to have been others.

Forget her, Stephen told himself. No man with a shred of pride would allow a woman so tainted and deceitful to get under his skin.

But Anna *had* gotten under his skin. And for some absurd reason, he still felt responsible for her. He imagined her alone in New York, speaking her mind as she did, getting herself in trouble. And he thought of Rory. The boy loved her. Anna wasn't fit to be a mother to him, what with all the men in her past, but she was damned good with the lad, made him toe the mark, gave him hugs and kisses.

Stephen blew warm breath into his cupped hands and thought of Anna's glorious smile, her fragrant hair, her sweet lips. Heaven help him, he still wanted her. He wanted her safe in his home. And he wanted her in his bed.

Stephen slammed his palm on the rail. By God, he wasn't going to stand by and stew. He'd find out the truth of her past once and for all, and he'd tell her that he planned to keep her—at least for a while.

Chapter 13

Anna wasn't in the cabin. Stephen glanced at Rory's bunk, where the curtains were still closed, and headed for the ladies' boudoir. There, he nearly collided with Miss Camberwell, who was on her way out.

"Why, Mr. Flynn," she exclaimed, her hand flying to her pretty breast, "you look to be in a purposeful frame of mind!"

Stephen nodded curtly. "I'm looking for my wife. Is she here?"

His abruptness caused Miss Camberwell to become more pink and flustered. "Yes, indeed. Shall I fetch her?"

"If you please."

Miss Camberwell hurried back inside, and Stephen poked his head through the door. The room was filled with enough chattering ladies to make a man shudder. He withdrew his head and satisfied himself with looking discreetly around the doorframe.

He watched Miss Camberwell speak to Anna, who sat on the sofa by the stern windows. Anna glanced at the door, then folded her handwork and tucked it into her workbag. She stood up and shook out her skirt. Stephen felt the back of his neck prickle. Even in her plain, faded dress, she outshone the others.

As Anna hurried toward the door, Stephen could tell from her sour expression and the flush on her cheeks that she was displeased at the interruption. Even her curls, vivid and bursting from their pins, looked angry. By God, she was lovely. Stephen watched the way her breasts moved beneath her bodice and thought, just once in bed with her, maybe twice, and he'd ask no more. Immediately, he knew it wasn't true. Once he started with Anna, he might never let her go.

"You should know better than to be sticking your nose in the ladies' saloon," Anna said, pulling closed the drawstring of her workbag with an angry jerk. "It's to be getting away from men that we have our own place."

"I want to talk with you in private."

"I've lace to finish, Stephen Flynn, and if I'm to pay you what I owe, I can't be wasting my time."

He took her arm and marched her into the main dining saloon. Empty of people and unlit by skylights or chandeliers, the vast chamber was silent and gloomy.

Stephen pulled out a chair and motioned for Anna to sit. "I told you I don't want your money."

She didn't budge. "Then I'll give it to Rory. He can spend it all at the sweetshop."

"Sit down. I want to talk with you."

"We have nothing to say to each other."

"I want to know about your husband, Anna. I want to know who he is and why he left you."

Anna felt a sharp spasm in her head, already aching after a sleepless night. "I won't be telling you what's my business alone. Not after the things you said to me."

Stephen crossed his arms on his chest. From the set of his mouth, it was clear to Anna that nothing short of a gun to his head would force an apology from his lips. "I had a talk with Shaw," he said. "He told me your husband ran off."

"How nice," Anna snapped. "The two of you, gossiping about me. I've never seen the likes of it, the way you men gossip." To herself she thought, By all that's holy, was there a man left in the world who could mind his own affairs?

"Who is he, Anna?"

Anna sighed in exasperation. Dear heaven, she might as well tell him what he wanted to know and get it over with. It didn't matter any longer what he thought. "Billy Massie. His name is Billy Massie, and he worked as a stoker at Bates Foundry. We were married at St. Brigid's by Father Rooney himself."

A steward entered the far end of the saloon with a cart heaped with rattling dishes. Stephen didn't even glance at him. "Why did you marry him? You had a good position with Dr. Wyndham."

"Oh, don't you just sound like herself! 'Stay in service, Anna,' is what my mistress said. 'It's a safeguard against poverty.' "

"And she was right, wasn't she?" Stephen demanded. "A girl like you, starving in the famine. You should know about poverty."

"A girl can starve for more than food," Anna retorted. "I was starving for a loving family of my own."

"A loving family? You picked a fine one for that, then. What did he give you? Not a blessed thing. He ran off and left you with nothing."

"And aren't you the one to be talking so!" Anna cried. "Didn't you run off and leave your Rose?"

Stephen's eyes lit up with anger. "By God, Anna, don't be speaking of her!"

"And why not? Am I not good enough to speak her sacred name? Me, who has murdered and lied and married two men? Oh, I know how you hold me up to her. And don't I come off the poorer for it! Me and every other woman in the world. After Rose, no one is good enough to be your wife or raise your son."

Stephen's face turned thunderous. "By hell, I'll be finding a girl for myself. A girl who's obedient and pure—"

"Who's a saint everywhere but in your bed. That's what you want, isn't it? As if you'll ever find one."

"Now, listen here—"

"And one more thing, while you're thinking to judge me. When I was a maid of all work at Mayhew's hotel, I slept in a room no bigger than a closet and with no bolt on the door. And what do you think happened one night? I woke up and there stood a man, one of the guests, stripped bare. Didn't he just force me that night? But that was my fault, I suppose. I suppose you'd say I was glad for it, that it goes to prove I'm lower than dirt. Well, I'll tell you, Stephen Flynn, a woman doesn't ask to be used and hurt, and that's a blessed fact."

Stephen stared at her, his face frozen, his eyes dark and

unblinking. He looked stunned, as if she'd clapped him on the head with a brick.

"I'll spare you the rest, God help me," Anna said. "The rest of it would show you for sure that I'm not worth a black curse."

Gathering up her skirts, she turned and hurried out of the saloon, past the startled steward, his arms full of plates.

In the cabin, where Rory was still fast asleep, Anna dropped her workbag and fetched her shawl. There was no point in staying there, she decided. Stephen would only come after her with more of his insults. There was only one place where she could think in peace, undisturbed either by Stephen or by the ladies who thought they were higher than the sky.

The deck air was raw and damp; it made Anna shiver. Few people were about. The foam-streaked swells broke against the *Mary Drew*'s hull, making her roll, but Anna was accustomed to the ship's motion and she didn't miss a step. As she headed forward along the rail, sailors in their loose trousers and pilot jackets stared at her. Anna ignored them, knowing they wouldn't utter a word against her. The few steerage men lounging on the forecastle, pipes in hand, watched her silently.

When she reached the cow shed, Anna paused to rub the cow's velvety nose, then went behind the shed to her own private place. She sat down on the coil of rope, unmindful of the tar, and leaned back against the bulwark.

She tried to empty her mind, but Stephen's words came back to her: "What did he give you? Not a blessed thing. He ran off and left you with nothing." Well, that was the truth, Anna thought bitterly. Not a blessed thing but heartache.

She closed her eyes. The regular rise and fall of the ship soothed her, the pitch and roll eased her turmoil. She pulled her shawl closer against the chill and thought of Dublin in the summer, of Sunday afternoons on the strand, the sun hot on her back, the cool water swirling about her ankles. She thought of wading in the water and hunting the pools for crabs, of walking on the beach out as far as the sandbanks.

She thought of the summer that had changed her life and sealed her fate.

There had been a gang of boys on the beach that one Sunday, boys only a few years older than she. They'd teased her, and she'd teased them back, but there had been no harm in it. The next Sunday only one boy was there, a dark-eyed, handsome lad named Billy Massie. He had a way about him that Anna liked, as if he wasn't afraid of a thing, as if he knew exactly what he was about. Billy bragged that he was one of the best workers at the foundry. And he told her that in the evening he and his mates liked to stir up a bit of trouble. But nothing wicked, or so he said.

Anna was lonely that summer, missing her family even after all the years, and she looked forward to the Sundays with Billy. She let him kiss her, but he wanted more, and when she resisted, he got angry. He sulked like a small boy and stayed away from her. Anna walked the strand alone. Then Billy came back and said they'd be married.

Married! Anna sighed at the memory of her foolish expectations. Oh, hadn't she thought she'd be happy, belonging to someone? Everything would be perfect when she was Billy's wife. She would love him and he would love her and they'd raise a brood of bright-faced children. She would again have a family, like her own that she'd lost.

They'd sent for their baptismal certificates, Anna from Killorglin and Billy from Cork. Almost one year to the day after they met, Father Rooney married them.

Mrs. Wyndham had been furious at Anna; she hadn't even said good-bye. Dr. Wyndham had been kinder. He'd slipped Anna five pounds, patted her hand, and wished her luck.

Billy found a flat in Loughton Court. It was a shabby place, the steps broken, the street filthy, but their room was large and had a lovely view of the mountains. Anna kept it clean and made sure there was a cloth on the table. She was able to sell lace to the shops and even did some mending for a few of her former mistress's friends.

Billy worked hard, coming home with his face black from the furnace. Anna could never fault him for being lazy, and he wasn't a man to drink, but he wanted her only for bed. He took her quickly, carelessly, and he wanted her all the time. Other than that, he lived for his mates, for gambling and fighting. He'd come home late, bloody and exhilarated, bragging about which man he'd fought, how much he'd won, and Anna would clean his wounds and put the torn, soiled shirt aside to mend. Then he'd want her again.

They didn't walk on the beach any longer. Most of their time together was spent on their bed. Anna tired of it, and more than once she gave Billy a good slice of her mind. But he told her it was her God-given duty, and the priest agreed with him. In time, it didn't bother her anymore.

Anna shifted on her seat of coiled rope and thought of Stephen. Surely it was the same with all men. They coaxed so sweetly until they had a girl, and then the tenderness vanished and it was all their own rough satisfaction, as if the woman counted for nothing.

After a few months of marriage, Billy had started talking of America. Gold in California, he said, was there for the taking. Anna told him he was daft, wanting to go halfway around the world when he had a steady job at the foundry. But Billy was always thinking of bigger things, things beyond himself. He was a gambler, while Anna liked things steady and secure.

One night he came home late, frightened. Anna had never seen Billy frightened, and his fear terrified her. He gathered together his few things and said he'd be sending for her. Then he was gone. Anna was still in her nightdress, staring out the window in confusion, when the police came. There had been a fight, and Billy had killed a boy. They'd fought over the boy's sweetheart, a girl whom Billy had spoiled.

Anna couldn't absorb the shock of it. Her husband had killed a boy in a fight, beaten him to death. Billy had killed over a girl who was not his wife. He'd broken his wedding vows.

Not until the next day did Anna discover that he had taken her money. Gone were her savings from working for the Wyndhams, her lace money, Dr. Wyndham's five pounds.

She'd screamed in outrage at Billy's betrayal. She searched the streets until she found his mates, then demanded to know where he'd gone. Reluctantly they told her he'd eluded the police and sailed to America.

Anna had returned to their room and fallen onto the bed, weeping her heart out. Billy had run off to his dream of California, leaving behind a dead man, a spoiled girl, and a penniless wife.

Worst of all, he would always be her husband. She was tied to him for life.

Anna felt a spatter of rain on her face. She pulled her shawl over her hair and squirmed on the rope, trying to find a more comfortable position. Billy Massie, she thought grimly, if I ever get my hands on you, you'll know trouble, that's sure.

"Anna? What are you doing sitting here?"

She came back to the present with a start. The freckled face of Davy Ryan looked down at her.

"I heard you was here," Davy said, pushing a lock of red hair away from his eyes, "but I didn't believe it."

"I'm enjoying being alone, Davy Ryan," Anna said. "So don't be minding my business."

Davy crouched beside her. His jacket was dirty and threadbare, his cheeks covered with a bright stubble of beard. "What's got into you, now?" he asked. "You're back of the cow shed when you've got the whole ship to sit in with all those fine people."

"Fine people!" Anna retorted. "I'm sick to the teeth of them."

Davy grinned. "I wouldn't mind it myself. I'd soak in a tub and scrape off my beard and kiss all the ladies' hands."

"Oh, Davy, they'd just laugh at you."

He gave her a skeptical look. "I hope it's not your husband you're sick of. He's as steady as timber. Never did meet a better one than him."

Anna picked at the worn threads on her skirt and changed the subject. "They say it's only a day or so till we reach New York. Where will you be staying?"

"Your Stephen told me there's boardinghouses for men in the Sixth Ward. When I'm settled, I'm to come by his place and he'll see about getting me work."

Anna saw pride and expectation in Davy's face and felt a ripple of affection. "You'll do fine in America. I know it."

He grinned. "And you will yourself. It's your Irish good luck that he took a fancy to you. You've got a rich husband now, and not a worry in the world."

The rain was coming harder. Anna stood up, clutching her shawl under her chin. With her free hand, she grabbed Davy's. "Good luck, Davy. And may God walk with you in America."

She set off at a quick pace as the heavens opened and rain poured down.

* * *

When she entered the cabin, Stephen was sitting on the couch, tight-lipped and tired-looking. He jumped to his feet. "Where the devil have you been? I looked all over."

"I've been on the forward deck, if you must know," Anna replied. "Talking to Davy Ryan."

"You're soaking wet."

"That's plain to see." Anna pulled off her damp shawl and cleared the wet strands of hair from her face.

"What got into you, going up on the forward deck?"

"I wanted some peace. Heaven knows, I can't find it within a mile of you." She gave him a cool glance. "If you'll excuse me, I'll be going up to take a bath." She pulled the curtain across the cabin and disappeared behind it.

Stephen sat down on the sofa and ran both hands through his hair. He felt shaken to the core. The exchange with Anna in the dining saloon had confirmed his worst fear—that she was vulnerable to a man's violence. It had happened to her in a Dublin hotel, it had nearly happened with Spinner, and she had yet to reach the streets of New York.

And there was more. "I'll spare you the rest," she'd said. Stephen suspected she'd spared him the worst, and he was glad of it. He didn't think he could bear to hear another word about what men had done to her.

Anna emerged from behind the curtain, her arms full of clean clothes, her nose in the air. As he watched her leave, Stephen thought of the day he'd met her behind the cow shed. Then he'd wanted her safe—safe from every man but him. Now he didn't know what he wanted, except that he could never leave her on her own.

He rubbed his forehead with his fingers. Somehow he had to persuade Anna to stay with him. Where else in New York would she be safe? Even if she found a position in a rich man's home, something could happen. A randy young son, a drunken guest, the master himself, might find her too tempting to leave alone.

Stephen wished he'd given her better instructions in self-defense. But more than that, he wished he hadn't spoken to her so cruelly.

Anna returned from her bath looking rosy and damp, smelling like blossoms, still in a temper. Stephen watched her arrange her wet towel over the washrack. "Where will you be staying in New York?"

"I'll find a place for myself." Her tone was curt.

"You know nothing of the city."

Anna took up her hairbrush. "Davy Ryan plans to find a place in the Sixth Ward—"

"You'd not last two minutes in the Sixth," Stephen said roughly. "A girl like you."

Anna pulled her brush through her hair. The wet curls became snarled, and she winced. "Mr. Shaw might help me."

"Shaw! By God, you take care with him."

"Oh, don't be foolish. He's kindness itself."

"Kindness? I see how he looks at you." Stephen jumped to his feet and began pacing.

"Oh, and how does he look at me?"

"You know how it is, Anna. I've no need to tell you."

No, he didn't have to tell her, Anna thought, putting down her brush. They all looked at her the same way, even Stephen himself.

She was beginning to worry. As Stephen said, she knew nothing of New York, and she had no idea where she'd be staying. She'd imagined a room in a respectable house on a peaceful street where no men would bother her, but she didn't know how to find such a place.

Anna ran her fingers through her hair, arranging it over her shoulders so it could dry. Something would come along, she told herself. She mustn't feel afraid. But her thoughts were braver than her heart.

"You owe me two hundred dollars," Stephen said.

Anna looked at him in surprise. Not two hours ago, he'd refused even to consider her offer to repay him. "You'll be getting your money," she said. "Every last penny."

He gave her a faint smile. "I've got a better idea."

Anna sat down in the rocker and picked up her workbag. "I know your ideas."

"Look after my place for me."

"Your house? Never!" Anna shook out the lace and studied the rent she was repairing.

"A maid can earn seven dollars a month in New York. I'll give you ten. In little more than a year, you'll pay off your debt and be free of me. And on top of it, you'll have a safe place to live."

"A year with you? You must be daft." Anna bent over her work and thought of living with Stephen, of being safe with him and Rory, of repaying her debt so painlessly.

"I need someone to look after Rory."

"No, Stephen."

"I bought a range for the kitchen. It's brand-new, never had a fire in it."

"Well, aren't you lucky?"

Stephen stopped his pacing and sat down. "I had water piped inside. You don't have to go to the yard for it." Anna heard the excitement in his voice. "There's two floors and a big sunny room for you to do your lace. It's only got a few sticks of furniture, but the paint's fresh and you can fix it up as you like. There are paperhangers and furniture merchants nearby. I'll have them call around."

Anna's needle darted in and out of the frothy lace. She tried not to think of what it would be like, living with a new range and inside water, having a big sunny room all to herself and fresh paint on the walls, and looking after Stephen and Rory.

"I'll get a girl to help you with the washing and the cleaning."

"I don't need a girl."

"You'll agree to it, then?"

Anna shook her head. She couldn't allow him to entice her deeper into their false marriage. "I won't be living with you."

"I want you safe. You'll only be safe with me."

"I've got mending to finish for the ladies," Anna said sharply. "I'd be pleased if you'd leave me alone."

Silence fell between them. Then, his voice low, Stephen said, "You'd stay alone for all your life?"

"I'll be living a virtuous life in America," Anna said, keeping her eyes on her work. "I'll work hard and not depend on any man. If that means being alone, so be it."

The words sounded sadly final to her ears. Alone. Afraid. Uncertain.

Stephen cleared his throat. "Anna, I'm sorry for last night. And for today, for all the things I said. I didn't mean one of them."

Anna stopped her stitching. She touched the delicate lace—pure, fragile, unsoiled—and wondered if she loved it because it was everything she was not. The thought of her own stained past reminded her of Stephen's cruel words. She jabbed the needle through the lace. He was trying to get back in her good graces, she told herself. He'd apologized only to make her soft on him, so he could start in with her again, so he could have his way.

"You meant every word," she said, not looking at him. "When we reach New York, you'll see the end of me."

"Will I, then?" Stephen was quiet for a moment. "I'd sooner send away the sunshine, Nan, than see the end of you."

Anna's fingers trembled. "I still know right from wrong," she said. "And I know what's best for me. So don't be asking for anything more."

PART II

New York

Chapter 14

The great Bay of New York offered a splendid panorama of blue sky, wooded hills, and a vast harbor flecked with sails. Fully rigged ships moved majestically through the shining water, sloops and schooners scurried about. Steamers, their wakes churning, trailed threads of smoke.

It seemed that the *Mary Drew*'s entire company of passengers and crew had crammed the decks. They were a noisily festive bunch, jostling one another for a place at the rail, pointing and shouting their excitement. But their high spirits and the spectacular view of New York and its harbor only deepened Anna's anxiety.

She clung to the rail, staring at the long sprawl of a city, a jumble of pitched roofs and gables, soaring church spires and patches of green parks. *New York*, she thought, her fear mounting with every turn of the ship's great screw. In no time at all, she would be on the street, alone with her boxes, her small treasure of cash, and her faltering courage.

She looked at Stephen standing at her side, pointing out to Rory the landmarks—Trinity Church, the Battery, Governors Island. When she had swallowed her pride and asked him for help finding a place to live, he'd replied with an offhand shrug. "I don't know, Anna," he'd said. "It's not easy finding a place that's safe and cheap for a woman alone."

Maybe he no longer cared what happened to her, Anna thought miserably. She couldn't deny he had reason. He'd seen her through the most perilous time in her life, and what had she given him in return? Nothing but back talk and the most blatant deception. More than once during the past few days she'd formulated expressions of thanks, but she feared if she opened her mouth, she'd reveal what was in her heart, not her head.

Oh, what a mess she'd gotten herself into! For the first time Anna wondered why she had left Dublin. Her life there had been hard, but at least it was familiar.

At the Battery they saw a round fortresslike building, which Stephen said was Castle Garden, the immigration depot where the steerage passengers would be taken. There the immigrants would bathe and change money and make arrangements for travel beyond New York.

Mrs. Smith-Hampton had told Anna that New York ladies often came down to Castle Garden looking for servant girls. The girls, she said, could earn good wages, because American girls refused to go into domestic service.

As the *Mary Drew* reversed engines, Anna's gloom turned to dizzying fright. The wharf teemed with activity, crowds pushing and jostling in their haste to move along. Life ashore seemed loud and confusing, and Anna realized with a jolt that the past weeks in the luxury of the *Mary Drew*'s cabin had been perhaps the most secure and comfortable of her life.

She tugged at the brim of her round straw hat, bought in a fit of extravagance on Grafton Street, and told herself that those peaceful days were over. She was once again on her own and she'd best be prepared for the worst.

The gangway crashed into place, and the steerage passengers pushed forward, dragging their bundles and frightened children. Anna watched as they were herded toward customs inspection, then onto barges that would transport them to Castle Garden. With mounting panic, Anna wondered if she had been too hasty, turning up her nose at domestic work. Even a laundress or a scullery maid had a place to sleep, food to eat, and perhaps a friend or two among the other servants.

Stephen touched her arm. "Come along, then," he said, hoisting her biggest box onto his shoulder. A porter would later collect his baggage, see it through customs, and deliver it to his place.

Rory began to speak, but Stephen shushed him and addressed Anna. "There's boardinghouse runners outside the gate who'll take care of you."

"Runners!" she cried, remembering the rough, fast-talking men in Liverpool. They'd wrested her belongings from her in their effort to get her to lodgings whose operators charged fantastic prices for filthy accommodations.

Stephen had already set off with Rory in tow. Anna scooped up her smaller box and hurried after them. "I'd best go to the depot," she said, as she stumbled down the gangway. "Maybe I should look for a domestic position. Mrs. Smith-Hampton said there's an agency for girls."

Stephen glanced at her, his expression bland and uncaring. "I offered you a good position."

"I can't live with you."

"You can work for me."

They were on the wharf, which was swarming with colliding multitudes of passengers, merchants, sailors, and dockworkers. Vehicles stacked with baggage rumbled by, tossing up clods of mud. Anna's ears were assaulted by the racket of carts, the screech of iron wheels on stone, the shouts of the stevedores. She was sweating under her wool shawl, though the late afternoon breeze was cool.

"I can't stay with you," she cried desperately, staggering on the muddy ground that was strangely free of the *Mary Drew*'s dip and roll.

"Suit yourself," Stephen replied, shifting her box to his other shoulder.

Anna thought longingly of Castle Garden, which had appeared so much safer than the chaotic streets. As a cabin passenger, she'd been subject to only casual inspection by the doctor and immigration officer who'd come aboard at Staten Island. Now she wished she were among the steerage passengers at Castle Garden, who would be carefully tended to by helpful officials. As it was, she'd be all on her own, lost in the city like a mouse in a hayfield.

A customs man stopped them and rummaged about in Anna's boxes. Then he waved her and Stephen and Rory out the gate and into the crowded street.

Almost immediately a man lunged at Stephen, grabbing his arm. "Cheap hacks! Come to the cheapest house in the world!"

Another man in a checked suit and bowler hat grabbed at Anna's box. Before she could tighten her grip, it had slipped into his arms. "Come along with me, girlie," he shouted.

"My box!" she cried.

The lodge touter set off at a quick pace. Anna ran after him, through the surging crowd, bumping into pedestrians who didn't spare her a glance. "Stop!" she shouted. "My box! Oh, stop!"

She kept her eye on the tout's green-checked back, and saw him halt a good twenty yards ahead, his keen eyes searching the crowd for her. She caught up with him, breathless, her heart thudding against her breastbone, her hat hanging by its ribbons.

"Give me my box!" she cried. "Give it to me or I'll call the constable."

The tout laughed, revealing stubs of black teeth. "It'll cost you a dollar, girlie. I carried it all this way."

Then Stephen was there, grasping the tout by the collar. The man dropped the box and swung a fist at Stephen's head, shouting, "Don't be touching me, ye bloody sod."

Stephen easily dodged the blow. Almost faster than Anna's eyes could follow, he boxed the tout's ears with the palms of his hands and gave him a kick to his backside. The man yelped and fled into the crowd.

Anna pressed the back of her wrist to her mouth and sank onto her box. "He'd have stolen it," she said, tears burning in her eyes. "All my lace would be gone!"

Stephen bent down and patted her shoulder. "Now, darling, he just wanted to cheat you. You'd have paid him his dollar and he'd have given your box back. The city's full of his sort, so be on your guard."

"I hate New York," Anna said, looking through a blur of tears at the hurrying crowd, the muddy tangle of traffic. "It's worse than Liverpool."

"Hate it!" Stephen exclaimed. "Why, you haven't even seen it yet. And there's lot to see."

Anna looked at his face, radiating easy confidence, at his broad, comforting shoulders, and wondered how she would

manage without him. "If only I had a place," she said, half
to herself. "If I knew where to go."

A kindly smile tipped the corner of his mouth. "Come along
with us, Nan. Just for a while."

Anna wiped at her cheeks with her palm. After all her
plans and defiant words, how could she agree to stay with
Stephen? Oh, what had become of her courage, her resolve?
"I shouldn't," she whispered. But even as she said the words,
she sagged in defeat.

"It's a rough place, New York," Stephen said, pressing his
handkerchief into her hand.

Anna gave her nose a good blow. "Where's Rory?"

"Back by the gate with your other box. Now, fix your hat
and come along, before a tout snatches him, box and all."

He took her arm and led her back to the pier entrance
where Rory sat on her box, his eyes fixed on a group of men
loading crates and barrels onto a cart. Anna had wondered why
Rory had been so quiet since their arrival. She suspected that
Stephen had told him to keep still until Anna agreed to go
with them.

"I could stay with you for just a short while," she said.
"Until I get my bearings."

"You're welcome to stay for as long as you like," Stephen
said. "Now, let's get going."

A hack took them along the waterfront, beneath ships'
bowsprits that thrust clear across the street nearly into the
windows of the red brick buildings that housed shipping
offices and warehouses. Rory, no longer restrained, bounced
from one side of the carriage to the other, gaping at the sights,
reading aloud the multitude of signs. "Peck's Slip Ferry!" he
shouted. "New Haven Line! Daily at three o'clock! Valentine
and Son Flour Store! Look, Da, Oriental Brewery!"

Anna covered her ears.

"Quiet down, sport," Stephen said.

The hack turned away from the waterfront and plunged
into a narrow, twisting street crowded with carts and wagons,
laborers and hurrying merchants. The sidewalks were heaped
with bales and boxes. Plain three- and four-story buildings bore
the signs of fur merchants, wholesale druggists, stove dealers.
Anna wrinkled her nose at the stench of garbage and manure
and stopped-up drains. New York looked crude and unfinished

and frighteningly chaotic, but it throbbed with activity like no place she'd ever seen.

"Da, look!" Rory grasped the window frame and pointed at a boy, no older than he was, carrying an armload of newspapers, bawling out at the top of his voice.

Anna saw a flicker of alarm in Stephen's eyes. "You don't have to work for your living, Rory," he said. "Be thankful for it."

Rory stared after the newsboy, his face full of longing.

The hack emerged from the narrow, hectic streets into a busy intersection. Anna saw a tree-shaded park with fountains that threw up columns of water. A wide boulevard was crowded with gaily painted omnibuses, private carriages, and throngs of people.

Broadway, Anna thought, sitting up to take notice. From listening to the ladies aboard the *Mary Drew*, she knew that Broadway was the most fashionable shopping avenue in New York, grander by far than Dublin's Grafton Street. And indeed, there were high buildings and handsome stores fitted with large plate-glass fronts. Bright awnings hung from beams that extended nearly to the edge of the sidewalk. Advertisements blazed everywhere.

Stephen pointed out City Hall, built of white marble, and Barnum's flag-draped American Museum. A sign on the museum advertising the appearance of a "Feejee mermaid" made Rory shout with excitement. But it was the passing scene on Broadway, lit by the early evening sun, that captured Anna's attention. She saw elegant ladies and gentlemen, singly and in pairs, strolling before glittering store windows that displayed jewelry and books, house furnishings and wines, toys and perfumes. The shops advertised the latest European articles—French, Anna decided, since Miss Camberwell had declared everything English *mauvais ton*. The strolling ladies were swathed in silks and satins of all colors, their hats streaming ribbons and feathers, and everywhere there was lace and more lace, on shawls and bonnets, on parasols and bodices, on flounces and gloves.

Surely, Anna thought with growing excitement, there would be one shopkeeper willing to buy her work.

The hack turned off Broadway, and there were no more plate-glass windows, no strolling ladies, no shining carriages.

Once again they were on a teeming street. Anna saw millinery shops and clothiers, but they were narrow and plain and stood among junk shops and warehouses and taverns. There were private dwellings, well-built houses two or three stories high, and dilapidated wooden houses that had seen better days. The stoops of the tenements were crowded with men and women enjoying the spring evening. The sounds of commerce were muted, the rumble of passing carts replaced by the raucous shouts of playing children.

Stephen, who had been pointing out the sights, fell silent. He crooked an arm around Rory's neck and stared out of the carriage, his face rapt with anticipation. Anna swallowed her disappointment at the inelegant surroundings. This was Stephen's neighborhood. She would live here only long enough to find a room on a quieter, tidier street.

The hack stopped before a corner building, painted a dark gleaming green. The ground-floor windows were covered with decorative wrought-iron grills. Geraniums bloomed in boxes on the sills. A boy burst out of the shuttered door carrying a foaming pail of beer. Rory stuck his head out the window and stared after the boy, then lifted his eyes to a gold-lettered sign on a green background that ran the length of building.

"The Emerald Flame Saloon," he announced. "Stephen Flynn, Prop."

Stephen grinned. "Here we are."

A group of men loitered on the corner, smoking and talking in the twilight. They spotted Stephen immediately.

"It's himself!"

"Flynn's come back!"

The men clustered around the hack while Stephen helped Anna down and paid the driver. They clapped him on the shoulders, offered their hands in greeting. Their faces and voices were familiar to Anna, work-hardened faces, Irish voices. Like the emigrants on the *Mary Drew*, they wore rough frieze jackets and cloth caps pulled low.

"Maguire's been missing you, Stephen," one man said. "Looking for another fight, he is."

"So he's come around, has he?" Stephen joked. "I thought he'd still be out cold."

"Young Mose licked one of Maguire's boys, licked him good."

The crowd grew larger, pushing to get close. Stephen greeted them warmly, with cuffs and soft punches and firm grips of the hand. Then the crowd's attention shifted to Anna. Voices trailed off and curious eyes stared at her. She glanced at Stephen, wondering how he would explain her.

He slid his arm around her waist. "This is my wife, Anna," he said. "And this here's my boy, Rory."

Anna's jaw fell open. *His wife!* She stared at Stephen, dumbfounded, her mind scrambling to find the words to express her astonishment. Why, he was announcing to everyone that she was his wife, when she'd just barely agreed to work for him, and for only a short while.

The men were snatching off their caps. "Mrs. Flynn," they murmured almost as one voice.

Then Stephen was identifying them to her. "Morrissey, Fitz, Delaney, Sayers, Lawler, Tully . . ."

They looked at her with admiration, almost with reverence, and Anna forced herself to smile at their greetings, as if she was pleased to be there, as if she was indeed Stephen Flynn's loving bride.

"Married," one man said. "Wait'll my missus hears."

Another looked her over carefully. "Aye, Stephen, she's a fine girl."

"And too bad for Peggy Cavanagh."

The last remark brought general laughter and a protest from Stephen. "Now, don't be making fun of our Peg," he said.

Then Rory was brought forward and exclaimed over, and Anna heard the whispers of approval. " . . . his wife." "Ah, now, isn't she a fine one. . . ." "And that's his boy, the one he went after. . . ."

Her face was hot with embarrassment. It was as bad as on the *Mary Drew*, with all the ladies examining her. There she had faced contempt; here it was too much admiration, but it was equally unpleasant. Anna pulled Rory in front of her and slid her arms down his chest. It was a comfort to hold him and to feel his small heart beating as hard as her own. She expected him to wriggle out of her grasp, but he leaned hard against her as if he also felt strange.

A young man made his way through the crowd, a dark-haired young man with striking good looks. He wore an apron, and his sleeves were rolled up to the elbow. He was smiling, but there was an intensity in his face that made Anna think he didn't smile often.

"Emmet," Stephen said. He flung an arm around the young man's shoulders. "Emmet," he said again.

"It's good to see you, Stephen."

Stephen drew Anna and Rory into the circle of his other arm. "This is Emmet Cavanagh, Nan. Emmet looks after things when I'm away."

Emmet looked at Anna, his smile fading.

"Anna's my wife," Stephen said, "and this one's Rory, my boy."

A look crossed Emmet's face that told Anna he was not at all pleased to meet her. The furrow between his brows deepened, and he nodded to her. "Welcome to you, then."

Anna replied with a wary smile. He was jealous, she thought. She was tempted to tell Emmet that before he knew it, she would be gone and he could again have Stephen to himself.

"How fares your fine mother, lad, and our Peg?" Stephen asked.

"Well enough. They've got your place clean and tidy. Come have a drink, Stephen. The lads will be wanting to see you."

Stephen shook his head. "I'll be showing my family their new home." He nudged Emmet's chin with his fist. "Always wanting to talk a little treason, aren't you, lad? Well, there'll be time for it later." To Anna he said, "He's a fine patriot, our Emmet. If I'd let him, he'd be off to Ireland to lift the yoke from our people all by himself."

He pushed Anna and Rory ahead of him through the crowd toward the saloon, reaching over Anna's shoulder to shake a hand or shout a greeting. They stepped through a doorway on the side of the building and into a hallway dimly lit by a gas lamp that hung next to the staircase. Two men carrying Anna's boxes placed them on the floor and, touching their caps, disappeared.

Anna stood with her hands on Rory's shoulders, bristling with annoyance. If it hadn't been for the boy, she would have given Stephen a piece of her mind before taking another step. His wife!

"I guess I should carry you up," Stephen said, looking

pleased with himself. "The bride should be carried over the threshold."

"Don't bother!" Anna snapped. Gathering up her skirts, she marched up the steps.

"It's the second landing," he called after her. "The top floor."

On the third floor she pushed open the door into a sizable room that smelled of new paint and varnish. Two windows let in enough light to show that the room was nearly empty. In addition to the range, as shiny new as Stephen had promised, there was a plain deal table and a sagging upholstered chair. Anna crossed the wood floor, gleaming with wax, and looked into the scullery, where she saw a sink, a small fireplace, a water cistern, and an icebox. A window opened onto a view of the backyard. It was too shaded to see clearly, but Anna could distinguish the shapes of some outbuildings and the remnants of a decaying garden.

She heard Rory and Stephen come in and walk toward the front of the flat, talking excitedly. Anna ran her hand over the immaculate sink edge and cautiously turned the faucet. Water spurted out, making her jump. She twisted it off. It wouldn't be so bad, she thought, cooking and cleaning in such a place, without having to haul water.

She left the scullery and again passed through the kitchen, admiring the range with its nickel-plated castings. Down the hallway she walked by a bedroom that looked fully furnished, passed a sitting room, and entered a spacious front room that looked out over the street. The lower windowpanes were filled with ground glass, which let in light but kept out prying eyes. Through the clear upper panes, which opened casement style, Anna could see the last of the sunlight clinging to the city's rooftops.

Stephen was lighting the lamp. There was a hiss of gas, and the flame jumped, brightening the room. "What do you think, Nan?"

She shrugged. "It's clean enough."

"Emmet's mother saw to that, and his sister, Peg."

"Peg's the one they talked about out there," she said, remembering the men's teasing. She wondered if Peg was

Stephen's sweetheart, a possibility that did nothing to cheer her up.

"You'll like Peggy," Stephen said. "She's a lively girl. Nothing like Emmet."

Anna glanced around the room, which held only one narrow bed, a clothespress, and a battered chair. "Where will I sleep?" she asked.

"Why, right here, darling," Stephen said easily. "With me. This is our room."

Anna set her mouth in a grim line. "Is that so?"

Rory, who had been pondering the view of New York from a chair drawn near the window, turned around, his eyes sharp with curiosity.

"Come here, sport," Stephen said. "I want you to run down to Mrs. Cavanagh's grocery store and get us a bite of supper." He pulled a handful of coins from his pocket.

"The store on the corner across from us?" Rory asked jumping off his perch.

"That's the one. Tell her who you are and that you need some sausage and bread and anything else that catches your fancy."

Anna intercepted Rory as he raced for the door. "Not an hour in the city, and you're covered with dirt," she said, wetting her fingers and wiping at a smudge on his face. "Mrs. Cavanagh and the whole neighborhood will think you've come from a Dublin workhouse."

Rory struggled against her, impatient to be gone. "Everyone's dirty in New York."

"Oh, are they, now?" Anna tried to tame his rake of hair with her hands. "Well, no one in this family will be dirty, not if I have anything to say about it."

When he was gone, Anna took off her blue jacket and opened the door of the clothespress. She felt self-conscious, being alone with Stephen in this bedroom. It was odd to feel so, considering how long she'd shared his cabin aboard the *Mary Drew*.

"We'll never fit in that bed," Stephen said. "I'd best be ordering a bigger one tomorrow."

Anna hung up her jacket. He could tease her all he wanted, she thought. But let him lie down with her tonight, then he'd see trouble.

"A brass bed," Stephen said. "From Rogers down on Water Street."

Anna's temper snapped, and she whirled on Stephen. "After all I've said, what gives you the idea I'll be sleeping with you? And what's more, you had no right telling the whole world I'm your wife when not an hour earlier you said I'd be working for you. If I'm to look after this place and Rory, then I'm your hired housekeeper, nothing more. And if I agree to work for you, it won't be for long, because as soon as I get to know this city and find a peaceful place, I'll be going off on my own."

Stephen smiled at her, an easy, confident smile that dismissed her every word. "You said 'family' just now, did you hear?" he asked, moving toward her. "A little family. You and Rory and me."

Anna backed away, pressing her hands tightly together. "We're not a family. And what's more, you deceived me, telling everyone I was your wife after we'd agreed—"

"One deception begets another, darling. You deceived me first, not telling me of that husband of yours. Let's call it we're square."

He put his arms around her, his hands sliding down to her waist. Anna braced her palms on his chest to keep him at a distance. Over his shoulder, she saw the narrow bed, and she imagined waking up there with him beside her, his body warm from sleep, his face rough with morning whiskers. She lowered her eyes so he wouldn't see anything that should remain hidden.

"You can't force me to be with you."

"I won't have to force you. I know that well enough." He spoke gently and rubbed her back. "Forget the past, Nan, and all the people in it. You've a new life now. No one will judge you here."

He kissed her cheek and nuzzled her neck. His whiskers prickled her tender skin, making her tremble, making her weaken. He found the sensitive little hollow below her ear and kissed her there, a gentle brush of his lips. Anna closed her eyes, her fingers crept up to his shoulders. It was like a sickness, the way he made her feel, the way his mouth lingered, the way his hands moved on her, without haste or harshness.

Anna thought of Rose, the saintly mother of his child, whose perfection grew with every passing year. How had she felt with

Stephen? Had she felt this powerful longing?

He drew her closer still and kissed her brow and then her lips. Anna vaguely heard Rory coming, his footsteps pounding up the stairs, but she didn't pull away. She slid her arms around Stephen's neck and returned his kiss, wondering if a person could lock up memories like old clothes in a trunk and forget they ever existed.

Chapter 15

Later that night Stephen looked around his crowded saloon and thought that the place had never looked better. Behind the bar, the plate-glass mirror shone without a smudge, the bottles had been carefully dusted, the gas lamps were clear of soot. On a calendar on the far wall a bare-shouldered lady sniffed a rose, compliments of Davis Brothers Whiskey. A framed engraving of the noble racehorse, Eclipse, hung on one side of her, and on the other the great fighters Hyer and Heenan squared off in facing posters.

By God, it felt fine to be back in the old place, Stephen thought. He leaned an elbow on the carved mahogany bar and savored the familiar smell of smoke and beer, the sound of loud Irish voices, a jingling piano, the sharp crack of billiard balls. Those uptown gents could keep to their Union Club. A man could relax in a Bowery saloon and find a measure of respect, away from the dock or the ditch where he toiled all day. He could enjoy a drink and a song, lose a few coins at cards, or have a look at the *Irish Times*. If he needed to burn off some anger, he could step into the back room and go a few rounds in the ring.

Stephen's gaze drifted toward the sparring room door and abruptly stopped. "What the devil?"

He stared at the poster of himself, chest bare, fists up. The poster had hung in the sparring room for years. Someone had moved it to a spot above the billiard table, right next to the life-size painting, *Susannah Surprised in Her Bath*. Stephen looked at the incongruous pair and laughed. He appeared to be challenging Susannah to lift her hands, one strategically placed at her shapely pink thighs, the other hovering near her blushing breasts.

Stephen nudged Emmet, who leaned beside him at the bar. "Will you look at that," he said with a chuckle. "I'm about to go a few rounds with our Susannah."

Emmet took a listless gulp of beer. "Tully's idea," he said. "It amused the lads."

Stephen caught the eye of the sleek-haired barman, busily wiping glasses. "I see your hand in this, Tully."

Tully's drooping mustache twitched as he smiled. "Figured it was time you took on a woman."

"I have a wife now, Tull."

Tully pulled at the beer faucet. "I seen her today, your missus. She's a lovely one. God's blessing on you both."

Stephen ducked his head in acknowledgment and said no more. Women were a lively topic of conversation in saloons, but not wives, and never Anna, especially not in the same breath with the naked Susannah.

He glanced at Emmet, glumly nursing his beer. Emmet had been sulking all evening. Even the raucous welcome Stephen had received from the packed saloon had failed to lift his spirits. He'd always been a moody lad, ready to look on the hard side of things, but Stephen sensed something deeper was troubling him.

"Surely you've got a smile in you somewhere," Stephen said.

Emmet shrugged and said nothing.

"You'd best tell me what's biting you."

Emmet stared at his mug of beer. "You won't be fighting again, having a wife."

So that was it, Stephen thought. That was why Emmet had looked at Anna the way he had.

"She's got nothing to do with it, lad. I gave up fighting because I haven't the heart for it any longer. And I don't want to end up like our Hammer." He nodded at the old fighter who sat contentedly amid a quarreling group of men, deep in their cards and their whiskey.

Emmet's jaw jutted out just enough to show his displeasure. "O'Mahony and Doheny organized a committee for the invasion of Ireland. They'll be holding a meeting at the Sixth Ward Hotel."

"Oh, so now it's the invasion of Ireland," Stephen said. "I thought we were speaking of prizefights."

Emmet pushed aside his half-finished beer. "I'm speaking of you, Stephen. You're a fighter and a patriot. You belong to the Irish cause as much as you belong in the prize ring."

Stephen contemplated Emmet's reflection in the mirror over the bar. The lad loved the notion of battle, as long as Stephen was doing the fighting. At the age of twenty-three, he had yet to become his own man.

"I belong to my family and to my good neighbors and friends," Stephen said. "That includes you, if you'll not be thinking of me as a hero out of the old legends. As for Ireland, freedom will come. Maybe not in our lifetime, but it will come, God willing, in Parliament, without the shedding of blood."

"It must come now!" Emmet said, his face flushing with passion. "How can we Irish earn respect in America if our own country is under the heel of the British?"

"You earn respect by working hard and living a decent life, Emmet, just as you're doing."

"But O'Mahony says—"

"O'Mahony and Doheny have bricks in their hats, both of them," Stephen said impatiently. "They left Ireland in 'forty-eight as failures, like all of us. Now they fancy themselves heroes."

"They *are* heroes," Emmet protested. "They rose up and fought! And so did you."

"Fought!" Stephen shook his head in disgust. " 'Forty-eight was a skirmish in a cabbage patch, nothing behind it but politics and poetry. I suppose they still think they can go after the queen's army with pikes and pitchforks and a mouthful of brave words."

"They'll be getting guns this time. Enfield rifles."

Stephen felt a jolt of alarm. By God, had word reached American shores so quickly?

"And there'll be a rising—"

"There'll be no rising!" Stephen said, angry now. "The Irish people have no stomach for it, not after the famine and all the sickness and sorrow in the land. The priests preach against insurrection, and the best men have come to America. No one in Ireland cares about risings any longer, not even the police. They let us old 'forty-eighters wander about, free as the air. They know it would take Saint Patrick himself to light the old fires again."

Looking at Emmet, Stephen was reminded of himself years ago, dizzy with hatred and hope. It was a shame the lad should waste himself on other men's causes. "Emmet," he said, trying to be patient, "you're American-born. You've never set foot on Irish soil. Revolution in a ruined land is a hopeless cause."

"It's not hopeless," Emmet said stubbornly. "I'll be going if they'll have me."

Stephen looked closely to see if he was serious. "You'd go over there and get into it?"

Emmet nodded. "I know they're organizing. There has to be communication between New York and Dublin, but the mails aren't to be trusted. I told O'Mahony I'll serve as a courier if they'd have me. I've already taken the oath."

So, Stephen thought, his passionate young friend was his own man after all, eager to give himself over to a lost cause. "You're serious, then."

"I am, Stephen."

Stephen thought of Padraic McCarthy's charge—to find a trustworthy man to carry money to Birmingham—and his mind began to work. Emmet wasn't reckless. He had brains to spare, and he was loyal to the core. He had a mother and a sister, but no wife, no children. And once he reached Ireland, Padraic would look after him.

Stephen leaned closer to his friend. "That group in Ireland is no more than a handful of men drilling in the Dublin mountains with pikes and staffs on Sunday afternoons. I wager it'll all come to nothing."

Emmet set his handsome jaw. "I have to do it, Stephen. I have to do something."

"What have you heard about guns?"

"Nothing for sure. O'Mahony is wanting to raise money to buy some. He's talking of issuing bonds and staging benefits and raising an army of five hundred to send over. But first he has to hear from the Brotherhood in Dublin."

Stephen glanced at the clock and saw that Tully's shift was over. He gave Emmet a cuff on the shoulder. "Roll up your sleeves and get to work. Later we'll be talking. And don't be giving drinks on the house to every Irishman who speaks against the queen."

Stephen left the bar and made his way through the crowd of men. The more he thought of Emmet serving as courier, the better he liked the idea. The lad was as sober as Bible covers, not a light-minded hair on his head. Padraic would approve of him, Stephen was sure of it. He would tame Emmet, mold him into a political thinker to rival the best of them. But O'Mahony had to be reined in. Padraic wanted operations directed from Ireland, not by the New York firebrands.

Stephen stepped into the sparring room, thick with spectators and cigar smoke. Over the heads of the crowd he saw two men punching and feinting in the roped-off ring in the center of the room. He headed for the corner where the heavy bag, stuffed to a man's weight, hung from the ceiling. That was where he loosened up and broke a sweat. During training, he worked on the bag for a good half hour at a time while Emmet held it still.

"So the Emerald Flame still burns," a familiar voice called out. "Welcome home, champ."

Stephen turned, recognizing Frank Gillespie, the rumpled, florid-cheeked Scot who reported for the *National Gazette*. "Gil," Stephen said, breaking into a smile.

"By Christ, you look fine," Gillespie said, pumping Stephen's hand. He gripped a cigar butt in the corner of his mouth. "Fit as a flea. Maguire's been waiting."

"He'll have a long wait, then. I've gone to ground."

"The hell," Gillespie retorted. He unscrewed the cap of his ever-present flask and without removing the cigar from his mouth, took a gulp. "The papers get wind you're back, they'll print Maguire's insults till you'll have no choice but to fight him."

"Sorry, Gil. There's not a challenge in the world that'll get me back in the prize ring."

"Ah, I don't believe it. You're in top form, champ. And by God, there's money to be made."

Stephen let the argument drop. "Come on, Gil, hold the bag while I give it a few whacks."

He pulled off his coat and shirt. Men stepped back to let him pass, nodding and murmuring their greetings.

"They say you're giving it up for a woman," Gil said. "Hard to believe you'd let a female get under your skin."

Stephen shot Gillespie a warning look. "Don't be mentioning my wife, Gil. Not in this place." He tossed his shirt and coat into the arms of a spectator and took a pair of light sparring gloves from a hook on the wall. "I said I was finished after the Maguire fight. I'm thirty years old."

"Hell, Yankee Sullivan was thirty-five when he beat Bob Caunt—"

"I said I'm out of it." Stephen thrust out his hands for Gil to tie the strings on the gloves. "Now lay against that bag before I lose my temper and knock you to the floor."

A group of men gathered around the bag. Stephen braced his legs and let fly a flurry of punches. His buckskin gloves smacked against the bag's buff leather cover, sending jolts through his arms and shoulders. A prickle of sweat started on his neck and back. He punched the bag with all his strength, keeping his eyes on Gil, whose face darkened as he struggled to keep himself and the bag steady.

As he worked, Stephen thought of the pressure he'd face in the coming weeks. The newspapers would be after him, reporting Maguire's challenges, hinting at his marriage, speculating about his physical condition. The papers would print anything to arouse interest. They portrayed prizefights as rivalries that went beyond the ring—American against Irish, Catholic against Protestant, northerner against southerner. At one time they'd touted Stephen as a bloody Irish revolutionary. But when he fought Billy Maguire, he'd been transformed into a respectable businessman, with Billy the villain, tied to gang violence and corrupt politics.

Stephen knew that the newspapers' lies were part of the game, a way to sell papers and give workingmen a diversion from their daily grind. But no amount of noise was going to change his mind. He had quit the ring for good.

He stopped his workout abruptly, his body drenched with sweat. Someone tossed him a towel and he wiped his face and neck.

Gil was puffing hard, his thinning sandy hair stuck wetly to his scalp. "You're hot, champ. Haven't lost that punch. How're the legs?"

Stephen ignored the question. "Emmet'll give you a drink, Gil," he said. "On the house."

"Later. I'll stick around and watch you work." Gil fell in step with Stephen as they headed for the ring. "How about an exhibition match? You and Maguire at Sportsman's Hall. Three sparring matches and a glove fight. At a dollar a head—"

"You going deaf, Gillespie?" Stephen snapped. "I said I'm through."

At ringside a husky dark-skinned youth paced, keeping an eye on two men flailing away at each other. The lad wore a red flannel shirt, and his hair stuck out from his head in a wiry black tangle. Stephen marveled at how Mose had grown. When he'd first turned up in the sparring room a few years back, he'd been a skinny, half-wild street boy working as a rat catcher for a Water Street rat pit. Now Mose was probably all of eighteen, but he looked fitter and was built bigger than most full-grown men.

Stephen nodded toward the ring. "They doing each other any harm?"

Mose shook his head. "Them two old goats ain't done nothing but fan the air."

Stephen tossed down his towel. "Let's you and me go a few rounds, Mose. For the lads."

Mose's eyes, normally flat and wary, brightened. "I don't mind."

Stephen signaled to the men to wind up their match. Mose stripped off his shirt, pulled on some gloves, and climbed through the ropes with Stephen. A murmur ran through the sparring room. Men who'd been milling around came to attention and pushed closer to the ring, their voices growing louder.

Stephen jogged on the wooden floor of the platform and assessed Mose's husky shoulders, his broad chest. "You're almost the size of me, lad."

Mose thrust out a sleekly muscled arm and laid it against Stephen's. "Seems you've darkened some."

Stephen laughed. "I spent a good many hours on that ship sparring in the sun." He peered out into the smoky room.

"Gillespie," he shouted. "Get up here and keep time."

The newsman elbowed his way through the crowd, pulling out his pocket watch. Stephen and Mose touched gloves and raised their hands to full position. The sparring room fell silent.

"Time, gentlemen."

"Look at me, now," Stephen said to Mose. "Look at me hard. Focus on business."

Mose's eyes narrowed. He had a fierce look about him that served him well in the ring, and he didn't lean back. He hung his face right in there bravely, ready to take the blows.

They circled each other. Stephen made a few feint swipes to test Mose's reaction. "Keep your head moving," he said.

He threw a right. Mose ducked and backed away. Stephen advanced, and Mose retreated farther. "I'm pushing you backward," Stephen said. "Don't let me do it."

Mose broke forward, driving a glove at Stephen's chin. Stephen tried to slide away, too late to escape the blow. His head snapped back and the jolt ran through him. He felt a second of blankness, heard a roar of voices, and saw Mose blinking, looking surprised.

Stephen shook his head to clear it. "Good lad." He threw a right and a left to the ribs that drove Mose back. "Don't stand there admiring your work," Stephen said. "Throw your punch and get out of the way."

Stephen dodged and feinted, finding his rhythm. Mose's footwork was less than artful, but he kept Stephen lively. By the second round, Stephen felt the familiar pleasure of going toe to toe with a decent fighter, concentrating hard, watching, reacting, every nerve sharp. Even after the blow to his chin, he felt alert, his legs strong and springy. Mose landed any number of stingers, but the boy was all attack and no defense. Stephen reached Mose's ribs and chest at will.

They quit after five rounds, despite loud protests from the spectators. Stephen loosened his glove strings with his teeth, dropped them, and flexed his shoulders. He felt weary but exhilarated, and pleased that his hip had not given him the slightest twinge. Mose looked fresh, and in his eyes there shone a quiet pride.

"Defend your body," Stephen said between gulps of cool water. "In a real match, the body punches are what'll wear you down."

Mose smiled slyly. "I found your chin easy enough."

Stephen cuffed the boy's head. "You did at that."

He went off to shower behind the wooden partition at the far end of the sparring room. As he stood on the stone floor beneath the spray of cool water, he thought about Mose's youth and strength and felt a pang of envy. Sure, it was a relief to have it finished. His body couldn't take the punishment of the prize ring any longer, and the anger that once ran in his veins was gone. Yet there was something about the fighter's life that he loved, the rough camaraderie among men, finding his worth in an explosion of violence, the glory of being a champion. And in even the most bitter rivalry there was respect, a blood bond of courage between two men.

Stephen dried himself and dressed. Exertion and the cold shower had left him feeling both fatigued and stimulated. He ran his fingers through his wet hair and thought of Anna. He pictured her asleep upstairs, warm and tousled. He imagined lying down beside her, kissing her awake. . . .

He pushed the thought out of his mind. He'd wait until he got a proper bed and she was more settled. Tonight he'd sleep in the kitchen chair.

He headed back to the sparring room, feeling aroused. He thought of other women in the city he'd known over the years; any one of them would have welcomed him. He considered each in turn and dismissed them all. It was Anna he'd been wanting these past weeks. He'd gladly wait one more night.

He noticed an odd silence in the sparring room, a current of tension mingling with the hot smell of cigar smoke and sweat.

"Evening, Flynn."

Stephen turned, his nerves jumping to attention. Billy Maguire stood before him, stroking his kidskin dress gloves smooth over his big hands. His black hair, cropped short as if for the ring, set off his handsome features. Over his checked suit he wore a full dark cloak, thrown back over one shoulder.

"Why, Billy," Stephen said slowly, taking in the arrogant stance, the insolent smile. "I didn't expect to see you so soon."

A half-dozen glowering young men surrounded Maguire. Their hair was long and laden with a pungent-smelling grease, and they dressed in the fashion of the Bowery—gaudy handkerchiefs knotted about the neck, full trousers turned up over heavy boots that were iron-tipped for cracking shins.

"I come by to welcome you back from the old country," Maguire said, flexing his leather-clad fingers.

"That's mighty nice." Stephen didn't bother to keep the sarcasm from his voice.

The gang's scowls deepened, and Stephen wanted to smile at their posturing. Like all Bowery gangs, these men were dangerous, especially at election time when they descended on polling places with clubs, knives, and brickbats to bully and intimidate the opponents of Tammany Hall. They had little to their credit but their clothes, their leader, and their enthusiasm for mayhem.

He nodded toward the door that led into the saloon. "Come on, then. I'll have Emmet draw you a beer."

The offer of hospitality seemed to take Billy by surprise. He looked at Stephen, his confident smile fading.

"Well?" Stephen asked. He enjoyed watching Maguire deal with the unexpected.

Billy shrugged. "Don't mind if I do."

Stephen set off toward the saloon, trailed by the clatter of hobnail boots.

The saloon's shuttered outside doors stood open, allowing the cool night air to mingle with the smell of smoke and spirits. A score of men lingered over their cards and drink, trying not to stare. Gil was knocking balls aimlessly around the billiard table. He took one look at Billy and his gang, dropped his cue, and reached for his notebook. Stephen could almost see his newsman's nose twitching.

Stephen leaned on the bar. "A beer for Mr. Maguire, Emmet."

Emmet gaped at Billy and reached for a schooner, then poured and slid the foaming mug across the bar.

Billy took a drink and wiped the back of his wrist across his mouth. "I want to meet you, Flynn."

"I figured as much."

Billy dug into his pocket and pulled out three golden eagles. He slapped them on the bar. "You name the spot and the date and the money's yours."

"I'm finished with the ring, Billy."

Maguire's face darkened. "I'm challenging you."

"Sorry."

Maguire's greased-haired men shifted ominously, shooting hostile looks in all directions.

"I hear you got married."

Stephen cocked his head, instantly on guard. "That needn't concern you."

"I hear she's a looker."

"Shut up, Maguire."

A smug smile crawled across Billy's face. He slipped his hands into his pockets and glanced at the picture of Susannah trying unsuccessfully to cover her breasts. "Your wife got titties like that?"

Stephen's fist glanced off Billy's jaw just as pain exploded in his side, stunning him, stopping his breath. Then men were between them, shouting. Stephen was pressed against the bar, held by Mose and Gil. Billy's sidekicks were making a gleeful show of holding their own man.

Stephen struggled mightily, but the pain was too much. He slumped against the bar, gasping, feeling as if he'd been stabbed.

"Son of a bitch has iron knuckles," someone said.

"Let me go, Mose."

Stephen pushed himself upright, his hand beneath his coat, holding his searing ribs. Everyone in the saloon was on his feet. Cards had scattered, fallen pool cues lay on the floor.

Billy backed away toward the door, his eyes darting about nervously. His smirking hoodlums jostled one another with excitement.

Stephen walked toward them, stopping only when the toes of his boots bumped Billy's. "You want to fight me, you bastard, we'll fight. Now. Open rules. Gouging and kicking. The man who's alive at the end of an hour wins."

Billy licked his lips, his eyes blinking in alarm. "I want a prize match."

"You want a prize match," Stephen said in a tone of flat contempt. "Prizefighters don't wear iron on their hands, Billy.

You're a disgrace to the boxing profession. But worse, you dumb Irishman, you forgot your manners."

Billy's eyes lit up with anger. "Don't you be calling me—"

Stephen drove a fist into the midsection of Billy's checked waistcoat. He followed with a right to the chin that sent a shot of pain through his fist. Billy stumbled backward into the arms of his men, his eyes glazed.

The saloon erupted into shouts and roaring curses. Men lunged at one another in a blur of waving arms and pummeling fists. Stephen saw Mose drag one of Billy's men to the floor by his neck scarf, his arm pumping like a piston. A knife flashed. Before Stephen could call out a warning, Mose had grabbed the gangster and hurled him to the floor. The knife spun away into a pile of sawdust.

"Maguire!" Stephen shouted. "Call off your men."

Billy gingerly touched the hinge of his jaw.

Stephen made for the bar, forgetting his bruised ribs and throbbing fist. "Emmet!"

Emmet reached under the bar and tossed Stephen a Colt revolver. Stephen cocked it, gave a shrill whistle through his teeth, and fired a shot into the wall.

The saloon fell silent. All eyes turned to Stephen and Billy.

Maguire attempted a careless smile but winced with pain.

"Get out, Maguire," Stephen said, laying the Colt gently on the bar. "And take your bullyboys with you. They're stinking up the place."

Billy glanced at the three gold coins, shining next to the revolver.

"Those coins'll just about cover damages," Stephen said, surveying the busted chairs, the broken glassware.

Billy made a show of smoothing his gloves. "We ain't finished, Flynn," he said, his voice muffled by his attempts not to move his jaw. "Not by a long shot."

"If you ever mention my wife again, I'll put a bullet through you."

Billy shifted his broad boxer's shoulders and rearranged his cape. "I'll be meeting you in the ring sooner or later."

Stephen laughed, a sound raw with contempt. "I'll see you in hell first."

Chapter 16

Anna woke to sunlight sparkling on the decorative crushed-glass windows. The bed seemed oddly still. Then she remembered that she was no longer aboard the *Mary Drew* but in New York City in Stephen's flat. In Stephen's bed. She jerked around in alarm. To her relief she was alone. The last she'd seen of Stephen, he was heading downstairs to tend business in the saloon. Anna wondered where he'd slept.

She raised her arms over her head in a long stretch, then pulled on her green silk dressing gown and went to the window. Pushing open the casement, she looked down three stories to Brace Street, where proprietors prepared for another day of business, washing and sweeping the sidewalk and unloading carts. A milk wagon and a baker's truck stood in front of Mrs. Cavanagh's corner grocery store. Beyond the shop's faded green awning, Anna saw a store hung with carpets that billowed in the breeze.

It was a lively, friendly neighborhood, she thought. After supper last evening, Stephen had taken her and Rory out for a walk along the gaslit Bowery, past cafés and little theaters, shooting galleries and oyster houses. There had been no end of sights, nothing like it in Anna's experience. The sidewalks had been thronged with brightly dressed shopgirls and swaggering young men. People on the street had recognized Stephen.

He'd stopped to talk, even to strangers, and introduced her and Rory.

The thought of Rory reminded Anna that she'd best be seeing about a school for him. She was relieved that the Curran twins were waking up somewhere other than Brace Street.

After scuffing into her slippers, Anna ventured down the hallway. Rory's door was ajar, the bed rumpled and empty. She entered the kitchen and came to a startled halt. Stephen lay sprawled in the old easy chair, head back, jaw hanging, snoring contentedly. A blanket had worked its way down about his spread thighs, revealing loosened trousers and a half-buttoned shirt.

Anna twisted the plait of hair that lay over her shoulder. Not once aboard the *Mary Drew* had she seen Stephen sleeping. Now she looked at his great body, restful as a stroked cat, and felt a familiar warmth flow through her limbs. How would it be with him in bed? she wondered. Quickly she scolded herself. Didn't she remember how it was, lying beneath a man's full weight while he thrust and panted and she waited for it to end? Did she think it would be any different with Stephen Flynn?

Stephen groaned and shifted in the chair, then settled back with a snort and continued to sleep.

Anna tossed her braid over her shoulder and glanced about impatiently. *Rory.* Now, where was that boy? She opened a door beside the scullery to a crude flight of stairs. Holding her dressing gown close about her, she went down the steps, past the second-floor landing, lit by a dingy window, to the bottom, where a short hallway led to the back door. She opened the door and surveyed the yard, cluttered with weeds and dilapidated outbuildings, but she saw no sign of Rory. The breeze plucked at her dressing gown. She shivered and shut the door.

Another door led off the hall. Anna pushed it open and stepped into a vast unpainted room with a scuffed wooden floor and walls covered with tattered fight posters. In the center of the room stood a simple roped-off platform lit by a shaft of sunlight that fell through the window.

The place reeked of stale smoke, sweat, and liniment. The sparring room, Anna thought. She tried to disapprove, but instead, she looked around with interest. It was Stephen's

place of business, big, stark, and purposeful. A sign painted
on the wall announced that any evening except Saturday a
man could pay fifty cents to step into the ring for seven
three-minute rounds of sparring. On Saturdays spectators paid
twenty-five cents to watch and wager on exhibition matches
featuring fighters of professional rank.

As Anna finished reading the sign, she heard a faint, high-
pitched cry coming from the far end of the room.

"Rory?" She hurried toward a slight figure hanging by his
hands from what appeared to be a metal horizontal rod fastened
diagonally across a corner.

"Rory!" she cried. "What on earth?"

He was bare-chested and struggling to pull himself up. His
legs kicked the air. With a hopeless groan, he relaxed his
bone-thin arms and hung, gasping for breath.

"Watch me," he said, panting. He grunted and kicked some
more, until his small chin topped the bar.

Anna smiled. "Well, I declare."

Rory released his hold and dropped to the floor, knocking
over the stool he'd used to reach the bar. A lock of black
hair stuck to his forehead, damp with exertion. Hitching up
his trousers, he raced for the other corner where a man-size
bag hung from the ceiling.

"Watch this!" he cried. Spreading his legs, he pounded the
leather with his bare fists. The bag creaked lazily. "And look
at these!" He ran to a wooden rack that held an array of
dumbbells. He dragged one off the rack and lifted it, his dark
eyes shining. "One hand," he panted happily. "I bet that's ten
pounds. The iron ones must be a hundred. My da can lift a
hundred in each hand."

"Ha," said Anna. "Nobody can do that."

"*He* can," Rory said with confidence. He replaced the
dumbbell and pulled Anna over to the wall where sparring
gloves hung in a neat row. He grabbed a pair and thrust them
at Anna. "Put these on."

"Oh, Rory, don't be daft."

"*Please*, Anna," he said impatiently.

The gloves were made of soft buckskin and bound with
leather. There were strings at the wrist and ventilation nets on
the palms. Anna pulled them on. Inside, the gloves felt gamy
with old sweat. She took a swipe at Rory, delighting him.

"Let's get in the ring!"

"Enough, now," Anna said, putting on a stern face. "Fighting is not something to play at. Why, you shouldn't even be here alone, swinging on that bar and lifting those heavy things. Your da wouldn't like it, and what if you got hurt?"

Rory didn't seem to be listening. He took a pair of gloves for himself and climbed into the ring. "He won't mind," he said. "Come on." He leaped about the ring, punching at an imaginary opponent.

"Now you get out of there," Anna scolded. "That ring is for men, not children. Or women, either."

Rory stopped jumping. "Come in for a minute. I won't hit you. Promise."

His cheeks were rosy with excitement, and his hair stood up like a field of grass. Anna looked down the length of him and noticed that his trousers stopped well short of his ankles. Heavens, the child was growing before her eyes. She'd best go through all his things or he'd be looking like one of the ragged crossing sweepers she'd seen last night on the Bowery.

"Anna?"

"Oh, well," she said with a shrug, "where's the harm in it? But only for a moment."

She climbed up the short set of steps to the platform. Rory held the ropes apart, and she stepped inside. "So," she said. "Now what do I do?"

Rory struck a fighter's pose, his legs apart, his gloves raised. His head bobbed about like a buoy. "Try to hit me."

"Hit you!" Anna put her gloved fists on her hips. "Rory Flynn, I swear you have the devil in you. Look what you've got me into now, standing in this ring when I should be seeing to breakfast and a hundred other things. And as for you, by tomorrow you'll be in school. Why, if you think for a minute you're going to spend your days playing in this place or fighting in the street, you'd best think again."

"Indeed you'd better, lad."

At the sound of Stephen's voice, Anna swung around, her gloves still on her hips. She thought how ridiculous she must look, standing in the middle of a fight ring wearing her dressing gown, with a braid hanging down her back and sparring gloves on her hands.

Stephen gave Rory a broad wink. "Giving our Anna a match, then, are you, sport?"

"He's giving me trouble," Anna shot back. "Wanting me to hit him, for pity's sake." She strode over to the ropes, which Stephen held apart for her.

"I doubt you have much of a punch," he said, his voice warm with teasing.

"Is that so?" Anna retorted. She was annoyed at the way her heart jumped at the sight of him, even though he was rumpled and whiskery and still bleary with sleep. "I have punch enough when I need it."

"Wrestling, now," Stephen said, taking her by the waist. "There, you'd give a fellow a match."

As he swung her to the floor, Anna heard him take in a sharp breath. A grimace of pain crossed his face. She looked at him, startled. "What's this, then? What's the matter with you?"

Before she could get a response, Rory was clambering out of the ring. "Show Anna how you can lift a hundred pounds with one hand, Da."

Stephen shook his head. "Later, sport. Take off your gloves and go along upstairs."

Rory looked hopefully at Anna. She nudged his cheek with her glove. "Listen to your da. We'll see his tricks later."

After he scampered away, Anna held out her hands so Stephen could pull off her gloves. "What happened to you that you're hurt?"

Stephen shrugged and tossed her gloves aside. "A bit of a muss last night, that's all. I took a punch in the ribs. I'll be hurting for a day or so, no more."

"A punch!" Anna exclaimed. "Who did it to you?"

Stephen looked at her thoughtfully, as if considering whether he should answer. "Maguire was in last night, trying to provoke me into a match."

"But you said you wouldn't be fighting again."

"I don't plan to."

"But this Maguire—"

"Believe me, darling, I'm finished with fighting. Maguire or anybody." His gaze drifted over Anna's face; his eyes met hers and stopped. "Does it matter so much to you?"

Anna pulled her dressing gown closer about her. She felt naked beneath her nightdress and a little breathless, the way she always felt when Stephen was near. "I don't want you hurt."

His eyes softened. "I'm glad to hear it."

Anna stared over his shoulder at the dust motes floating in the shaft of sunlight, achingly aware of his eyes on her. "We'd best go upstairs."

"Tonight there's to be a celebration of our marriage," Stephen said. "Mrs. Cavanagh and the neighbors want to welcome you."

Anna wondered how she could pretend to be Stephen's wife, yet keep him at arm's length. "We can't have a wedding party," she said in a small voice. "We're not even married."

"We're married all right."

"But you said—"

"The past is gone, Nan, left behind in Ireland. It's time for us to be man and wife."

Anna looked away, awaiting the familiar press of buried memories. Billy Massie. Her family lying dead in the ground. The shattering evening in a Killorglin shop that she could never atone for. But the power of her sorrows had somehow faded. She was no longer in Dublin or Kerry or aboard the *Mary Drew*. She was in New York City, in Stephen Flynn's home. His words, the touch of his hands, the smell of his sparring room, seemed more real to her than the life that lay years behind her and miles beyond the sea.

Anna looked back at him. He studied her intently, as if awaiting an answer. When the time came, she knew there would be only one answer to give, an answer he could surely see in her eyes.

"It's time for breakfast," she said abruptly. "And you need a shave."

Stephen grinned and rubbed his cheeks.

"And another thing," Anna said, gathering her emotions under control. "Rory shouldn't be playing here alone. He could drop one of those dumbbells on his foot or fall from the bar."

"Aye, you're right. I'll have a talk with him."

"And I'll need to be going to market." Anna set off across the sparring room with a purposeful stride. The larder was bare and the range stone cold. There was work to be done, and she'd better get to it. "You'll have to tell me where to shop."

"Anna."

She stopped.

"One more thing." Stephen came up beside her.

"Oh? And what's that?"

He ran his hand down her braid, twining it around his fingers. Then, before Anna knew what he was about, he bent down and covered her mouth with a hard kiss. It took Anna so much by surprise that by the time she thought to struggle, Stephen had pulled away.

"There," he said with satisfaction. "Now I'm ready to face the day."

Anna sent Rory off to Mrs. Cavanagh's for flour and coffee and a few other staples. Within the hour everyone was washed and dressed, a coal fire burned in the black Thompson cooking range, and Anna was serving up a breakfast of pancakes and oatmeal. She set a platter of pancakes on the wide wooden table and glanced around at the empty cupboard and clean shelves. "You lived in this big place with hardly a fork or a broom to your name, Stephen? Why, there's not even enough plates for all of us to eat at once."

Stephen's forkful of pancakes, dripping butter and honey, halted in midair. "Now, what would I need with any of that? I took my meals out, and Peggy came in twice a week to clean up."

Anna wiped her hands on her apron. "Weren't you spoiled, then."

"Aye, I was spoiled, and I've no plans for changing." A smear of honey shone on his smiling lips.

Anna turned her attention to Rory, who was concentrating hard on his food, his cheeks bulging. "As for you, young Mr. Flynn, there'll be no spoiling of you. I'll be expecting you to be a helper to me. Starting today."

Rory's eyes widened. Anna heard a distinct sound of protest emerge through his mouthful of pancakes.

"You mind our Anna, you hear?" Stephen said. "Whatever she tells you to do, you do it or you'll be answering to me." He scraped back his chair. "I'll be off, then. I've got brewers and distillers to talk to and more than one argument to settle among the neighborhood lads. If you need anything, go over to Mrs. Cavanagh's. She and Peg'll be friends to you. There's money on the dresser for whatever."

He slipped an arm around Anna's waist, giving her a quick squeeze and a kiss on the lips. He whispered in her ear, "It's good to have you here, Nan."

"Get along with you," Anna said, pushing him away. She busied herself with the dishes so Rory wouldn't see her bright cheeks.

While Anna cleared and washed the breakfast things, Rory slouched in the easy chair, leafing through one of his books about fighters, awaiting her instructions. She glanced out the window and took pity on him; it was too sunny a day for a boy to be cooped up, she thought, especially when he'd only just arrived from Ireland. In a day or two he'd be tied to a school desk.

"I'll not be needing you for chores today," she said. "Run along now and call the day your own."

Rory's face brightened. "You mean it?" He bolted from his chair and ran for his jacket and cap.

"Mind you, be home for dinner," Anna called after him. "And I'll be making ginger biscuits this morning, so come by later for a taste."

He flew out the door, tossing off an unintelligible response. As his footsteps pounded down the stairs, Anna went into the front room and looked out the window. Rory appeared on the corner outside the saloon, his alert posture reminding her of a hunting dog catching the scent of its prey. Then he broke into a full run and disappeared in the direction of Broadway. That boy was too curious by half, Anna thought. Sure enough, it would get him in trouble.

She brushed her hair, fastened on her flat straw hat, picked up her shawl, bag, and the money Stephen had left, and set off down the stairs. It would be only neighborly, she decided, to invite Mrs. Cavanagh and Peggy for a cup of tea. And while she was out, she might as well find herself a pastry board and a baking iron for the ginger biscuits and look for some cabbage and beef for dinner. She ran through the inventory of kitchenware. There was a pot for boiling and a teakettle, but no saucepan—she'd need at least two—and no rollers or storage jars, not even a bread bin. And she'd not found a coffee mill or a flat iron. Stephen was short of everything. And the furnishings! Why, the man had no place to lay his head, and the kitchen would need a worktable, and there was nothing but a sagging sofa to sit on in the parlor.

The thought of making a home from scratch and being in charge of it quickened Anna's step. In Dublin she'd done just about every kind of work, whether it was in the scullery or the dining room or the mistress's chamber. At the Wyndhams and at the hotel, she'd hauled and scrubbed and polished enough for a lifetime—but all at someone else's beck and call, and never with inside water. In Stephen Flynn's home, she would be both mistress and maid. She'd answer to one but herself, and she'd have all the conveniences.

Anna stepped into the cool May sunshine and took a deep, spine-straightening breath. In time she would get back to her lace. She would make the rounds of the shops and show samples of her designs, then set to work creating opera bags and tea cloths and whatever else the ladies of New York might fancy.

A man with a scissor grinder pushed by, ringing his bell. Down the street, carpets flapped outside the carpet store, and delicious smells from a bakery filled the air. Anna thought of her first impression of the neighborhood yesterday, how disappointed she'd been. This morning it looked ever so fine, bustling and clean. And temporary, Anna reminded herself. It was only temporary, living with the Flynns, and she mustn't grow too fond of it.

She stepped briskly across the street and went from store to store, collecting items she needed for the kitchen. Every merchant seemed to know her. They addressed her as Mrs. Flynn and welcomed her to the neighborhood. They spoke of Stephen with extravagant kindness and insisted on delivering her order so she wouldn't have to carry a thing.

Anna was embarrassed by the attention. Never in her life had she been treated with such respect. When she dug in her bag to pay for her purchases, she was assured that Mr. Flynn's credit was sterling, that a bill would be sent around at the end of the month.

By the time she walked into Mrs. Cavanagh's grocery, Anna had decided that the Bowery must be the friendliest place on earth.

The grocery store was dim and cluttered with barrels and casks. It had a smoky smell of bacon and cheese, sweetened with the scent of currants.

"Why, Mrs. Flynn! A good morning to you!" Mrs. Cavanagh hurried out from the back room. She was short and stout with wispy dark hair shot with gray. A dusting of flour whitened the sleeves of her black dress, but her apron was immaculate.

"La, don't you look pretty in that hat!" she exclaimed, her softly creased face beaming. "Peggy! Come along out and see Mrs. Flynn!"

It took a moment for Peggy to appear. She looked to be about eighteen, a buxom, well-proportioned girl with light brown hair and merry eyes. She had her brother Emmet's good looks, but she shared none of his reserve.

"Oooh, what a lovely hat," she said, gazing at Anna with admiration. "It came from Dublin, then?"

Anna nodded, wishing to heaven she'd never worn the wretched thing. The Cavanaghs probably thought she was putting on airs, wearing a hat to cross the street. "I'm pleased to meet you, Peggy," Anna said, feeling shy. "Mr. Flynn speaks most kindly of you."

"Does he, now?" Peggy crossed her arms beneath her full bosom and turned a flustered shade of pink.

She fancies him a little, Anna thought. Just as she'd expected. But to her relief, Peggy didn't seem to harbor any ill will. "I'd be pleased if you'd both come up later for a cup of tea," Anna said, trying not to sound like too grand a lady. "I'll be making ginger biscuits and getting the kitchen in order."

"Oh, I'd like that," said Peggy.

Mrs. Cavanagh seemed to approve. "I'll be minding the store, but Peg'll come along. Now, what can we get for you today, Mrs. Flynn?" She eyed Anna's basket. "That scamp of a lad's been in here twice, but surely you'll need something for dinner."

Anna gladly turned the subject to groceries. By the time she left the store, she'd filled her basket with enough ingredients for a hearty stew, and she'd learned which days to expect the iceman, the ragman, and the soap-fat man.

When she reached the flat, her order from the dry goods store had arrived and she set about her tasks—unpacking and organizing, stirring up the biscuits, washing cabbage and carrots, cutting the meat. She stopped every few moments to add to her list of items to buy—a salt box, a ladle, a pan for frying bacon.

While the ginger biscuits were baking and the stew boiling, Anna went into Rory's room and retrieved his trousers from his trunk. She measured the length and looked at the hems, all neatly stitched by his gran, no doubt. Tonight she'd stand him on a chair and let them down.

As she left Rory's room, she caught a glimpse of herself in the mirror over the dresser. Gracious, she was still wearing her flowered hat! Anna snatched it off and hurried into the front bedroom. She opened the wardrobe and stuck the thing far back on the darkest shelf. She would not have people thinking her proud. Already they had her higher than she deserved, just because she was married to Stephen Flynn, the prince of the neighborhood. Why, he was famous throughout all of New York, and if Rory was to be believed, throughout all of America. It made her uncomfortable to think people admired her just for being with him. If they knew the truth of where she'd come from and what she'd done, they'd think differently, that was sure.

Anna jumped at the sound of knocking at the door. "Mrs. Flynn! Oh, Mrs. Flynn! You'd best be coming down here."

She hurried to the door. Peggy stood there, her eyes bright with excitement. "It's Mr. Lawler. He's come with the delivery wagon."

Anna looked at her, bewildered. "Who's Mr. Lawler?"

But Peggy was halfway down the stairs, calling for Anna to follow. Anna ran to the range and, using her apron to protect her hands, snatched the ginger biscuits out of the oven. Without removing her apron, she flew down the stairs.

Three men stood by a cart loaded with something made of brass. It gleamed beneath the torn wrapping. A small crowd had gathered to stare.

"What is it?" Anna asked, holding her apron down in the breeze.

A thin grizzled man stepped forward and lifted his cloth cap. "Why, 'tis a bed, missus. A bed from Rogers down on Water Street."

"A bed?"

"Your husband asked for a big brass bed." The man jerked his thumb at the cart. "This here's the biggest, brassiest one they got."

"Oooh," cried Peggy, almost jumping. "Oh, Mrs. Flynn, aren't you in luck! A brass bed from Rogers."

Anna twisted her hands in her apron, trying to ignore the grinning faces all around her. "Well, then, you'd best be taking it up, hadn't you?"

"Aye, missus," Mr. Lawler said, motioning to the men to help. "You show the way."

The men brought the bed up in parts, along with the mattress. Peggy accompanied them, chattering with the grizzled Mr. Lawler the entire time. It was Peggy who directed the men to the front room and suggested they set the bed up facing the window. "See how it catches the light, Mrs. Flynn," she said. "Why, won't it look beautiful, shining in the sun!"

"You need a sizable bed to hold Stephen Flynn," Mr. Lawler commented as the men screwed the parts together. Anna was thankful he didn't mention the bed holding her as well, but from the looks on the men's faces, she knew what they were thinking.

"Thank you, Mr. Lawler," Anna said when they were finished. She was already rehearsing what she would say to Stephen. Oh, she would give him a piece of her mind! Ordering a big shiny bed with scrolls and knobs fit for a king, and having it delivered to her in broad daylight with all of the neighbors watching and thinking their thoughts!

"I'll be seeing you again real soon, missus," Mr. Lawler said, touching his cap. There was a mischievous gleam in his eye.

Anna smiled politely, determined to maintain her composure.

When the men had gone, Anna leaned against the door and glared at Peggy. "Wait till I get my hands on that Stephen Flynn. A bed like that, and everybody grinning."

Peggy made a sympathetic sound. "Men think anything to do with a bed's a fine joke," she said. She cast a longing look toward the front room. "Even so, it's a lovely bed, Mrs. Flynn."

Anna sighed. "It is at that. Now, come and have a cup of tea. And please, my name is Anna."

Chapter 17

Anna had no sooner started the kettle and put the next batch of ginger biscuits to bake when there was a pounding of feet on the stairs. Rory burst through the door.

"Anna! Anna! Look who's here!"

They all pushed into the kitchen together, Rory and two skinny, grinning, dirty-faced Currans.

Anna nearly dropped the teapot. "Lord save us. The Curran twins."

"I found them on Broadway!" Rory shouted, jumping for joy. "They were coming for me and I was going for them! We met right there in the street."

"But how did they know where you lived?"

"I gave them one of Da's cards! I told them where to come!"

The Currans' feet were bare and black with dirt, and their shaggy flaxen hair stuck out in all directions. They wore the same tattered jackets they'd probably slept in for three weeks in steerage.

"La, what dirty boys," Peggy said, wrinkling her nose.

Anna decided to make the best of things. "Well, then, a good day to you, Eddie. Michael."

Two pairs of sharp blue eyes darted about, no doubt looking for something to steal. "It's your place, then?" one of the boys said.

213

"This is Rory's place" Anna answered. "Rory's and his da. Now, where are your manners to say good day to Peggy and me?"

The Currans sniffed the air, smelling the stew. They eyed the plate of ginger biscuits. Quick, grimy hands reached out, and before Anna could make a move, the plate was snatched clean. Ginger biscuits were shoved into mouths and pockets, and crumbs showered the floor.

"Hey!" yelled Rory. He jumped on one of the Currans, and the two of them tumbled to the floor in a blur of flailing arms and legs.

"Rory!" Anna waded into the tussle, reaching for the nearest limb. She grabbed at a sleeve, then a shirttail, but the boys rolled out of her grasp.

"Take them by the hair!" Peggy shouted.

Anna found a yellow cowlick and pulled. The Curran boy came up howling. Peggy dragged Rory, red-faced and kicking, to the easy chair and pushed him down.

"He took all the ginger biscuits! I'll knock his head for it."

"Not a word, young man," Anna scolded, pointing a finger at Rory. "And you!" She gave the Curran boy a shake. "Which are you, Mike or Eddie?"

The boy wiped his nose on his sleeve and licked a row of crumbs from his upper lip.

"It's Mike," Rory cried.

"Don't you know your manners, Michael Curran?" Anna demanded.

Mike shook his head. Crumbs fell from his hair.

"He knows nothing," Rory said, kicking the floor with his bootheel.

"Rory, you watch your tongue and stop scraping the floor or you'll be the one polishing it. Now, young Mr. Curran, you sit down there." Anna pushed Mike toward a chair. "It's time you learned some manners, both of you. I declare, I've never seen such wild boys."

She looked around for Eddie, but he was nowhere to be seen. The door stood ajar.

Suddenly, Mike lunged out of his chair. Peggy shouted and grabbed for him, but too late. Flashing a rude sign that made

Anna gasp, Mike dodged around her and fled the room, trailing crumbs.

"Oh, the devil!" Anna exclaimed, throwing up her hands. "Two sewer rats if I ever saw them." She looked at Rory's pout, then her eyes met Peggy's, dancing with merriment, and the idea of the dirty Currans and the flying crumbs made her want to laugh.

Peggy giggled first, then Anna, and the more Anna laughed, the more Peggy laughed, until they were both holding their sides and gasping for breath.

"Oh, Peggy," Anna said, pressing her palms to her waist. She hadn't laughed so hard in years. "Those boys are enough to make a priest swear."

Peggy wiped her eyes. "They should be whipped, those boys."

"Shouldn't they just?"

"They're hungry," Rory said. "They wanted some dinner."

Anna looked at him, at his rosy cheeks, his clean shirt, his polished boots. She thought of the dirty Currans, poor as mice, and sobered quickly. "They were so hungry?"

Rory nodded glumly. "I told them you'd be having a good dinner and ginger biscuits. Now they spoiled it, and you'll never let them come again."

Anna exchanged a look with Peggy. "Well, who was it that started the fight, then?"

Rory ignored the question. "They only had a bit of oatmeal last night."

"Poor little scraps," said Peggy.

Anna went to the stewpot and poked at the meat. She thought of her own days of hunger, of her little brothers crying from it, and of the Currans without a penny to bless themselves with. "You bring them back, Rory, and I'll feed them a proper dinner. But if they eat here, they'll have to learn their manners."

Peggy found a broom behind the door of the larder and brushed the crumbs into a pile. Thoughts of the Currans' plight dimmed the gay atmosphere, but each time Anna met Peggy's merry eyes, she had to stifle a smile.

A jaunty rap sounded at the door. Anna looked up. "Now who's coming?" She put aside her spoon and wiped her hands on her apron.

She opened the door, and there at the top of the stairs stood Davy Ryan, wearing his old cloth cap and a big grin. "Why, as I live and breathe," said Anna.

Davy tugged off his cap, baring his thick red hair. "A lovely morning to you, Anna. They said below Stephen might be here."

"He's not here now, but you're welcome, Davy. Come in."

"Davy!" Rory was on his feet, legs spread, fists up.

Davy raised his own fists. "Watch out, bucko." He faked a quick right and left at Rory's belly. Rory covered himself and backed away, giggling.

"A cup of tea, Davy?" Anna asked. "And some ginger biscuits?" She smiled at Peggy. But Peggy was staring at Davy, taking in his heavy frieze coat, cut in the old-fashioned way, and his corduroy trousers that bagged around his boots and made him look like a bumpkin.

"Peggy," Anna said. "This here is Davy Ryan. Davy, Peggy Cavanagh."

Davy grinned at Peggy and swept his cap into a low bow. "Peggy," he said. "Lovely Peggy." He raised his eyes to the ceiling and began to whistle. Peggy's face grew stern. It was obvious that a Paddylander straight off the boat was not to her fancy.

"Sit down, then," Anna said, pushing at Davy's back. But instead of sitting, he dropped to his knees and held the pan as Peggy swept in the crumbs. When he stood up again, his eyes moved from her face to her shapely figure.

Peggy turned red. "Who are you to look at me so?" she snapped.

"I'm only admiring you, darlin'. I'm a Connaught man. We from the west country are well known for our way with the girls."

"You're a greenhorn," Peggy retorted and snatched the pan from his hands. "You'd best be learning the ways of New York." She crossed the kitchen to empty the pan into the cinder box, twitching her ample hips as she walked. Davy all but licked his lips, watching her.

"Davy!" Anna hissed. "Mind your manners." She glanced at Rory, relieved to see him engrossed in a fighter book.

Footsteps sounded on the stairs. "Mrs. Flynn! Mrs. Flynn!"

Dennis Lawler stood at the door, cap in hand, his wrinkles lost in a gray stubble of whiskers. "Delivery again, missus."

"Another? What now?"

Dennis looked into the kitchen and saw Davy. "We could use that young fellow. You stay here, missus, and point where you want things put."

It was more furniture, and it kept coming. Side tables with tapered legs, shield-backed chairs, a chest of light wood inlaid with a darker wood, a wardrobe, a huge kitchen dresser. For the sitting room there was a sofa upholstered in lemon yellow with a walnut frame, and a flap table for the kitchen. There was a lovely armless mahogany chair, its back and seat covered with velvet the color of ripe cherries. Last came a mirror with a gilt frame crowned by an eagle.

Anna hadn't seen such beautiful furniture since she worked at Dr. Wyndham's house in Dublin.

Rory scurried among the men, getting in the way. Peggy stood by, clasping her hands, exclaiming over each piece. "La, aren't you the lucky one," she said to Anna, "to have such a generous husband as Mr. Flynn."

Anna smoothed her apron, feeling embarrassed. "It's too much."

When everything was in its place and Mr. Lawler had made his final inspection, Anna said, "If I had enough cups, I'd offer you men a drink of tea."

"No need, missus, we'll be taking our lunch downstairs in the saloon."

"Wait, Mr. Lawler." Anna wrapped the second batch of ginger biscuits in a clean piece of butcher paper, tied the bundle, and bit off the end of the string. "They're fresh from the oven. Take them along for the men."

Mr. Lawler lifted his cap. "Why, that's kind of you, missus."

Anna saw the men down the back stairs, then walked through the flat from room to room. The place had been transformed. It looked settled, like a home. It needed only a few final touches—a cloth on the table, some dishes to fill the kitchen dresser, curtains and pictures. A coverlet on the brass bed.

Peggy stood in the bedroom doorway, her face soft with smiles. "All blessings on you and your husband in this room, Anna Flynn."

Davy poked his head in the door, stared at the bed, and whistled. "That's big enough for whatever."

Peggy jabbed him in the ribs with her elbow. "I've had about enough of you for one day. I'll be getting on home to my own dinner."

"I'll see you home, then," said Davy.

Peggy cocked her head and looked at him, her glare somewhat softened. "It's only across the street."

"All the better."

Peggy cast an exasperated look at Anna. "Green," she said. "Green as the country he came from."

Anna laughed. "If you don't want him, leave him here and I'll feed him." She slipped her arm around Peggy's waist. She knew she'd found a friend. "Come up often, Peg."

"I'll see you tonight at the wedding party for you and Mr. Flynn."

Anna had forgotten. She looked at Peggy's smiling face and felt a stab of guilt. With all good intentions, Stephen's neighbors were planning a wedding party for two people who were not truly married.

"I'll be there," Davy said, brightening. "I'll dance a jig with you both."

Peggy gave him a look. "Oh, you, inviting yourself!" But she was smiling when she left.

Anna walked around the spacious front room, seeing how the light struck the brass bed, how the wood of the dresser shone. She sat on the armless chair of cherry-colored velvet. Here she would do her lacework, in the sun. Oh, it was lovely.

"Am I so green?"

She looked at Davy's glum face and held back a smile. "Not so green as some."

Davy ran a hand through his flaming hair. "Peggy's a fine ball of a girl. Just like I dreamed American girls to be."

Anna got up and smoothed the nap on the velvet chair. "Go along and wash up, and I'll give you some stew."

Davy seemed to be struggling for words. "I just took one look at her and knew she was for me. I could see our whole life together. Even the babies."

"Oh, Davy," Anna said. "Don't be thinking about babies and Peggy in the same thought, or you'll have Emmet Cavanagh down on you. That brother of hers is a glum fellow if I ever saw one."

She steered Davy to the scullery to wash and then sat him down at the table. After the blessing, Rory slurped his stew and happily tore into slabs of buttered store bread, but Davy didn't seem to have an appetite.

"It costs plenty to keep a wife," he said. "I haven't a penny in the world."

"Aren't you getting ahead of yourself," Anna said. "Peggy's surely got a sweetheart, an American boy, so don't get your heart set on her." She laid a place for Stephen, wondering where he was. "Eat your dinner, Davy, or you'll waste away with worry."

Anna was pouring Rory's buttermilk when she heard footsteps and voices on the back stairs. The kitchen door opened, and Stephen stepped in. He carried a basket of flowers, pale yellow early roses and white and yellow tulips with little violets.

Stephen looked at Davy, sitting before his bowl of stew. "So, Davy," he said. "You've wasted no time finding a good meal."

Davy got eagerly to his feet. "Hello, Stephen."

Stephen came to Anna and put the basket of flowers in her arms. "To welcome the summer, darling. And to bless our home."

Anna took the basket, too surprised to speak. In Ireland it was a custom to decorate the doorstep and ledges with May boughs. She wanted to thank Stephen, but he was talking with Davy. Emmet Cavanagh stood beside him, looking grim and unhappy.

Anna looked at the third young man and her eyes widened. He had brown skin and curly hair that stuck out from his head like a wreath. Rory was also staring, his jaw hanging down a mile. Anna moved toward him to give him a nudge, to remind him of his manners.

"This is Mose," Stephen said. "He looks after the sparring room when I'm not around." He gestured to Anna and the wide-eyed Rory. "My wife and my boy, Rory."

Mose was all muscles and broad bones, nearly as big as Stephen. He wore a red flannel shirt and a serious expression.

He crossed his heavy arms over his chest and nodded to Anna. "Ma'am."

Anna found her voice. "You're welcome here, Mose," she said.

"Are you a fighter?" Rory asked, still gaping.

Mose nodded. "That's how I'm aiming." His voice was deep but soft.

Anna saw Rory swallow hard, at a loss for further words.

"Please, sit down," Anna said to the men, wondering how she would feed them with only half a pot of stew and not enough bowls or spoons.

"No need, Nan," said Stephen. "Mrs. Cavanagh puts out a lunch in the saloon."

"Peggy was here," Rory said.

Stephen glanced at Anna. "Was she, then?"

"The Curran boys turned up, too," she said. "As dirty and hungry a lot as I've ever seen."

Rory squirmed out of Anna's grasp. "They took all the ginger biscuits. Then Anna chased them off."

Stephen started to laugh, then grimaced and touched his ribs.

"What's wrong?" Davy asked.

"Maguire was in last night," Emmet said scornfully. "The bastard wore iron knuckles. Stephen got him back, though, clean on the jaw—"

"Emmet," Stephen said. "Enough."

"Billy Maguire?" Rory cried, his eyes popping. "He came here?"

"Maguire wants a match?" Davy asked.

Stephen nodded. "So he says. But he won't be getting one from me."

Rory swung a fist into the air, the force of it lifting him off his feet. "You'll beat him, Da!" he cried. "One punch. Pow!"

Anna pushed Rory down in his chair. "You tell Mr. Maguire you'll have no more of his fights, Stephen. You're too old for it, and you've got a son to think about."

Stephen grinned. "Just so, darling. I'll be telling our Billy my wife says no more fights. That should end it."

"You can beat him," Rory said, wriggling with excitement.

"This time he'd probably beat me, sport." Stephen paused and gave Anna a look. "Seeing how old I am."

"You're not old," Emmet said fiercely. "You're as strong as you were against McCleester and Maddox—"

"Emmet," Stephen cautioned.

Emmet glared at Anna. "He can beat Maguire. He can beat any man living."

"He can fight any man living, just to please you, I suppose," Anna said, returning Emmet's hard look with one of her own. "At any price to himself."

"Nan," Stephen said sharply, "leave it alone, now. You too, Emmet."

Davy spoke up. "Don't be getting on the wrong side of our Anna or she'll take a knife to you, like she did to that sailor."

Anna whirled. "Don't you be bringing that up, Davy Ryan—"

"Stuck him right in the heart, she did, killed him dead. One less Englishman for the world to worry about."

"Davy, it's you I'll kill if you don't shut your mouth."

Emmet looked uncertainly from one to the other.

"She did it," Rory piped up. "Killed him dead."

Anna turned to Stephen for help, but he was watching Emmet, who stared at her in disbelief.

"It's all behind us now, thanks be to God," she said, rolling her hands in her apron.

"Well, doesn't that beat the devil?" Emmet said, his voice soft with awe. "Murdered an Englishman. Is it the truth, then?"

"A nice article I married," Stephen said.

"How did it happen?" Emmet asked.

"That's enough of that," Anna said sternly. It was shameful the way they were all looking at her. "It's not a thing to be proud of. And I'll thank all of you not to be spreading it around."

Stephen grinned. "We'll try to keep it quiet." He took Anna's arm. "Now, show us the new furniture. To hear Dennis Lawler tell it, he and his gang broke their backs carrying it."

Chapter 18

❧

The crush of guests spilled from Mrs. Cavanagh's kitchen into the store and out the back door into the yard. Men with heavy clothes and worn, outdoor faces drank whiskey and argued politics while plain-faced mothers held howling babies and scolded the bigger children who ran about like dogs at a fair. Young men wearing gaudy silk neckcloths and black frock coats jostled one another around the kitchen table, which was laden with bottles and jugs, and eyed the girls in their best bright dresses and shawls.

Through all the commotion a fiddler scraped away, mostly unnoticed, while Davy Ryan, flushed with porter and wearing his cap sideways, bellowed love ballads in a clear tenor voice.

Anna was relieved at the confusion. She'd been afraid it would be like a country wedding party with a priest and a sit-down supper and embarrassing games. There had been a few toasts and bawdy jokes, and Mrs. Cavanagh had broken a small cake in half above Anna's head, a mother's duty to ensure her daughter's luck and prosperity. But after Stephen had kissed her, to the raucous delight of all, the guests seemed more interested in enjoying themselves with drink and talk than with teasing the bride and groom.

The men all wanted to talk to Stephen. They crowded around him, asking about Ireland, about Billy Maguire, telling him their troubles with an employer or a landlord or the Manhattan Gas Light Company. Stephen listened to their complaints, making promises to some, admonishing others. He called each one by name, tossed off harmless insults, and cuffed the younger ones. He seemed to know something about each man's family, his troubles, his vices. Anna saw how much the men depended on Stephen, and it made her proud.

"Champ!"

A stocky sandy-haired man pushed through the crowd toward Stephen.

"Bless me, Gil," said Stephen. "It's near nine o'clock and you're still standing."

"Wanted to meet the lady who put an end to Stephen Flynn's glorious boxing career." The man grinned at Anna, his broad rosy face glistening with sweat.

"Frank Gillespie," Stephen said to Anna. "He's not good for much, but he writes a grand news story. Murders, robberies, forgeries, frauds—Gil's an expert on all of it."

"Charmed, Mrs. Flynn. Charmed, I'm sure."

A faint Scottish accent emanated from Frank Gillespie, along with the thick smell of whiskey. "By God, champ, she's a beauty," he said, shoving his bottle under his arm. "Can't blame you for wanting her." He grasped Anna's hand in his great damp paw and gave her tight blue jacket a furtive glance.

Anna blushed. The other men had acknowledged her with only a polite nod. Mr. Gillespie's pushy friendliness and his frank stare made her self-conscious. "You're a newsman?"

"That's what they tell me."

"The *National Gazette*," Stephen said. "Gil's covered my fights from New Orleans to San Francisco to Bangor, Maine. Now that I'm quitting, he'll be out of a job. He'll have to find honest work."

Anna gave Stephen a nudge. "Go on with you. There's more in this world to write about than you."

Gillespie laughed. "You're right, angel. When the sportsmen quit on me, there's always the criminals and politicians." To Stephen he said, "Hammer's come. Dennis Lawler's got him out front. You'd best show him your bride." Gil hoisted his bottle at Anna. "I'll be on my way, angel, I've got a story to write."

Stephen put his hands on Anna's waist and headed her through the crowd toward the store. She glanced back at Gillespie, who had paused at the back door to take a pull at his bottle. "It's a shame, Stephen, his drinking like that. Why, his eyes are all red and he stinks of whiskey."

Stephen gave her waist a squeeze. "Don't worry about Gil, darling. He holds it all right."

A blunt finger appeared from nowhere and poked Stephen on the shoulder. "Boss, Mrs. Cavanagh says Hammer's waiting on you." Dennis Lawler, his toothless jaw working on a chew of tobacco, waved toward the hallway leading into the store. "And she says it's time you stopped dragging the missus about and let her sit down for a spell."

Stephen pushed Anna ahead of him into the shop. Women stood talking in groups. Small children perched on the counter, swinging their boots, while others played among the barrels and produce crates.

Mrs. Cavanagh hurried out from behind the counter, her gray-streaked hair wound tight against the back of her head, her well-lined face bursting with a smile. "La, Mr. Flynn, the poor girl's been on her feet all night listening to the prattle of men."

"I want her to meet the lads, Mrs. Cavanagh."

Mrs. Cavanagh scoffed, waving her hands in the air. "You don't want to let her out of your sight, that's what, keeping her all to yourself." She beamed at Anna. "I hope you didn't listen to those useless men, Mrs. Flynn. They tell lies fast as a pig would gallop."

"Oh, the men hardly peeped to me," Anna said. "It's Stephen they fancy."

"Isn't that the truth? Get a gang of Irishmen together and they don't care a jack rat about women, especially if there's a fighter or a politician about. Now, you go sit with Mr. Moran. I've a nice plate of boiled chicken and bacon and a glass of porter for you. And after, there's strawberries from the market and a jug of cream."

"I'm obliged," Anna said. She smiled at the other women, who jiggled their babies and stared at her as if she were the queen of Spain.

Stephen led her toward the rear corner of the shop where an old man sat at a small round table. He was broad-shouldered, and his hair was thick and dark. When she got closer, Anna realized he wasn't old; he was just stooped and worn. The man raised his head and stared at her until Stephen said, "Hammer, it's my wife, Anna."

The man blinked, and a smile of comprehension crawled across his flat blank face. "Ah, laddie," he said, his speech slow and slurred. "She's a fine girl, then, isn't she?"

Anna watched in dismay as Hammer moved his big broken hands toward his glass. It took several attempts before he could grasp the glass and raise it in salute. "There's no finer man in the world than your laddie, God bless him. He's the best I've seen in the ring." He looked at Stephen as if an idea had just struck. "By God, Stephen, you should fight Sullivan. I fought him in 'forty-three."

Stephen pulled out a chair, and Anna sat down. "Yankee Sullivan's long dead, Hammer."

"Dead!" Hammer's smile faded. "I'd take my oath I just saw him."

Stephen grinned. "Then you saw him in your dreams."

Mrs. Cavanagh set a steaming plate before Anna. "Don't pay Mr. Moran no mind," she said in a low voice. "He's as sweet as a child. Just smile and he'll love you for it."

Anna forced herself to eat. She'd been hungry up to a moment ago—when she saw Hammer Moran's frailty and heard his slurred speech. She looked at Stephen, lounging in his chair, and imagined his fine, strong body bent and crippled, his keen mind dulled. The idea of it filled her with fear. She thought of Billy Maguire's iron knuckles, his insistence that Stephen fight him again. She thought of Stephen's hip that gave him trouble when the weather was damp, and she thought of the blows he'd taken on his head and face. She knew that Stephen must never fight again, no matter what Billy Maguire and Emmet Cavanagh and this poor creature across the table might want for him.

Anna took a gulp of porter, then another. The ale warmed her insides and eased her mind. It also sharpened her appetite. As Stephen spoke patiently to Hammer, Anna picked her chicken bones clean. Then Mrs. Cavanagh was at her side again with a big bowl of berries.

"Oh, but I'm stuffed!" Anna protested.

"Hush, now," said Mrs. Cavanagh. "You've hardly eaten a thing. And when you finish, you come back in the kitchen for the dancing."

When Mrs. Cavanagh departed, Anna touched Stephen's arm. "Eat the berries. I can't fit in another bite."

Stephen smiled at her, a smile of such pride and affection that Anna felt uneasy. "Don't look at me so," she said, embarrassed. It was desire she saw in his face, desire as pure as light.

He touched her knee beneath the table, and then his hand found hers and he twined their fingers together. Anna glanced at Hammer staring off into space. "You should be whipped for what you're thinking, Stephen Flynn."

"If you know what I'm thinking, darling, then you're thinking it, too."

Anna imagined lying with Stephen in the new brass bed with its scrollwork and shine. She disentangled their hands and stood up, feeling warm and breathless. "I'll be going. They're having games in the kitchen."

Stephen didn't take his eyes off her.

"Good by, Mr. Moran," Anna said loudly.

Hammer stared at her, puzzled. Then his face broke into a smile. "You're Stephen's girl."

"My wife," Stephen said. He caught Anna's hand again and brought it to his lips. She pulled away, worried that the other women might be watching. When she reached the kitchen door, she looked back and saw a gang of men racing for her empty chair, eager to sit beside Stephen.

In the kitchen a space had been cleared, and several couples were dancing to the fiddler's tune. They stepped in toward each other and out again, and as the music quickened, their feet matched the tempo. Davy, in his red knitted jersey and corduroy pants, looked like the yokel he was, but he danced with vigor. Anna smiled at the way he lifted his feet, nearly high enough to get his toes in his pockets. Peggy watched him, too, laughing. She wore two silver combs in her light brown hair and a blue and yellow dress that flattered her figure.

Mrs. Cavanagh nudged Anna. "Look at that red-haired one, the great thick fool."

"It's Davy Ryan," Anna said, wishing he wasn't quite so much the Paddylander.

As he whirled around, Davy caught sight of Anna and pulled her onto the dance floor.

"It's her husband she should be dancing with!" Mrs. Cavanagh cried, but Davy paid her no mind. The fiddler struck up a reel, and Anna passed from man to man, laughing as the pace became faster. Peggy was there too, and Davy shouted and kicked his feet high. Anna danced until she couldn't breathe for the exertion and the laughing. When she stopped to catch her breath, another girl took her place.

Anna was making her way out front to the shop to look for Stephen when a man called out, "Peggy's the next to be married. Tell us who he's to be, Peg."

"Peggy's my gal, so don't be asking," cried another masculine voice.

"I'm not your gal, Peter Crowley. I don't belong to any man."

The fiddle went silent. Anna turned to see Peggy, hands on her hips, glaring at a young man with a brawny neck and a flashy satin vest. His hair, like the others', was cropped short in back, rolled into long curls in front, and greased to a bottle shine.

"Oho!" Peter Crowley said, throwing back his shoulders. "You'll do as I say, Peg, if you know what's best for you."

Anna didn't join in the laughter that followed. Something about Peter Crowley's arrogant tone and sneering smile made her uneasy. She knew the banter was harmless, but she also knew how a rough man could turn dangerous when a girl didn't let him have his way.

"Give Peggy an apple and we'll see who she'll be marrying." It was Davy talking. He was looking at Peggy with the same stare he'd had that afternoon.

"Oh, Davy," Anna whispered to herself, "don't be foolish, now."

Someone tossed an apple to Davy. He pulled a folding knife from his pocket and handed it to Peggy.

She gave him a mocking look. "Aren't you still back in the old country," she said, but Anna saw her smile.

According to Irish tradition, if a girl peeled an apple in one long strip and the peel fell on the floor, it would form the initial of her future husband. There was silence as Peggy worked the knife around the apple. A cheer went up when the long skin fell to the floor.

Davy stood over it, staring down. "It's a *D* for sure," he shouted. "Sleep with a garter under your pillow, Peggy, and you'll have me in your dreams." He took Peggy by the waist and tried to kiss her, to the uproarious laughter of his audience.

Peggy struggled away from him, her face scarlet. "That's no *D*," she said. "You're a Connaught man. Everyone knows Connaught men don't know their letters."

Her remark brought on more laughter. Peter Crowley gave Davy a shove that was not good-natured. "You're fresh off the boat, greeny, still stinking of Irish manure. Peg'd just as soon look at a crow as the likes of you."

From the expression on Peggy's face, it seemed she was regretting her harsh words. She turned her fury on Peter Crowley. "You're nothing but bottled wind!" she cried. "I'd rather die in a ditch than marry the likes of you."

Peter looked surprised, but only for an instant. He gave a hitch to his trousers and swaggered over to her. "I've got rights to you, Peggy Cavanagh," he sneered, "and don't you forget it."

"She won't be wanting you, I can tell you that," Davy said, thrusting out his chest and his chin. The other men laughed and heckled, urging Peter and Davy on.

"God's mercy, if only Mr. Flynn was here," Mrs. Cavanagh muttered. She pushed past Anna and grabbed Peggy by the arm, giving her a smart jerk. "That'll just do, now, Mary Margaret Cavanagh." To Peter and Davy she said, "If you two want to fight, go across the street to Mr. Flynn's saloon and do it where he can keep an eye on you. I'll not have it in my place."

Mrs. Cavanagh led the sullen Peggy through the laughing crowd toward the shop. "By all the saints," she muttered, "two Irishmen are never at peace unless they're fighting each other."

Anna watched Davy standing alone at the table, downing another glass of porter while Peter Crowley and his gang glared at him. Oh, Davy, she thought.

"Mrs. Flynn, you'd best leave the lads to themselves and come along."

"Yes, Mrs. Cavanagh, here I am."

Anna followed Peggy and her mother out of the kitchen and down the short hallway that led to the store. She looked around for Stephen, thinking he'd know what to do with Davy.

"Oh, wasn't that a red-haired fool?" a woman said, laughing. All the women were smiling and teasing Peggy. "Is he your new sweetheart, Peg?"

Anna jumped to Davy's defense. "It's Davy Ryan, and he's no fool. He's a brave lad, I'll tell you that. Peggy couldn't find a better sweetheart."

Mrs. Cavanagh clucked her tongue. "Our Peggy can do better than a green boy off the boat. Peter Crowley, now, he's got a fine position, apprentice to Sontag, the German butcher over on Mulberry Street."

Peggy scowled. "Peter Crowley stinks of blood. What's more, just because he takes me about, he thinks he owns me."

"He'll earn a good living one day," her mother said, adjusting the combs in her daughter's hair.

"He's a jackeen," Peggy said scornfully. "All of them are. They think they're as dandy as uptown gents. They take a girl out and afterward try to get what they think is their due."

Mrs. Cavanagh's mouth fell into a disapproving line. "You behave like a wanton, you're asking to get your due." She turned to Anna. "Dance halls and theaters and outings to Long Island, that's all the young people think about, and then the girls wonder why the boys act like they're married."

"Davy's not like that," Anna said. "There's none more gallant than Davy Ryan. Why, on the ship coming over, the sailors had a mind to use me for sport, and it was Davy who tried to save me."

The other women stopped their chatting and stared at Anna. "Davy did that?" Peggy asked in wonderment.

Anna nodded. "The sailors beat him. Threw him into the hold for his trouble."

"Oh!" Peggy looked shocked. "He didn't save you, then?"

"I . . ." Anna began, realizing she'd opened a subject she'd just as soon have left closed. "I fought the man."

"*You* fought him?"

"He tried to use a knife on me. It . . . it ended up in his heart." Anna mumbled the last part, hoping it would pass unnoticed. A gasp rose from the women.

"You killed him?"

"Oh, he was a filthy devil," Anna hurried on. "He was after me from the start, said he'd won me in a wager with his mates."

"God's mercy," murmured a woman, blessing herself.

"I was sick one night. When I went on deck, the seaman grabbed me. He held a knife to my throat and meant to have his way. I fought him, and the knife . . . He fell on it." Anna glanced at Peggy, whose face had gone as white as a mushroom. "It was Davy who came to help me when I screamed. But the mate and the sailors thrashed him."

"Faith, you were brave altogether," Peggy said softly. "Killing that man."

From the looks on the women's faces, Anna saw that instead of making Davy a hero, her story had made a heroine of her. "Davy tried to save me," she said again.

"So he did, and he's a brave lad for it," Mrs. Cavanagh said. "But you, Mrs. Flynn—why, you were the brave one."

"What happened after?" Peggy asked, her eyes wide.

Anna squirmed with embarrassment. She wished she'd never begun the story. "The captain himself came, angry as a swarm of bees. He looked me over. Would have had me himself, had it not been for Mr. Flynn interfering."

The women pursed their lips and shook their heads.

"Mr. Flynn took me into his own cabin." Anna paused, wondering how to proceed. In a soft voice, she added, "He didn't force me, though I expected it."

There were murmurs that Mr. Flynn would never be so dishonorable as to force a girl. Why, anyone in the neighborhood could tell you that.

"But the other passengers!" Anna exclaimed, warming to the tale. "Oh, didn't they complain to the captain? To them, we were living in sin, the two of us in the cabin, even with his son. The captain listened to them and decided to send me back to the steerage hold, back to the other sailors."

Peggy gasped, her fingers over her mouth. "Send you back! What did Mr. Flynn do then?"

"He offered to marry me."

The women glanced at one another and back to Anna, their faces rapt.

"The captain himself did the ceremony."

"You're not married in the church, then?" Peggy asked.

Anna shook her head. She wished she could tell the whole truth. She hated having these good-souled women look at her with such admiration, thinking her so high and brave. "It was a marriage to save me, you see."

"To save you," Peggy said with a sigh. "How lovely."

"Isn't that like Mr. Flynn, always helping a body," said a woman jouncing a baby wrapped in a red shawl. "When my man was hurt, he saw we had food and coal, and he spoke to the landlord about the rent. He sees to things, Mr. Flynn does."

"Now that you're here, you'll go to the priest and have a real wedding," Peggy said.

Anna moistened her lips. "I . . . I don't know."

"Well, you're Mr. Flynn's wife and that's all there is," Mrs. Cavanagh said. She looked sternly at the other women, as if daring any one of them to disapprove.

"Not in the sight of God," Anna said, feeling ashamed.

"It'll come soon enough," Mrs. Cavanagh said. "He'll not be turning you out, I can tell you that. Why, he eats you up with his eyes, that man does, and from what I see of his son, God bless him, the little lad loves you like his own mam."

"But if we're not married by a priest, people will think—"

"People won't think anything of the sort," Mrs. Cavanagh said. "That's the way it is in the Bowery. If you're just out of prison, we forgive you. If you don't wear a bonnet in the street, we pay it no mind. If you've got a past worth forgetting, we'll forget it with you." She scanned the faces of the other women, who were nodding their agreement. "It's none of our affair that you're not married in the church."

Peggy took Anna's hand and gave it a squeeze. "Your troubles are behind you now, Anna, thanks be to God."

Stephen glanced into the kitchen and saw Anna dancing. He watched for a while, admiring her bright cheeks, her hair shining red and brown, her lovely figure. She seemed so happy and well occupied that when John O'Mahony arrived, he decided he could slip away.

"We'll go across the street, John," Stephen said. "To my office."

O'Mahony was a bearded, stern-faced, heavy-browed man, who wore his hair nearly to his shoulders. "Aye, Stephen, 'twould be best to speak privately, rather than risk being overheard by informers."

Informers, Stephen thought with an inward sigh. Whenever the Irish exiles disagreed over how to accomplish the liberation of the homeland, they accused one another of spying for the British. The leaders were so busy looking for informers among themselves, they'd most likely miss the genuine article, should he come along.

They crossed the street in the cool night air and entered the Emerald Flame Saloon. Most of the regulars were at Mrs. Cavanagh's, so the barroom was quiet. O'Mahony stopped at the bar to speak to Emmet, bringing a look of pride to the young man's face. Stephen watched with bemusement. O'Mahony was a decent man, but he was a scholar by nature, not a fighter. During the 'forty-eight rising, he'd had more liking for words than for weapons. So had all the other leaders, even Padraic McCarthy.

Stephen ambled into the sparring room and watched Mose bat an uptown gent around the ring. After a few moments, O'Mahony joined him.

"Young Emmet's a fine patriot, Stephen, with a thirst for justice."

"He's a dreamer."

Stephen led the way up the back stairs to the second floor where he kept his office and Mose had a room. He lit the gas lamp in the hall and another in his office.

The room was gloomy and cluttered. The walls, covered with yellowed fight posters, hadn't seen fresh paint in years, and the furniture was old and scratched, but the place suited Stephen. It was here that he kept his books and conducted his business. Within these walls, he entertained distillery agents and fight promoters with a few hours of talk and whiskey, listened to his neighbors' troubles, or just put his feet up and thought.

Stephen took the key from his desk and wound the battered cherry clock that had come with the building. "There's a bottle in the bottom drawer, John, if you've a thirst."

O'Mahony waved away the offer and seated himself. "Maguire had a benefit for the Committee. He staged a sparring exhibition at Sportsman's Hall. We collected nearly five hundred dollars."

Stephen tossed the clock key onto a stack of ledgers. "So even Maguire's turned into a patriot. I didn't know he was an Irishman at heart."

O'Mahony ignored Stephen's sarcasm. "He made a speech that moved all who listened. 'May we have the grace of God and die in Ireland,' he said, 'the land of our brave forebears.' "

Stephen sat down behind the desk and braced one foot on the edge. "Touching."

O'Mahony's beard quivered with disapproval. "Better to die with a purpose, Stephen, than to live with the British yoke on our necks."

"By the grace of God, I'll die right here in this land, preferably in the arms of my wife. Now, I've got a message from Paddy McCarthy, and I'd best be giving it to you."

O'Mahony sat forward, attentive.

"They've named you supreme organizer and director of the Revolutionary Brotherhood in America," Stephen said. "They want you to raise eighty pounds a month and train two thousand men. But you're not to take any action or make any plans for invasion. Dublin will be deciding what's to be done and when."

O'Mahony's deep-set eyes dampened at the troubling news. "There are brave lads right here, Stephen, trained and ready to go over. It will be hard to hold them back, and they won't like taking orders from Dublin."

"I know it, John," Stephen said patiently. "But those in Ireland think there are too many hotheads in New York with more hatred for England than love for Ireland."

O'Mahony shook out his handkerchief and dabbed at his eyes. "There's no shame in earning respect in this country by having a free and strong homeland."

Stephen wished he could ease his old leader's distress. "It'll come one day, John. Have faith in it."

"And what of the guns?"

"The guns will come from Birmingham."

"From England!" O'Mahony exclaimed. "By God, Stephen, we'll be operating right under their noses."

Stephen shrugged. "The arms merchants care nothing for politics. They're in business for money, nothing else."

"But the authorities—"

"Birmingham manufactures most of the world's guns. Crates of them are stacked along the canals and in the railway stations. With so many guns coming out of Birmingham, the authorities won't notice our little shipment."

O'Mahony stroked his beard. "What sorts of arms?"

"Breech-loading rifles, muzzle-loaders, revolvers. There'll be ammunition, too, and bayonets." Stephen shifted in his chair. He hated to think of the carnage if the rising ever came to pass. And he was uncomfortable revealing the details. But he had to trust O'Mahony; Padraic had instructed him to do so.

"There's plenty of patriots among the Irish in Birmingham," Stephen went on. "They'll meet with the courier and see to the rest of it. The shipment will be packed in American flour barrels and consigned to a Cork merchant by way of the Newport-Cork steamer. The stationmaster there will see them on to Kilkenny."

O'Mahony's heavy brows drew together. "The money's to come from us?"

"Where else does money come from besides America?" Stephen said with a wry smile. "All communication from this side goes through you by way of a courier. Anyone writing to Ireland on his own is to be looked upon as a traitor."

O'Mahony sat back in his chair and closed his eyes, no doubt imagining the glorious moment when masses of Irishmen would rise up with those Birmingham guns and drive their oppressors from Irish shores.

"For now the arms are for drilling, not for battle," Stephen cautioned. "Padraic insists there'll be no quick action. They won't have another failure like 'forty-eight."

O'Mahony opened his eyes; they blazed with a fanatical light. "We're the Fianna Eireann of our time, Stephen, the warrior bands of the old legends. We will vanquish the enemy and lead the people out of famine and disgrace."

Stephen drummed his fingers on the desk top. "We're a bunch of damned fools, that's what we are. The country is hopelessly weak."

O'Mahony looked sad. "I pity you, Stephen, for your lack of faith."

"There'll be no political squabbling and no loose talk. If the British get wind of what I've told you, men like Paddy McCarthy will rot in Kilmainham prison. Or swing at the end of a rope."

"Aye, lad, I know it well. No one will know but the leadership here in New York."

Stephen let out his breath slowly. "Paddy told me to choose the courier. God help me, I've chosen Emmet Cavanagh."

O'Mahony nodded solemnly. "A fine choice. And an honor for the lad."

Stephen swore softly, wondering if this "honor" would doom his young friend. "Emmet's never been away from his mother, and he's never set foot on Irish soil. Now he'll be in the thick of it, carrying messages back and forth, learning to practice treason."

O'Mahony rose from his chair, his beard trembling. "Emmet Cavanagh will work honorably to crush the power of the tyrant foe."

"He's a boy, for Christ's sake," Stephen snapped. He felt a sudden disgust for involving himself in this patriotic madness. "He's got shamrocks for brains."

"He's taken the oath. And he bears the name of Robert Emmet, the grandest patriot of them all." O'Mahony laid a hand on his breast and gazed into the distance. " 'When My Country takes her place among the nations of the earth, then, and not till then, let my epitaph be written.' "

"Aye, John." Stephen got to his feet, feeling immensely weary. "There's nothing like the noble speech of a dying Irishman to make the English tremble."

Chapter 19

Anna brought Rory home shortly after nine o'clock, early enough for him to have a good sleep before he started school the next day. She'd hardly glimpsed him all evening, running around as he'd been with all the other boys.

Stephen had disappeared completely. Mrs. Cavanagh said he had gone off to talk Irish politics. Anna was annoyed that he'd left her all to herself, but Mrs. Cavanagh had only laughed.

"You know how men are with their politics," she'd said.

Anna knew. She remembered her father sitting with the neighbor men before the peat fire, talking far into the night. Men and politics went together like tea and milk.

Rory finished his prayers and kicked his way under the covers. "I wish I didn't have to go to school."

"Of course you're going to school," Anna said, arranging the quilt over him. "And you'll like it, too."

"Eddie and Mike don't have to go. They're going to work."

"Then Eddie and Mike won't amount to much. Where would you be if you couldn't read and write."

"I already know how to read and write."

Anna smoothed the hair off Rory's damp forehead and thought of the Curran boys, so dirty and wild, with no clean clothes or proper food, and a mam and da with no time to look after them. It was going to be a sad life for the little lads.

"You bring those Currans for dinner whenever you want to," she told Rory. "They could use some meat on their bones and a good scrubbing, too. I just might stick them in the bath."

Rory looked doubtful. "They won't like that much."

"I daresay you're right," Anna said. "Now let's have a kiss good night."

Rory screwed up his face and allowed Anna to kiss him on both cheeks and on the tip of his nose. Once, he'd complained of being hugged and kissed too much. Anna had said it was good for him, that one day he'd give all those kisses back to the girl he loved, a notion he'd found shocking.

Anna turned off the lamp. The room fell into darkness, but she continued to stare down at the small figure in the bed, feeling warm all through.

When she went to the door, Stephen was there, silhouetted against the light from the hallway. He stepped aside to let Anna pass, then reached behind her and closed Rory's door.

"Where were you?" Anna asked.

"Downstairs, talking with John O'Mahony."

"Politics, was it?"

Stephen looked tired, too tired for her to be angry with him. "Politics. I'm sorry I left you alone, Nan."

Anna patted his arm. "Come have some tea, then." She led the way into the kitchen where the boiling kettle rattled on the stove.

Stephen sat at the table and rubbed his hands over his face. "It wears a man out, talking about Ireland, fighting the same battles again and again."

Anna put tea in the brown pot and poured hot water over it. She set out two chipped cups, sugar and milk, and the few remaining ginger biscuits. "I remember Dublin before the 'forty-eight rising," she said. "Oh, didn't the patriots make beautiful speeches, talking of democracy and free land. Then the soldiers were all over—red tunics and kilted Scotsmen, big, well-fed boys, strutting about with their guns. And before you knew it, it was finished." She shook her head. "It's a shame how the patriots always end up in defeat."

Stephen stretched out his legs and watched her arrange the tea things. Anna had loosened her jacket. Her shapely breasts filled the white blouse, pulled tight into the narrow waist of her blue flowered skirt. A long hank of curly red-tinged hair had fallen from the knot on her head. It shone in the gaslight.

"I was saying to Mrs. Cavanagh, politics doesn't matter so much to women, not like it does to men," she said. "Women leave Ireland with a light heart. We know we're going to a better life, and we don't look back. Men, though! Oh, they dwell on their defeat as if it was a curse on their manhood."

Anna added milk to the two cups, sat down, and rested her chin on her palm. In the subtle light, her eyes looked large and solemn, her lips softly full. Watching her, Stephen felt the hard ache of longing. She was the loveliest woman in the world, there was no question of that. He thought of the way she'd looked standing by Rory's bed and felt something more than desire. Something gentle and soft and deep. He picked up his spoon and ran his thumb over the handle.

"Aye, darling, you're right about that. Men never leave Ireland behind."

They sat quietly while the tea brewed. Stephen couldn't recall ever having felt as content as he did now, sitting in his kitchen with Anna, knowing his boy slept nearby, safe and happy.

"I want you to buy whatever you need for this place," he said. "Dishes, carpets, pictures."

"Oh, I plan to. I'll fill the dresser with things."

Stephen looked at the loose bundle of hair on her head, the strong shape of her brows, the fine straight nose. She was beautiful. Beautiful as a dream. "And I want you to have things for yourself. Dresses, shawls, bonnets. Go down Broadway and look in the shops. I want you to have anything you want."

"Listen to you, now," she admonished. "Aren't you extravagant."

"I mean it."

Anna reached for the teapot. "I'll not be turning myself into the grand lady, flaunting myself before your neighbors. And I'll not have you buying things for me. In no time I'll be earning American dollars with my lace and paying you back what I owe."

Stephen watched her pour the steaming tea into his cup and thought of telling her again that he wouldn't take her money. But he didn't want to start a quarrel. "Tell me about tonight. Did you enjoy yourself?"

"It was a lovely time. Everyone made me welcome. But that Davy Ryan! Oh, Stephen, he has hope of Peggy, but he'll never win her by playing the fool. He nearly fought with her sweetheart."

Stephen smiled. "I'll speak with him."

"And I told the women about Spinner and how I came to be with you. I didn't mean to tell them, but it all came out."

"It's no matter, Nan. I have no secrets from these people."

Anna looked at him anxiously. "No secrets, except about my—"

"Hush, darling. Let's not talk about hard things. Not tonight."

Stephen looked wistful, his eyes full of longing.

"Drink your tea," Anna said.

His expression didn't change. "A few sips. Then it's time for bed."

He wasn't going to ask, Anna thought. He was going to take her to the shiny brass bed and do what he'd been wanting to do all these past weeks. She wouldn't refuse him. She was in America now, in New York. The past was far away, so far away it might have been another life. And she owed him too much.

Anna took her teacup in both hands and wondered how it would be. Billy had come to her often, but he'd been quick about it. He'd been so eager to get down to business that he'd hardly kissed her, hardly touched her. Even in the early weeks when he couldn't get enough of her, he'd never touched her intimately, and she'd been thankful for it. But Stephen was different. She looked at his hands, broad and flat, and imagined them on her body. If he was kind, she wouldn't mind it. If he didn't squeeze and pinch her, if he didn't hurt her with his fingers, it wouldn't be bad. She wondered if she could ask him that, if she could ask him not to put his fingers inside her.

Stephen yawned and Anna saw he was growing impatient. She took quick sips of the hot, sweet tea until he stood up.

"Did you see our bedroom?"

Anna shook her head. "Not since this afternoon."

"Come, then." He held out his hand.

In the bedroom the brass bed was made up with fresh sheets and a bright quilt, turned down. The basket of yellow and purple flowers sat on the plain oak dresser. The crushed glass on the lower windows sparkled in the soft lamplight.

"Oh, it looks pretty," Anna said, astonished that Stephen had taken the trouble to prepare the room himself. Until this moment she hadn't thought about making the bed. "When did you do this?"

He looked pleased with himself. "Earlier."

Anna went to the window and touched the rough sparkling glass. "Can anyone see in?"

"Not through that glass."

"I'll have to be making curtains."

Stephen came to her and put his arms around her waist, drawing her close. Anna's body tensed. Stephen rubbed her back; his lips touched her hair. "Don't you want me, Nan? Just a bit?"

Anna rested her forehead against his shoulder. "Yes," she whispered, knowing that was what he wanted to hear.

He lifted her chin and kissed her. His lips moved slowly on hers, and on her checks and forehead. Anna closed her eyes. She didn't want him to see her apprehension; she didn't want to spoil his pleasure. But the more he kissed her, the less wary she felt, and when he went back to her mouth and touched her lips with his tongue, she opened for him and grasped at his shirt with her fingers. If only they could just do this, she thought, kiss and hold each other—nothing more.

Stephen drew away and reached for the lamp, lowering the light. Anna watched him remove the studs from his cuffs and drop them onto the dresser. He pulled off his shirt. His torso and arms were thick with muscles, his chest covered with swirling golden brown hair.

He caught Anna looking and grinned. "Did you ever see such a man in your life?" He ran a hand over his chest.

"Spoiled," she said, concealing a smile. "Spoiled and vain." She slipped off her jacket and arranged it over the back of a chair.

Stephen drew her toward him. "You know I like being spoiled."

Anna curled her fingers around the warm hardness of his upper arm. She looked at the curve of muscles on his shoulders, the broad expanse of chest, the steady pulse throbbing in his neck.

"Trust me, darling," he said softly.

Stephen caught her lips in his own. He nibbled and sucked at her mouth and played with her tongue until Anna slipped her arms around his neck and kissed him back. He pressed her close, crushing her to his chest. Then he stepped back and ran his hands down the front of her blouse, searching for buttons.

"Let's get you out of this rig."

His voice sounded rough, impatient. Like all men, once they got going, Anna thought.

She turned her back and unfastened the buttons with shaky fingers. She pulled off the blouse and laid it on the chair. When she lifted her hands to unfasten her camisole, Stephen slipped his arms around her and drew her hard against him. He held her firmly, one arm beneath her bosom, the other at her waist. His lips touched her neck, her shoulder, sending little shivers down her back.

"Lovely," he murmured, nuzzling her. "Christ Almighty, I've been dying for this."

His hands moved over her ribs and closed on her breasts, squeezing. Anna tensed and grasped his forearms. A babyish sound came from her throat.

"What is it, Nan?" Stephen asked. "What's wrong?"

She forced herself to lean back against him. She was breathing quickly, and her heart raced. It would hurt. After so many years it would surely hurt.

"I . . . don't know," she said.

Stephen was silent for a moment. Then he spoke softly. "Close your eyes."

Anna swallowed hard and closed them.

"Don't think of anything but how this feels." He caressed her breasts through the sheer linen of her camisole. Anna squeezed her eyes tighter.

"How is it?" he asked.

"I . . . I don't mind it."

The more he touched her, the more she felt. On her skin, down to her bones, and beyond. He was rubbing the tension out of her, bringing on the lovely, hazy pleasure she'd felt with him before, all down her belly and thighs.

"Will you mind the rest of it, when I go into you?"

"No," she lied, aware of him pressing hard against her back-side. There was no point in telling him how she hated it.

Stephen unbuttoned her camisole and slipped his hand inside. Callused fingers traced the swell of her breast, played with her nipple. Anna's lips parted with a soft sound of pleasure. She relaxed against him, her legs trembled under her weight. "Oh, Stephen."

"I'll please you tonight," he whispered against her hair. "Oh, Nan, I'll be sure to please you."

He opened the camisole completely. He caressed her with both hands, not pinching or squeezing, but holding her, stroking gently. Anna's back arched, her palms pressed back against his thighs. He made her feel tight and aching and full of heat.

He turned her around to face him and slipped the camisole off her shoulders, running his hands down her bare arms. Anna felt a quiver of pleasure as he studied her, his face serious and intent.

"Take down your hair."

She reached up and pulled out pins.

"Slowly, Nan, so I can look at you. Ah, what a picture you are." His voice was low and soft; his eyes consumed her.

She did it as he asked. Slowly. Letting him look at her, until every heavy strand had fallen, covering her chest, brushing her back. Stephen cleared it away. He pushed her masses of curls over her shoulders and caressed her breasts with his hands. His tongue wet her, his lips teased and tugged. Anna grasped his arms. She was wavering on her feet, feeling a warm heaviness settle over her limbs and a throbbing excitement deep inside. Her eyelids fell half closed. She'd never known such pleasure, never imagined it.

Stephen pulled at her skirt fastening, the ribbons on her petticoats. One after the other, they fell to the floor.

His eyes lingered everywhere. Anna felt drowsy and wanton, as if she were falling into an enchantment.

When her drawers were gone, he crouched down and pulled off her stockings, leaving her naked. He ran his hands lightly up her thighs. Anna stood transfixed, her eyes closed tight, feeling wicked and beautiful. She dug her fingers into his hair.

He held her hips and nuzzled the juncture of her thighs.

"Oh!" Anna's eyes flew open. "Stephen . . ."

She felt the thrust of his tongue, seeking, and then a lovely sensation that made her cry out in surprise.

"Don't do that!" She pushed him away.

He stood up and smiled, his eyes dark and liquid. "It does no harm."

He tried to catch her in his arms, but she pulled away. She was trembling, ashamed of what Stephen had done, more ashamed of the way it had made her feel. She picked up her petticoat from the floor and covered herself. The spell had been broken, leaving her confused. She felt a sudden urge to cry.

"You do everything different," she said. "You look too much. And touch. And that . . . what you did. It's not right."

Stephen heard her out, a smile on his mouth. "From now on I'll do it right, Nan." He began unfastening his trousers.

Anna held her petticoat firmly over her chest and averted her eyes. She wasn't going to look at him. She couldn't. But when he tossed his trousers aside, she found herself staring at his naked hips, his long-muscled thighs, the thick male part of him thrusting out like a lance.

She turned away, gripping the petticoat tighter. She didn't want to lie under him, wide open and helpless, waiting for him to be finished. He wasn't really her husband, she told herself. It wasn't really her duty.

"Stephen, I can't."

He eased the petticoat out of her hands and draped her arms over his shoulders. When he drew her close, Anna leaned hard against him, pressing her lips to his shoulder, feeling the pounding of his heart. "I'm afraid," she whispered.

"I know it, Nan."

She wanted to please him. She wanted to kiss him and feel his hands on her. She wanted everything but to have him force himself inside her, where his passion would turn wild and rough and he would hurt her and forget she existed.

"I won't hurt you," he said. "I swear it. If I do, tell me and I'll stop."

He eased her back onto the bed, on the cool linen sheet, and looked down the length of her. Anna could feel her pulse beating in her throat, in her ears. She didn't close her eyes; she didn't dare. She had to watch him so he wouldn't lull her into another enchantment.

He bent over her, bracing himself above her, his hands on either side, and kissed her, his mouth hot and open, his tongue gently probing. He lowered his chest onto hers, barely touching, and rubbed against her breasts, making her shiver. He drew back, then slid an arm beneath her hips and moved her up fully onto the big soft bed. "There, now. Here we are."

He stroked her and kissed her breasts, his tongue wet and warm. Anna closed her eyes, her fear fading. Other feelings rose through her, those lovely wanton feelings.

Stephen's fingers slid between her thighs and Anna stiffened. She remembered rough hands probing tender flesh, the sharp bite of ragged nails. She grasped Stephen's wrist, trying to pull his hand away.

"It's all right," he said. "Let me show you."

She lay still, her body tense, her eyes open wide. Slowly, gently, he caressed her, searching out the sweet place his tongue had touched. "You're beautiful, Anna. The loveliest woman in the world." His voice was soft, breaking.

His fingers raised sensations that were all new, feelings that might have been wicked if they weren't so lovely. Anna opened her legs more, hoping he wouldn't notice.

"Ah, darling," he said. "I think you're wanting me now."

His fingers moved boldly, pushing deep, and suddenly Anna was struggling in panic, trying to push him away. "No," she cried. "Don't do that. Oh, don't." She struck out at his arm.

Stephen grasped her wrist. "There, don't run away from me now."

She lay still, panting. Stephen was looking at her in alarm, as if there was something wrong with her. Anna covered her chest with her arms and turned away.

He smoothed the hair from her face and shoulders and spread it out on the pillow. He turned her face back to his. "I won't do it again."

In the lamplight his expression was baffled but kind. Anna was glad it was Stephen beside her and not some other man. Any other man would have been on her already, not bothering to care how she felt.

He kissed her for a long time, on her mouth and her breasts, making her feel drowsy and liquid. When he touched her again, Anna felt an ache inside her like an illness, like a hunger in her womb. It grew until she could barely stand it, and her hands were all over him, her fingers digging into hard flesh, and she was sighing with pleasure.

When he came to her, she bit her lips and pressed her face to his throat, willing him to hurry.

But he didn't hurry. He slipped his hands beneath her hips, down the backs of her thighs, lifting, separating. He eased into her slowly, carefully. "Anna," he whispered. "Oh, Nan."

He opened her legs wider still, fitting himself snug and deep. It didn't hurt. Not at all. It felt wonderful. He raised himself and looked at her, his face naked with passion. Anna clutched at the sheet and turned her head, not wanting to see him. But, oh, she felt him. The feeling of him went all through her, making her lips part, making her breath come short.

He moved on her, satisfying her hunger, making it worse. "Oh, please," Anna whispered, not knowing what she wanted. The feelings grew and swelled, and she felt a tiny quiver, and another. She arched her back and grasped at Stephen, whimpering like a child. He collapsed on her with his full weight, thrusting, growling with pleasure, digging his fingers into her hair. He kissed her so hard she felt his teeth on her lips.

"Anna. Oh, Jesus."

He was fierce and full inside her. Anna twisted upward, shameless and wild, and suddenly his great body thrust and shook with a power that seemed to wring the life from him, that left him gasping.

Then he was utterly still, save for his pounding heart, his back heaving. Anna lay beneath him, holding him, stroking his hair. She felt relieved, but also a bit sorry. She wondered why she felt sorry, when she should have been thankful it was over, and with no harm done.

Stephen rose up and gazed at her with a soft, misty smile. He looked happy and very young. Even with his scars and lines and his beard making shadows on his cheeks and chin, he looked like a young man.

The expression on his face made her whole body tingle. "Why are you looking at me so?"

"My Nan," he said softly. "My beautiful Nan." He moved away gingerly and lay back with a satisfied groan.

Anna waited for him to roll over and sleep. Billy had never said a word after being with her; he was snoring the moment he was finished. But Stephen was very much awake, watching her, one thick hairy arm thrown across her soft white middle.

"The inside of you feels like petals," he said. "Flower petals covered with dew."

Anna played with the crisp hair on his arm, embarrassed by his intimate talk. "What a thing to say."

"Did you mind it so much?"

Anna felt too shy to look at him. "You know I didn't mind it." Her voice was barely a whisper.

Stephen fondled her breast. "You're a glorious woman altogether." His voice turned husky. "Oh, what we're going to do, you and I, here in this bed."

He put his lips to her breast. His hair tickled her skin, his tongue made her squirm. She was still all stirred up inside; the ache between her thighs hadn't gone away.

"It's time to sleep," she said.

Stephen drew back and looked at her, smiling. "Aye, darling, it's time to sleep."

When Anna moved to get up, Stephen's hand tightened on her hip. "Where are you going?"

"To get my nightdress." Never in her life had she slept without something on.

"I'll keep you warm."

"But, Stephen—"

"No nightdress. I want to feel you against me, all those soft, round places you have, all those places I might want to touch."

He pulled the covers up and drew her into his arms. He twined his legs about hers, fitting their bodies together, making them comfortable. Anna nuzzled his cheek, rough with whiskers, and inhaled his musky scent. She liked the way he felt, large and warm against her.

"The lamp," she whispered.

"We'll leave it on. I might want to look at you."

"I'll thank you not to be waking me up every minute with all your looking and touching." Anna tried to sound stern, but she knew she wouldn't mind if he wanted to take her again.

Stephen laughed and kissed her and wished her sweet dreams. Long after he slept, Anna lay awake, thinking how very strange it had been with him, how different. How truly lovely.

*   *   *

Anna floated in a dream. Rough, warm hands stroked her. She writhed slowly. Her body moved in a quickening rhythm that matched the beat of her heart, that bored into the very depths of her. She opened her legs, and he touched her. Through the foggy bliss that clouded her mind, she knew it was not a dream. "Stephen."

"Darling. It's all right."

She felt his heartbeat against her own, the rise and fall of his chest. She sought his mouth with her lips. His kisses were deep and slow, and then his mouth left her. "Let me kiss you, Nan. Will you let me?"

"Yes." Of course, she would let him—what did he mean?

His lips moved over her at a leisurely pace. All down her body. His tongue lingered and stroked. Anna felt herself melting from the inside, sweet and warm like hot honey. He parted her thighs. Too late she understood what he wanted.

"Stephen." Her heart leaped, her scalp tingled. "Stephen, don't." She could manage no more than a whisper. She felt drowsy and dazed, too weak to stop him. She let him feast his eyes; she let him kiss her where he looked.

"No more," she said, too softly for him to hear.

He put his lips and then his tongue, on the sweetest place. Anna closed her eyes. "No. Please, don't." She grasped his hair until her fingers ached; then she forgot about trying to stop him.

He didn't make a sound. Anna could hear only her own little sobs, the blood pounding in her ears.

She felt a tremor inside her and cried out. Stephen stopped and moved over her.

"I want to feel this," he said. "This first time."

He pushed hard into her, and Anna took him hungrily, feeling the fullness of him. She clutched at him, heard his quickening breaths, her own little cries. She felt wide and endless and powerful, like a great river. She didn't realize how she was moving until Stephen grasped her hips.

"Don't move so, darling. Let me do it."

She forced herself to lie still, sobbing against his mouth, her nerves tearing like silk. She was desperate to move again, to feel the power of it, to make it end. "Please stop," she cried.

His hands tightened on her hips. He held her close, held himself deep and still. "Nan. Oh, Nan, the way you feel."

He drew back and came full into her. Again he pulled away, hesitated, drove hard. The force of him pushed her down. She was overflowing, drowning. She couldn't hold on any longer.

"Stephen!"

He thrust again, breaking her open, shattering her into a million pieces, and then she felt him, huge and bursting, heard him call her name.

When she came to herself, she was weeping. She couldn't stop her tears. She didn't know what it was—relief or joy or shame or sorrow. Stephen held her close in his arms. He played with her hair and said nothing.

"It's too much," she said at last, wiping her cheeks with her palm. She couldn't bear such feelings. "It's too much to feel that way."

Stephen lifted her hair and gathered it into long coil. "It shows we're made for each other, that's all."

"It's like falling," Anna said. "From a mountain. From heaven."

He nuzzled her cheek. She felt his smile. "I'll be there to catch you, darling. I'll make sure you don't fall too far."

Chapter 20

Anna spent the following week organizing and decorating the flat. She hung pictures on the walls and white lace curtains at the windows, and filled the kitchen dresser with mugs and jugs and flowered plates. She chose carpets for the floors, laid antimacassars on the sofa, and spread her mother's thick lace coverlet on the bed. Stephen brought more flowers, which she arranged in pots on the oak chest in the bedroom. The flowers added a spot of bright color to the room's white lace and polished brass. And the fragrance was lovely. It was most intense at night, Anna thought, when she lay in bed with Stephen.

The bedroom was for the two of them, the kitchen for everyone. Anna kept a chicken simmering in the pot, a pie cooling on the table, and the kettle boiling for tea. Peggy came to gossip, Davy was always looking for a bite to eat, and Dennis Lawler stopped by for a slab of pie after his free lunch in the saloon. Gil appeared daily, sometimes twice, to drink whiskey and entertain Anna with grisly newspaper stories while she worked on her lace or prepared the dinner. After school, Rory and the Curran boys would burst in, shouting loud enough to wake the dead.

Anna loved the company, but Stephen complained about the constant activity. At odd times of the day he'd come up from the saloon or his office and find her laughing with Gil or feeding the boys or offering Peggy some piece of advice.

He talked with whoever was visiting, but he kept his eyes on Anna, watching her with an expression that embarrassed and excited her.

One morning he found an excuse to take her into the bedroom for a few words. A few words turned into a breathless embrace, and before she knew it, Stephen had her on the bed with her bodice open and her skirts hiked up. It was swift and thrilling and so wonderfully indecent that Anna blushed for the rest of the afternoon.

She had fallen far and fast; there was no question of it. She dwelt on impure thoughts that no virtuous woman would ever entertain, and at night she was incapable of either modesty or restraint. But she didn't have time to consider the state of her soul, what with getting the laundry done and dinner on the table, and seeing Rory off to school, and teaching the Curran boys how to polish a window and clean the range. Why, she barely had a moment to sit down for a cup of tea with Peggy or pick up her crochet hook, let alone think about her sins. One day soon she would consider what she was doing and where she was headed, but for now—for the first time in her life, it seemed—her mind was empty of worries.

Anna was thinking these thoughts one sunny June evening while she knelt on the parlor floor, brushing the cheerful yellow and blue carpet. The room looked pretty, with the lace curtains stirring at the open window and bright pillows snug in the corners of the lemon-colored sofa. It was a lovely home she had to care for and lively children to fuss over and a man who petted her and praised her to the skies. The home wasn't hers, nor were the children, or even the man, when it came right down to it. But she was happy in a way she'd never imagined, a deep solid happiness that could only be contentment.

"Anna, you work too hard."

She glanced up from her brushing. Stephen leaned against the doorframe, his fingers shoved into the waist of his trousers. He looked vital and handsome, and there was a new softness about his eyes and mouth that Anna knew had something to do with her.

She sat back on her heels and wiped her damp forehead with her sleeve. She raised her arms to secure the hair falling out of its knot and saw Stephen's gaze drop to her breasts.

He always looked at her as if he thought she was the most desirable woman in the world.

"That's what I'm here for," she said. "To take care of your home."

Stephen's face darkened, and Anna remembered that he hated any mention of her debt. "You're my wife," he said irritably. "You don't have to work so hard."

"This is what wives do," she said, getting to her feet. "They work. Besides, I have plenty of help. The Curran boys cleaned the range today and hung out the laundry, and Mose was up three times, asking if I needed anything tended to." She held out her hand. "Come, let me show you something."

She led him into the bedroom and pointed out a new braided rug. "Do you think it's too small? I didn't want the floor covered so much. I like to lie in bed and look at the sun shining on the wood."

Stephen slipped his arm around her waist. "When I lie in bed with you, darling, I don't care what's on the floor."

"Oh, you," Anna admonished gently. She gave him a flirtatious little glance, and Stephen watched her cheeks bloom pink. The evening sunlight sparkled on the windows, and the polished bed shone with a brilliant light. Stephen imagined Anna lying on white linen, naked, her glorious hair spilling over the pillow, while he touched her and kissed her and made her body blush.

"Lie down with me, Nan. Just for a minute."

She put her hands on his shoulders and pressed close, making his pulse leap, making him feel weak.

"Don't you just want that all the time, Mr. Flynn?"

He brushed his lips against hers. "Every minute of the day." He kissed her slowly, savoring the taste of her, feeling her softness against him. She moved ever so slightly, a little squirm and a sigh, and he felt himself drop into a place where nothing existed except Anna and his endless hunger for her. He grasped her hips and held her as the heat seeped into him, making him hard.

The kitchen door opened and slammed shut. Rory and Davy shouted out a greeting. Anna pulled back, bright-eyed and breathless. "It's suppertime."

Stephen muttered an oath, his hands tightening on her. "I'm taking you away. I'll have you to my bloody self for a change."

Anna rose up on her toes and ran her hands over his hair. "Spoiled," she whispered against his lips. "Spoiled and greedy." She kissed him boldly, her hand lingering on his cheek before she slipped out of his arms. "You rest now," she said. "I'll be calling you for supper."

After she left, Stephen loosened his collar and lay down on the bed. He folded his arms beneath his head and stared at the ceiling, trying to calm his mind and body, no easy task when it came to Anna. She had done something to him, gotten so deep under his skin he could hardly think straight. And now that he had her, he lived in terror that he would lose her. The way she talked sometimes made him think she might repay him and leave.

He wished he could marry her properly. When it came to Anna, he cared nothing for the finer points of church law. He would have lied in God's face to keep her, and he knew how she felt about him—she'd told him often enough when they lay together, spent of passion but too happy for sleep. But he also knew that Anna believed she was sinning with him. She never spoke of it, but sometimes he could feel her hesitation, just for a moment when he first touched her. And sometimes she got a distant, thoughtful look on her face, as if she was considering her sins. It frustrated Stephen that he could give her the comforts of a decent home and the passion she'd never known, but not the blessing of God, which she seemed to need to be completely happy.

He thought of the one obstacle that kept Anna from being his true wife—a man named Billy Massie, her bloody church-wed husband. Massie could be anywhere—in New York among the thousands of Irish immigrants in the Fourth and Sixth wards, or out west working on the canals or digging ditches or laying rails. Stephen had an urge to make inquiries, to track the man down. But what if he found him? What then? Stephen felt the familiar clench of muscles in his shoulders and arms, the stir of anger in his gut. Thinking of Billy Massie brought on primitive feelings that never failed to spoil his mood.

"Stephen?"

Anna stood at the door, wiping her hands on her apron, an anxious look on her face. "Emmet says Mr. Curran's downstairs looking to see you. I hope it's no trouble with the twins."

Stephen got to his feet and fastened his collar button. In all the time the Curran boys had been coming around, their father had never once stopped by, not even to the saloon.

"I hope they've not been pilfering down at the docks again," Anna said.

"Don't be worrying about your little lordeens, darling," Stephen said, pulling on his coat. "They may not be able to read and figure, but they're too quick to be caught at their mischief."

In the kitchen, Rory and Davy were consuming a stack of pancakes and a pitcher of buttermilk. Davy had filled out, Stephen noticed. He looked fit; handsome, too. His red hair was trimmed and brushed, and he wore a shirt and trousers of Stephen's that Anna had altered. She had persuaded him to donate the clothes. "Peggy will never take to him if he looks like he just came off the boat," she'd said.

Next she'd had him giving Davy a job as a waiter in the saloon, and the small room next to the office to sleep in. Stephen hadn't been pleased to do either, but Davy had worked out well in the saloon. He was a friendly lad and could jolly a troublemaker out of a fight. But what Davy liked best, as far as Stephen could tell, was to lounge around doing nothing.

"I see you haven't starved to death yet, Davy," Stephen said.

Davy grinned. "Anna won't let me."

"I can tell that from the grocery bills Mrs. Cavanagh sends me."

"Hush, Stephen," Anna said. "Davy is always welcome."

Stephen laid a hand on Rory's head. "As for you, sport, you'll soon be out of school for the summer, and it's going to be work for you. Mrs. Cavanagh could use an errand boy, and I know you can run fast."

"But I'd rather do chores for Anna," Rory said through a mouthful of pancakes. "With Eddie and Mike."

Stephen caught Anna's eye. "I'm told the three of you together don't do the work of one. Too much carrying on."

"But, Da . . ." Rory looked hopefully at Anna. " 'Tisn't true, is it?"

"You know it's true," Anna said, dropping a spoonful of batter on the griddle. "Put the three of you together, there's not a turn of work done, and I'm wasting my time scolding." She looked at Stephen. "You ask Mr. Curran upstairs for some pancakes. If the poor man's like his boys, he didn't get much of a dinner."

Curran was a string bean of a man, his face lined with care. Stephen vaguely remembered sparring with him on the *Mary Drew*, and remembered how his children had howled with excitement all through the match. Now, as he stood by the bar, twisting his cloth cap in his hands, Curran looked nervous and somewhat lost.

"Mr. Curran." Stephen held out his hand.

The man took it and smiled. There were more than a few gaps in his teeth. "I'm obliged you taking the time, Mr. Flynn."

Stephen motioned him to a table. "Have a drop, then. Ale? Whiskey?"

"No, thank you kindly. I took the pledge back when I was married. The wife insisted."

"Good man," Stephen said as they seated themselves. "I hardly touch the stuff myself. Now, what can I do for you? Are those lads of yours in trouble?"

Curran shook his head. "No, sir. But I want to thank you for what you've done. I know you feed them and let them play in the sparring room. And the money for the chores, well, it's a blessing to us."

Stephen waved aside Curran's gratitude. "It's no trouble. Those two work hard for my wife, and they mind her, too."

Curran looked surprised at that piece of news. "At home the only thing they mind is the strap."

Stephen thought of the way Anna managed the Currans, fussing and scolding and cuddling them until they blushed and beamed like cherubs. "Mrs. Flynn would never lay a hand on your boys. But she can scold the devil out of his pitchfork, and those lads know it."

Mr. Curran looked impressed. "More power to her, then."

"She's got a soft spot for boys," Stephen said. "She lost three little brothers in the hunger."

Curran's face fell. He stared at his cap, twisted in his hands. "Aye, 'twas a sad time, the hunger." He swallowed a couple of times, and Stephen wished he hadn't mentioned it.

"What's your business with me, then, if it's not those rascals?"

"It's what I heard. I thought you should know." Curran's voice dropped so low that Stephen had to lean across the table to hear him.

"What did you hear, then?"

Curran glanced around the saloon. Since it was suppertime, the room was barely a third full. "I'm no snitch, Mr. Flynn, telling tales behind a man's back."

Stephen waited.

"It's Maguire," Curran said at last. "Maguire and his gang from the Big Six Saloon are coming here to bust up your place."

Stephen sat back in surprise. He hadn't heard from Maguire in weeks. He figured Billy had accepted the inevitable, that there would be no prize match. Stephen gave his saloon a quick protective glance. Bust up the place, he thought grimly. By God, that would provoke him. If Billy's gang tore up the Emerald Flame, that would provoke him a great deal.

"Where did you hear this, Curran?"

"I'm digging for the city, the gas lines, you see. When we get a rest, the lads talk."

So it's just gossip, Stephen thought. But he wouldn't put it past Maguire. "When are they planning to come by?"

Curran moistened his lips. "Don't know that. Didn't want to ask, neither, drawing attention to myself."

Stephen nodded. If Billy's men thought a man was a spy, they'd break him in two. "I'm obliged to you. Much obliged. I'll be calling on Mr. Maguire. I'll try to get things straightened out before any harm's done."

Curran looked suddenly fearful. "You won't be speaking my name?"

"May God wither me if I do. Now, come on upstairs. My wife stirred up a batch of pancakes. If we hurry, there'll be a few left for us."

Curran hesitated. "I don't know about that. I'd best be getting along—"

"She told me if I didn't bring you by, there'd be the devil to pay," Stephen said, getting to his feet. "When all's said and done, it's no treat for a man, being in trouble with his wife."

Curran grinned. "You have the right of it there, Mr. Flynn."

They passed through the saloon and into the sparring room. Curran glanced at the posters on the wall, at the heavy bag and the small one, at the rack of dumbbells. Then he stopped in his tracks, his eyes fastened on the ring, where Mose, his dark torso gleaming with sweat, sparred with another muscular young giant before a sparse but noisy group of spectators.

"You're welcome here any evening," Stephen said. "Saturday night there's two lads from Boston coming through for a bare-knuckle match. There'll be a mob here. You might fancy the excitement."

Curran tore his eyes away from the ring and glanced at the notice that listed the price of admission.

"You're my guest," Stephen said quickly. "Anytime, no charge. And if you want to take a chance in the ring yourself, there's plenty of lads in the saloon who'll be wanting to knock the smoke out of you."

A smile broke across Curran's worn and weary face. His eyes brimmed with sudden life. "I don't mind if I do that, Mr. Flynn. It's a long time since I've been out with the lads."

"I'll look for you, then," Stephen said. To himself he thought it was a sorry life for a country-bred man, digging ditches all day in a city like New York, living in a rabbit warren of a tenement, worrying about how to feed his family.

"By the way," Stephen said as they climbed the back stairs to the kitchen. "Have you run across an Irishman named Massie?"

"Massie," Curran said thoughtfully.

"Billy Massie. He comes from Dublin, though he was born in Cork. Must be twenty-some years of age. A rough sort of lad."

Curran shook his head. "Can't say I've heard of a Billy Massie at all."

* * *

Anna filled Mr. Curran with pancakes and buttermilk and wrapped some poppy seed buns for him to take to his wife. After Stephen saw their guest down the front stairs, he took Anna into the parlor.

"Curran warned me there might be some trouble downstairs. I want you and Rory to stay inside for the evening."

"What sort of trouble?" Anna asked in alarm.

"A bit of a muss, that's all. I'm going out now and try to stop it."

"Oh, Stephen, it's not Maguire, is it?"

"I'm not going to fight him, Nan. I'm going to talk to him."

Anna rolled her hands in her apron. Her cheeks were pink from working over the stove, and she looked tired.

"I may be late, so don't wait up," Stephen said.

Anna's eyes clouded with worry. "I don't want you hurt."

"I won't be hurt." Stephen drew her into his arms and kissed her, wishing he didn't have to go out, wishing they could lie together and talk and touch and let their passion rise. He released her reluctantly, his hand lingering on her breast. "I'll be taking Davy along."

"Davy!" Anna clutched at his sleeve. "Davy won't be any help to you. You'd be better taking Mose."

Stephen shook his head. "The Big Six boys don't like colored men. Besides"—he gave her a smile—"I've got to get Davy out of your kitchen, so you don't make him as fat as a parson's pig."

Stephen went downstairs and spoke to Mose and Emmet, telling them to alert the sergeant at the Spring Street police station if anything should develop.

Mose crossed his arms on his chest and made clear his displeasure at being left behind. "Don't see why we got to wait for them to come here. We can raise a gang and pay our own visit."

Emmet agreed. "Davy Ryan will be about as much help as a flea."

"I'm not looking for a fight," Stephen said. "Now, try to keep your hair on, both of you, and if anything happens, don't be forgetting Anna and Rory upstairs."

Twilight had fallen when he and Davy set off down the Bowery. The streetlamps were lit, and crowds thronged the sidewalk. Stephen moved along amid the brightly garbed shopgirls and their swaggering boys. People recognized him and wanted to chat, but he'd learned how to grasp a man's hand and exchange a greeting without missing a step. Beside him, Davy threw out his chest and returned the girls' admiring glances.

The Big Six Saloon on Chatham Street was a dingy hole compared to the Emerald Flame. The bar was made of plain rough pine, and the shelves behind it were crowded with dusty bottles. There were no mirrors or framed pictures to decorate the walls, only aging political placards and smudges of black from the smoky kerosene lamps. Men sat on barrels, their fists around mugs of ale, arguing in loud voices and spitting on the sawdust floor. They were a rougher lot than Stephen's clientele, men who dug and hauled all day and lived in crowded tenements where water had to be carried in from the public pumps. Some worked hard to keep their families together; others had given in to violence and despair.

But they were all Irishmen, and they all loved a fight. Even the ones who backed Billy Maguire admired Stephen. So when he stepped up to the bar, they crowded around him, pushing one another to get closer, except for a few of Billy's Big Six gang, who lounged against the far wall, their faces impassive.

Jimmy Haggerty, the florid-faced barman, waved a dirty rag over the bar. "Would you be looking for himself, then, Stephen?"

"That's so, Jimmy," Stephen said, dropping a handful of coins on the bar. He signaled to Davy to order a drink. "Where might our Billy be?"

The barman deftly swept the coins into his palm. "Seeing a fancy girl up at the St. Nicholas."

"The St. Nicholas, now." Stephen gave a low whistle. "Isn't he up in the world?" He glanced around at the rugged Irish faces, nodding their agreement, and wondered how Billy had managed that. The best men in New York kept their mistresses at the St. Nicholas. Seeing a woman there did not come cheap.

"He don't go there much," Jimmy said, "but when he does, he brags on it. He don't stay long, our Billy. In and out, you might say."

The remark was greeted with lewd and knowing laughter. Even the gang members cracked a smile. Davy flushed scarlet, and it occurred to Stephen that he was probably as innocent as a chick just out of the egg.

"Ye've come to arrange a match, Stephen?" a man asked.

"No, Tim, no match. I heard talk of a rumble at the Emerald Flame. I wanted to know when you lads were planning to visit." He looked from face to face, smiling easily, keeping an eye on the gang against the wall.

The men shifted their feet and looked at the floor. Jimmy Haggerty reddened. "Aye, there's been talk. He's wanting to provoke you, Stephen. It's nothing personal, you know. It's just that the lads love a good brawl, and if you and Billy went at it like you did on that island, why, it would give us all a grand lift."

"A grand lift," the men agreed almost in unison.

And it would be the making of Maguire, should he win it, Stephen thought. He glanced around the rank, tobacco-fogged saloon. When you came right down to it, Billy didn't have much. He kept the Big Six, though the brewery owned it, and he hired out as a thug and a strongman during election time. As the bare-knuckle champion, his very presence would terrorize the party's enemies at the polls, come November, and secure his spot with the Tammany crowd. He would have the admiration of powerful men, and later, if he kept his health and his wits and did as he was told, he might even be put up for public office himself.

Stephen wouldn't deny him any of it. As far as he was concerned, Billy was free to run for mayor, as long as it didn't involve him. He wasn't about to risk his well-being in a championship match just so Billy Maguire could have a soft future.

Stephen was formulating his response when the crowd began moving back and a murmur went up. "It's himself. It's Billy."

Davy all but flattened himself against the bar. "Easy, lad," Stephen said. "Drink up and enjoy yourself. It's nothing to fear."

Billy wore a gold and black checked suit and a brushed felt hat tipped back on his head. He looked fit and clear-eyed, and his cheeks were ruddy with health and arrogance.

He grinned, flashing white teeth, and stuck out his hand. "What's got into you, Flynn, coming down here so?"

Stephen grasped his hand, applying more pressure than was necessary. "I heard you were stopping by my place with your gang. Up to no good, it seems."

Billy's eyes swung to the gang against the wall, but his cocky expression didn't change. "Where did you hear it?"

"The walls and the wind have ears, Billy. You know how Irishmen talk."

"I thought we'd finish the muss we started back when."

"And bust up my place?"

Billy slapped a hand on the bar. "Whiskey, Jimmy," he said to the barman and jerked his head toward the table at the rear of the saloon. The men already seated there scrambled to their feet.

"Come along, Davy," Stephen said.

Billy glanced at Davy. "Who's the yoke?"

"Davy Ryan, my second." Stephen gave Davy a wink. "He's stronger than he looks."

Billy looked Davy over and shook his head. "You've a sorry lot for a gang, Flynn, that's all I can say about it. Aside from the nigger boy, not one of them can fight worth dirt."

Davy flushed, and Stephen gave his shoulder a reassuring thump. "The only trouble with my gang is they fight fair."

Once they were seated and Billy had offered whiskey around, Stephen said, "I hear you did a sparring exhibition for O'Mahony."

Billy nodded. "Me and Patsy Kelly raised a fair sum. What's the Committee doing with the money?"

Stephen shrugged. "You've got me there. O'Mahony's not saying, and it's just as well. One Irishman opens his trap in New York, and the next thing you know, Dublin Castle's heard everything."

Billy sat back, crossed his big arms on his chest, and gave Stephen a mocking look. "You know where the money's going, Flynn. You're just back from the hearth of Padraic McCarthy. You must be in on it."

Davy cleared his throat. "I heard it was for the defense of the patriots that've been arrested in Dublin."

Billy looked at him scornfully. "My bloody eye, it is. It's for guns."

Stephen's heart jumped, then quickly steadied. He's bluffing, he thought. It didn't take a genius to make that wild guess. He laid his hands on the notched and scarred tabletop and thought of the consequences if word got out about the Birmingham connection and the plan for transport. There would be a welcoming committee of British soldiers at Cork when the steamer docked. It would be the end of Emmet and Paddy and a fair number of other Brotherhood men.

"Davy's got the right of it," he said easily. "From what I can make out, that is."

Billy tossed back his drink and pushed his tumbler away. By God, he looks strong, Stephen thought. Strong as a bull, and in his element down here with his gang close by. There was none of the nervousness he'd shown at the Emerald Flame or in the ring at Guardian Island. Billy Maguire had reached his prime, and Stephen was glad he wouldn't have to fight him.

"Let's you and me do a benefit, Flynn."

Stephen shook his head. "I'm out of it, Billy. I already told O'Mahony."

"I take it you don't approve of the cause, then."

"I'm not fighting."

"It's a sparring match. I won't hurt you." Billy was grinning, a little too broadly, a little too knowingly. "What's got into you, Flynn? A hero of 'forty-eight turning his back on the cause. You haven't gone over to the British, now, have you?"

Stephen met Billy's eyes. They gleamed dark and hard. Stephen had never seen him so assured, so full of pride. He's on to something, Stephen thought, and it made him uncomfortable.

"All right, Billy, I'll take a match."

There it was; he'd agreed to the exhibition and he wasn't sure why.

Billy poured another tumbler of whiskey and tossed it down, looking pleased. "Until then, so," he said and stuck out his hand.

This time it was Billy who applied the squeeze.

Walking back to Brace Street in the warm night air, Stephen said nothing.

Davy spoke only once. "Anna will kill you for this."

"It can't be helped," Stephen replied, and Davy said no more.

At home things were quiet, the gas lamps turned low. Anna had left some supper warming in the oven and a pot of tea, grown cold. Stephen took off his boots and sat at the table with the plate of beef and cabbage. As he ate, he looked around the kitchen. Anna's touch was everywhere—the dresser crammed with sparkling dishes, the brass candle holders, the clean cloth on the table, ready for tomorrow. Stephen knew nothing about decorating, but he was pleased that Anna liked things light and cheerful. And she didn't clutter the place up with the fringes and figurines that were all the fashion uptown. She left plenty of empty spaces, so a man didn't have to worry about where he swung his elbows.

Anna. He'd never imagined that a woman could so consume him. But she was no ordinary woman. She understood life; she understood him. She'd made his home beautiful and his neighbors feel welcome, and she loved his son. Thinking of all she'd done filled Stephen with such gratitude that he had to frown hard against the emotion of it.

But he knew that Davy was right—Anna would kill him for stepping into a ring with Maguire, even for a sparring match.

Stephen pushed the last of the cabbage onto his fork. He wasn't sure why he'd let Billy get to him, why he'd agreed to the match. Partly it was for the cause, to do his bit for John O'Mahony, and partly he'd been distracted by Billy's odd confidence. But there was more to it. For all his resolve to quit, the ring still attracted him. Stephen imagined the mob filling Sportsman's Hall. He smelled the sweat and liniment, heard the rough banter of the other fighters on the card. He thought of the acclaim when he landed a blow, the thunderous shouts, the stamping feet. Stephen ran his hands down the front of him, over his chest, his hard belly, and gripped his thighs. The ring had been his life, his youth; he was the champion. Giving it up wasn't easy.

He got up from the table and carried his plate to the scullery. He straightened the cloth the way Anna had left it and snuffed out the lamp. On his way down the hall, he stopped in Rory's room. The boy lay sprawled on his stomach, the covers kicked off. Stephen laid a hand on Rory's back, feeling the slow rise and fall as he breathed. The lad was happy and thriving. He had a big heart and a clutch of new friends, and Anna loved him like her own. Thank God for it, Stephen thought. He didn't know if he could bear his son's unhappiness.

In the front room, Anna slept, her fist tucked under her cheek, her thick braid curled on the pillow. The lamplight brought out the reddish shine of her hair. Stephen stripped off his clothes and thought of it loose, entwining them as they clung to each other.

He lay down on the bed, gently so not to wake her, and stared at the ceiling, feeling a growing unease. Anna would be furious about the match. She would accuse him of breaking his promise. What if she left him because of it? What if she paid off her debt and moved away?

Stephen closed his eyes. The dread in his gut moved up to his chest, almost like panic. He tried to push away his fears. He'd never been a man to brood about what might come to pass. He took things as they came, as a challenge, like any fighter.

Anna stirred beside him. "Stephen," she said sleepily, reaching for him. "You're home, thank God. What happened?"

"Nothing happened, darling. Nothing at all."

She wriggled her way into his arms and kissed his neck. Her hand slipped down his belly and closed around him. Stephen felt himself swell under the pressure of her fingers; his anxiety eased, melting into desire. He kissed her mouth until it grew warm and open, he filled his hands with her breasts. He wanted to lose himself in her silky heat.

"Nan, I need you."

She gave him a squeeze. "Come, then."

He threw back the covers and ran his hands over her. He pressed her down with desperate kisses. She sensed his urgency and moved so he could take her quickly. He rushed into her, a frantic joining, sharp and blinding. Stephen had hardly begun when she surged against him, crying out his name, and he felt a shock of excitement that dragged him deep, like an undertow, drowning his senses.

Coming out of it, he felt half numb, his limbs prickling, his head in a fog. Anna stretched beneath him, sighing in the aftermath of pleasure. Her soft thighs hugged his hips. She was hot and as damp as dew.

"I love you," she whispered. "Oh, Stephen, I do."

He eased away from her, and the dread came thudding back, leaving him spent but not soothed, satisfied but still in need.

"Something happened, didn't it?" Anna was watching him. She pressed her fingers to his brow, smoothing it. "Tell me."

Stephen looked into her eyes and stroked her breasts, flushed and full, and it came to him in an instant. A child. A child would keep her with him, bind them forever. "Nan, I want us to have a child."

Her hand stilled on his face. She looked stunned for an instant, then glanced away, her eyes glittering.

Stephen raised himself up on an elbow, alarmed. "What is it? You don't want a baby?"

"I can't, Stephen."

He waited for her explanation, dreading it.

"It was the hunger. It ruined a lot of girls, dried them out inside, left them barren."

Barren. Stephen let out his breath. Thank God it had nothing to do with her feelings for him. "You're sure, then?"

Anna nodded, a little pinch between her brows. "I was married for nearly a year and never conceived. I went to see Dr. Wyndham once when his wife was away on holiday— he'd always been kind to me—and he said it was probably the hunger that made me barren."

Stephen studied his fist, huge and brown against the white bed linen. He didn't want to think of her with Billy Massie, trying to conceive.

"I'm sorry, Stephen. I always wanted babies. Everyone else in my family is dead."

The sadness in her voice reminded him of how much she'd suffered. Stephen rubbed her cheek, then kissed her brow and nuzzled her hair. "It's no matter, Nan. We have Rory."

"And each other."

He drew back and looked at her. "We do at that," he said and smiled. Her words warmed him, calmed him, satisfied his soul. He took her chin in his fingers and gave it a little wag. "You won't be leaving us, then, will you?"

Anna smiled, that glorious smile that creased her cheeks and softened her eyes. "Oh, you," she said, giving his chest a push. "How could I ever?"

Chapter 21

Anna pushed Stephen's old felt hat off her forehead and wiped her face with one of his big red handkerchiefs. Even at nine in the morning, the late June sunshine beat down, clear and hot.

"Where did you learn about gardening, Mose?" Anna asked.

Mose stopped chopping the ground they were preparing for Anna's garden. He leaned on his pickax and looked off down the yard. "Might look nice to plant some trees down yonder by that fence."

Anna followed his gaze. It might look nice at that, she thought, and give the place some shade, too. She wanted a pretty yard to sit in, and a garden for vegetables—tomatoes, onions, potatoes, and cabbage. Maybe some sweet corn. The Curran boys had cleared the yard of bottles and tins, tangled rope and torn boards, and Stephen had turned the outbuilding into a garden shed for tools. Now Mose was breaking up the earth while Anna trailed behind him, whacking at the big clods with the back of her hoe.

"Cherry trees," Mose said. "And plum."

Anna shaded her eyes and looked at him. He'd removed his red shirt, and his muscular torso gleamed with sweat. He seemed like a man, not a boy, though Stephen had said he was only eighteen.

"Did you work on a farm once? Is that how you know so much?"

Mose continued to gaze off toward the back fence where his fruit trees would one day blossom. "My daddy worked at a big place out in Brooklyn. Gardening."

"Did he, then?" Anna said, encouraging him. Stephen had told her that Mose's past was no one's business, but Anna couldn't help being curious. Mose was like family, sitting down to dinner with them every day and living downstairs in the room next to Davy's.

"Slave catchers got him," Mose said. "Took him and my mama back down south."

"Oh, how dreadful." Anna whacked dismally at a clump of dirt. Slavery was so cruel, especially in a country like America, which made so much noise about freedom.

"They didn't catch me, though. I run too fast for them slave catchers."

Mose swung the pickax high, then drove it into the packed earth with a fury that made Anna flinch. She gripped her hoe and resumed her chopping, watching Mose's gleaming back and the play of muscles as he worked.

Stephen had told her that before Mose came to work in the sparring room, he'd hunted rats on the garbage hills along the East River. He'd sold burlap sacks full of them to a sporting dive on Water Street where men wagered on which dog could kill the most rats. Anna had never heard of anything so filthy and disgusting. The rat pit was even worse than the livery stable the Curran boys had discovered where women stripped bare to the waist and wrestled with each other for the amusement of men.

Mose turned suddenly, brandishing the pickax. "Someday I'll go down there and find my mama and daddy," he said fiercely. "And kill them slave catchers, too."

The rage and hatred on his face shocked Anna. She stood very still, staring at him. Mose must have seen her surprise, for his anger vanished and he looked simply sad. "Don't mind me, Miz Flynn," he said, ducking his head. "I've got no place saying those things."

Anna thought of her own fury at Spinner and his mates, the helpless rage of being powerless. "You say anything you like, Mose," she said. "You're entitled, after what you've been through."

They resumed their work in silence. Anna thought how different Mose was from the other men who surrounded Stephen, noisy Irishmen who voiced their opinions whether or not anyone cared to hear. Mose rarely spoke, but beneath his calm he bore a deep, dangerous anger, the sort of anger that Stephen said every fighter needed to succeed in the ring.

"Mrs. Flynn! Mrs. Flynn!"

Anna turned to see a skinny, towheaded Curran standing at the back door, his bare toes curled on the sill.

"Eddie Curran, don't you set one foot out here without your shoes on! Haven't I told you every minute about wearing your shoes?"

Eddie waved a white paper. "It's a letter. Come by a different carriage than the one before."

Anna rested her hoe against the shed and wiped her hands on the red handkerchief. She glanced at Mose. "This garden will never get done with all the coming and going."

"No need for you tiring yourself out here in the sun," Mose said. "We'll take care of it, me and the boys."

Anna pulled off her hat and tossed it into the shed with a sigh. "Those boys."

Mose offered one of his rare smiles. "They ain't so bad, them little devils."

Anna hurried inside, thinking of the burden she'd taken on, training the Currans to do chores, teaching them their letters, keeping them clean and their bellies full. When she had enough of them, she turned them over to Mose, who let them play in the sparring room or put them to work in the yard. He scared the Currans and Rory half to death with stories about a place called the Tombs, a prison on Centre Street where criminals— even boys—could rot for years. Anna didn't favor scaring little boys, but if Mose's tales kept them out of trouble, she wouldn't complain.

In the kitchen, Eddie bent over his tablet of paper, his tongue poking out of the corner of his mouth. Eddie had taken to learning more than Mike, who squirmed and complained when she tried to teach him.

Anna glanced into the parlor where Mike stood on a stool, gazing out the window, a rag in his hand. "What's this,

Michael Curran?" Anna asked. "Staring at it won't get it clean."

Mike looked glum. His yellow hair stuck out from his head, uncombed and not especially clean, reminding Anna that it was time for a bath. "I'm resting is all. And hungry for me dinner."

"Aren't you always? Now get busy on that window and watch your fingers. I don't want to see any smudges. When you finish, I'll have a plate of biscuits for you."

Mike perked up. "Ginger biscuits?"

"What else?" Anna smiled, remembering.

Back in the kitchen, she sat down at the table across from Eddie and picked up the envelope, this time from Miss Camberwell. She had already received several notes from Mrs. Smith-Hampton, asking her to call. Mrs. Smith-Hampton had lace mending to be done, and she'd seen a fetching little lace bolero in *Journal des Modes* that she wanted Anna to make.

Anna had written back, promising to call soon. For now, though, she was swamped with work. She had the flat to look after, and men and boys to feed and keep clean, and the Crystal Palace Emporium had engaged her to supply them with crochet lace shawls. She was able to work on her lace for a few hours in the morning and at night before Stephen came upstairs. But there were too few hours in the day to do all she had set out for herself. Sometimes she found herself crossing the line from busy to frantic.

The door opened and Stephen stepped into the kitchen. "I've got Sully down in the office, trying to talk me into some boys from Providence. He's parched, asking for buttermilk."

Sully was one of the promoters who arranged Saturday night fights in the sparring room. He was partial to buttermilk and Anna's berry pie.

"Davy finished the pie," Anna said, putting down her letter, unread.

"Don't get up, Nan." Stephen disappeared into the larder.

"Bring out the pitcher," Anna called after him. "The boys will be having some milk. And take Sully a plate of biscuits."

Stephen returned, pitcher in hand. "I don't think he's one for biscuits." He peered over Eddie's shoulder at his carefully formed letters. "Well now, that's coming along. Rory can't do much better."

Mike ran in from the parlor. "I finished, Mrs. Flynn. I finished the window."

Anna would have gone in to inspect his work, but she was busy studying Miss Camberwell's letter, which included a picture of a stunning three-quarter length lace coat done in a chrysanthemum spray. Miss Camberwell wrote that she would be obliged if Anna would stop by for her measurements and complete the garment by August, when she planned to depart for Saratoga.

"Oh, how lovely," Anna said to herself, smoothing out the picture. The sleeves stopped at the elbows and the waist fit tight.

"What is it?" Stephen asked.

"A lace coat Miss Camberwell wants me to make. The loveliest you'd ever want to see." Anna glanced up, her eye catching Mike, who knelt on his chair, stuffing biscuits into his mouth. "Sit down properly and eat the biscuits one at a time. And save a few for your brother. Eddie, stop for a minute and have a bite."

She looked at Stephen, pouring buttermilk for the boys. "Where's Saratoga?"

"About two hundred miles north of here."

Anna looked back at the picture and thought of Miss Camberwell and Mrs. Smith-Hampton going off to Saratoga in their lovely clothes. "I suppose it's a grand place for a holiday."

"It's a grand place all right. Grand for doing nothing but drinking water and watching the gentry watch each other. We'll go there one day, Nan. Just you and me."

Anna gave him a look. "Oh, you're daft, Stephen Flynn. Taking me to Saratoga when I'm worried about looking decent enough to go uptown to Mrs. Smith-Hampton's place."

Stephen set the pitcher down. "Why, darling, don't you worry about looking decent enough. Once they've seen the beauty of you, Gramercy Park and Saratoga will never be the same."

"Hush your Irish nonsense," Anna said. She pushed the letter aside. "Wait here and I'll show you what I've been making."

She hurried into the bedroom and changed into a nearly finished blouse of cream silk, decorated at the neck and sleeves with a scallop of lace. The dark brown skirt, trimmed with black piping, was plain and narrow by fashion's standards, but fuller than what Anna was accustomed to. For this costume, she'd sewn a small bell-shaped hoop into the underskirt.

Back in the kitchen, she slipped on the short jacket, which matched the skirt, and spun before Stephen. "Does it look respectable so?"

He looked her over. "Respectable's not the half of it." The tone of his voice and the expression on his face told Anna that he would have come after her, had the Currans not been there.

"You look like them ladies on Broadway," Eddie said and licked his milk mustache.

"Like a picture outside the theater hall," Mike chimed in.

Anna felt embarrassed by the compliments. She busied herself folding Miss Camberwell's letter. "Fine feathers don't make a fine bird," she said. "It's time to get back to work. Eddie, I want you doing the front windows and Mike will work on his numbers."

"Aw—"

"No back answers, Michael. I'll not have you growing up too stupid to put two and two together." She looked at Stephen. "And you, Mr. Flynn. You should be getting back to business yourself. What's Sully thinking, being left all alone?"

Stephen grinned and backed toward the door. "Aye, Mrs. Flynn," he said, mimicking Mike Curran. "I'll be going along, then."

That night, as they sat in the kitchen with their tea, Anna couldn't help but fret. "There's not enough minutes in the day."

Stephen reached over and rubbed her neck. "I'll get you a housekeeper, Nan. Then you can work all day on your lace."

"I'll keep my own house, thank you very much. And do my own cooking and wash my own clothes, too. Besides, no one else would look after the Currans properly."

Stephen's fingers kneaded her shoulders, easing the tension. "It's you they want, all right. Every morning those boys are coming up the stairs calling for you."

"Oh, go on," Anna said. "It's only a good meal they're wanting. Or Rory to play with and help stir up trouble."

But she had to admit that whatever they came for—a few coins in their pockets, a good dinner, a bit of attention— Eddie and Mike showed up every day without fail. Anna fed them and Rory breakfast, and once he was off to run errands and unpack crates for Mrs. Cavanagh, she put the Currans to work. She let them sleep after dinner, for she knew they didn't get much rest at night in their noisy tenement, and when Rory came home they all played in the street or in the sparring room until supper.

"If you won't send the laundry out, why don't you and Peggy do it together?" Stephen suggested. "That way you can get your visiting done while you work."

Anna thought that was a grand idea, and so did Peggy. The following Monday the two of them bent over their washboards and steaming tubs of water in the room by the back door, laughing and talking. The Currans had turned up sick, so Anna had fed them some stewed chicken and sent them home to bed. Davy agreed to help in their place, but all he seemed good for was clowning around with the washing paddle and juggling blocks of yellow soap.

"You, Davy," Anna said, stepping back from the washboard. "Use your muscles here while I do the delicate things."

Davy thrust out his chin. "It's not man's work, scrubbing."

"I suppose it's more manly to stand around playing like a boy," Peggy said.

"Stephen said I was to haul the water from the copper," Davy said. "He said naught about scrubbing."

"All right, then, no scrubbing," Anna said. "But you have to hang things out. And be sure you hang them high, so they're not dragging in the dirt. Now pour out that bucket that's bleaching and give the things here for a scrub."

Davy went reluctantly out to the line. Peggy watched him through the window, pushing her sleeves up on her plump red arms. "Look at that man. Why, Peter Crowley would sooner drop dead than hang out a wet pair of drawers."

From the tone of her voice, Anna couldn't tell if she was complimenting Davy or not. "He doesn't mind so much," Anna said. "Davy's about as easy as an old shoe."

"Oh, he's a fool," Peggy said, turning away from the window.

"He's fond of you, Peg. It's plain to see."

Peggy shrugged. "Well, he looks a sight better than he did at first. Why, that first day he looked like he'd just rolled out of a bog."

Peggy's cheeks glowed from the heat, and sweat dampened her brow. Such a lovely, healthy girl, Anna thought, perfect for Davy. She'd shame him into working, and he'd make her laugh for the rest of her years.

"He'll never be rich like Peter Crowley," Peggy said. "Peter will be owning a butcher shop one day."

Anna twisted the water out of a lace-trimmed petticoat. "Davy may never own a shop, but he's got a light heart and a good mind, and he hardly drinks a drop. In time, he'll find his place here, Peg, and make something of himself."

Peggy ran her finger along the edge of her brass-bound tub, a thoughtful expression on her face. "He isn't always putting his hands on my front and rucking up my skirt, either."

Anna stared, shocked. "Never! Oh, Peggy, sure Peter Crowley doesn't do that!"

Peggy looked embarrassed. "He wants me to give in to him. He says everybody does it before they marry. 'Twould be a sign I love him."

"Oh, but you wouldn't!"

"No." Peggy's voice was tentative. "It's a mortal sin, I know that, and more than once I've slapped him good."

Anna bent over her washtub, biting her lips. *A mortal sin.* She thought of lying with Stephen, doing things that made her heart nearly stop with delight, when all the while she was married to another.

"Now you think I'm wicked for speaking so," Peggy said.

Anna looked up. "Oh, no, I don't, Peg. I swear I don't."

"I've got no one else to tell. My mam would kill me if she knew I let Peter touch me so." She hesitated and flushed pinker. "I don't like him so much, but I don't mind his hands, you see. I don't mind at all how it feels. It's a sin all right, feelings like that with no love."

Anna scrubbed hard at her board. She wished she could speak frankly about a woman's feelings, but she had yet to sort out her own. "You keep yourself for the man you love, Peggy. That's all I can say."

Peggy gazed back toward the window, watching Davy struggle with a petticoat. "That Davy Ryan, I'm a fool to even look at him. I'd sooner take the Holy Orders than marry a man like him." But there was a softness in her eyes, and she cocked her head and smiled.

They finished the laundry by midafternoon, so Anna had time to put the final touches on her new costume. The following morning she tidied up the breakfast things, sent the Currans outside to work in the garden, and caught the omnibus uptown.

She had been out in the city any number of times. On fine afternoons she and Peggy strolled west to Broadway, arm in arm, gorging their eyes on displays behind plate-glass windows guarded by polished brass bars. They watched the uptown ladies dismounting from carriages in front of A. T. Stewart's and H & L Peck and A. Arnold & Co., their silks and taffetas sweeping the pavement. Sometimes, Anna would pull Peggy into Stewart's vast vaulted palace to gaze upon acres of goods and hundreds of salespeople. Afterward they'd sit at a marble-top table at the Vienna Bakery, on the corner of Broadway and Tenth, and eat pink ice cream and dainty little cakes.

When Stephen took her out, it was much different. He wasn't a man for elegance, so they ate at Bowery oyster bars and in cafés that catered to shopgirls and mechanics. They listened to loud music and bawdy stories at the Bowery Theater or Niblo's Garden. Stephen loved the Bowery night-life, and when Anna was with him, it suited her just fine.

She no longer thought of leaving him. She had saved nearly a hundred dollars in the Bowery Savings Bank, and she would make another fifty from Mrs. Smith-Hampton's bolero and Miss Camberwell's coat. A few more opera bags and shawls for the Crystal Palace Emporium and she could pay Stephen his money and go off on her own, supporting herself with her lacework.

But she didn't plan to leave.

She was an adulteress, she knew, and in the eyes of the church she was living in infamy. She'd not dared attend mass since the night she'd first lain with Stephen, and she hardly ever prayed any longer, not wanting to attract God's attention. It was Peggy who took Rory to church.

But while she missed the ceremony and comfort of religion, Anna had never felt so happy. The past had somehow slipped away, taking with it memories of loneliness and struggle. For too long she'd had no love, no companionship, no one but herself. Now that she'd found a safe and loving home, she wouldn't give it up.

The omnibus bell rang. Anna saw that they were passing a tree-filled park with sturdy iron fences, which had to be Union Square. Stephen had instructed her to get off the bus four blocks past the square. Anna fumbled in her bag and took out Mrs. Smith-Hampton's card, then looked out the window again. The neighborhood was beautiful and peaceful in the morning sunshine, like being in the country. There were trees and gardens and shrubs and great piles of houses—more being built, too, from the look of it. All over New York, houses were going up and new streets were being laid out. Anna marveled at the city's restless energy, the sounds of commerce and construction, the endless bustle. It seemed that nothing stood still for a minute.

At Twenty-first Street, a man jumped out and handed Anna down, then left her alone in the lazy sunshine. She heard birds chirp and the faraway sound of chimes. A policeman in a blue uniform studded with brass buttons and a baton in his belt, touched his cap and wished her good day. Anna returned the greeting, straightened her straw hat, then proceeded across East Twenty-first. She studied the house numbers, smelled the fragrance of roses, listened to the distant shouts of playing children. The uptown children didn't seem to make as much noise as Bowery children. Anna thought of evenings on Brace Street, standing on the curbstone with the neighborhood women, gossiping as they watched the children at their rackety games.

Anna stopped before a four-story house across from an enclosed park. Like the others beside it, number 9 was a plain brownstone with a cast-iron rail. Anna glanced at the downstairs entrance and decided to go straight up the scrubbed stone steps to the front door.

She twisted the polished brass knob in the center of the door, and a bell jangled inside. The door opened and a maid in a black dress and long white apron welcomed her with a cheerful greeting.

It was lofty and quiet inside the entryway, but dimly lit. As she followed the maid toward the staircase, Anna peered through the darkness at the severe paintings on the walls, the drab, serious carpets on the floor and thought of her own bright sunny place, with neighbors and children coming in and out and the smell of cabbage and onions and baking bread.

Bless me, she thought, I'll keep that life for this any day.

The upstairs sitting room was stuffed with great dark pieces of furniture, and everything seemed to have fringe on it, from the draperies to the lampshades.

Mrs. Smith-Hampton rushed to greet her. "How lovely to see you!" she exclaimed. "Don't you look well. Why, surely New York agrees with you." She took Anna by the shoulders and pressed her cheek with her own.

"Oh, yes'm," Anna said, standing stiff in Mrs. Smith-Hampton's embrace. "Sure, it agrees with me."

"The heat is dreadful this time of year, don't you think? I can hardly bear it."

"It is at that," Anna replied. The poor woman would feel better, she thought, if she let in a bit of sunlight and opened a window or two.

"Do sit down. We'll have some tea, and I want you to tell me all about yourself and Mr. Flynn and how you're getting on. Then we'll discuss the little projects I have in mind for you."

By the time tea arrived, Anna's eyes had grown accustomed to the dark, and she found that she was enjoying herself. She told Mrs. Smith-Hampton about Rory and the Currans, about Davy and Peggy, and how Stephen was keeping his promise not to fight again. She talked about the lacework she was doing for the Crystal Palace Emporium and mentioned that she'd heard from Miss Camberwell.

"I have wonderful news myself," Mrs. Smith-Hampton said, smiling mysteriously. "I'm to have a child." She covered her cheeks with her palms, as if the idea of it filled her with unbearable excitement.

"Oh, isn't that grand!" Anna exclaimed, feeling a genuine delight at the lady's good fortune.

They talked about the baby, not due for months, and Mrs. Smith-Hampton's good health and her husband's happiness.

"He'd quite given up on me, I'm afraid," she said and blushed with pride.

Anna felt a brief pang of envy, thinking how complete she would feel having Stephen's children. Then she reminded herself that it was a blessing she was barren, that she couldn't conceive a child in sin.

When they'd said all that could be said about the baby, the conversation turned to lace jackets and opera bags and freshening summer bonnets with ribbons and trim. Anna was so enjoying herself that when the clock chimed eleven, she realized she'd talked with Mrs. Smith-Hampton for nearly an hour without once feeling shy.

They said their good-byes upstairs, and Anna departed with the maid. At the bottom of the staircase, the girl said, "The master would like a word."

"Mr. Smith-Hampton?" Anna asked, surprised.

"Come this way."

They went down a dark paneled hallway to an office that reeked of cigar smoke. Mr. Smith-Hampton, seated behind his desk, heaved himself to his feet. He looked plumper and rosier than ever, his second chin folded into his collar. He glanced over Anna's skirt and jacket, a playful sparkle in his eyes. "Good morning, Mrs. Flynn. Don't you look handsome."

Anna lowered her eyes and stared at her new cream-colored gloves. "Go on, Mr. Smith-Hampton. Your wife, now, she looks lovely."

"Quite so, quite so."

"And such grand news. The baby, I mean." Anna flushed, remembering it was improper to mention unborn babies in the presence of gentlemen.

"Indeed," Mr. Smith-Hampton said, rocking back on his heels. "I hope the little creature makes her happy. Now, Mrs. Flynn, I know a lady who is most anxious to avail herself of your lace-making services."

"Oh, that would be grand, sir," Anna said, wondering how she would fit this new client into her busy schedule.

"She lives at the St. Nicholas Hotel, a suite on the second floor. She's available most mornings. Would it be convenient for you to stop by on Thursday?"

"Thursday would be fine, sir."

"Good." Mr. Smith-Hampton took out a visiting card and scrawled something. "There," he said, handing it to Anna. "I'm sure Mrs. Sinclair will have plenty for you to do."

"Thank you, sir," Anna said, taking the card. "Good day, then."

She didn't look at the card until she was out in the sunshine. She stopped at the curbstone and stared at Horace Smith-Hampton's name, engraved with abundant flourishes. She turned the card over, where he had written,"Mrs. Violet Sinclair, Suite 210, St. Nicholas Hotel, Broadway between Spring and Broome."

How odd that he would know a woman who lived at a hotel, Anna thought. Perhaps she was the wife of one of his associates. Then the truth dawned. Anna's felt a rush of astonishment that caused her jaw to drop.

His mistress! Dear heaven, it could be no other!

She felt such a surge of indignation that she almost tore the card to pieces. But on second thought, she decided to show it to Stephen, to show how brazen Mr. Smith-Hampton was, how utterly without moral character, and then she'd tear the blasted thing to bits and throw it in the trash bin.

Anna stuck the card in her bag and set off at a brisk pace. She fumed all the way across Twenty-first Street. The cheek of the man, she thought, expecting her to serve his mistress in the very same way she served his wife! As if she had no loyalty, no loyalty at all.

She made a turn at Fifth and headed south, following Stephen's directions to Miss Camberwell's place, too annoyed to enjoy the fine buildings, the passing carriages, the elegantly mounted ladies. When she reached the mansion at the corner of Fourteenth, Anna was sweating hard and nearly faint from heat and thirst. But she stomped up the steps, gripping the balustrade of solid granite, and sailed between the fluted columns flanking the doorway.

Miss Camberwell received her in a downstairs sitting room, offering a welcome glass of lemonade. As Anna gulped down the cool, tart drink she thought that Miss Camberwell didn't appear as smug as she had aboard the *Mary Drew*. She looked pouty and bored; perhaps she'd always been so, Anna thought, and she'd been to intimidated to notice.

But she felt no nervousness now; she felt annoyed. She took Miss Camberwell's measurements while the young lady babbled on about August in Saratoga.

"We'll be going there ourselves," Anna said, pausing to make a notation of Miss Camberwell's admirable waist measurement.

"To Saratoga?" Miss Camberwell sounded incredulous. "You?"

"Me and Mr. Flynn and Rory, too." Anna glanced at her startled face, damp with perspiration, and wondered why the gentry didn't open their windows and get a breeze in. "We'll be staying in a big hotel."

"No one will speak to you," Miss Camberwell said frostily. "I hope you realize that."

Anna took Miss Camberwell by the shoulders and turned her abruptly. "I'll not be going there to talk. I'll be taking the water and watching the horses with Mr. Frank Gillespie, the famous sporting writer. He promised to educate me about horse racing."

That seemed to shut Miss Camberwell up. She barely said a word for the remainder of the measuring session. She even came up with an advance payment for the lace jacket when Anna requested it.

When Anna stepped out into the Fifth Avenue sunshine, she felt more than satisfied with herself. When it came to dealing with the gentry, she decided, she could quite hold her own.

Chapter 22

Stephen roared with laughter that night when Anna told him about Mrs. Violet Sinclair. "Of course you'll call on her," he said. "And why shouldn't you? If you don't do her lacework, she'll find someone else. You'll not be better off by refusing."

"But it's like I'm approving of her," Anna protested. "Why, it's terrible, Mr. Smith-Hampton going up to that hotel, and herself at home carrying his baby. And imagine what he called his own child—a little creature, that's what, like it was a kitten or a wee pup for her to play with."

Stephen pushed aside his teacup. "Don't be too hard on the man, darling. Your standards are too high for this world."

His words seemed to give Anna pause. When she spoke, her tone was thoughtful. "It's true, isn't it? Here I am judging a man and his mistress when I'm no better myself."

She looked so melancholy that Stephen reached out and covered her hand with his. "Now, what are you saying?"

Anna traced the edge of her cup with her finger and made no response. Stephen watched her with growing apprehension, wondering if she was thinking of herself living with him or of some unspeakable thing in her past. Nothing would change the way he felt about Anna. But he worried about her, that she would think too deeply and judge herself too harshly, then run away from him in shame.

"Tell me, Nan. What is it?"

She looked up, and the expression on her face alarmed him. She was remembering something terrible, he knew it.

"There's things about me, Stephen. Things I want to tell, but I'm afraid to."

He steeled himself for the worst. "Come on, then. There's no secrets between us."

Her blue eyes darkened with tears. "You'll hate me."

Stephen squeezed her hand. "Never, darling."

Anna wet her lips and began to speak, haltingly, her voice uncertain. "It happened to me when I was a girl. During the hunger. Soon after we buried my mam and the little boys. I went into town with my da and my brother, Sean. Da wanted to sell his books, his last precious things. The shopkeeper wouldn't take them. No one would want old books, he said."

She stopped speaking and wove her fingers with Stephen's, holding tight. He didn't take his eyes off her troubled face. "Go on, then," he said.

She told him. His kindness made it all spill out of her. She told about the smell of blight and starvation as they walked to town, about her exhaustion and hunger, her father's silent grief. At the shop, full of tantalizing smells, her father left the children and went to see the priest about the books. The shopkeeper pinched Anna's cheek and told her to come back one evening. In exchange for a kiss, he said, he would give her a sack of meal and two chickens.

A kiss, she'd thought, was a small price to pay for enough meal to feed them for a week.

She returned two nights later and waited in the rear of the shop. When the shopkeeper came to her, it wasn't a kiss he wanted. He shoved her to the floor and tore her dress. He put his hands on her legs and pushed his fingers inside her and squeezed and bit her. He climbed on her, and the pain was terrible. She struggled, but she was too weak from hunger to fight, and her screams were no more than whimpers. When he finished, he was angry. He gave her a sack of meal, but no chickens, and she stumbled away, stunned and weeping.

Anna bowed her head. Her fingers gripped Stephen's hand. He stared at her in horror.

"I was only twelve," she said, "and so hungry. I couldn't fight back."

Stephen glanced away, not trusting himself to speak.

"My da knew right away. He looked at my dress, at my face. He saw the blood. Oh, I hardly had any bosom to bother with, yet that man had scratched and bit me there." She spoke very softly. "My da looked at me with such sadness, and then he sat down and wept. You see, I was his treasured girl."

Stephen's sorrow boiled into rage. He pounded his fist on the table. "What father wouldn't weep, not able to feed his family or take revenge when his daughter is dishonored?"

"He died of it. My da died because of what I did."

"For the love of God, Anna!" Stephen was on his feet. "Sure, you're not blaming yourself?"

She looked up, startled.

"Listen to me," he said, trying to keep his anger in check. "England starved you. English policies. The potato crop failed, and still they took Ireland's corn and wheat and livestock for themselves. They let the people starve rather than give away one grain of meal, all in the hallowed name of protection."

Stephen sat down and dropped his head into his hands. He was ranting about political injustice because he couldn't bear to think of Anna being violated on a shop's dusty floor.

"English policies had nothing to do with it," Anna said sadly. "We all have a will of our own, don't we? I went to the shop. I took the meal and carried it home. My da was shamed to death, thinking I'd traded myself for it."

Stephen sat back in his chair and sighed. "You didn't trade yourself, Nan—" He stopped abruptly, understanding what was behind her confession. "Before God, you think your father died because of you?"

Tears shone again in her eyes. "He never spoke of that night, but I saw how he looked at me. Ever after, he was as silent as doom. He had no heart left. When he died, he died of shame."

"Christ. You really think that."

Anna wiped her cheeks. "We took to the road, heading to Dublin. My da said we couldn't stay in our place anymore, not after what happened. He said we'd go to England to work in the factories. We went with another family who had a cart. My brother Sean took sick with road fever. He was dead by Limerick. My da died near Kilbeggan." Anna paused. "He was walking and he fell down. He lay there, gasping, trying to talk. But he said nothing. And I forgot to say good-bye. I forgot to tell him I was sorry."

She wept softly. Stephen went around to her and pulled her to her feet. He kissed her wet cheeks, her eyes, her lips. She wrapped her arms about him and pressed her face against his shoulder.

Stephen held her close, his throat tight with pity. "Ah, Nan. It's all past. There's nothing we can do." He wished he could say more, he wished he could offer some comfort, but Anna's feelings were buried deep, beyond his reach.

They prepared for bed in silence. When they lay together, Anna went on with her story, telling Stephen how she'd reached Dublin, nearly dead from exhaustion and sickness. She found her way to a workhouse where she stayed with other poor girls, sewing for paupers. Dr. Wyndham, who treated the workhouse children for their ailments, was a kind man. He praised Anna's lacework and took a sample of it to his wife. Then he brought her to his home.

"They were good to me, the Wyndhams, but I was lonely, missing my family. I wanted to make a family of my own. I didn't want to be in service all my life."

She rested her cheek against Stephen's chest and told him about meeting Billy on the strand, their courtship, her mistress's anger when she left.

"Did he treat you well?"

Anna could tell from Stephen's voice that he hated Billy Massie, that he wanted to forget his existence. "He never raised a hand against me."

"Did he know about what happened in the shop?"

"No. It wasn't like that with us, talking of such things. He was always out and about, brawling and boasting with his mates."

Stephen said nothing. When he spoke next, his voice was tense. "Did you love him?"

She'd expected the question. "I did my duty by him. I thought I would grow to love him, but I didn't."

He smoothed her hair, and Anna sensed his relief. "Your father saved you, Nan, leaving Kerry when he did. Otherwise, you'd have starved."

Anna nestled closer, laying her palm on his warm belly. She moved her hand lower and stroked him. Stephen kissed her mouth and thought how much he wanted to keep her safe and make her happy. He took her hand away from him. "You don't want that tonight, not after all you've remembered."

"Oh, yes," she said, twining her leg about his. "Tonight especially. It would be a comfort."

Despite the bright morning sunshine, the saloon was dim, kept so to lessen the scorching heat that had descended on the city. The door to the street was propped wide open, seeking a breeze but instead admitting Brace Street's sounds of commerce and the hot, fetid smells of summer.

Light from one open shutter fell across the table where Stephen, in his shirt-sleeves, sat with the newspaper. He looked up at the sound of clinking glass. Emmet stood on the walking board behind the bar, dusting and measuring bottles.

Emmet seemed to be in fine spirits these days. No doubt he was dreaming about his role as hero of the next Irish rising, or at least as hero of the scheme to deliver guns from Birmingham to Cork.

Stephen yawned and turned the page, scanning an article about the fight over Kansas, whether it should be admitted to the Union as a slave state or free. He enjoyed this part of the morning, when the saloon was quiet. As was his custom, he'd gotten up at five o'clock for a workout with Mose. He'd seen to the unloading of a shipment of beer later on, and then he'd taken the brewery agent, a large, good-natured German, upstairs for a piece of pie, a glass of cold buttermilk, and a vigorous argument over the rise in the price of a barrel of beer.

"Da, Anna's asking if you want some lemonade."

Stephen looked up as Rory, bare-chested in the heat, trudged through the door from the sparring room. His hunched posture and hangdog expression aroused Stephen's suspicions.

"What's doing, sport? Why aren't you off to Mrs. Cavanagh's?"

Rory's expression grew more pained. "My belly hurts, but Anna says I can't stay home."

Stephen grinned. "I'd say nothing ails you but the notion of work."

Rory leaned on the table beside Stephen's elbow and stared with interest at the newspaper, his pains forgotten. "Did Gil write a story today?"

Stephen pointed to an item. "The yacht regatta at Montauk Point."

"Oh." Rory sounded disappointed. "Nothing about you?"

"Now, why would Gil write about me when I'm not doing anything?"

Rory squirmed impatiently. "I wish you'd fight, Da."

Stephen hooked an arm around the boy's shoulders. "Anna would kill me if I did. Besides, you know I'm through with fighting."

Rory sighed, and Stephen tickled his skinny ribs. "I'll say yes to the lemonade. And bring some for Emmet."

"And for me," said Davy, who wandered sleepily into the saloon. He grabbed the broom and began pushing sawdust across the floor. "A slice of pie would be grand. The one with the berries."

"It's finished, Davy," Stephen said.

Davy leaned on his broom. "But Anna promised it to me. I only had one piece."

"Sorry, Davy," Stephen said, raising his arms in a satisfying stretch. "If I'd known, I wouldn't have taken a bite."

Stephen looked back at the newspaper but found he couldn't concentrate. He wished Rory hadn't brought up the subject of fighting. Plans for the exhibition match with Maguire wouldn't be sorted out until John O'Mahony returned from a speech-making trip to raise money for the cause. But Stephen would have to tell Anna, and tell her soon, before she heard about the match from someone else. Sure as he was born, she'd not be pleased.

Rory returned bearing a sweating pitcher and a plate of currant cake. "Anna said no more pies. It's too hot for baking, and she won't be making a fire until it's cool again."

"No fire at all?" Davy said in dismay. "What will we be eating, then?"

"You'll be eating the free lunch we put out on the bar every day," Emmet said in disgust. "Is that all you can think about, your belly?"

Davy went back to his sweeping, red-faced and glum. Stephen felt sorry that Emmet had spoken so harshly. For all his passion for justice, Emmet felt superior for having been born in America. He looked down on Davy and the other greenhorns. Emmet would never understand that like all those who'd starved during the famine, Davy would never take food for granted.

The thought of the famine reminded Stephen of Anna's confession last night, and his anger flared. By God, he thought fiercely, he could do nothing to change the past, but he would see to it that Anna never suffered again.

"You're really going to Ireland to fight, Emmet?"

Stephen looked up from his paper. Rory stood on the brass footrail, his arms on the bar, watching Emmet polish the woodwork with his chamois cloth.

Emmet exchanged glances with Stephen. "How d'you know about it, Rory?"

"Peggy says you hate the English and want to drive them out."

Emmet bent over his work. "I'm not the only one hates the English."

"You're not even Irish, not like you were born there."

Stephen got up from the table. He went to the bar and poured himself some lemonade. He wondered if Rory was just talking or if he'd heard something about the plan for the guns and Emmet's role in it.

"I'm as Irish as you are," Emmet said to Rory, his face taking on an earnest flush. "My own father came here from Ireland, forced out by the landlord wanting his land. My da was a good man when he left there. He came here and died in a brawl."

Rory maintained a respectful silence while Emmet rubbed the bar vigorously, his anger growing more visible as he worked. "The English broke his heart and drove him from his home. Because of them I grew up not knowing my own da. They forced him and my mam out of Ireland, and he died, drunk and fighting."

After a thoughtful pause, Rory said, "I never knew my mam, neither. But I never really minded, because I had my gran and now I have Anna. Just because your da's dead don't mean you've got to fight the English. You've still got your mam and Peggy and us, too."

Emmet scrubbed at the beer taps and said nothing. Stephen could see him getting red in the neck, evidence that he'd heard enough of Rory's views.

"Where did you learn all this, young Flynn?" Stephen asked. "About Emmet going off to fight?"

"Peggy was telling Anna. She said their ma don't want him to go." He lowered his voice. "I heard some about the guns, too, but I won't say nothing."

Stephen looked at Emmet. By God, he couldn't believe he was hearing this, that Emmet had been so careless. "Get along with you, Rory," he said. "And you, too, Davy. I want to talk to our Emmet."

Davy looked up from his sweeping. His red hair was plastered to his sweating forehead. "But what about this I'm doing? You want it done before the lunch crowd."

"Later," Stephen said, more sharply than he'd intended.

When they were alone, Stephen exploded. "What under the shining God are you doing, telling Peggy and your mother about the guns? I thought you had a brain, Emmet. Don't you know if word gets out, some informer will be behind closed doors with the British consul? Back in Dublin they'll be preparing cells in Kilmainham prison to welcome a new crop of Irish martyrs."

Emmet's flush darkened. "She was crying when I told her I was going. I had to explain."

"And isn't she crying more now, knowing of the guns? And more still if you're locked up in prison? By God, Emmet!" Stephen was appalled that he would tell even his dearest kin about so serious a matter as transporting guns. "It could be worse than prison for you. At least there's hope from a prison. There's none from the grave."

"I'm sorry, Stephen."

Stephen ran a hand over his face. "I'll be speaking to your mother and Peggy and Anna, too. I'm sure they'll keep their tongues still. But Rory, now, he'll be tempted to brag to the Currans and all the other little lads. And then won't the news spread."

That evening Stephen talked to the Cavanagh women, warning them of the danger to Emmet if word got out about the purpose of his mission. For appearances, he was going to Ireland to visit his relatives, to take them money and encourage them to emigrate to America.

Pale with fright, Peggy and her mother agreed. They promised not to breathe a word of the scheme.

Anna was less docile. "Didn't you just get him into this, Stephen!" she scolded later that night. "And now his mother and Peggy are crying their eyes out."

Stephen lay back on the bed, his arm crooked over his eyes. "Emmet wants to go. He's his own man when it comes to this."

"His own man!" Anna brushed angrily at her hair. "Emmet wouldn't so much as bless himself without looking to you for approval."

"He's man enough to do what he thinks best," Stephen said. "It may even be good for him, put some years on him. And Paddy McCarthy has the sense of ten men. He'll let nothing happen in haste."

Anna laid down her brush and ran her hands over her hair. She wasn't so much angry as frightened, for she'd grown fond of Emmet. And Peggy and Mrs. Cavanagh were her dearest friends.

"And what of Rory?" she asked. "Did you speak to him?"

Stephen lifted the arm that shielded his eyes. The lamplight lit the gold in his hair and deepened the lines of worry between his brows. "I told him it's not a boy's game and that he'd best forget what he heard. I only hope to God he takes my warning."

Anna saw Stephen's distress and heard it in his voice, and she wished she hadn't spoken so harshly. She thought of his tenderness last night when she'd unburdened herself of her terrible secret. Stephen had learned the worst of her, and he'd accepted it. More than that, he'd offered her comfort and soothed her guilt.

She went to the bed and sat down beside him.

He looked at her. "I'm worried, Nan."

She ran her hands down his deep-muscled chest, covered with soft golden-brown hair. He wore nothing but his snug fighting drawers. Anna was tempted to unfasten the buttons and do what always made him smile, but the time was not right. Instead, she pinched his big bare toes.

"Rory's a sensible child. And he loves Emmet. He'll not say a word."

Stephen sighed. "I hope so, darling. I hope it all comes out right in the end."

Stephen was working in his office above the sparring room when he heard unfamiliar footsteps on the back stairs. He looked up from his ledgers and ran a shirt-sleeved arm across his forehead. It was the third day of breathless heat. The door to the hallway stood open, as did the window at his back, but not a breath of air stirred.

The footsteps came closer, and a slim, dapper figure appeared in the doorway. He leaned on his walking stick and surveyed the disorderly room. "Untidy, I'd say. A bit like my own office at college."

Stephen slapped his palms on the desk. "Shaw," he said, getting to his feet. "By God, I wondered what happened to you. I figured some pug tossed you in the gutter weeks ago."

"I've been spared—for the moment, at least." Despite the weather, Shaw's tie was tight, his collar stiff, and his hands encased in leather gloves. "I took an unexpected journey to Washington. Guest of your esteemed Senator Preston King." Shaw removed his brushed beaver hat, drew a handkerchief from his breast pocket, and dabbed at his brow. "Beastly weather. Worse in Washington. Can't understand why you Americans selected that swamp as the site for the capital of your nation."

Stephen poured a tumbler of water, which Shaw drank down gratefully, then motioned his guest to a seat. "I suppose you've had your fill of the politicians' noise about Kansas," Stephen said.

"Fascinating debate." Shaw set the glass on the desk, peeled off his gloves, and smoothed his mustache with two fingers. "This slavery business gets quite nasty when it comes to admitting new states to your union. Free-soilers on one side and proslavery chaps on the other. From what I hear, the Irish favor the institution, afraid the freed black men will run north and steal all the jobs."

Stephen drummed his fingers on the arm of his chair. "There's plenty of Irish hypocrites, that's for sure. In Ireland, they cry out for insurrection, for freedom from the English slave masters. Once in America, they decide slavery's not such a bad idea, at least when it comes to keeping the black man in chains."

"Speaking of insurrection, there's all sorts of rumors flying about. Guns, I hear. Invasion. A peasant rising." Shaw folded his hands on the head of his walking stick and gave Stephen a shrewd look. "Surely you're not ignorant of the talk."

"Do you think I'd tell you, one way or the other?"

"Of course not," Shaw said with a small smile. "Wouldn't be wise at all, seeing as how I'm to dine with the British consul this very evening."

Stephen stared at him stonily, feeling a rising anger. "What do you want here, Shaw? Is it information you're sniffing out to pass on to your English friends?"

Shaw raised his eyes to the ceiling. "My dear Flynn, let me make it quite clear that I'm in search of nothing more than a few sparring lessons for the purpose of defending myself in this wretched city. I have no interest in betraying your cause, whatever it might be."

Stephen knew he would be mad to allow Shaw anywhere near the Emerald Flame Saloon, where men talked treason at all hours, where Emmet stood behind the bar, his dreams of guns and spilled English blood all but visible to anyone who might glance his way. But by God, Stephen liked Shaw. During their long talks aboard the *Mary Drew*, he'd grown to admire the man, even trust him—more than he did some Irishmen with mouths too big to stay shut.

"All right, then. But I'll be keeping an eye on you."

Shaw smiled. "No doubt you will. Now tell me. How fares that wife of yours, our lovely Anna?"

The heat continued. On Saturday morning, after a stifling, sleepless night, Stephen said to Anna, "How would you like to go to a place where there's a cool breeze and an ocean of water to wade in?"

Anna moaned against her pillow. She felt sticky and exhausted. "Wouldn't I love that?"

"It's the island where I fought Maguire. It's lovely and cool there. Let's go out for a few days, you and Rory and me."

Anna rolled over and looked at him. "Oh, Stephen, do you mean it?"

"There's a pretty beach, and lots of paths and lakes. And an inn with big comfortable beds and breezes in every room."

"We could sleep."

Stephen wiggled his eyebrows. "And do other things."

Anna pulled his head down and gave him a hard kiss on the mouth. "I'd like that."

Rory wanted the Curran twins to go. And when Davy came up for breakfast, he looked so crestfallen at the prospect of being left behind that Anna said, "Oh, Davy, come along, then."

Davy said, "If Peggy came, she and I could look after the young ones."

Anna looked at Stephen. He threw up his hands. His plan for a holiday alone with Anna had turned into a neighborhood outing.

They took a steamer to Bridgeport, Connecticut. From there, they took a launch across the glistening waters of Long Island Sound to Guardian Island. It was a glorious place, breezy and ever so peaceful. Anna fell in love with the windmills and rolling hills, the old tombstones and fishing huts. Stephen took them to the meadow where he'd fought Maguire. Davy and the boys listened wide-eyed as Stephen recounted the fight, while Anna and Peggy gazed out at the broad, sweeping Atlantic, where steamers and white-sailed pleasure craft passed back and forth and gulls coasted on the air.

After a picnic in the meadow, they went down to the beach. The men and boys stripped to their trousers and plunged into the water, diving and wrestling and tossing one another about, while Anna and Peggy waded along the shore, their skirts tucked up to their knees, daring each other to sit down in the waves and get their drawers wet.

That night they dined on oysters and salmon at the inn. The boys, worn out and sunburned, were asleep as soon as darkness came. Peggy slept in a room with Rory, and Davy looked after the twins.

When they were alone in their own room, Stephen took Anna in his arms. She leaned against him, listening to the curtains snap in the breeze, smelling the salt-laden air coming through the window. Neither of them spoke, but Anna could sense Stephen's contentment. She'd watched his face all day, eager as a boy's as he wrestled and shouted with Davy and the children. She blessed the island for giving him a rest from his worries about politics and guns and loose-tongued Irishmen.

Stephen rested his lips on her hair, and she knew he wanted to say something. When he spoke, his voice was soft and hesitant. "The day I fought Maguire, I looked out over the Sound and imagined coming here with Rory. I thought to myself, I'm not alone any longer. I have a son. I'm beginning a grand new life." His voice drifted to a whisper. "Dear God, I was happy, thinking of that boy."

Anna rubbed his bare back. It radiated warmth, as if he had absorbed the sun.

"And now I have you, Nan. With the two of you, I feel I have the world."

Anna pulled back and looked at him. The sun had turned Stephen's face a deep brown and had streaked his hair with gold. He looked breathtaking in the soft lamplight, a rough beauty, with his scars and lines and the tough skin around his eyes. Anna touched his cheek. "You're beautiful."

The melancholy expression vanished, and his eyes filled with mischief. "And skillful, too. Never has there been such a lover of women."

Anna pressed a finger to his lips. "Only me. I don't want you loving anyone else."

His arms tightened around her. "By all that's holy, darling, I couldn't get stiff for anyone but your own sweet self."

Anna hugged his waist. She thought of their glorious afternoon, of the boys' quick bodies, their happy shrieks, of Davy and Peggy exchanging secret smiles and touching hands. She thought of Stephen bare-chested in the sun, his powerful torso glistening wet, and the expression on his face when he'd looked at her. She wondered what it would be like to live here on the island, far from real life, with the sun and the breeze and the sea, with Stephen making her laugh, and doing things that no longer seemed wicked.

"I love this place."

Stephen pulled a pin from her hair, then another. "I'll build a house for us. Down on the south cove."

"A house! Stephen, you're daft."

"A little house. It wouldn't cost much. You and Rory could come here for the summer, away from the dirt and heat of the city."

Anna thought how it would be to have a little house of their own, here on the island. But she could never stay away from Brace Street for the whole summer. What would happen to her lace business, and how could she live without seeing her neighbors each day, without Stephen in her bed each night? "I couldn't live here, Stephen. I'd miss everyone. I'd miss you."

He was taking down her hair, smoothing out the tangles with his fingers. "Then we'll come here together. All of us. The whole neighborhood, if you like. We'll take a holiday and fill the place. We'll have lanterns outside and steam oysters on the shore. But once in a while, it will be just you and me, Nan. We'll come to our little house and take off every stitch of clothing and swim naked."

Anna drew in a breath. "Never!"

"And then I'll lay you down on the sand and come inside you and we'll roll around like puppies. I saw just the place today."

"In broad daylight, for anyone to see?"

He grinned at her. "And who's to see but some tired old gulls?"

Anna laughed, feeling excited.

"Look at this, now," Stephen said, stepping back. "Just talking about it and I'm as stiff as a poker."

Anna laid her hand there, feeling the swollen heat of him. Stephen drew her close and kissed her. His lips felt smooth and hungry. He spread his fingers in her hair, gripping hard, and the more she stroked him, the more desperate were his kisses.

"Nan." His voice was ragged, breathless. His passion made Anna's insides quiver and her knees go weak. Each time it was new again, the way Stephen wanted her, the way he made her feel.

He crushed her to him. Anna kissed his cheek and caressed his rough, damp hair. Touching her lips to his ear, she whispered to him, telling him what she wanted. In one smooth motion he scooped her into his arms and carried her to the bed.

Anna slept hard, too deep for dreams. When she woke, the sun was bright in the sky. Stephen was already awake, his hands folded behind his head, staring at the ceiling. Anna slipped her hand between her cheek and the pillow and gazed at him. "What are you thinking, then?"

"About Davy. I'm thinking of having him take Emmet's place at the saloon when Emmet goes to Ireland." He looked at her. "What do you think of it, darling? Is our Davy clever enough to manage things?"

Anna rose up on her elbow, wide awake. "It would be grand for him. I know he could do it if you gave him the chance."

"The lads like him, and he's got an easy manner. I was thinking of Tully, but he hasn't a head for figures."

"Davy can figure well enough," Anna said. "He's helped Rory with his schoolwork and the Currans with their sums."

Stephen reached out to push Anna's hair off her face. She'd slept with it loose last night, a wild mass of curls that had felt like feathers against his skin. He took a handful and crushed it in his fingers. "We'll try it, then," he said. "I'll speak to Davy and Emmet and have him start learning the business."

Anna's eager face told him that he'd made the right decision. "Davy will work hard," she said. "If only to win the admiration of Peggy."

"He'd best work hard to win the admiration of me," Stephen said. He lay back on the pillow and resumed his observation of the ceiling. "Nan," he said after a moment, "you're sure Shaw is to be trusted?"

He had told her about Shaw's visit and his concerns about the man. Anna had sworn that Mr. Shaw was honorable, but his association with the British still worried Stephen.

"Mr. Shaw would never abuse a man's hospitality," Anna said. "He would never come to our place to spy."

Stephen rubbed his rough-whiskered cheek. "When it comes to politics, darling, hospitality doesn't count for much. Men do terrible things for the sake of their cause."

"But in Dublin, Mr. Shaw was always taking the radical stand at dinner parties. When he and Dr. Wyndham and the other guests argued about home rule, Mr. Shaw always argued in favor."

Stephen looked at her lying beside him, lovely and tousled, tempting beyond reason, and tweaked her sunburned nose. "Perhaps he did it only for the sake of argument. But if you stand up for him, I'll take your word."

Anna snuggled closer. "Mr. Shaw is a decent man altogether."

Stephen inhaled the scent of her hair and thought of their intimacy last night. He propped himself up on an elbow and pushed back the covers.

"Oh, you," Anna said. But she let him gaze upon her long-limbed beauty, her graceful womanly curves. Her body was the color of cream, save for her deep-hued nipples and the saucy curls between her thighs. He laid a hand on her breast and felt the fire creep into his loins.

"Nan," he said, looking into her eyes.

She gave him a blushing smile. "We'd best be quick about it," she said, opening her arms. "In a minute there'll be three boys banging at our door."

They went home on the late steamer, crowded with merrymakers. No sooner had they set off than Peggy and Davy disappeared into the crowd, hand in hand, and the boys raced away to find a clear spot to play running games. Anna and Stephen stood at the rail, watching the Connecticut coastline in the still summer evening. Anna, drowsy from too much sun, leaned against him. The vibrations of the steamboat throbbed through her body, making her sleepier, even more content. She hugged Stephen's arm and closed her eyes.

Next thing she knew, he was lifting the brim of her straw hat and peering at her face. Anna blinked up at him. "Now, what are you staring at?"

"You fell asleep. You were snoring."

"Never!" Anna straightened her hat. The sun had turned her cheeks the color of apricots, and her nose was bright pink. The sight of her made Stephen feel ridiculously happy. "You're lovely as sin, Nan. It's a mystery of nature how you ended up belonging to me."

Anna gave him a teasing look. "You're smitten, that's sure."

"I'd rather be here with you than in heaven itself."

"Oh, you speak nonsense." But Anna felt the same thing, a sort of giddy joy, like nothing she'd ever known, a pure enchanted happiness.

Chapter 23

Anna hurried through her chores so she could get to Mrs. Sinclair at the St. Nicholas Hotel by early afternoon. As usual, there was one interruption after another. Mose wanted to show her the shoots poking up through the soil in the garden; then Dennis Lawler stopped by to say he'd be delivering uptown and could he have his after-dinner pie early. It was the junkman's day, so there were rags and bottles to be gathered for the Currans to take out. Just when Anna began kneading a batch of bread dough, Peggy came over to talk about Davy, how lovely he'd been on the island, how well behaved.

"You're sweet on him, I can see that," Anna said, slapping at a mound of dough. "What will you be telling Peter Crowley?"

Peggy sniffed. "I'll tell him to go to the devil."

Anna brushed flour from her hands and took a sip from her cup of tea. Peggy looked to be in love, or maybe it was just the color in her cheeks. She was wearing a pretty flowered dress and a yellow ribbon in her hair, and everything about her glowed—her skin, her eyes, her light brown hair. She kept glancing at the kitchen door.

"Davy's busy all day," Anna said. "Stephen and Emmet are teaching him a new job."

"Oh?" said Peggy. "What job is that?"

"He'll be telling you later." Anna didn't want to spoil Davy's grand news. He'd be sure to go bragging to Peggy first thing, hoping to get a kiss for his new responsibilities.

Peggy tossed her head. "It isn't fair to lead me on so."

"You'll have to wait and hear it from him. Now, run along, Peg. I've got lots to do before I see Mrs. Sinclair, and your mother will be wanting you to mind the store."

Peggy stood up and gathered the tea things. "I'll come in later and put the bread in the oven."

"Thanks, Peg. And tomorrow we'll wash the laundry."

"I don't suppose Davy will be helping us, then, not if he has a new job."

Anna tucked the dough into the pan. "The Currans will be hauling the water. Davy's got more important things to do."

"So it's an important job that Stephen has for him?"

"Oh, you might say so." Anna patted the last of the loaves. "Now, don't be dying of curiosity, Peg. Davy will tell you in good time."

Once Peggy had gone, Anna sat down and rested her head on her arms. The weather had cooled, but still she'd felt tired since the visit to the island. Last night she'd fallen asleep before Stephen finished undressing. He'd teased her this morning. "You've grown tired of me, Nan. I knew it would come to that sooner or later."

Anna yawned and rubbed her face. It was the sun, she decided, that made her sleepy. Too much sun on the island after the heat of last week. She forced herself to her feet and looked at the chicken stew, simmering on the back lid of the stove. She wet a rag and scrubbed the table, put on a clean cloth, and took an armful of plates. She'd begun laying the table for dinner when she heard a rapping on the back door and Gil stuck his head in.

"Morning, angel."

"Oh, Gil, don't mind me. I'm busy, but you're welcome to sit."

Gil looked hot from climbing the stairs. He sat down heavily and opened his flask. Anna set a tumbler before him. "Dinner will be ready soon. I'll lay a place for you."

Gil waved away the invitation. "Thanks, angel. Can't stay a minute. I stopped by to see about plans for the exhibition match, but I can't get near your husband. He's got his head together with Davy and Emmet." Gil settled back and took a gulp of whiskey.

Anna stopped her work. "What exhibition match?"

"The one between Stephen and Maguire. The news is spreading like a rash. Didn't you . . ." Gil stopped speaking and his freckled face took on a florid hue. "Christ Almighty, he didn't tell you yet, did he?"

Anna felt a chill that went right to her bones. "Gil," she said, "Stephen's not fighting anymore. He gave me his word."

"Jesus God, I'm sorry, angel. Holy Christ on the cross, he'll kill me for this. Goddammit, here I am swearing in front of a sweet girl like you—" He broke off and took a long slug of his drink.

Tears prickled Anna's eyes. She sat down, clutching the plates to her chest. "He won't fight. He said so."

Gil leaned over and patted her arm. "It's not a bare-knuckle match, angel, it's a sparring exhibition. For the Committee, you know, O'Mahony's gang. It's just to please the lads and raise a few dollars for the cause. Stephen won't get hurt; he won't have a mark on him. Now, put down those pretty plates before you drop them on the floor."

He took the plates from her. Anna wiped her eyes. She felt fragile suddenly, and frightened. *Oh, Stephen, how could you do this . . . ?*

The door opened, and they were all there, Stephen and Emmet and Mose. And Davy, looking proud, bursting with news of his new responsibilities.

"Gil, you good-for-nothing," Stephen said, punching his shoulder. "What are you doing here, bothering my wife?" He looked at Anna and his smile faded. "Nan, what is it?"

The men were staring at her. Anna felt tears running down her cheeks. She stood up and tried to compose herself, tried to smile, but it was no use. Stephen came toward her. "Anna?"

"I'm sorry," she said softly, backing out of the kitchen. "I . . . There's corn bread in the oven."

"Nan!"

She turned and ran to the bedroom, slamming the door. She fell onto the bed and lay there, her hand on her mouth, her body limp. Stephen had lied to her. She'd trusted him with her heart and her future, and he was going to fight again.

The door opened. Anna felt the bed sag as he lay down behind her. He rested his hand on her back, moving it in small, soothing circles. "I'm sorry you heard it from Gil, darling. I meant to tell you myself."

"You promised me!"

"It's only a sparring match. No one will be hurt."

Stephen kissed her hair, then the back of her neck. Anna rolled onto her back and looked at him. He smiled at her, a hopeful smile, and wiped at the tears drying on her cheeks. "You feel better now. I can see it."

"No," she said, her throat tight with hurt. "I don't feel better. You promised you'd not fight again."

She saw a grimace of annoyance cross his face. "I agreed to do this. It's for O'Mahony and the cause. It's what I have to do."

Anna turned her head away.

"Darling." Stephen leaned down and nuzzled her neck. He put his hand on her breast.

"Don't." She pushed at his hand. "I don't want that."

Stephen was silent. Anna didn't look at him. She turned onto her side. "Please go."

He sat on the bed for a moment before getting up. When he left, he closed the door gently.

Anna felt worse after a nap, groggy and dispirited. She washed her face and put on her new brown skirt and jacket. In the kitchen the dinner things had been cleared away, the dirty plates rinsed and stacked in the larder. She checked her rising loaves of bread and forced herself to eat a bowl of stew. Then she fastened on her flowered straw hat and set off for the St. Nicholas Hotel.

The sky was gray and the breeze damp, but the air was refreshing. By the time she reached Broadway, Anna had pushed away disturbing thoughts of Stephen. She ventured across the busy thoroughfare, mindful of the carriages and cabs whirling past, the fast-trotting horses, the wagons laden with merchandise. At one time, crossing Broadway had terrified her; now she faced the deafening rumble and squeals, the shouting drivers and the impatient hacks with hardly a thought.

When she was safe on the far sidewalk, she shook out her dusty skirt and joined the pedestrians jostling their way south.

She stepped along briskly, admiring the bright banners floating before plate-glass windows and the huge, colorful signs hanging over the sidewalk. Broadway, the teeming heart of the city, never failed to excite her. What was more, Anna thought, she soon would be stepping inside the St. Nicholas Hotel—actually welcomed into one of the suites.

Despite her anticipation, however, Anna couldn't help feeling a twinge of disloyalty. She was calling on the mistress of Mrs. Smith-Hampton's husband. She tried not to think about it, for she knew it was wrong.

A vast marble edifice with green Venetian shutters, the St. Nicholas looked more like a European palace than a hotel. Anna hurried up the steps, trying to act as if she belonged there. But it was hard not to stare. She looked sideways at men in light suits, smoking slim cigars—southern plantation owners, Stephen had said, in town on tobacco and cotton business—and the western men with their slow talk and pointed boots.

In the grand lobby, the air was thick with tobacco smoke. Anna gazed at the tremendous staircase, the dripping chandeliers, the thick draperies embroidered in gold. Deep plush sofas held loud-voiced men, and huge ferns sprang out of porcelain pots. Magnificently gowned ladies strolled about, their taffeta swishing, their laughter gay. Mistresses, Anna thought, like Mrs. Sinclair. Oh, they were elegant.

She couldn't stand around gawking all afternoon, she told herself, and headed for the staircase. She'd hardly mounted two steps when she noticed a man descending, a broad-chested, well-built man with rough black curls tight to his head. Anna looked at him and something leaped inside her, taking away her breath. She stopped dead still, her gloved hand gripping the balustrade. Dear heaven, if she weren't in New York, if she weren't a million miles away from her old life, she would have sworn it was Billy Massie.

His dark eyes darted about, as if on the lookout for something. A hot flush sprang to Anna's cheeks. Billy did that, looking around, making sure no one was crowding him. The man's eyes came to rest on her. Anna made a little sound in her throat, a cry of disbelief. Mother of God, oh, sweet Mary!

Billy.

He stared at her. She heard him say her name. Slowly, as if walking on glass, he came down the steps, close enough for her to see the dark shadow of whiskers on his cheeks and chin.

"Anna Kirwan, is it you?"

Anna felt numb, as if every bit of her had been dunked in a tub of ice water.

"What are you doing here, Anna?"

"I . . . I came to see a lady." Her voice was a mere whisper. "About making some lace."

Billy's expression cleared. "Oh, you're still doing that so?" He didn't find it strange that she was in America.

"You look grand, Anna."

Thoughts came to her in bursts, like firecrackers going off in her head. This man was her husband, the husband she'd sworn to honor until death. He'd killed a boy and betrayed his marriage vows and stolen her money, and now he was chatting her up on this staircase as if they were mere acquaintances.

"I'm a fighter now, a prizefighter." Billy thrust back his shoulders. He wore the smug expression of a boy bragging to his mates. "I'm not called Billy Massie any longer. I'm Billy Maguire."

A shock ran through Anna, from her brain to her toes. She clutched the balustrade with both hands, only vaguely aware that her workbag had fallen to the steps.

"I was afraid the police might catch up with me," Billy explained. "The police and you." He looked proud. "But it's no matter now. Nobody's going to bother about what happened back then. I know important men from Tammany Hall. Bill Tweed, Mike Walsh, John Kelly. I have friends who live right in this hotel." He glanced around. "It's a grand place, isn't it? America's a grand place."

He looked back at her and frowned. "Are you all right?"

Anna swallowed hard and swallowed again. She gathered her strength, every remnant of her sanity, and her body tingled, a sign that it was once again coming to life.

What was left of her life.

Billy Maguire. Dear God.

He was talking again. "It's a surprise for you, seeing me, that's sure. Where are you staying? Are you married?"

Anna's eyes hazed with tears. She wanted to scream at him, scream and shake him. He was acting as if they hadn't shared a life and a bed, as if he hadn't tried to destroy her. "I'm *married* to you."

Billy grinned sheepishly. "Aw, Anna, now—"

"I have to go." She couldn't bear this, not for another instant. "I have to see Mrs. Sinclair."

She pushed past him. Billy grabbed her arm. "Your bag. You dropped it." He pushed the workbag against her chest. He was smiling at her, his face bright with anticipation. "Meet me afterward, down there by the desk. I'll take you to Delmonico's. We'll talk of the old days."

He looked her over, appraising her. Billy's face had always been easy to read, and right then Anna knew that he was thinking of the little room at Loughton Court and all that had passed between them. She turned away, feeling sick.

"By God, you're sweet." His voice softened, his hand tightened on her arm. "No girl can hold a candle to you. I should never have left you behind."

Anna extracted her arm from his grip and fled up the carpeted stairs.

She managed to get through the session with Mrs. Sinclair. They talked of lace and looked at samples of Anna's work. Only in passing did Anna notice her client's graciousness, her fair-haired beauty, the luxurious appointments in the rooms.

They had tea. Anna's hand shook so she could barely hold her cup. The cakes tasted like ashes. Thoughts of Billy kept jumping to the front of her mind, demanding her attention, reminding her that everything was spoiled, ruined to dust.

Mrs. Sinclair ordered a yoke and cuff set done in a blackberry pattern. As Anna left, she asked if there was a rear door out of the hotel.

"You needn't bother with that, Mrs. Flynn," said Mrs. Sinclair.

Anna insisted. She wasn't about to go down the grand staircase and encounter Billy Massie-Maguire in the lobby. She never wanted to see him again. Not ever. Nor would she again set foot in the St. Nicholas Hotel. By coming here, she had betrayed Mrs. Smith-Hampton and had reaped her reward. When she finished Mrs. Sinclair's order, she would send it around with a note saying that her lace-making services were no longer available.

Outside, the clouds had lowered. Rain spattered Anna's straw hat and brown jacket. She walked in a daze, as if she weren't walking on the same earth as other mortals; she felt utterly empty and alone.

Outside the Emerald Flame, the usual group of men loitered in the drizzle. They touched their caps and murmured a greeting. Anna answered them, forcing a smile. As if nothing was wrong.

She climbed the stairs and stepped into the flat. Peggy was in the kitchen, pulling fragrant loaves of bread from the oven. She was smiling, her face flushed. Davy leaned against the dresser, his arms folded across his chest, looking pleased.

"There you are, Anna," Peggy said. "Did it go well, then?"

Anna looked around the kitchen, so cheerful and cozy, the kitchen she loved so much, that she was about to lose, and a rushing started up in her head. She felt a flood of despair. Her face crumpled, and she heard her own anguished cry. "Peggy! Oh, Peggy!"

Then her legs went soft, and everything turned gray; she was falling, and Peggy was screaming her name.

She was lying on the bed and Mrs. Cavanagh was bending over her. "There's a girl. There you are, now. You had a bit of a spell, that's all."

Anna blinked at the crushed-glass windows. The panes were a dull gray in the cloudy afternoon. "Stephen," she whispered.

"He's just outside," Mrs. Cavanagh said. "Poor man. Worried half to death, he is. He says you've been tired, working too hard, he says."

"Tired." Anna closed her eyes, trying to collect in her mind the pieces of her shattered life. She longed to see Stephen, to feel the strength of his arms. But she no longer had a right to him.

"You frightened us." Peggy wiped her teary eyes with the back of her hand.

"Have a sip of tea, Mrs. Flynn. Take a sip and you'll be your own self."

Anna glanced at Mrs. Cavanagh and looked back at the windows. Billy Massie is Billy Maguire, she thought. Oh, Stephen, how this will hurt you.

"You'll be needing your strength," Mrs. Cavanagh said. "Mark my words, there'll be a wee one come winter."

It took a moment for Anna to understand the meaning of Mrs. Cavanagh's words. "A baby?" she asked, her voice barely a whisper. "Oh, surely, not a baby!"

Mrs. Cavanagh beamed. "I know the signs. Kill me if I'm wrong."

Anna turned her head on the pillow. A baby! It wasn't possible. It *couldn't* be.

Peggy touched her shoulder. "Anna?"

Tears slid down Anna's cheeks. "Please God. Please, not now." She couldn't conceive, not when she was barren, not when after all those months with Billy, there had been nothing.

"Leave her be, Peg," Mrs. Cavanagh said. "Every woman acts a bit strange, starting her first. Now, Mrs. Flynn, you just go along and cry. I'll be getting your husband."

Anna sat bolt upright. "You didn't tell him!"

Mrs. Cavanagh and Peggy exchanged glances. "That's your place, Mrs. Flynn. He's your husband."

"We mustn't tell him. Not yet. Not . . . until I'm sure." Dear Lord, not ever, Anna thought frantically. If she had a child, it would belong to her church-wed husband. To Billy. She put her hands to her face and sank back on the pillows. Oh, Sacred Heart of Jesus, pity me. . . .

"Nan."

Stephen sat on the bed and took her hands from her face. He looked hard into her eyes. "What's troubling you, darling?"

He looked handsome and vigorous, his hair streaked a lovely gold. He was her solid and comforting husband, her true love, and he was lost to her.

Anna pressed her trembling lips together. Already she missed him; already she wanted him in her arms.

"It's the match, isn't it?" he asked. "I should have told you. I should have explained. It's nothing, you see. Only a glove match, an exhibition. No one will be hurt."

She stared at him, her eyes full of tears and burning hot. She touched his lips, his cheek, his brow, tracing his scars.

"There's something else, Nan. What is it?" He looked tense, the fine lines around his eyes cut deep.

She couldn't tell him, not yet. She hadn't the strength. "I'm tired now. I want to sleep."

Stephen tucked a strand of hair behind her ear. "I'll leave the bed to you tonight, then. You need a good rest."

Anna had to stop herself from crying no! She wanted to grip Stephen's hand and tell him that more than anything she wanted him next to her tonight. But instead, she turned her head on the pillow and said softly, "That would be best."

The next morning Anna felt drained of energy and emotion. She went about her morning chores, conscious of Stephen's eyes on her, aware of his concern.

Rory was feeling rambunctious. When the Curran boys turned up, the three of them started galloping and yelling down the hallway. Then at breakfast they took to shoving one another off their chairs. Stephen lost his temper and threatened to take the strap to the lot of them. Anna snapped that no one would lay a strap on any one of those boys, not while she had a breath left in her.

Stephen got up from the table and stamped out, slamming the kitchen door. The boys fell quiet, turned into angels by the exchange of harsh words, and Anna fought the urge to cry.

She laid a hand on the Currans' yellow-haired heads. "I want you helping Mose in the garden this morning."

"Yes'm," they answered softly, in perfect unison.

"And you, Rory, you're off to Mrs. Cavanagh's, and ask her for strawberries and rhubarb when you come home."

Rory's face brightened. "For a pie?"

Anna nodded. "A fine pie for all of you. I'll be going out this morning, but after dinner I'll give you each a penny for ices."

The boys grinned and nudged one another. Anna looked at their sweet faces, all cheekbones and big eyes, and gathered the three of them into a big squirming hug. She held them tight, feeling their sharp shoulder bones, their skinny ribs. There was no more meat on them than on a tree, she thought. Who would be feeding them when she was gone?

She sent the children out of the kitchen and tidied up the breakfast things. As she dressed, she considered again the plan she'd decided upon. It was the only thing she could do; she had no other choice.

She pinned on her straw hat and took up her bag. Then she set off for Broadway and the omnibus to Gramercy Park.

Chapter 24

For dinner Anna served griddled potato cakes and cold ham. For Stephen, the meal was a test of patience. Rory played with his food and fretted about having to work when he wanted to play. Emmet sniped at Davy over the casual way he'd supervised the morning's brewery delivery.

"You'd best be watching him, Stephen," Emmet said. "With Davy Ryan looking after things, the place'll be going to mischief in a week."

"For the love of God, Emmet, give it a rest," Stephen said. "In a month you'll be gone from us. You'll be worrying about other things than a dozen barrels of ale."

Davy winked at Rory. "He'll be worrying about holding off the forces of the queen's army. All by himself."

Stephen shot Davy a look. "Hold your tongue before the whole world hears you."

Emmet's face reddened. "It's because of men like him who care nothing for the cause that we Americans have to rekindle liberty's fires."

"It's hard to kindle a fire when there's no wood for burning," Davy said, looking around the table for approval.

"Do I have to tie your mouths shut to keep you two quiet?" Stephen demanded. He pushed away his plate. With Rory complaining, and Emmet and Davy quarreling, only Mose and the Curran twins seemed content with their lot. The Currans kept their faces a scant inch above their plates, as if they expected their food to escape out the door, while Mose, as usual, didn't seem to hear a thing.

Stephen looked at Anna, turning potato cakes at the range, and his annoyance shifted to unease. He worried about yesterday's fainting spell and their exchange of sharp words. They had not made love together for two nights. He needed Anna in his arms; he needed her reassurance that all was well between them.

He got up from his chair and went to her, taking the spatula from her hand. "Sit down and let me finish this."

Anna gave him a tired smile. The expression on her face, trancelike and distant, was so strange that everyone fell silent. Even Mose stopped eating and stared. Looking at Anna reminded Stephen that it was she who kept this odd assortment of people in order. When Emmet and Davy quarreled, it was Anna who smoothed things over. She distracted the boys from their mischief and brought the rare smile to Mose's face. She'd even brought Peggy to see the good in Davy. As for himself, Stephen knew that Anna was the heart of his life.

"Finish up," Stephen said to the men and boys. "I want all of you gone. Look at Anna. We've worn her out."

Anna protested. "No, it's all right."

"Anna said we could have pennies for ices," Rory said.

"Never mind about that. Clear off. Now!"

"I promised them, Stephen." Anna went to the penny jar on the dresser. The boys leaped from their chairs to follow. She pressed a penny into each upturned palm. Then, to Stephen's surprise, she took Eddie Curran's face in her hands and kissed him on both cheeks. Before Mike could escape, she did the same to him.

"Be good boys," she said. She rested her hand on Rory's thick black hair. "I'll want to talk with you later, treasure."

The boys bounded out the back door. Davy and Emmet and Mose shuffled their feet self-consciously, then made for the door, bumping into each other in their haste to leave. When the door closed behind them and their footsteps faded down the stairs, Anna turned to Stephen.

"Stephen, sit down."

He felt a fist close on his heart. She was going to leave him. It came in a flash of intuition that gripped his guts, that froze him in panic. She was going to leave him because of the exhibition with Maguire. By God, he'd cancel the match. To hell with O'Mahony. To hell with the whole Irish cause.

He pushed the griddle onto a cold stove lid, then picked up the jug of buttermilk and put it down again. He looked around for something else to do, anything to delay hearing what Anna had to say.

"Stephen, please."

He pulled out a chair for himself. Anna sat across from him, across the dirty plates and tumblers half filled with milk. Her face was pale, all the liveliness gone. Stephen thought of the nights they'd sat here, drinking tea before bed.

"I saw Billy Massie yesterday. At the St. Nicholas."

It wasn't the news he'd expected. He had steeled himself for something worse. "Are you sure? Maybe it was someone who looked like him."

"I wasn't mistaken," Anna said, her voice calm and soft. "We spoke to each other."

Something in her face made Stephen's heart gallop. Christ, what was she going to say? That she would go back to Massie? Would guilt drive her back? "Don't worry, Nan," he said. "I'll take care of him. I'll work something out."

"He's Billy Maguire. He took another name when he left Ireland."

Stephen stared at her, unable to speak. He felt as though someone had put a hand on his throat and was slowly tightening it.

"He doesn't know about us," Anna said. "He doesn't know where I live. I got away from him before he found out anything." Her eyes filled with tears. "I can't go on living here. I found a place on Fourth Street. It's a respectable boardinghouse. Mrs. Smith-Hampton recommended it."

All Stephen's muscles had frozen. He could do nothing but sit and stare. Then the pain came, digging into him without mercy, clawing away at his vitals.

"I tried to run away from the past, Stephen. We both did. But it found us, didn't it?"

He turned his head toward the window. The rooftops of his neighborhood swam before his eyes. He could see nothing but Maguire and Anna. Together. That big dumb ox of a man with his beautiful Nan. Stephen rubbed his eyes, clearing his vision.

He looked around the kitchen, so marked with her touch, but he couldn't look at her.

His gaze came to rest on the table, its neatly starched white cloth cluttered with dishes and food. With his arm, he could clear it. Smash everything to the floor—those pretty flowered plates, the cut-glass tumblers, the jug of buttermilk, the pile of potato cakes. Smash everything.

"I'll ask Dennis Lawler to take my boxes on his wagon."

Anna was talking again. Stephen heard her, but he couldn't look at her. Once, he had talked himself into accepting her past. He'd tried to understand what she'd been through. But she'd lain with Maguire. The faceless husband was none other than Billy Maguire. The thought of it filled him with disgust.

"I'll be telling Rory. I'll try to explain. Fourth Street is only a few blocks away, so I'll want to see him often. Stephen, is it all right?"

He shrugged. What did he care?

"Billy will find me sooner or later. He's sure to find out about us. But I'll be on my own then. You won't have to be responsible."

Stephen clutched his head. Christ, she was babbling. Why didn't she shut her mouth and get out of his house? She never should have been here, a woman like that, a woman who would sleep with Maguire.

"Say something, Stephen." Anna's voice was giving out, dissolving in emotion.

He got to his feet and walked out of the kitchen. Without a word, without looking back. Downstairs in the sparring room, Mose was preparing for a lesson. A half-dozen men loitered around the ring, talking and smoking. They hailed him. Stephen kept going.

The bar was full of patrons, quaffing mugs of ale, eating the salty lunch—pickles and egg sandwiches, cold meat and cheese. Stephen stepped up to the bar. Men saluted him with raised mugs.

"Afternoon, Stephen."

"That Davy Ryan, now, he's a card. Ye've done well to take him on, Stephen."

He forced himself to grin. He clapped a man on the back. "Everyone in their health," he shouted.

It was good being here with the men. Things went easy with men. Women were good only for the bed, to play with and forget. His mistake had been letting a woman get under his skin, making him think he loved her.

Stephen leaned against the bar and gazed at the painting of *Susannah Surprised in Her Bath.* He studied her lovely pink body, her startled expression as she tried to cover herself. A thought slipped through his defenses, the memory of Anna, shy that first night, frightened. He wondered if he'd hurried her too much. He remembered what he'd done to her, how upset she'd been, and knew that he'd reminded her of the shopkeeper who'd violated her.

Stephen turned abruptly away from Susannah and pounded on the mahogany bar. "Barman!"

Davy hurried over, a white towel in his hand. "Boss?"

"Whiskey."

"Stephen, it's busy as hell here."

"Whiskey, goddammit! John Jameson and be quick about it."

Davy stared in alarm. "You're having me on. You don't drink."

"What the devil does a man have to do to be served in his own place?"

Nearby conversations faded; men stared. Davy slammed down a bottle and a glass. He turned away, avoiding Stephen's eyes.

Stephen filled the glass to the rim and tossed it down. The liquor hit his stomach hard. He felt the heat moving into his limbs. He refilled the glass and tossed down another.

"Say there, champ. What's going on?"

Gil stood beside him, a hand on his shoulder. Stephen shrugged it off. "Shut up, Gil. Have a drink."

"Stephen—"

"I won't be listening to you. Drink if you want, but don't talk to me." Stephen stared at the plate-glass mirror behind the bar, at the lemons and glasses, the magnums of champagne. He thought how it would feel to smash it all, then recoiled at the thought. Destroy his saloon? The Emerald Flame? Tears welled up in his eyes, and he filled his glass again.

"I don't like this, champ."

Stephen drank off his glass and reached for the bottle. "By God, Gil, have a drink. It'll start a fire in the cellar." His tongue felt thick in his mouth.

Gil said, "Davy, what the hell?"

Davy said. "Emmet, there's something wrong with Stephen."

Then Emmet was beside him, taking his arm.

Stephen pulled away. He stared at Emmet, trying to get him in focus. "You know what your trouble is, young Emmet? You don't love your countrymen. You expect them to be clever like you, but they're just men, getting along, some dumb, some not so dumb. They're all greenhorns over there, like our Davy. You can't free them unless you love them. And if you don't love our Davy, you can't free them." He was getting mixed up. He knew what he wanted to say, but it was hard to piece it together.

"Jesus," said Gil. "What's that all about?"

Emmet smiled. "Aye, Stephen. I know what you mean. Have another drink."

"Another?" asked Davy, incredulous.

"He'll pass out. We'll drag him upstairs."

Stephen pushed the glass and bottle. "Take it away. I don't want to pass out." The bottle tottered and Davy grabbed it.

"I'll get Anna."

At the mention of her name, Stephen reached across the bar and took Davy by the front of his shirt, almost lifting him off the floor. "You get her and I'll have your sacred life."

Davy's face went white. Then Gil was pulling Stephen away, and someone whispered, "Mose. Get Mose."

Stephen held up his hands. "No, no. Never mind." The words slurred over his tongue. He arranged his face in a smile and turned to Davy. "Laddie, I'm sorry." He bowed to Gil. And to Emmet. "Emmet the Liberator, following in the shoes of our beloved Dan O'Connell."

The entire saloon was silent. Some men smiled, others looked uneasy.

"If you lads will excuse me, I have some business to attend to." The words came out perfectly. To his own ear, Stephen sounded stone sober.

He walked to the door, maintaining a straight course. It was more of an effort than he'd expected. At the door he turned and spoke slowly, so as not to trip over his tongue. "I'd be obliged if no one follows me. It's personal business I'll be tending."

He stepped out into the sunlight, shading his eyes against the sudden glare. The liquor had dulled his senses, yet the wild thoughts in his head were perfectly clear. He would find Maguire and kill him. If Maguire was dead, he'd no longer be Anna's husband. Perfect logic. So perfect that Stephen felt tears spill from his eyes. He wiped his cheeks and aimed himself south, toward Chatham Street.

Maguire, I'm coming to get you.

He avoided the Bowery and walked down Crosby Street. He crossed Broome to pick up Elm, ignoring the shoulders he bumped, his little stumbles. He stopped at a saloon on Grand Street, where he knew the barkeep, and chatted with him for a while, then at another place on Canal, where he didn't talk to anyone. He drank his whiskey and thought about Anna, what had happened to her in the back of that shop. He hated to think of it, but he couldn't get it out of his mind. He took out his handkerchief and wiped the tears off his face. She'd only been a little girl, for Christ's sake, a half-starved little girl.

He banged on the bar and demanded another whiskey.

By the time he left the saloon, the shopkeeper who'd hurt Anna was mixed up in his mind with Billy Maguire. To his way of thinking, they'd both violated Anna and they both deserved to die. When he reached the Big Six, he was in a fine rage and barely standing. He looked around the saloon, peering through the smoke, trying to focus on something that wasn't wavering.

He heard Jimmy Haggerty say, "Holy Mother of God— Flynn." And then he glimpsed Maguire leaning on the bar, a foaming mug at his elbow. Maguire was smiling, acknowledging something one of his gang had said, and the sight of that smile made Stephen growl with fury. The smoky room turned a dangerous shade of red, the barrels went fuzzy, the walls shimmered and heaved. Stephen curled his two hands into fists and ground them against his thighs.

"Maguire!" he bellowed. "I'm going to kill you!"

Anna knelt on the floor of the front bedroom, placing piles of white linen and lace in her basket. She would take no more from Stephen's place than she'd brought—her lace and her few clothes. Her father's books she had given to Rory. Better he keep them; it only made her feel sad to handle them herself.

It took hardly a minute to pack, and just as well. The room she'd taken at Mrs. Tuttle's was clean and well lighted, but tiny by anyone's standards. Anna was grateful she had any place at all. A genteel ladies' boardinghouse in so fine a neighborhood as Fourth Street would normally not welcome an Irish girl, but Mrs. Smith-Hampton had sent a note around with a glowing reference, attesting to Anna's upright character.

Stephen would hardly agree, Anna thought. Judgment had been written all over his face when she'd told him about Billy. He'd worn the same expression on the ship when she'd confessed she was married—the hard, tight-lipped expression that appeared whenever he looked at her and thought of Rose. He'd been thinking of Rose, Anna was sure of it—thinking how pure Rose had been, how worthy, and how soiled Anna was, how thoroughly used.

She got to her feet and went to the dresser, pausing to sniff the pot of daisies and buttercups and small pink roses. After all they'd been through together, it broke her heart to see that expression on his face again. It made her so tired and sad that she barely had the strength to lift a handful of lace.

"Anna!"

It was Davy, coming through the kitchen, running down the hall to the bedroom. He was red-faced and excited. "Anna, something's wrong with Stephen."

"What's he done?"

"He's drunk." Davy's voice rose to a frantic quaver. He looked around wildly, at the piles of clothes, the open basket. "What are you doing? Why are you packing your things? What's happened?"

Anna took the last of her belongings from the drawer and pushed it shut. She would lose all her friends. No one would ever understand how a girl could marry twice. She would lose everything she cared for, and once again she'd be alone.

"Davy, sit down and let me tell you."

Maguire's fist exploded in his head, blinding him with a bright burst of red. A hand on his throat thrust him backward over the bar. A fist drove into his midsection, knocking the life out of him. Stephen's legs buckled, but he was pinned

to the bar, wide open to blows that pounded his body. He
no longer felt pain, only jolts as fists hit flesh and bone. He
heard the frenzied shouts of men. He tasted blood. Sickness
rose in his throat, and he longed to drop to his knees, to hear
the cry of "Time." But this wasn't a prize match with umpires
and referees. There would be no end until Maguire decided it
was over.

Maguire grabbed him by the shirtfront and dragged him
along the bar. "Your wife!" he shouted. "What do you mean
she's your wife? You son of a bitch, Flynn!"

Stephen wished he would stop talking about Anna. Sweet
Nan, he thought. I would die for you. *I'm dying for you.*

Maguire let him go, and Stephen fell to his knees. The floor
rose up and smacked his face. He lay there, dreaming of her.
All through Maguire's shouts, the blows from his boots, he
thought of Anna, shy and eager in his arms. Anna holding
Rory's face. Anna scolding. Anna smiling.

He was slipping away. He loved her. He hoped she knew
it. A vast darkness took him gently, swallowed him up.

Anna stood by the bedroom door, shaking with fear.
Stephen had gone after Billy. He was drunk and he'd gone
after Billy.

And now Davy had gone after Stephen, to save him.
"I'll find him," he'd said. "I'll bring him back myself,
you'll see."

Davy wanted to be the hero. Davy! Anna shook herself back
to her senses. Billy had killed a boy in Dublin, fighting over a
girl. It was bad enough that Stephen had gone after him. But
Davy? Davy built his muscles helping women do laundry.

Anna ran down the back stairs and burst into the saloon.
Ignoring the glances of astonished patrons, she searched the
dim room for someone, anyone, who could help. "Gil!" she
cried. "Oh, Emmet. Mose! Stephen's gone after Billy Maguire,
and Davy went to help him. You've got to do something!"

He was jolted back to consciousness by cold water splashing
on his face.

"Stephen! Stephen!"

He opened his eyes and tried to focus. He couldn't make out
anything but a mass of red hair. A second deluge of water hit

him, bathing him to life. He gasped awake, struggling to catch a breath. Davy stared down at him, his face slack with horror. Maguire was there, too, looking at Stephen with disgust. Stephen rose up on his elbows and blinked hard, trying to clear the buzzing in his ears, trying to see out of his swollen eyes.

"You've been sticking my wife, Flynn," Billy shouted. "My *wife!*"

"You bastard!" Davy doubled his fists and lunged at Maguire. Billy threw a punch, and Davy flew backward. He crashed into a barrel, sending mugs of beer to the floor.

One of Billy's thugs yanked Davy to his feet and shoved him to one of his mates. They played with him like a rag doll, pushing him back and forth, cuffing his head, punching his arms. The gang shouted with laughter. Davy tried to duck the blows, a look of terror on his face.

Stephen managed to get his legs under him. He pushed himself into a crouch. Maguire was laughing at Davy when Stephen drove his head into Billy's midsection. Billy stumbled backward with a grunt, his arms waving. Stephen staggered after him, his breath bursting from his lungs. Just as Billy regained his balance, Stephen planted his feet and let fly a punch that seemed to come up from the floor. His fist caught Maguire square on the chin, snapping his head back. Billy wavered for an instant, then crashed down.

The commotion in the saloon quieted. The gang stopped playing with Davy and gathered around Billy, struggling on the floor.

Stephen staggered around, trying to keep his balance, but the room was rising and falling like the deck of a ship, making his stomach queasy. Through his pain and sickness, he realized he was still drunk.

"Mother o' God, Flynn," one man said. "I'd take my oath you was dead."

The men helped Billy to his feet. He spat out blood and wiped his mouth. His eyes burned with hatred. "I'll be putting a card in the newspaper, Flynn. I'm challenging you to a prize match."

There was a huge ache in Stephen's head. The whiskey and Billy's blows made it throb like a pulse. "Can't," he said through panting breaths. "Can't fight. Anna'll kill me."

The men started to laugh. Even Maguire's hard-eyed gang

members nudged one another and grinned until Billy shot them a hard look. "You're crazy, Flynn. Crazy."

Stephen tottered to the bar and leaned there, gazing around until he found Davy. "Won't she, Davy? Won't she kill me if I fight?"

Davy's bruised face was growing puffy. "Anna's leaving. She's packed her boxes."

Stephen put his hand over his eyes and fought the urge to cry. Of course she would leave. He wanted her to go. After what she'd done, he could never touch her again. He took a huge gulp of air that sounded like a sob and pushed off from the bar. He staggered over to Davy, bumping against men who reached out to keep him upright. He hooked an arm around Davy's neck. "Take me home, Davy. Take the old man home."

"We're not finished, Flynn," Billy shouted. "You'll see my card in the paper. You back down and everyone'll know you're yellow."

Stephen leaned heavily on Davy. "Isn't that the damnedest?" he said. "She's married to Billy. Christ, to think I got mixed up with Maguire's wife."

Chapter 25

At Grand Street they met Mose and Emmet and Gil, trailed by a gang of Emerald Flame regulars. It was a ragtag crew, mostly small wiry men and a few big ones. Billy's thugs would have smashed them to bits—except for Mose, whose thick brown arms were bared and ready. Seeing Mose made Stephen grateful they hadn't reached the Big Six. If Mose had raised a fist against those Fourth Ward Irishmen, they'd have shot him dead in a minute.

"Seems you run into some trouble, champ," Mose said, stepping in to replace Davy as a support.

Stephen leaned on him, feeling dizzy and sick and terribly sad. "I'm too old for this, Mose."

"Ain't that the truth. Let's get you home and clean you up."

They made their way up the Bowery, a sober gang bearing their fallen leader. People in the street stopped to stare. Stephen was aware of their shocked expressions, but he paid no attention. "Our Anna's married to Maguire. D'you know that?"

Mose hitched Stephen's arm up higher on his shoulder. "So I hear."

At the Emerald Flame, the men helped him up the back stairs and into the kitchen. Stephen dropped down onto the big easy chair and groaned. He hurt all over. His body felt as if everything in it was broken.

Mose sponged off his face and chest. Somebody plunged his torn and bloody fist into salt water, and Stephen let out a yell. He struggled to pull away, but Mose held him still.

"You just sit there, now," Mose said.

"Goddammit. Christ!" Stephen gritted his teeth as the water burned into his hand like acid.

"Tomorrow you'll be feeling worse."

Stephen swore mightily.

Mose's fingers probed for broken bones. "Don't look to me like Maguire done too much damage."

"Jesus, he nearly killed me. I thought I was dead a couple of times."

Mose grinned. "Take more'n Maguire to put you away, champ."

Anna watched from the kitchen doorway as Mose rinsed Stephen's bruised and swollen face and bathed his puffy eyes. He opened Stephen's sweat-soaked shirt and inspected his torso, marked with knuckle prints. Dried blood matted the hair on his chest, and his hand was a mangled mess. When Stephen started cursing, Anna retreated to the hallway, heartsick. She leaned against the wall, listening to the men's voices as they went about caring for Stephen.

Emmet touched her shoulder. "He'll be well in time. There's nothing broken."

"Thank you, Emmet."

Anna was grateful for his concern, but more, she was grateful that he was even speaking to her. Surely they all knew about Billy and her. They knew that she was to blame for what had happened to Stephen.

Emmet returned to the kitchen, and Gil came out. From the smell of him, he'd calmed his nerves with a fair amount of whiskey. He put his arm around Anna's shoulders and gave her a hug. "He's as tough as an old boot, that man of yours."

"I'm married to Billy."

"I know it, angel."

"I'm leaving Stephen. I'm going to live on my own."

Gil patted her. "That won't change anything. As soon as he comes to his senses, he'll be wanting you back."

"He'll never want me."

Gil drew back and looked at her. "I wouldn't bet on it. He went down to the Big Six and fought Maguire for you."

"Oh, Gil, it wasn't for me. It was for his own pride; you know that. He'll never forgive me for ever belonging to Billy. He compares me to Rose, and I can never be like her."

Gil looked surprised. "He got over Rose when he found you."

Anna sighed, wishing it were true.

"I know Stephen, angel. We traveled the country together back when he was fighting. Why, I wrote the book on Stephen Flynn, the one Rory carries around—Frank Gillespie, it says right on the front." Gil paused. "Matter of fact, I wrote a book on both your husbands."

Anna covered her face. Both my husbands, she thought. Oh, how could she have made such a mess of things?

"Billy's a damned decent fighter," Gil said, "but as a man, I'd chose Stephen any day."

Anna didn't care to hear more of Gil's comparisons of Billy and Stephen. "I'd best be getting over to Peggy's," she said. "I have some explaining to do, to her and Mrs. Cavanagh. And to Rory, too, when it comes to that."

Peggy wept softly. "I don't believe it. It can't be true."

Mrs. Cavanagh folded her arms across her apron. "We're none of us saints, Mrs. Flynn."

Anna told them of her plans to move up to Fourth Street. In time, she would leave New York altogether and start fresh in a new city. Mrs. Smith-Hampton had suggested Albany. She said Anna could find plenty of customers for her lacework there.

Mrs. Cavanagh heard Anna out, her plump face grim with disapproval. "Now's no time for you to be leaving Mr. Flynn. You've got a baby coming. You tell him that, and then you stay by the father."

"If there's a baby, it would belong to Billy Maguire," Anna said. "He's my church-wed husband."

Mrs. Cavanagh considered Anna's words, and her face took on a darker look. "You'd best be saying nothing about the baby, then. Not just yet."

"We don't even know if there is a baby," Peggy said, wiping her eyes with her fingers.

"There's a baby all right," Mrs. Cavanagh said. "Peg, see to the customers. You come right along, Mrs. Flynn, and I'll fix you a cup of tea."

Anna had just sat down in Mrs. Cavanagh's cluttered kitchen when Rory burst in from the shop.

"Mrs. Cavanagh! Mrs. Cavanagh!" He looked distraught, his hair wild, his small chest heaving. He saw Anna and threw himself at her. "Something's happened to my da. Emmet won't let me upstairs. He sent me here."

Anna turned in her chair and opened her arms. "Come here, treasure. Now, don't you worry. Your da's going to be just fine."

Stephen settled into the big easy chair, sore from the beating and sick from the whiskey. It was just as well he couldn't sleep; the best thing to do was to move around, so as not to get stiff.

Davy had wanted to stay with him, but Stephen had said no. He had to do some thinking, and he wanted to be alone. Maguire had whipped him soundly, but that meant little, since he'd been flaming drunk and all but defenseless. What bothered Stephen was making a fool of himself in front of his friends, babbling and crying over Anna like a lovesick boy. He was all right now, thank God. When Emmet told him that Anna would be moving up to Fourth Street and eventually leaving the city, Stephen had calmly accepted the news. Anna wasn't his concern any longer. He would make sure that she had money, and he'd have the sparring room boys keep an eye on her until she left New York. Someone had better be nearby in case Maguire decided to make trouble for her.

Stephen looked around the kitchen. Dirty cups and plates with remnants of strawberry pie littered the table. Crumbs and muddy boot prints soiled Anna's once-immaculate floor. He'd have to find someone to keep the place clean, he thought, some woman to look after him and Rory.

He got to his feet and cleared the table with his one good hand. His bandaged right fist throbbed like hell. It had always hurt after a fight, but never like this.

Stephen went into the front bedroom and lit the lamp. Anna's boxes and basket sat on the floor, packed and lashed. Stephen looked at the flowers on the dresser, flowers he'd brought for her. Anna said she liked the smell of flowers at night when she lay in bed with him.

Suddenly he was remembering the morning he'd awakened as stiff as a pike, wanting her, and she'd decided to decorate him with daisies. He'd let her do it, though he'd felt foolish and damned impatient, lying there as big as life with her hands all over him and daisies sprouting between his legs. Anna had told him he looked lovely, pretty as a Maypole. Then she'd rewarded him so sweetly, he'd nearly passed out from the pleasure of it.

Stephen pushed away the memory and sat down on the bed. He looked at the clock. Half past two. He longed for Rory. He needed his boy tonight, looking at him in his worshipful way, as if his da was the finest man alive. It would take but a minute to go over to Mrs. Cavanagh's and bring him home. But Stephen knew the lad shouldn't see him like this, all beaten and bruised. He had the awful fear that once Rory knew his da wasn't invincible, he would look at him differently, a thought that Stephen couldn't bear.

He wandered back to the kitchen, his thoughts moving to Emmet. He wouldn't rest easy until Emmet and the guns had safely reached Kilkenny, until Paddy McCarthy had everything in hand.

Stephen lowered himself into the easy chair, groaning with pain. Things would look better in time, he told himself. The future seemed bleak only because it was night, and he felt so sore and sick.

He closed his eyes, letting his mind wander, trying to doze. He heard a distant sound. Like glass breaking. He sat up and cocked his head, listening hard. Breaking glass. Muffled thumps. Jesus, the saloon! Stephen felt a jolt that sent blood pumping through his veins, that triggered his every nerve.

He struggled to his feet and headed for the back door. He tried to run, but his legs, so thoroughly kicked by Maguire's studded boots, seemed to move at a crawl. He gripped the rail and limped, step by step, down the stairs.

"Mose!" he shouted. "Davy! Jesus, they're busting up the place!"

They came tumbling out onto the second-floor landing, Davy and Mose and Emmet, blinking sleep from their eyes, fastening their trousers as they raced down the stairs.

Stephen followed, cursing, praying they wouldn't be too late. He made his way painfully through the sparring room, hearing the smashing sounds of destruction, the sound of clubs splintering wood.

He stepped into the saloon and let out a roar. Broken glass littered the floor, the felt of the billiard table was split and torn, busted chairs lay strewn about like fallen men. The gang numbered a half dozen. Even in the half-light of a single lantern, it was easy to recognize Maguire's greased-haired boys, their jackets shed, their teeth bared like animals'. Stephen stumbled toward the mayhem, toward the sound of fists on flesh, the crunch of boots stomping glass. Then he saw Susannah, slashed through lengthwise, her nipples poked out, and his anger blazed into fury, numbing his pain like a drug.

Stephen grabbed a broken chair arm and swung wildly, but his blows were feeble. He cursed his weakness, his helplessness to defend his place and help his men. There were too few of his own and too many of them. He saw Davy, his head bloodied, staggering near the bar. Emmet grappled with a man who butted his chin like a Connemara ram—the sound alone made Stephen wince. Emmet wobbled to his knees and sprawled on the floor.

He sought out Mose in the dim light. Billy's men were all around Mose, six of them, grunting and pounding and kicking. Stephen threw himself at the group, swinging his bandaged fist. He connected with a burst of pain that made the room rock, that made his feet slip out from under him. He crashed to the floor, landing hard on his shoulder.

As he scrambled to his feet, it occurred to Stephen that they hadn't come for him. Maguire would have ordered him saved for the prize match. The gang was sent to provoke him, to wreck the saloon and amuse themselves by beating up his boys. If they decided to kill Mose, so much the better.

They had Mose against the wall, punching, their fists armed with iron knuckles. Mose's face was bloodied and dazed, he sagged and slipped, and they hauled him up for more. Stephen floundered toward them, laboring for each breath, brandishing a piece of glass that he could barely grasp in his throbbing hand. Then he saw the knife. It flashed upward in front of Mose's face. They jerked his head back, exposing his throat. Stephen hurled himself forward, howling with fury and terror.

At the same moment, he heard a shattering roar, and one of Billy's men screamed.

An instant of silence followed. Stephen stood still, the smell of gunpowder filling his nostrils. A second roar sent Billy's men scrambling for the door, dragging their wounded comrade. Stephen whirled around to see Davy standing behind the bar, his eyes wide, his face slack with fear, gripping the Colt with two hands. Davy looked at Stephen and his mouth moved but no sound emerged. Then, abruptly, his eyes closed, and he disappeared behind the bar in a dead faint.

Stephen made his way across the crunching glass. Mose had slid down the wall, his back propped against it, his legs spread wide. Stephen gingerly lowered himself, wincing with pain, and fumbled at Mose's neck. His pulse was strong; he had not been cut. His face was swollen, and blood ran from his smashed nose and mouth, but his ears were clear, a good sign.

Stephen called to Emmet, who was moaning and stumbling, trying to find his footing. "Bring that lantern here!"

The light swung closer. "Davy's out cold," Emmet said, wiping at his eyes.

"So were you, a minute ago." Stephen ran his fingers over Mose's chest and ribs, and touched his face. His nose was broken, and they'd probably cracked his jaw and his cheek. His ribs would be hurting, too, but he'd live. Mose's eyes opened, white slits amid puffy flesh. He blinked and mumbled something. Stephen leaned closer.

"Sorry, champ."

Stephen laid a hand on Mose's hair and looked up at Emmet. "Round up some men. We'll get him over to your mother's kitchen. Send Dennis or Tully for Doc Finley. And give me the Colt. They might get it into their heads to come back and finish us off."

Once Emmet had gone, Stephen settled himself against the wall beside Mose, the revolver between his knees. He was as stiff as an old man, and his side was on fire—one of Maguire's men must have hit him, though he couldn't recall it—and his legs were killing him. He glanced at Mose, who looked back at him, stunned and scared. Two wrecked fighters, Stephen thought, and one wrecked saloon. He gently flexed his throbbing fist and stared at the jagged black hole in the mirror behind the bar. The shelf beneath it was swept clean of bottles. The place had been destroyed. He had no choice but to fight Billy—not after Anna, and surely not after this.

"I'll be meeting Billy in the ring, Mose."

Mose stirred and moaned. "You're'n no shape for that."

Stephen could barely make out his words, mumbled through pain and swollen lips, so he ignored them. "September," he went on. "Poole's Island in the Chesapeake Bay, where Sullivan met Heyer."

Mose said, "McCoy," and Stephen understood immediately. Fifteen years ago, Chris Lilly had met Tom McCoy at Hastings, twenty-five miles up the Hudson. After being knocked down eighty times in a hundred and nineteen rounds, the young, muscular McCoy had died, drowning in his own blood.

"I won't be dying in the ring, Mose," Stephen said. "I can promise you that."

It was hours past midnight, but Anna couldn't sleep. She lay with Rory in Emmet's narrow bed in a small, stuffy room above Mrs. Cavanagh's shop. Emmet had given up his bed, saying he would sleep with Davy. Everyone had been kind, surprisingly kind, Anna thought, considering the trouble she'd caused.

She laid a hand on Rory's hair, smoothing it. Since the afternoon, she'd thought of little else but how to help him through this ordeal. Rory had been confused and disbelieving when she'd told him she was married to Billy. Then he'd turned quiet. She'd tried to explain the unexplainable—that life played cruel tricks, that fate appeared in strange guises. She'd told him he mustn't give up his faith or give way to despair. He would never lose Stephen, she'd said.

Rory had listened. Then he'd said he was tired, that he wanted to sleep.

Anna heard footsteps on the stairs, then voices—Emmet's and his mother's, and Peggy's, rising to a wail. Anna's heart soared with fear. She lay still, not daring to move, as the three Cavanaghs passed in the hallway, whispering, and went down the stairs. Something dreadful had happened. Some new catastrophe had befallen Stephen, a catastrophe that would be too much for her to bear.

Silently, so not to wake Rory, she slipped out of bed and groped for her dressing gown. She stepped into the dim hallway, listening, hearing new voices drift up from the kitchen. Men's voices. And among them, Stephen's.

He was there. *Alive*. Anna sagged against the wall and offered a prayer of thanks, all the while thinking that there was no need to go down, no need to see him. But already she was on the staircase. She ran soundlessly down to the kitchen, her heart racing, as if he were still her lover, her husband, as if she had a right to call him her own.

They were all there in the kitchen. She counted them with her eyes—Emmet and Davy and Stephen and Mose. At first it didn't register that they were dazed and bruised, that Peggy was weeping, that Mrs. Cavanagh, a thick gray braid hanging down her back, was sponging blood from Mose's face. Then Anna looked more closely, and her hand flew to her mouth. Mose had been beaten, horribly beaten. Her eyes sought out Stephen. He rose from his chair and with painful slowness came to her.

"Maguire's men," he said, leading her into the hallway. "They tore up the saloon. Tried to kill Mose."

Anna gasped. "Never! They didn't!"

"The doctor will be coming."

"He must tend to you." Anna looked at Stephen's swollen eyes, his bruised lip, his bandaged hand stained with fresh blood. The sight sickened her, and she felt a sudden anger—at him and Mose and Billy and all men for their endless fighting, their wars and risings. Men's quarrels brought nothing but heartache to women and children, and Anna would have said so, except for the weariness in Stephen's eyes. The look on his face reminded her that this quarrel between him and Billy was not an empty one but had everything to do with her.

"I'm so sorry, Stephen."

He rested against the wall, not taking his eyes off her. "We'll put the place back to rights. It's no more than broken glass and broken furniture."

But it was much more. Anna could see that Stephen was heartsick over what had happened to Mose and to the Emerald Flame. It seemed that Billy would take everything he held dear—his men, his saloon, her.

"It's because of me," she said.

"No, Nan. It's not you. He wants a fight, a prize match. It's a way to provoke me."

"Dear God, Stephen, you won't agree to a fight! Not after what he did to you."

Stephen closed his eyes. "Christ, don't start with me. Not now."

Anna wanted to scream at him for even thinking of stepping into the ring with his body so punished and his son needing him more than ever. But she held her tongue and when she spoke, she forced a normal tone. "I told Rory."

Stephen nodded and glanced away, as if the thought pained him. "Emmet said you'll be leaving New York."

"I'll be going to Albany once I finish my work for the ladies. Mrs. Smith-Hampton says I'll find plenty to keep me busy there. She'll give me a reference."

He took a deep breath and expelled it. "I'll have someone keeping a eye out for you in the meantime. Billy may be looking to give you trouble."

"Oh, that's foolishness—"

"I won't have you taking chances with him," Stephen said sharply. "One of the boys will be watching you, and that's that." He glanced behind him to the kitchen. "The doctor's come. Now go on to bed."

"But Peggy and Mrs. Cavanagh will be needing my help."

Stephen shook his head. "They'll be getting along without you."

He turned away and returned to the kitchen. Anna remained in the doorway, uncertain whether she should follow. Then the meaning of his dismissal sank in. They didn't need her any longer, not Peggy or Davy or Emmet or Mose. She was unnoticed and unwanted. Because of Billy, she no longer belonged.

During the following week a question nagged at Stephen: what had Billy Maguire been doing at the St. Nicholas Hotel? He couldn't have a woman there. The women who lived in the hotel's luxurious apartments were not Billy's sort. They belonged to the wealthiest men of New York, to foreign businessmen and diplomats. Stephen scratched his forehead and thought of Billy's curiosity about Emmet's mission, his speculation about the guns.

Ah, he'd been thinking too much these days, thinking all night, unable to sleep. Now it was dawn and he was wasting his time thinking of Maguire. When Anna had been with him, he'd had no trouble sleeping. Waking after a night with her, he felt as if he'd died and been reborn. Now his eyes felt sandy all the time, and he couldn't seem to relax.

Stephen got out of bed and went to the kitchen. Davy lay sprawled in the easy chair, snoring contentedly. In the week since the fight at the Big Six and Mose's beating, Davy had assumed the role of Stephen's bodyguard, following him around and sleeping close by in case he was needed. Davy was proud of himself for braving the Big Six and for shooting at Billy's greasers and saving Mose's life. He'd won the respect of the whole neighborhood for his actions; even Emmet had been impressed.

Davy had won Peggy, too, and more than just her respect. Peggy had been looking after the flat for the past week, which meant that Davy spent a good deal of time with her in the kitchen. Stephen wasn't sure they confined themselves to the kitchen. Sometimes he'd come up from the saloon and find them looking so guilty, he'd wonder what they'd been up to. Seeing the embarrassed lovers reminded him of Anna and how passionately he'd loved her, and it made him feel old and sad.

Stephen sat down at the table and looked around the kitchen. It seemed a long time ago that she'd sat across from him and told him about Maguire. Stephen couldn't remember what he'd said when the truth sank in, only that it must have been terrible.

He heard a sound at the doorway. Rory stood there, rumpled with sleep, his bare feet sticking out from beneath his nightshirt. Stephen pointed at Davy, put a finger to his lips, and motioned for Rory to come closer. The lad was having a bad time of it, with Anna leaving and his own da so thoroughly beaten up. Stephen had tried to talk to him, to comfort him, but Rory would have none of it. He'd retreated into a wounded silence that even Davy couldn't jolly him out of.

Stephen drew Rory between his knees. "How about I take you and Eddie and Mike over to Hoboken and we'll see a baseball game?"

Rory gave a dispirited shrug.

"Say, sport, when are you going to come around to the way you used to be? You can't feel bad forever, you know."

Rory's chin trembled. "You don't care that Anna's not here," he said accusingly. "You never talk about her. You don't even miss her."

Stephen gently kneaded the boy's shoulders. "Anna's gone. There's nothing to be done, and there's no use crying about it."

Fat tears rolled down Rory's cheeks. "But I miss her, Da."

"You see her almost every day. You go up there to Fourth Street and visit her all the time."

"It's not the same as when she was here."

"Hey, sport." Stephen tried to gather the boy close. But Rory fought him, pushing and squirming until Stephen released him and he fled the room.

Living alone on Fourth Street was a boon for Anna's work. She had a clean room, plenty of time, and no distractions. She finished the yoke and cuffs for Mrs. Sinclair and was well along on Mrs. Smith-Hampton's bolero and Miss Camberwell's lace coat. Word had spread among the ladies' friends, bringing even more business, business that Anna didn't want, now that she was planning to leave the city. But she did a little mending and designed trim for bonnets, and at Mrs. Smith-Hampton's behest she began a massive dining tablecloth in a shell pattern. She had so much work that she no longer had time for the Crystal Palace Emporium, which was just as well, since she earned more money working for the ladies.

Busy though she was, not an hour passed that Anna didn't worry about Rory—how he was faring, how he would suffer when she left for Albany. She saw him nearly every day after he finished his errands for Mrs. Cavanagh. Late in the afternoon he ran the five blocks to Mrs. Tuttle's boardinghouse and sat by Anna in her room while she did her lacework. He seemed sullen, but he must have found some comfort in her company, since he continued to come. Maybe it was the treats he liked; Anna took him out for ices or to Taylor's on Broadway for cream cakes.

As for Stephen, she hadn't heard a word from him. Not one. Yet he made his presence known in a manner that annoyed Anna no end. Wherever she went about the city—to Gramercy

Park, to Miss Camberwell's home, along Broadway for some shopping—one of the young men from the Emerald Flame sparring room was nearby. The boys kept a discreet distance, but they were there, hopping on and off omnibuses, lounging at street corners, touching their caps when she glared at them.

The day she visited Mrs. Smith-Hampton's doctor, it was Mose who appeared.

Anna had agreed to the appointment at Mrs. Smith-Hampton's insistence, even though her spells of tiredness had passed, and she felt remarkably well. The doctor performed an embarrassing examination and pronounced her in perfect health. A waste of time, Anna thought as she walked down the stone steps into the sweltering July heat. When she reached the sidewalk, she glanced next door and there was Mose, conspicuous with his dark skin, his red shirt, and his great head of hair, bending over a wrought-iron fence, admiring a gloriously colorful garden.

Anna tugged on her gloves and joined him. "Well, I declare. Are you following me now?"

Mose didn't glance up. "This garden here's mighty pretty."

He wore a white bandage across his nose, but Anna was pleased that he seemed to be healing. "Every day there's somebody following me," she said. "I'm tired of it."

Mose touched his bandaged nose self-consciously. "We just follow the champ's orders."

"Well, you needn't bother. I can very well take care of myself, and you can tell that to Stephen."

She set off at a brisk pace. Mose easily matched her stride. "He don't want nothing happening to you."

"Nothing's going to happen to me."

"Missus, I got to talk to you."

Anna stopped abruptly. "What is it?"

Mose shifted his feet and stared at the sidewalk. The expression on his face filled Anna with alarm. "Mose?"

"He's set on fighting Maguire. He put a card in the paper. They'll be signing the articles soon."

Anna pressed a gloved palm to her forehead. Despite Stephen's words, she hadn't believed it would come to this. "Sweet heaven, have mercy. He'll have himself killed."

"That's what I tell him, but he don't listen. Even Gil don't like it; he says give it up. The champ thinks he can fight forever, but he ain't so strong, not like he was. Maguire hurt him bad, and next time he'll hurt him worse, I know it." Mose looked at Anna imploringly, his anguish visible. "Missus, even I could whip him, if I put my mind to it. I could hurt the champ, but he don't know it, 'cause I won't never do it."

Anna felt a mixture of anger and panic. Would this madness never end, she wondered, Billy and Stephen and their masculine need for revenge?

"Missus, you come back," Mose said. "We all of us need you, and the garden's growing, and the place just ain't the same. You can talk some sense into the champ. He listens to you."

Anna had never heard Mose speak so forcefully or at such length. The fact that he'd come to her meant that he was terribly worried. Anna looked away, trying to blot from her mind the image of Stephen, beaten and bloody, the memory of the boy Billy had killed. Her eyes met those of a passing lady, who glanced at Mose, her mouth pursed in disapproval.

"I can't come back, Mose, you know that. I'm married to Billy, and Stephen doesn't want me."

"He wants you all right. He just don't know it."

"That's not so—"

"And them boys." Mose shook his head sorrowfully. "Them boys are running wild without you. They took Rory down to that livery stable where the ladies fight with no clothes on. I hear them talking."

"Oh, no!" Anna clapped a hand over her mouth.

"And they'll be visiting the rat pit soon enough, if they ain't already. Peggy's hollering at them, saying they're the devil himself. I could whip 'em but it wouldn't do no good. Whipping never did nobody no good."

Sweat slid down Anna's back and down her front, brought on by nerves as much as by the broiling sun. She took out her handkerchief and wiped her forehead. It was hard enough to keep that household in order when she was there every day; living on Fourth Street, it was impossible.

"Come back, missus."

Anna turned up her palms helplessly. "I can't come back. You know I can't. But I'll be giving Rory a piece of my mind. And Stephen, too. That's all I can do, Mose. That's really all I can do."

Chapter 26

Rory stared glumly at his golden-crusted, cream-filled horn. "Peggy says Eddie and Mike can't come to our place anymore."

Anna's spoonful of ice cream stopped in midair. "Oh?"

"She said she gave them another chance, but we're all of us mischief-makers and criminals and should be sent to the House of Correction."

Anna's heart sank. She'd only just spoken to Peggy and calmed her down. "Peggy was in a temper, Rory. Surely, she doesn't mean it."

But Anna was afraid that Peggy meant every word. No amount of explaining about the Currans' need for hugs and full stomachs and things to keep them busy seemed to make any difference. "Those roughneck boys deserve to be whipped," Peggy had said. "And that Rory is just as bad."

Rory squirmed in his chair, craning his neck to look at himself in one of the gilt-framed mirrors that covered the walls of Taylor's ice cream saloon. He tilted his head back and stared at the ceiling, ornamented with gilding and scrollwork. "We were up on the roof throwing eggs. Peggy gave us a swat in the head and told the Currans not to come back."

"Oh, my soul!" Anna cried, appalled that the boys would get up to such mischief. "Rory, how could you? Surely you know better than to do such a thing."

"Eddie and Mike nick stuff down at the docks. They take brass doorknobs off houses and sell them. They smoke cigars, too. Pick 'em up off the street."

There was a note of defiant pride in Rory's voice that filled Anna with alarm. She thought of the Currans out in the streets, learning to be criminals, and Rory right there with them. "Does your da know about the stealing?"

Rory's heels drummed on the chair legs. "It ain't stealing, it's nicking."

"It's stealing all right," Anna said sternly. "And I don't want you having any part of it. I don't want you putting a filthy cigar in your mouth, either, and I don't like the way you're talking— rough, like a street boy. What would your gran say if she knew what you were doing?"

Rory shrugged and poked at his pastry, as yet untasted.

"Now, you listen to me, Rory Flynn. You're a good boy at heart, and a lucky one, too. Why, look at all you have—a fine place to live and a da who loves you and all the food you can eat. Those Curran boys are devils because they're poor and their mam and their da have no time to teach them right from wrong. It's your place to make them better, not for them to make you worse. Do you hear me?"

Rory huffed out a sigh. "Can't you come back? Can't it be like it was before?"

"You know I can't come back, treasure. I've told you a million times."

Rory kicked his chair hard, his face writhing with resentment. "Why did you marry Billy Maguire? Why did you spoil everything?"

"Hush, now," Anna said, aware that nearby ladies were glancing in their direction. "When I married him, I didn't know I'd be meeting you and your da." She reached out to stroke Rory's hair, but he jerked away, glaring at her with black-eyed stubbornness. Anna withdrew her hand and pressed her lips together. Rory deserved a good scolding for his behavior, but she didn't have the heart for it. It was Stephen who should take his son in hand, and the Curran boys, too.

"I'll be having a talk with your da."

Rory turned his attention to his pastry, stabbing at it halfheartedly with his fork. "My da don't care what I do. And he don't talk about you. He's forgotten all about you."

Forgotten? Anna felt a stab of disbelief that she hastily dismissed. What did she expect, for pity's sake? He'd washed his hands of her; surely, it was all for the best.

She stared out the window at Broadway's passing scene, her ice cream forgotten. From now on, her life would be the one she'd planned for before Stephen came along—making her lace in peace. Except now she would be raising Stephen's child, the baby created from their passion. Sudden memories rose to the surface of her mind, memories of his strong arms, his big heart, the way he'd loved her, and she missed him to the core.

"I miss my gran. And my uncle Paddy."

Rory's wail of misery jolted Anna from her thoughts. He sagged in his chair, his thick lashes wet with tears.

"Whisht now, Rory." Anna dug for a handkerchief and pressed it into his hand. "Your gran is dead, but your uncle Paddy writes to you all the time. He's not forgotten you." She smoothed his hair, and this time Rory allowed it. He leaned against her, pressing closer as she stroked him.

"I want to go home."

Anna smoothed his forehead. "In a minute, treasure. Why, look at your cake, you've barely touched it."

"Not *that* home." Rory snuffled. "To Ireland. I want to go home to Kilkenny."

Stephen pushed aside his teacup and glanced into the hallway to make sure Rory had gone to bed. He leaned across the kitchen table toward Gerald Shaw. "What did you find out, then?"

Shaw swallowed a bite of Peggy's custard cake and dabbed at his mustache with a napkin. "The second secretary's mistress has a suite on the fifth floor."

"By God!" Stephen exclaimed. "Is she seeing Maguire?"

Shaw gave a scornful laugh. "My dear Flynn, d'you think the mistress of a consular official on Her Majesty's service would be carrying on an affair with an ignorant Irish prizefighter?"

Stephen let the comment pass. "He's not stoking her; he's using her as a contact. Maguire's an informant. I'm sure of it."

Shaw looked surprised.

"He's passing on what he can learn about O'Mahony's Committee," Stephen explained.

Shaw's mustache quivered. "My good man, I can understand your distress about this business with Maguire and your wife, but you're going a bit far, making him out to be a spy."

"Find out if she sees Maguire."

"If you think they would give me such information—"

"Blast you, Shaw, find out if Maguire's passing on information!"

A resigned expression crossed Shaw's face. "Abuse and lack of manners, I have discovered, are two of your primary American customs."

Stephen rubbed his forehead. He had never felt so harried. Emmet was due to sail in ten days' time, and before he went, Stephen had to know what, if anything, the British knew of the mission. Besides that, he was overseeing repairs to the saloon, making arrangements for the match with Maguire, all the while trying to get into fighting condition. The newspapers were referring to "a certain lady" behind Maguire's challenge, which infuriated him. And as if he didn't have enough to worry about, Rory was sullen and Peggy complained every minute about his behavior.

"Sorry, Shaw. I'm a bit on edge these days."

"So it would appear." Shaw gathered his hat and walking stick and got to his feet. "Because you're such a charming man, Flynn, and so persuasive, I'll ferret out what I can. But may I suggest that you speak to your wife. She might have some insights into this fellow Maguire's political leanings."

"No," Stephen said. "I won't be involving her in any of this business." He was trying not to think about Anna, and he certainly didn't want to talk to her. He could hardly wait for her to finish up her business and leave the city so he could forget about her altogether.

"She knows Maguire better than anyone, old man."

Stephen slammed his fist on the table. "Goddammit, I said no!" But even as he shouted the words, he knew that Shaw was right.

He brought up the subject with Rory the next morning at breakfast. "When will you be seeing Anna, sport?"

Rory looked up from the lumpy, unappetizing porridge Stephen had made. "This afternoon."

"I want to talk to her. I'll go with you."

Rory broke into a huge smile. "She'll be taking me and Eddie and Mike to Battery Park. Will you be asking her to come home, then?"

Rory's sudden transforming joy hit Stephen like a slap in the face. He glanced away. "She won't be coming back. Better get used to it."

Rory drooped back in his chair.

"We'll get on fine, just you and me," Stephen said, trying to sound cheerful. "I'm counting on you to help me train for Maguire."

Rory's mouth twisted in an effort to hold back tears.

"Hey there, sport," Stephen said. "You want me to fight, don't you? You used to keep saying, 'When're you going to fight Maguire?' Remember?"

"I just want Anna to come back."

Stephen thought of suggesting a visit to Guardian Island or Barnum's museum, or maybe a fishing expedition to the Catskills, but he held his tongue. There would be time for that later, after the fight. Once serious training began, Rory would forget about Anna and regain his good spirits. They would again be father and son.

Stephen decided against accompanying the boys to Fourth Street to meet Anna. The walk from her boardinghouse to Broadway and the long omnibus ride to the Battery would be awkward. So he sent Rory and the Currans to Anna's place by themselves, telling Rory he'd find them later at Battery Park.

It seemed foolish to go all the way downtown when he could simply walk the few blocks to Fourth Street, ask about Maguire, and leave it at that. But Stephen decided it would be better to see Anna in a public place with the boys nearby. Sitting down with her in a quiet room might be too much for him.

Before leaving for the Battery, Stephen put in a painful hour-long workout with Mose, then showered, shaved, and dressed in a dark suit and crisp white shirt. As he brushed his damp hair before the bedroom mirror, he saw that his bruises were fading, blending in with all the other scars and lines. Despite the improvement, he didn't look good. He looked tired, as if the life had gone out of him. He felt it in the ring, too, a heaviness in his arms and legs, a lack of interest. Stephen tugged on his cap at a jaunty angle, as if that might lift his spirits, and headed down the stairs.

Battery Park was shady and inviting. Stephen strolled along the promenade, looking at the sail-flecked bay sparkling in the sun. The view brought back memories of the *Mary Drew* passing the point and heading up the East River. Stephen remembered how frightened Anna had been, arriving in New York, and how pleased he'd been when she'd agreed to live with him and Rory. In light of what had happened, it would have been better if he'd let her go her own way.

He saw Rory and the Curran boys hanging on a fence, watching wagons dumping rubbish and construction scrap, landfill for the extension of the park. Anna sat on a bench beneath a nearby elm tree, leafing through a journal. A new straw hat with yellow and pink flowers tilted on her pile of red-brown curls, and she carried a pale yellow parasol that Stephen hadn't seen before. Every few moments she looked up from her journal to check on the boys.

Stephen stepped closer. "Hello, Anna."

She glanced up. Her lips parted, and Stephen thought he saw a flash of something in her eyes, but she turned away quickly. Stephen felt heat pour through him—heat and desire, regret, despair—all the emotions he'd so deliberately suppressed these past few weeks. He had to stop himself from reaching out and touching her.

Anna busied herself with closing her parasol and setting aside her journal. "Rory said you'd be coming." Her tone was brisk, neutral. She moved to make a place for him on the bench.

Stephen sat down. The sight of her brought on a flood of loneliness that verged on desperation. "You're looking fine," he said. It was an understatement. Anna was blooming—her skin glowed; her hair was polished to a russet shine. She looked as if sunlight ran in her veins.

The breeze gusted, and Anna reached for her hat. The front of her brown jacket lifted and Stephen saw the thrust of her breasts into the silky stuff of her blouse. His heart thumped in his chest. He remembered how sweet she tasted, how soft and helpless she became when he touched her. For one crazy instant he wanted to put his arms around her and beg her to come back.

Anna pinned her hat more securely and assessed Stephen disapprovingly. "You're not looking so fine yourself."

"Maguire gave me a real beating," Stephen said and attempted a laugh.

"So you plan to fight again." Her voice was filled with accusation.

Stephen looked at the ground "Don't start on that."

"It's nothing to me if you want to cripple yourself," she said. "Go right ahead. Don't think about your health. Don't think about Rory."

Stephen rubbed his palms on his knees. "I don't want to quarrel with you, Anna."

She said nothing. Stephen could feel her watching him from a cool distance. Did she feel anything for him? he wondered. Did she care for him at all? He reminded himself why he was there. "I have to ask you about Maguire," he said, forcing himself to look at her. "Tell me about his politics."

"Why on earth do you care about his politics?"

"I have to know, Nan."

Her lips tightened. She looked off toward the boys, absorbed by the bare-armed men with their pickaxes and shovels. "Billy had no politics, no loyalty to anything but himself."

"Did he ever say anything about the rising, about the sentencing of Meagher or Smith O'Brien or Padraic McCarthy?"

Anna shook her head. "He scorned the rising and the men who led it. To him, they were fools who had failed."

Typical of Billy, Stephen thought. Be on the winning side or on no side at all. "Did he ever say anything about loyalty to the Crown?"

Anna looked puzzled. "I don't remember it. Why? What are you thinking?"

Stephen shrugged. There was no point in getting Anna involved. "Has he been bothering you?"

"No. He must be nervous of the boys you have watching me." Anna's voice took on a new edge. "When are you going to call them off? I'm tired of being followed every place I go."

"I want to be sure you're safe, darling."

Anna looked away from him, and Stephen realized what he'd said. *Darling*. The word had just slipped out. He felt himself flush.

"Rory's very unhappy, you know," Anna said.

"The fight will cheer him up. He'll be helping me train."

Anna turned on him, her gloved fists clenched in her lap. "For the love of God, Stephen, don't you know what your own son is feeling? He doesn't want you fighting Billy. He doesn't want you fighting anybody at all."

"What the devil are you talking about?"

"Rory saw what Billy did to you. He saw what happened to Mose. He's afraid if you fight you'll be crippled like Hammer. Or killed, lost to him. He's frightened to death, I can tell you that."

A sudden tension gripped Stephen's insides. He didn't believe her; he couldn't. His mind raced over the reasons why she was wrong. "Rory's been begging me forever to fight Maguire. There's nothing wrong with him but a spell of moodiness. He's missing you, that's all."

"Missing *me*! He sees you every day, and I pay him some attention, which is more than he gets from you. When you're not down in your office chatting up Sully or your brewery agents, you're whaling away in the sparring room or running off on O'Mahony's business. Why, from what Rory says, you hardly ever set foot upstairs—"

"Now wait a minute," Stephen said. "We're great together, Rory and me. He comes to the sparring room whenever he wants, and we eat out, and I take him to baseball games. . . ." His voice trailed off, and he felt the wetness of sweat on his back and under his arms. He ran a finger around his collar. "When did he say that he didn't want me fighting?"

Anna didn't answer right away. When she did, her tone had softened. "He didn't say it, Stephen, but I know he's feeling it. He's afraid of loving you any longer. He's afraid of losing you."

"He'll not be losing me. I'm not in the finest condition, but by God I will be. I'll be whipping Maguire, and that's the truth."

"You wouldn't know the truth if you were bang up against it," Anna said, angry again. "You don't know how close you are to ending up like Hammer Moran."

Stephen's heart started a slow, furious pounding that he could feel in his head. He struck out blindly. "You're turning him against me with all your harping about the fight."

"Oh, isn't that nice, then! I show a bit of caring and I'm turning the boy against you." Anna made a sound of disgust. "Sweet heaven have mercy."

Emotions were moving through Stephen too fast to control. What if he lost Rory, his beautiful son, the only person left to him? What if Anna was right, and Rory stopped loving him? Suddenly Stephen felt cornered and helpless. More, he was furious at Anna for speaking so. "You care so much about me and Rory that you leave us."

She stared at him in disbelief. "How can we live together when I'm married to Billy?"

He'd lost the logic of the argument; he wasn't even following his own thoughts.

"You want me out of your life," Anna went on in her accusing tone. "You made that clear enough. Don't I see it in your face whenever you think of me being with Billy? Don't I know I'm not as good as Rose?"

"Don't bring her into this!"

"I know what's in your heart, Stephen. I've always known it. You want a woman like Rose to mother your son and care for your home, but you want me in your bed."

"Goddammit, I won't listen to this—"

"All your sweet words when you're loving me don't mean dirt if you can't look at me when I tell you my troubles. I told you about Billy and your face filled with disgust. Don't think I didn't see it. And then you walked out with nary a word about how I was suffering."

"And what did you expect? You're married to Maguire, for Christ's sake. He had you in his bed."

"Yes, he did," Anna retorted, her blue eyes dark with anger. "He was my husband, and I did my duty by him. Then all these years later I came to you. Willingly. I went against everything I believed to be right and good, because I loved you. I lived with you, Stephen; I sinned with you. And what did I get from you? Your scorn, because I'm not pure enough."

Stephen bowed his head, overcome by dark, confusing thoughts. She was murdering him—with truth, with lies, he didn't know which. He didn't know anything any longer. He especially didn't understand his feelings for her. Perhaps he'd only wanted her for the bed; perhaps he'd always compared her to Rose. Perhaps. The only thing certain was grief over his loss, lodged so deep inside him he would never be rid of it. His only hope was to bury it. Bury it under the rage and violence of the fight ring. By God, he needed this fight. It was the only thing that would save him.

Stephen managed to get to his feet. He looked down at Anna's grim face, her dry, accusing eyes, the yellow flowers on her hat. Then he walked away, aching from the words she'd flung at him. It amazed him how words could hurt, worse even than the blow of a fist.

Anna opened her door to a soft knock. Mrs. Tuttle's maid thrust out an envelope. " 'Twas just delivered, Mrs. Flynn."

Anna took the envelope with trembling fingers. It was from Stephen, it had to be. Maybe he wanted to see her again; maybe he wanted to clear the air after their dreadful argument in the park last week. She wished she hadn't spoken so harshly, but seeing him again had aroused in her such feelings, such futile longings, that she'd lost all patience and said things that were unbearably hurtful.

With a whispered prayer, she tore open the envelope. She glanced at the signature and her heart sank. The letter was written in Billy's childish scrawl. She skimmed it, wincing at the misspelled words.

"Anna," it read. "I dont want to be bothring you at yore place so I will be asking you to come meet me at the oyster house on the corner of Bowery and Prince. I have importent things to tell you and aks you that bare on our marrage. dont worry I won't be looking to do you harm. Yore husband Billy (Massie) Maguire."

Anna read it again, thinking of Stephen's fear that Billy would come after her. She folded the letter and replaced it in the envelope. An oyster house was a safe meeting place, she decided, although it hardly mattered. Billy would never hurt her. In all the months they were together, he'd never raised a hand against her.

She looked at the little gold watch she wore on her dress. It was half past eight. Stephen's boys would have gone home long ago; they never expected her to go out at night. She opened her wardrobe and took out a light shawl, pinned on her hat, and slipped down the stairs and out the front door. Mrs. Tuttle's man, Jones, snoozed in the kitchen late into the evening. She would have to count on him to let her back in.

Anna hurried the five blocks to her destination. The Bowery was crowded and raucous on the late July evening. Sounds of revelry poured from dance halls and theaters; the calls of hot corn girls and strawberry sellers were all but drowned out by the rumble and clatter of traffic. Anna kept her eyes straight ahead and her step purposeful. The few men who tried to engage her in conversation were quickly put off by her withering glare.

When she reached the oyster house's distinctive red lantern, she descended the stone stairs to the cellar entrance. Inside, it was dim and smoky, crowded with young people. Billy sat alone in one of the rear boxes, a mess of oysters and an iced drink before him. Catching sight of Anna, he jumped to his feet, mopping his mouth with a napkin.

"I'm glad you came, then, Anna." He looked her up and down as he wiped his fingers, greasy with mustard and oil. "I didn't know if you would, after you left me waiting that time at the hotel."

Anna seated herself, declining Billy's offer of refreshments. He looked strong and ruddy, his short black hair gleaming in the lamplight, his collar clean and his coat well brushed.

"How did you find out where I lived?" she demanded.

Her question seemed to insult him. "I'm not so dumb I don't know where you're living. I knew it the day you moved up to Fourth Street. Flynn's got his spies watching you, but I've got mine, too."

Anna glanced at her gloved hands, folded in her lap, and felt a pang of memory. Billy had always been worried about being slow. She'd decided long ago that his eagerness to prove himself with tests of strength was a way to make up for his mental shortcomings.

"So then," she said, looking at him, "what have you to tell me?"

Billy didn't answer right away. He stared at her with the yearning look he used to get when they were courting, when he wanted to have his way. "You're a fine-looking girl, Anna, prettier even than when I first saw you."

"Don't be getting any ideas. If it's me you're after, you're wasting your time."

Billy laid his hands flat on the table. They were big and clumsy like Stephen's, but not nearly so broken. "I thought of taking you back."

"You think I'd go back to you after all that's happened?"

He thrust out his jaw. "I could take you. I could snatch you away from that place where you're living. It wouldn't matter if you wanted me back or not."

"Is that so, then?" He was bragging, Anna thought to herself. Just like a small boy.

"But I won't do it. I've no quarrel with you. You were a sweet girl to me. You kept our place clean, and you fed me and my mates, and you saw to my needs like a good wife."

Anna waited, tapping her heel impatiently.

"The only dumb thing I did in my life was leaving you behind." Billy stared at the table for a moment, then glanced up. "D'you want Flynn, Anna? Do you fancy him for your true husband?"

Anna stiffened, her every nerve alert. "Stephen Flynn can never be my husband."

"You can have him. I'll free you so you can have Flynn. It'll make us square, after what I did, running off and taking your money."

Anna's eyes narrowed. Billy appeared serious. There was no threat in his face or in his voice, nor did he seem to be playing a trick. "Oh, so you'll free me from my marriage vows. Are you the pope now, Billy?"

Billy's face reddened. "By God, you always had a sharp tongue. I never did like that about you."

"And do you think I liked you stealing my money and leaving me high and dry?" Anna snapped. "Do you think I liked being tied to a husband who'd abandoned me? And do you think I like you telling me you'll free me, when you know very well we're tied together to the grave?"

Billy hunched over the table and ran his rough fingers over the words carved into the wood. "What if I told you we wasn't really married?"

Anna rolled her eyes. "I'd say you're daft. I stood at the altar before Father Rooney and said my vows and heard you do the same."

"We're not really married, not like you think."

"Is that what you brought me down here to hear? After all these years without a letter or a thought, you suddenly find me and say we're not really married? Before God, I could roast you, wasting my time so." Anna got to her feet, gathering her shawl, straightening her hat.

Billy looked up. "Don't run off on me."

"And why not?"

He squirmed like a nervous schoolboy. "Sit down, Anna. Please. I've got more to say."

Anna paused. He was begging her. Odd, for Billy to be so desperate.

She sat down with an impatient sigh. "Say it, then. But be quick about it."

"I need some information."

"What information?"

"About the guns."

Anna sat very still. "Guns?"

"You know, the guns for Ireland."

Anna thought of Stephen's request in the park—"Tell me about Billy's politics." Slowly the purpose of his question was becoming clear to her, and as it did, Anna felt the blood turn cold in her veins. "I . . . I don't know about any guns."

"You lived with him. Surely you know." Billy's eyes implored her.

"I don't." Anna tried to think of some response, some way of dealing with this situation that would help Stephen, but her mind was blank.

"I know they're sending guns to Ireland, O'Mahony and his gang. I need to know when the shipment's going and where it's to be landed. You've got to help me, Anna. You help me and I'll free you, I swear I will. And I'll pay you back every penny I ever took, and more."

A spy. Billy was a spy. Anna thought frantically. What should she do? Oh, what should she say? "I can't tell you what I don't know. I . . . Give me some time, Billy. Give me some time and I'll try to find out."

He grimaced impatiently. "I don't have time. They want to know now. They're afraid the shipment will go off before they know the plan."

A spy. "Why are you doing this?"

Billy lowered his eyes, looking sheepish. "Them who ask the questions pay me good money to get the answers."

Anna was aghast. "Money? Oh, Billy."

"I didn't think I'd get to fight Flynn. I thought I'd be left with nothing. Now the fight'll make me rich, but they still want the information. They won't let me back out now. If I do, they'll tell O'Mahony what I've been up to, and somebody'll kill me for sure."

"You sell secrets to the English? How *could* you?"

Billy tugged at his cuffs. "It's no matter to me, the Irish cause. I never favored rebellion."

"No," Anna said, remembering. "No, you didn't."

"Will you help me find out about the guns? I'll free you, Anna. I swear I will. And I'll pay you, too."

Anna slid out from behind the table. Her legs felt wobbly, but Billy would never have known it from the steady look she gave him. "I'll find out what you want."

Billy grinned with relief. "You were always a girl to count on." He got to his feet and dug around in his pocket. He thrust his card into her hand. "Send a message around and I'll meet you. Soon, Anna. I need to know soon."

Anna crushed the card in her fingers. "Finish your oysters, Billy. You'd best be building up your strength for the fight."

Chapter 27

The oyster house was just a few blocks from Brace Street. Anna turned the corner of Bowery and Brace and hurried toward the yellow-lit windows of Mrs. Cavanagh's grocery. The door stood open to the summer air. Inside, a few customers leaned on the counter, passing the time with a drink and a chat. When Anna walked in, they straightened in surprise.

"Lord, it's Mrs. Flynn," Mrs. Cavanagh said. She stopped wrapping a bundle and seemed to be at a loss for words.

Anna nodded around a greeting. "I need to see Mr. Flynn."

There was a long silence, during which everyone stared. Then one of the loitering men said, "I'll bring him around, missus," and darted out the door.

Peggy stepped in from the back room, smiling. "Anna. I thought I heard your voice."

"Mrs. Flynn's husband'll be coming around to see her," Mrs. Cavanagh said. "Mind the store, will you, Peg?" She laid a hand on Anna's arm and drew her back to the kitchen. With a glance at her middle, she asked, "Are you well, then?"

Anna smiled. "I'm well."

"There's a gathering tomorrow night for our Emmet. He'll be leaving soon. We'd be honored if you'd come."

Mrs. Cavanagh's eyes filled with tears. Anna grasped her hand and gave it a comforting squeeze. Emmet had never been far from his mother's side.

"I'm gone from here now," Anna said. "I can't be coming back, even for our Emmet. But I'll see him myself and wish him Godspeed."

Mrs. Cavanagh wiped tears from her cheeks and blew her nose. " 'Tisn't the same without you over across the street, Mrs. Flynn. Your husband is lost without you, and that Rory—why, he misses you something fierce."

Anna lowered her eyes. Mrs. Cavanagh's words stirred strong emotions that were hard to keep down. "It's all in the past now."

"It needn't be so. Everyone in the neighborhood thinks the world of Mr. Flynn, and of you as well. We don't make judgments here; we're not holier than Rome. You could come back, Mrs. Flynn, and no one would blink an eye."

Anna put an arm around Mrs. Cavanagh's shoulders and gave her a hug. "You're a good friend to all of us. God bless you for it."

Then Stephen was there. He stood in the doorway, big as a bear, his hair burnished gold in the lamplight. He looked so handsome and sad that Anna almost ran to him. Then Mrs. Cavanagh spoke a greeting, and her voice brought Anna back to herself.

"I just saw Billy," she said once Mrs. Cavanagh had left. "He wants information about the guns."

Stephen said nothing for a moment, his face as unreadable as stone. When he spoke, his eyes looked dangerous. "Did he touch you?"

"No."

"By God, Anna," he said, his voice rising. "I told you—"

"He didn't harm me! We only talked."

Stephen's shoulders sagged. He sat down on the kitchen chair, his legs splayed wide, one arm resting on the table. His expression didn't change, nor did he take his eyes off her.

"What did he say, then?"

Anna related the conversation exactly as she remembered it. Once she finished, Stephen looked thoughtful. "It's good he's asking."

"He's a spy!" Anna exclaimed. "How can that be good?"

"I suspected him for a spy. Now there's proof. But more important, it tells me that they don't know the details. Emmet can go off and there'll be no surprises at the other end."

Anna saw his reasoning. "What will you do?"

"I'll see Emmet off and then I'll deal with Billy."

Will you still fight him? Anna almost asked. But she didn't. She had no wish to hear the answer. "What shall I tell him?"

Stephen slumped lower in his chair, rubbing his forehead as if it pained him. "Nothing. Don't contact him again." He looked at Anna. "What did he mean, you aren't really married?"

"He was lying, that's all. Billy would say anything to get his own way."

"You're sure of it?"

Anna sighed. "Stephen, I was there when we spoke our vows."

He smiled a small resigned smile and got to his feet. He came to her, standing close enough for her to touch, close enough to make her skin tingle and her breath come short, close enough for her to feel the heavy tug of longing.

"I'll see you home, then," he said.

"No, I'll take a cab. But I'd like to see Emmet, to say good-bye."

"I'll send him over, and Davy, too. Davy's been missing your cooking, always complaining he's not getting enough to eat."

"Oh, that Davy."

She gave Stephen a smile, and his expression changed abruptly. He stared at her with a strange stricken look, as if he'd seen a ghost. He opened his mouth but seemed lost to speech.

"Stephen? What . . . ?"

But before Anna could say more, he turned on his heel and bolted from the room.

"Really, Mrs. Flynn, it's quite unacceptable, a gentleman calling so late in the evening. We discourage gentlemen from calling on our ladies, you know that perfectly well—"

"Please, Mrs. Tuttle." Anna tried to dislodge the landlady, who stood stolidly before her door. "It's an emergency, I'm sure of it. You see, there's been some trouble."

Mrs. Tuttle stepped aside, resigned and disapproving. "I expressed my concern to Mrs. Smith-Hampton, but she assured me that you were quite different from the normal Irish element,

Mrs. Flynn. Quite different indeed."

The rest of Mrs. Tuttle's words were lost to Anna as she raced for the staircase. Stephen had come. He'd come to claim her, to take her home. . . . Anna stopped herself. Oh, didn't she have the brains of a buttercup to think so, even to wish it, after all she'd said and done, after all he'd said to her? Surely he'd only come about her meeting with Billy.

Anna slowed to a walk and descended the stairs, feeling glum.

He stood in the middle of the plain, tidy sitting room. He looked at her, his eyes despairing, and Anna felt a shiver of terror race up her spine. "Stephen." She could manage no more than a whisper. "What in heaven's name happened?"

He appeared close to tears. "Rory."

Anna's heart plunged. "Oh, dear Lord!"

"He's gone. Run off."

"Run off!" Anna sagged with relief, her hand to her heart. Thank God, she thought. Thank God for sparing the boy, for not having him dead. "You frightened the life out of me."

"I've hunted all over." Stephen's voice was hoarse. "Davy, Mose, Emmet, all the boys are out looking. He's nowhere, not with the Currans, not with Peggy, not here. I even went after Billy, but he's got nothing to do with it." Stephen ran a hand down his haggard face. "I haven't seen him all day. I didn't think to worry till suppertime. Now, it's near ten."

Anna regarded him sternly. "And why didn't you come to me before?"

"Davy came by here earlier, asking about him. The landlady said she'd not seen him." Stephen's gaze dropped to the floor. "I said not to bother you."

Anna's temper stirred, but she held it in check. "Rory's gone missing and you didn't want to *bother* me?"

Stephen turned his hands out helplessly. "You think I'm neglecting him. I didn't want you on me, getting me down."

Anna glanced away. It hurt her that he hadn't come to her first, that he'd feared she would scold or blame him. She thought of the things she'd said, all spoken in anger, and regretted every word.

She looked back at his face and saw that his strength had ebbed. He was at a loss; he had no idea what to do.

"Am I so hard on you, Stephen?"

He attempted a smile. "You're not easy, Nan. You've never been easy."

The sadness in his voice was too much for Anna. She went to him and put her arms around his waist. She laid her head against his chest, longing to give him comfort. "It's a wonder you put up with me so long."

Stephen's big hands stroked her hair. "Put up with you?" He gave an empty laugh. "Without you, I don't know how to live anymore."

There was a weariness in his voice, as if he'd suffered a loss that was too hard to bear, that left him too tired to fight. It was as if he'd battled fate all these years with his fists, and he'd always won. Now he'd lost his son, and fighting would not be enough.

Anna tightened her arms around him. "Stephen, I'm so sorry."

His fingers slipped from her hair to her back. He pulled her in a huge, crushing hug that squeezed the breath from her. She felt his body tremble.

"Help me, Nan. Help me find my boy."

The kitchen was full of milling men who didn't seem to know what to do with themselves. Emmet's farewell gathering had turned into a search party. O'Mahony was there with some men Anna had never seen, and Davy and Emmet and Mose and men from the neighborhood. They'd been scouring the city, looking and asking, to no avail.

Peggy and her mother busied themselves at the range, stirring and pouring, keeping cups and plates full.

"Rory, the poor little scrap," Mrs. Cavanagh said to Anna. "He hasn't passed a happy day since you left."

Peggy looked angry. "It's those Curran boys. I know they're in on it."

Anna thought so, too. She went to Rory's room, opened and slammed drawers, pawed through clothes, counting the missing items—a few shirts, underwear, two pairs of stockings. She rifled through the fighter books. The only one missing was Stephen's. The packet of letters from his uncle Paddy was gone, as was the poster of Stephen that had hung over Rory's bed.

"Is any food missing?" Anna asked.

Stephen looked bewildered. "I don't know. We don't have that much food around anymore."

No wonder he ran away, Anna thought. "We'd best go see the Currans."

"I've been there. They say they know nothing."

"Those little devils are masters at lying."

"You think so?" Stephen appeared hopeful. "I got nowhere with them."

"They'll talk to me," Anna said.

On the way to the Currans, Anna mulled over what she knew. There was no doubt that Rory was trying to get back to Ireland and his uncle Paddy. The question was, where was he now—somewhere at sea or in hiding, waiting to sail? One thing was sure: the boy knew where to hide on a ship; he and the Currans had explored the *Mary Drew* down to the last cubbyhole.

The Currans' tenement house was bleak and noisy. Late as it was, the corridor resounded with children's voices, a man's labored coughing, a shrieking argument. Anna wrinkled her nose at the smell of grease and overflowing privies. It was no place for a child to grow, she thought.

Stephen banged on the door until Mr. Curran growled at them to go away.

"It's Mrs. Flynn, Mr. Curran," Anna called. "Forgive me for disturbing you, but could you please open up?"

There were voices and stirrings within, a baby began to cry, and then Mr. Curran, sleepy and disheveled, opened the door a crack. "Why, missus," he said, raising his lamp to look at her. "If ye've come for the boy, he's not here."

"I'm wanting to speak with Eddie and Mike, if you please, Mr. Curran."

Mr. Curran hesitated, glancing from Anna to Stephen.

Anna understood his reluctance to admit them to his over-crowded, underfurnished rooms, strewn with sleeping children. "I'll just come in for a moment," she said, pressing Stephen's arm, a signal for him to wait outside.

Mr. Curran stepped back. "My wife . . ." he began.

"Don't be disturbing your wife, now," Anna said as she slipped through the door. "Just those twins."

Mr. Curran headed off to a second room, his trouser legs visible beneath his nightshirt. It was dark in the room, but from the light of Mr. Curran's lamp, Anna glimpsed a bed in the corner where Mrs. Curran was soothing a baby.

"Is it Mrs. Flynn, then?"

"Yes, Mrs. Curran, it is."

"Bless you for caring about my Eddie and Mike. They were doing so well with you. Now they're getting up to their mischief again. The police are bothering me every day."

"I'm sorry for that. They're good enough boys at heart."

"That's what I'm telling myself, but he's always after them with the strap."

The lamp returned, followed by Mr. Curran and the twins in their tattered nightshirts. The boys' hair stood up in clumps, their fists dug at sleepy eyes. They tried to look sullen, but Anna saw smiles struggling to escape.

"You tell Mrs. Flynn the truth, now, you hear?" Mr. Curran said, giving the boys a shove toward her.

Anna held out her hand, drawing the boys off to a corner. They were none too clean, and their faces looked thin. Oh, she'd missed the little devils. She wished she could take them home and give them a bath and a hug and a big bowl of stew. Instead, she gave their father a look, a plea to keep his distance.

Anna crouched before the boys. "Now then, Eddie, Mike, where's Rory got himself to?"

"Nowheres," Mike said, wearing a little smile.

"Won't you miss him when he's back in Ireland?"

Mike looked surprised. "How'd you know about that?"

"I just know, that's all. Now, tell me where he is, so I can fetch him."

"Can't."

Anna looked at Eddie, who remained mute. She saw him give his brother a hard nudge.

"You're breaking my heart, the two of you," Anna said. "Rory's like my own boy, and now he's lost to me."

Mike gave her an accusing look. "Why'd you leave us, then? Why'd you leave Rory?"

"It has nothing to do with Rory. Or you boys, either."

"You comin' back?"

Anna studied the two of them. They were up to something, and she thought she'd best play along. "What if I did?"

The boys exchanged a look that signaled agreement. "We might tell you where he is," Mike said.

"Might," said Eddie, wiping his nose on his sleeve.

Anna ran her hands down each boy's arm. They were as thin as rakes. "You tell me where Rory is. We'll worry about the other later."

Mike stared at the floor, as if considering. Eddie cast him a worried look. "He'll kill us for telling."

"No, he won't," Anna said. "Rory's scared to death and wanting to come home right now. I'm sure of it."

Mike looked from Eddie to Anna, then seemed to come to a decision. "The ship *Thunder* at Peck's Slip," he said. "It's the one Emmet's going on tomorrow."

Anna gasped. "No one knows when Emmet's going or on what ship," she said in a harsh whisper. "It's a secret."

"*We* know," Eddie said proudly. "We all of us heard him 'n' Mr. Flynn talking."

"Good Lord, you little devils—"

"But we kept mum. We know all about the guns and all, but we didn't say nothing, did we, Mike?"

Mike agreed. "Didn't say nothing."

Anna thought how much Billy would give for the information these boys had known all along.

"Rory's going to England with Emmet to get the guns," Mike explained. "Then he's going with the guns back to his uncle Paddy."

Anna closed her eyes. "Saints bless us."

"We scouted out the ship one day when we was down there nickin' stuff off the docks. We got aboard and looked around."

Anna felt overwhelmed. If any boys deserved to be punished for their mischief, it was these two. But she gathered them into a hug, crushing them in her arms until they groaned and squirmed.

She released them and stroked their freckled cheeks. "It's time Rory's da went to fetch him."

"You'll be asking Mr. Flynn if you can come back, then?" Eddie asked.

"First we'll find Rory, treasure."

Anna returned the children to their father and said good night. In the dark, fetid hallway, Stephen was pacing. He turned abruptly when she stepped into the corridor. "What did they say, then?"

Anna leaned back hard against the door. The thought of what the boys had done made her almost giddy with fright. "He's on Emmet's ship. The *Thunder* at Peck's Slip."

Stephen lowered himself into the gloomy darkness of the *Thunder*'s between-decks. His nerves and muscles were tense, and there was a taste of fear in his mouth. He wanted to shout for Rory, to tear the ship apart. But Anna had warned him to go gently with the lad, and Stephen would do as she advised.

The hold stank of must and dampness and emigrant travelers long gone from their steerage bunks. Stephen raised the lantern the watchman had given him and peered into the darkness. The deck was filled with ship stores, spare sails and masts, coils of rigging. There would be only a score of steerage passengers on the voyage to England, the dockmaster had said, men going home to fetch their families.

"Rory." Stephen spoke strongly to keep the anxiety out of his voice. "Come along now, sport. I know you're here."

The response was silence, save for the squeak of timber as the *Thunder* swayed lazily in her berth. Stephen hung the lantern on a spike driven into the bulkhead and sat down on a wooden bunk.

"You frightened the life out of me, lad," he said into the darkness. "Out of all of us."

His hands were shaking. He rubbed them on his knees and thighs. He felt stupid talking to the walls, but he sensed that small ears were listening.

"We've got a hard fight coming up, and I need you. If you go back to Kilkenny, I'll be all alone." Stephen attempted a laugh. "How can I beat Maguire without your help, then? I'll bring you into the ring with me, you and Davy and Mose and Hammer. With all of you there, I'll have an easy time with Billy, I'll take my oath on it. How about it, sport? How about coming out and talking to your old da?"

The faint scratch and scurry of a rat sounded overhead. The ship's timbers groaned. The lamp's orange glow spilled and receded over the water casks with the swaying of the ship. Stephen waited, wondering if it was all for nothing, if he had lost his son for good. He thought of Rory's strong spirit, his pure and honest soul; he thought of how the lad had loved him. Rory had made him feel like the worthiest of men, decent and proud.

"I'll ask Anna to come back," he said. "You and me together, we'll get her back."

There was a rustling sound from behind two large water casks not fifteen feet away. Stephen's nerves jumped. Another rat, he told himself, not daring to hope. But then a small, accusing voice spoke from the darkness. "She won't come back. Not ever."

Relief rushed through Stephen's limbs. He gulped down his emotions, trying to steady himself.

"I know she won't come back," Rory said again.

"We can ask her, then, can't we?"

"She married Billy Maguire. You hate her for that."

"Hate her?" Stephen said in surprise. He had never once spoken against Anna to anyone. "Now, where did you get that notion?"

"You told me there's two kinds of women, the good ones like my ma and the bad ones. Like Anna."

Stephen's heart started a hard, slow pounding. He tried to remember what he'd said, so carelessly, so full of easy judgments.

"I know what happens when you're married." Rory's voice was muffled by his hideaway but still painfully clear. "Eddie and Mike said good women do it only to get babies, because the priest says they have to. Bad ones do it with lots of men. That's why you think Anna's bad."

A numbness settled over Stephen. He didn't know what to say.

"Don't you?" Rory asked.

Stephen shifted on the hard wooden platform and ran a nervous hand through his hair. He'd never felt so confused and embarrassed. "You'd better come out here, sport."

There was a good deal of rustling and bumping behind the water casks; then Rory stepped into the lamplight, dragging a sack made from one of Anna's tablecloths. He looked no worse for his adventures, save for dirty tracks of dried tears on his cheeks and tired circles under his eyes. Stephen forced himself to sit still, not to leap up and embrace his son.

"I don't hate Anna," he said.

"But you think she's wicked."

Stephen stared at his hands.

"You did that to her, the same as Billy Maguire did, the same as Spinner tried to do before she killed him. You made her wicked, Da, doing that, and then you blamed her for it."

Stephen opened his mouth to say that Rory was a child who couldn't understand such things. He wanted to explain that one day Rory would learn about judging women and choosing a worthy one for himself. He wanted to say that what went on between Anna and him was none of Rory's business. But he held his tongue. Somewhere within himself, Stephen knew that Rory was speaking something close to the truth, and that he would have to respond.

He watched the lantern swaying in the gloomy cavern between-decks and considered his feelings for Anna. He'd never admitted to anything other than sheer desire. Thinking of her now brought back the joy of being with her, the deep-down passion.

He looked at Rory. "Anna and I made each other happy," he said. "You see, sport, a man can hurt a woman, the way Spinner wanted to do, but he can also make her happy. I never hurt Anna. We were happy together."

Rory's accusing expression didn't change. Stephen reached out and drew him closer. He rubbed his hands up and down the boy's thin arms. "It's hard to figure, but you'll understand it when you get older. I promise you'll understand."

"You blame her for being married to Billy Maguire," Rory persisted. "It's not her fault she knew him before she knew us."

"You're right. It's not her fault." Nevertheless, thinking of her with Maguire stirred his deepest anger.

"You think she's not as good as my ma."

"Your ma was the best sort of girl." Stephen was beginning to tire of Rory's questions and accusations, but he forced himself to be patient. "She was like an angel; she was that good and pure."

"Were you happy with her, like with Anna?"

"Of course I was happy. She was your mother." But he knew he was lying. Rose hadn't made him happy; she'd made him miserable. Stephen stopped his thoughts before they veered into sacrilege. By God, he wouldn't turn his back on Rose.

He wouldn't deny her after the sacrifices she'd made, giving her body to him, giving up her life for his son.

"Uncle Paddy says my ma was so good she should have been a nun. He said she expected everyone to be as good as she was."

"She did at that," Stephen said.

"I'd rather have Anna, Da. I think Anna's better for us than my ma—"

"Listen to you!" Stephen jumped to his feet. "Your mother was a saint, she was that good. Anna can never be . . ." Sweat dampened his back. The hold was unbearably stuffy, so close he couldn't breathe. *Blast her to hell's flames*, he thought. Blast Anna and the lust he felt for her. The lust . . . the love. Oh, God, he loved her—not only in bed but in the kitchen and in the garden and out walking. He loved her with a lapful of lace and an armload of laundry, he loved her talking to Davy and Gil and scolding the boys. He loved her on the island, with her skirts blowing and her face smiling and at night, whispering in his ear. Anna wasn't a saint, and bless her for it. She was a decent and loving woman who understood him better than he understood himself, and when he took her in his arms, she made him feel like a god.

"I once heard Uncle Paddy and Gran talking," Rory said, his voice sorrowful. "Uncle Paddy said you weren't happy with my ma."

Stephen slumped down on the berth. Memories rushed into his mind before he could stop them—how it had been with Rose, how hard he'd tried to stifle his desire and crush his revolutionary passion, all for her. He'd been a young man, full of fire and lust and political fervor, married to a beautiful, pious girl whose family had given a wild orphan boy a chance at a decent life. She'd been innocent, and he'd taken her lustfully. He'd wanted to enjoy her, and he'd tried to make her want him. But she'd wept each time and prayed through the ordeal, killing his passion, making him angry. When the Brotherhood called, he'd defied her wishes. He'd taken the oath and gone. He'd wanted to go, desperately. It was a liberation to him, getting away from Rose's soft-voiced piety, her sacrificing sighs.

Then he'd returned and she was dead, leaving behind a screaming child and a final legacy—searing, consuming guilt.

Rose had always made him feel guilty—about his lust, the satisfaction he found in violence, his passion for revolutionary justice. When she died, that low-simmering guilt had risen to a boil, nearly driving him mad. He'd had no choice but to flee.

"Uncle Paddy told Gran you needed a lively, jolly girl to make you happy," Rory said.

Stephen rubbed his temples. Paddy had said that to him, too. "Find a good wife for yourself, Stephen," he'd said. "A mother for the boy. Find a girl who knows how to laugh and love you."

Anna knew how to laugh. And love him. She also knew how to scold him, but usually for good reason, and she never made him feel guilty.

Stephen looked at Rory. It was strange how the lad seemed to understand things that could baffle a grown man. "Let's go home, sport," he said. "Anna's waiting for us."

Rory lowered his eyes, his jaw stiffened in a stubborn line. It's not settled, Stephen thought. There's something more. "What is it, then?"

Rory ducked his head. "I don't want you to fight."

Stephen felt a jolt of surprise. Then he remembered his angry exchange with Anna in Battery Park, when she'd said that Rory was afraid he'd end up dead or like Hammer. He hadn't believed her; he couldn't imagine his boy not wanting him to fight.

He drew Rory between his knees, cupping his chin, forcing it up from his chest. "You were always after me to fight Billy Maguire."

Rory kept his eyes lowered. "That was before."

"Before Maguire whipped me so bad?"

Rory nodded. "It scared me."

"Didn't like seeing your old da busted up?"

"Not much." Tears welled up in Rory's eyes.

Stephen looked at his son's trembling lips, his tear-smudged cheeks, and words dried up in his mouth. The boy loved him, not for being a fighter but for something much more, something so precious Stephen didn't even know what it was.

Then he thought of Billy, of all he had done. He'd married Anna and deserted her. He'd stolen her money. He'd had her in his bed. He'd wrecked the Emerald Flame Saloon and betrayed the Irish cause. Could such outrages go unanswered? Stephen wondered. Could he, as a man, give up revenge and pride and honor, all for the sake of his son? Could he deny Billy's challenge and call off the fight, just because his boy loved him?

The answer came quickly.

"Let's say I tell Billy the fight's off," he said. "And I'll ask Anna to come back. How would that be?"

Rory attempted a smile, but instead tears fell from his eyes and slid down his cheeks. "She won't come back, Da. I know she won't."

Stephen drew the boy into his arms. "We'll see, then. We'll just have to see."

Chapter 28

❧

Anna jumped to her feet when they came into the kitchen. "Look at you," she cried, grabbing Rory. "Oh, you made us worry! God's ears are hurting from all the praying we've done. And you spoiled Emmet's party. . . ." She couldn't stop kissing him, pressing his face to her bosom, while he wriggled and complained. Not until she'd had her fill of hugs did Anna hold him at arm's length to look him over. She wet her fingers and rubbed hard at his cheek. "There's more dirt on you than in a potato patch," she scolded. "Davy'd better take you downstairs and give you a good scrub in the shower. And using my tablecloth for a sack!"

People gathered around, trying to get their hands on Rory. Mrs. Cavanagh pressed a cup of chocolate into his hand, while Mose and Emmet cuffed him affectionately. Gil stumbled about, stone drunk; Peggy wept. Chocolate spilled, men jostled one another, and everyone hugged Rory and tickled him, while he blinked with happy exhaustion.

Anna watched, eyes blurred with tears of relief. Stephen slid his hand around her waist. His smile made her go soft inside. She reached for him, just to pat him, but then her arms were around his neck, her face pressed to his shoulder, and she began to cry. As voices buzzed about them, she clung to him, sobbing, feeling the tension melt out of her. He held her close, running his hands up and down her back. "Nan," he murmured into her hair. "It's all right now."

When he released her, she wiped her cheeks with her fingers. "Look at me, crying for happiness. Faith, it's good to have him back."

Stephen appeared fresh after the ordeal. He looked as he had during those weeks before Billy, when they'd been together every night.

"Come to the front room, Nan. I have something to say to you."

He took her arm. Anna pulled back, suddenly apprehensive. She didn't want to be alone with Stephen; she felt too weak, too vulnerable. "I'd best be getting Rory to bed."

"Peggy will see to him."

His expression was so adamant that she gave in and allowed him to lead her down the hallway.

In the bedroom, a pitcher of wilted flowers sat on the dresser. The brass bed was unmade and sorely in need of a polishing, and everywhere the dust was an inch thick. Anna ran her finger over the dresser top and clicked her tongue.

Stephen leaned against the wall beside the window, watching her. "We want you to come back to us, Nan."

Anna tried to feel nothing; she tried to ignore her throbbing heart. She reminded herself that the joy Stephen brought her had also caused terrible pain.

"Nan?"

Anna gave him a sharp look. "How can I come back when I'm married to Billy Maguire?"

"We want you. Rory and I agreed to it."

He was asking her to continue living a lie. "So you think it's that easy. Just come back, with no thought to my marriage vows."

"We can't live without you."

He rested against the wall, his rolled-back sleeves showing his muscular forearms covered with golden brown hair. Something was different about him, Anna thought. Even with his thick late-night stubble of beard, there was a softness about his face that she hadn't seen before.

"And what about Rose?" Anna asked, anticipating an explosion.

"She's dead, darling. Rose is dead."

"I know she's dead!" Anna cried, bewildered by his calm

manner. "But she's alive in your heart. Don't I see it in your face when you compare us? Don't I hear it in your voice, shouting at me not to mention her name?"

Stephen looked pained. "Forgive me for that."

"When you compare me to Rose, you make me feel . . . worthless." Tears started up, and she wiped her eyes.

"Rose made me feel that way myself."

Anna stared at him, startled.

"She was a good girl," he said. "Everything I've said about her was true. But she was too good for me."

Anna bristled. "And I'm not?"

Stephen laughed, an easy laugh and surprising, because he never laughed about Rose. "No, Nan, you're not too good for me. You're just like me, no better, no worse. Neither one of us is as good as Rose, but she never had to suffer or make hard decisions like you and me."

Anna twisted her fingers together, watching him, suspicious.

"To tell the truth, she made me miserable."

Anna drew in a breath. "Never!"

Stephen shrugged. "I never admitted it to anyone, even myself, until tonight. She made me feel bad about everything. She didn't want me fighting. She didn't want me in the Brotherhood. I couldn't be with her in bed without feeling ashamed."

"Why, you're never ashamed in bed."

"Not with you."

Anna glanced away, thinking of their leisurely kisses, the gasping excitement. Never once had he forced her to do anything against her will. She couldn't imagine a woman not wanting him.

"It's more than bed, how I feel about you. The way you are, the way I am—we're the same. You understand me better than anyone in this world or out of it. I can't let you go."

He was courting her again, luring her back. "And what of Billy? I'm his wife."

"You may have been, once. But no more."

"Till the grave, Stephen. I'm his wife forever."

"You're mine, Nan. You and Rory and me, if one of us goes missing, it throws everything off. It's like we keep each other in balance, the three of us."

Anna went to stand beside him. The barriers in Stephen's heart had crumbled; her own were as fragile as glass. "There's to be four of us. I saw Mrs. Smith-Hampton's doctor."

He was silent for a moment. "You told me there would be no babies."

"I didn't think I was able."

Stephen slid his hands around her waist, down her belly. Anna leaned back against him, letting him feel where his child grew. He kissed her hair, her neck. She closed her eyes and let his hands caress her, all over the front of her, tempting her, making her hot.

"Why didn't you tell me before?" His voice was husky.

"I was afraid of Billy. I was afraid he'd claim the baby."

"He'll be claiming nothing of ours."

Anna turned in his arms. "Are you sure, then?"

"Billy is a spy against his own kind, Nan. His life is worth nothing if word gets out. So don't be worrying about him. He won't be bothering us about anything."

Anna thought of the baby she carried, her family's only legacy, the bit of life that would tell the tales of them all. A baby fathered by a man who was not her husband.

As if he read her thoughts, Stephen said, "Do you think your da and mam would want you to be alone rather than with the father of your baby?"

Anna leaned her forehead against his shoulder. It pained her to think of her parents knowing the sins she'd committed. But her mam had always said that a girl should choose for a husband a man who would best provide for her babies. And Da—he would surely have wanted her to find happiness after all her trials.

"They would tell me to stay with you."

Stephen stroked her hair. "I thought so."

His kiss was gentle at first, then more urgent. Anna clung to him, welcoming his familiar taste, the feel of heat and muscle beneath her hands. Stephen's heart pounded against her own, and deep within herself she sensed the secret heartbeat of their child. She felt a happiness that was pure, beyond doubt, almost beyond feeling.

He undressed her with kisses. His lips touched everything he laid bare. When she caressed him, he took her hands away.

"This time is for you, Nan. All for you."

He laid her on the bed, on linen that glowed in the lamplight, and looked at her. He made love to her with sweet words, with kisses and caresses, until her hazy pleasure grew to a knife-edge of need.

"Stephen." She could barely gasp out his name.

He throbbed with heat, yet he didn't go to her. He wouldn't be taking until he'd had his fill of giving. He listened to her soft, despairing sighs, he watched her beautiful body blush and writhe. He knew that Anna's pleasure was his greatest joy, and his heart overflowed with love.

When her hips sought him, he went to her blindly, bunching her hair in his hands, driving as deep as he dared. She grasped him with thighs and arms, greedy for his hard thrusts, for the fainting delight that was familiar yet ever new.

And it came in glorious waves, an ecstasy of sensation that seemed to go on forever, that left her sobbing for air.

They lay together, entwined and exhausted, the throbs of pleasure fading. Stephen stroked her cheek. "I love you, Nan."

The look in his eyes told her it was true. He'd never said it before, even during their most tender moments.

"I know you do."

"I loved you from that first time behind the cow shed. I saw you and knew I wanted to keep you safe and happy. And, Nan, I swear to you I'll do it. Nothing will hurt you again."

The next morning Stephen rose before dawn to accompany Emmet to the *Thunder*. At the wharf, Emmet was bursting with pride and excitement. He shook Stephen's hand a half-dozen times, and they laughed and slapped each other's arms and ducked each other's punches. When the steam whistle blasted, Stephen caught Emmet in a giant embrace. The lad was headed for danger, but Stephen could do nothing more than wish him Godspeed.

He walked home through the sticky dawn of another day, watching the city awaken. He'd hardly slept a wink all night, what with Anna in his arms and thinking about getting Emmet off. He'd gotten up in the night to look in on Rory. He'd stroked the lad's hair, and suddenly Rory had laughed in his sleep, a short, gleeful laugh. The sound of it had done something to Stephen, something warm and healing that made him want to weep with gratitude.

He'd sat by his son's bed in the darkness and thought about their conversation in the hold of the *Thunder*. He thought of Rory's accusation that he'd seduced Anna and then blamed her for her wickedness. Perhaps it was true, perhaps not. But one thing was sure—he had held Anna up to Rose's standards so he wouldn't have to hold himself up. He'd blamed Anna for her shortcomings so he wouldn't have to consider his own. Just figuring that out had lifted a burden from Stephen's soul. In fact, he'd shed so many burdens that he felt lighter than any man with all his limbs and his wits had a right to feel.

As he passed through the Fourth Ward, Stephen bought a bunch of flowers for Anna. He considered going to the Big Six, but he decided to deal with Billy later. He wanted to come in on Anna tousled with sleep. The memory of her last night, so sweet and eager, made him quicken his step. He ran up the stairs to the flat and was relieved to find the place quiet.

He went to the kitchen and stuck the flowers in a pot, then headed for the bedroom. Anna opened her eyes when he entered. "Is he gone, then, our Emmet?"

Stephen bent over her and kissed her. "He's on his way."

Anna sat up, yawning, and gave a mighty stretch. She was naked beneath the covers, and the sight of her lifting her arms and arranging her hair made Stephen come alive with longing.

"Look at you," he said, sitting down on the bed. "So beautiful." He put his hands on her breasts and kissed between them, and then her throat and her mouth, until he was hot and full with desire. He reached beneath the covers.

When he touched her, Anna rumpled his hair. "Oh, aren't you greedy, then?"

Stephen hesitated. "It's all right to do it so much with the baby in you?"

"Now's a good time to ask," she teased. "After last night."

"I didn't think of it then."

Anna ran a finger along his cheek and across his lips. "It's all right, I'm sure of it." She gathered him close, rubbing her palms on his back, feeling his warmth through the damp cloth of his shirt. She could smell the scent of last night's passion, and she thought how lovely it was to have him again.

He drew back. "I'll be going to see Maguire."

"Oh, no, Stephen. Not today."

He propped himself up on his elbow and looked at her. "I have to tell him you're staying with me, don't I? And that the fight's off."

They spoke of Billy and Rose easily now, without anger or shame. It was a relief, Anna thought, to feel so free. "I guess you'd best do it, then."

"And there's a few more questions he'll have to answer."

"About spying?"

"That and more."

Anna played with Stephen's hair, curling a strand around her finger. "Poor Billy. He's got ambition enough to make the sun rise, but at heart he's a bungler."

"How he can give you up is beyond me."

"Oh, he doesn't want me, Stephen, not really. He doesn't care about having a woman. He wants to be admired by men. He married me because his mates thought I was pretty and they wouldn't have minded taking me for themselves. For Billy, winning me was like grabbing the biggest cake on the plate."

Stephen leaned over to kiss her breast. "If you're a cake on a plate, darling, then I'm a starving man."

"Be quiet yourself," Anna said, feeling a delicious shiver. She reached down to find the fastening of his trousers.

Anna cleaned all morning, scrubbing and dusting until the windows sparkled and the furniture gleamed. She made Davy his favorite breakfast—white shop bread soaked in hot milk and flavored with sugar and cinnamon. While a stew simmered on the stove, she peeled a bowl of ripe, rosy peaches for a cobbler. Gil stopped by, red-eyed and irritable from last night's whiskey. While Anna worked, he drank coffee and yawned into the newspaper. After a second trip to Mrs. Cavanagh's for groceries, Rory ran off to find the Currans, reminding Anna to make an extra cobbler for Eddie and Mike, who would surely be starving.

Anna sang to herself as she mixed the dough. She was back in her bright, cheerful kitchen, back in Stephen's arms and in his bed. Rory was safe and happy, and tonight her neighbors would fill the kitchen to welcome her home.

But beneath her contentment there ran a current of anxiety. After breakfast Stephen had gone off to see Billy. He'd promised there would be no fighting, but there was no predicting what would happen when the two of them got together.

"Look at that, now, Gil. Isn't that a fine-looking cobbler?" Anna stepped back to admire the neatly tucked dough.

Gil averted his eyes. "The sight of it makes me sick."

"Aren't you as sour as lemons?" Anna said. "If you drank tea instead of whiskey, you'd be in a better temper in the morning. Here, let me mix you some soda and water."

Gil rubbed his face. "It's good to have you back, angel. No one takes care of me like you do."

"If you stopped that drinking, you'd find a good wife. Why, you're as clever a man as there is, and not bad to look at. I'll see about finding you a girl, if you give up the whiskey."

Gil looked wistful. "Show me the girl and I'll consider it."

Just as Anna put the cobbler in the oven to bake, she heard footsteps on the back stairs. Stephen. She wiped her hands on her apron and looked up with anticipation.

Stephen stepped into the kitchen. "Nan—"

Gil was on his feet. "By the living Jesus! Maguire, what in hell are you doing here?"

Anna took a step backward, her hand at her throat. Billy stood in the doorway, his eyes darting about.

"It's all right, Nan," Stephen said. "He's come to talk to you." Stephen jerked his head toward the door. "Gil, it's best you leave us."

"Hell, Stephen, you can't expect me to miss a trick like this."

Stephen gave him a hard look. "I said clear out."

Gil got up from his chair and glanced at Anna. "If you need help, angel, just shout. I'll be right outside." He brushed past Billy, shaking his head.

"Billy might like a cup of tea, Nan," Stephen said.

Anna moved as if in a trance. "Forgive me," she said, pulling out a chair. "You're welcome in our home, Billy."

Billy's cocky demeanor had vanished; he looked contrite, even frightened.

Anna glanced at Stephen, longing for some explanation, but he gave her no more than a reassuring smile. She reached for the teapot on the dresser as Stephen said, "Go ahead, Maguire. Tell her what you told me."

Billy shifted his big shoulders. "We're not married, not really. Never were."

Anna felt a tremor, and her hands began to shake. Stephen took the teapot from her. "Sit down and hear him out, Nan."

Billy stared at the table as he spoke. "It was all a trick, marrying you. I did it on a wager. I only wanted to have you there behind the rocks where we used to sit on the strand. The lads said you'd never let me, and when you wouldn't, they thought it a grand joke. I got mad and decided to go them one better and marry you."

Anna felt heat flow into her cheeks. She gripped her elbows and forced herself to be calm. "We *were* married," she said, her voice a whisper. "For whatever reason, we were married."

Billy squirmed and ducked his head. "I'm not Catholic."

"What?" Anna turned to look at Stephen. He stood behind her, arms folded, absorbed in Billy's account.

"I'm not Catholic," Billy said again. "My great-granddad quit the church. He said 'twas the only way to avoid the laws that kept a man of the old faith from getting anywhere in Ireland. He brought up his boys Protestant, and that's the way it's been in our family ever since." He glanced at Anna. "When it came time to marry you, I paid the clerk at St. Brigid's two pounds to forge a baptismal certificate for me. Father Rooney hardly looked at it."

Anna felt prickles run up her back. "What does it mean, then?" But she knew what it meant: in the eyes of the church, she and Billy had never been married. It meant that their marriage had never existed.

Anna's confusion was turning to anger. All her beliefs about herself were upside down. She thought of those nights in Billy's bed, the despair when he left her, the guilt over Stephen, the remorse for living in sin. It was all for nothing. Her marriage had been a lie, a wager among a gang of Dublin toughs.

Before she knew what she was doing, Anna was on her feet. She leaned across the table and, with all her strength, slapped Billy's face. The blow caught him by surprise, tipping him in his chair. The force of it sent a stinging pain from Anna's palm up her arm.

Stephen grabbed her from behind. "That's enough, Nan."

Billy jumped up, his fists doubled. "By Christ, I don't take that from a woman."

"Shut up, Maguire," Stephen said.

Anna writhed in Stephen's arms, trying to break free. "Have you no shame in you?" she screamed at Billy. "I swear by the black curses you belong in hell!"

"Anna! Stop it, now. I'll not let you go until you have proper use of yourself."

She was boiling with rage. She wanted to get her hands on Billy's throat and choke the life out of him.

"Stone mad, that's what she is," Billy said, adjusting his tie. "You're welcome to her, Flynn. Bold as a cat's claw, with a mean temper, too."

"Gil!" Stephen shouted.

The back door opened and Gil poked his head in. "Need some help there, laddie?"

"Show Maguire out."

Gil looked at Anna and his eyes popped. "Jesus, Maguire. Looks like she's a mind to take your life."

"May the devil scald you for all time!" Anna cried as Billy hurried out the door. She pushed Stephen away and fled to the bedroom, slamming the door behind her. She sat on the bed, trembling, cold with shock, trying to absorb the meaning of it all. She'd cleaned Billy's home and cooked his meals and mended his shirts. But worst of all, she'd lain with him whenever he wanted. She'd thought she was fulfilling the holy sacrament of marriage, when all she'd been doing was acting like a whore.

Stephen came in. "Nan, let it go, now. It's all in the past."

"I'd like to kill him!"

Stephen sat beside her and touched her shoulder. Anna turned away. "He hurt me. He spoiled my life."

"He didn't spoil your life. It's all in the past, what he did. You've got a new life now, a bright one, with me and Rory and a new baby coming. Don't let what Maguire did make you bitter."

Anna dropped her head into her hands. Wasn't this what she'd prayed for? Something that would free her from Billy so she could truly be Stephen's wife?

"In a week we'll be going to Saratoga," Stephen said. "You'll rest and grow fat and watch the horse races with Gil. We'll have a fancy hotel room to ourselves, and there'll be no work for you, though I don't know how you'll manage without a gang of men to look after."

Anna barely heard Stephen's words. Not married to Billy, *never* married to Billy. In the space of a second, she'd become a different person with a different name. She had never been Anna Massie, only Anna Kirwan. And Anna Flynn. Abruptly she realized that her marriage to Stephen was real, while the marriage to Billy had been a charade.

"Nothing is spoiled, Nan," Stephen was saying. "We'll be together always."

He took her hands away from her face and held them in his own. He didn't do more, and for that she was grateful. She needed time to sit quietly and think.

Gradually she became aware of the smell of simmering stew, the sweetness of baking peaches. She thought of Rory coming to dinner with the Currans, and Davy and Mose, too.

"I've got work to do," she said, getting to her feet.

Stephen followed her to the kitchen. She took the kettle of stew from the fire and picked up a pile of plates. As she laid the table, she thought of Stephen's words and knew he was right. No matter how angry she was at Billy, she mustn't be wasting her time with bitterness and curses. She shouldn't be thinking of the past when so much was happening in the present.

"Peggy says now that Emmet's gone, Davy will propose any minute," she said. "And Gil said he'll stop drinking if I find him a pretty girl to marry. Oh, Mrs. Smith-Hampton sent a note by. She's got a mind to have me make all her baby things."

Stephen watched her. "Well, then. There's lots doing, isn't there?"

Anna stopped her work and looked at Stephen. "What made him confess? Sure, he didn't do it willingly."

"I used a few threats."

"About his spying?"

"There's evidence from Shaw, and from others as well. All it would take is for me to spill it and Billy would be a dead man. He knows it."

Anna frowned. "How did you know he married me falsely?"

"Didn't he say so himself? He wanted information about the guns in exchange for your freedom. I told him to tell me the truth about your marriage or I'd put the word out about his spying. He blustered a bit, but he didn't fight long. He's agreed to stay in New York to see the annulment through. It'll take time, Nan, getting proof from Ireland. But one day it will be over, and then Billy will be leaving. He says he's always yearned for California."

Anna finished laying the silver. She took the pot of fresh flowers from the kitchen dresser and placed it in the center of the table. "He always spoke of California."

"He knows that if he makes a run for it, we'll track him down. The Brotherhood doesn't take kindly to spies, and one day he'd end up with a bullet in him, or a knife. He's not so brave, our Billy, when it comes to that."

Anna took a bowl and ladled in some stew. Already her heart was lifting, her anger fading. "And then we'll be married properly. In the church."

"In St. Patrick's itself, I promise." There was a husky tenderness to Stephen's tone and a smile on his face that reflected deep into his eyes.

Anna set down the bowl and looked at him, the last of her anger melting away. "Oh, Stephen," she said.

She started for his arms, but stopped when she heard the pounding of feet on the stairs, the babble of young voices.

"God bless us! It's Rory and the Currans." She reached for another bowl. "Go now and call Davy and Mose. And Gil, too, if he can eat. And you wash up yourself. I don't want my stew getting cold."

Stephen's hands circled her waist. "Let them wait. All of them."

"But Stephen—"

"Kiss me."

He drew her close and kissed her. And then he kissed her again. Anna clung to him, tangling her fingers in his hair. "The dinner . . . " she whispered against his mouth. "The boys . . ."

"Be quiet yourself," Stephen murmured, and Anna was quiet. His lips were warm and open, his great arms clasped her tight. He kissed her until she was limp with happiness, until she slipped into that private place they shared, that belonged to them alone.

When the kitchen door burst open, and Rory and the Currans tumbled in, shouting and jumping, Anna didn't hear a thing.

Epilogue

"Indian summer."

Anna repeated the expression. It was new to her, but it had a lovely sound, perhaps because the season was lovely, with the red and gold tints of foliage, the clear air, and the sun's kindly warmth.

"That's what they call it," Stephen said. "Though what it has to do with Indians, I don't know."

Anna rested her head against the wicker back of her porch rocker and looked at him. He was as hard and brown as a native himself after a summer of hammering and sawing and sweating in the sun. He'd brought a gang of men out to the island to get their cottage started, then finished it himself, with help from Davy and Mose and the three boys. Now it was early October, their last visit of the season.

"I wish we could stay one more day, Stephen."

He reached across the space that separated their two chairs and caught her hand in his own. "Do you, now, Mrs. Flynn? Why, I'd wager you're tired of your honeymoon and ready to get back to Rory and the Currans and all those friends you've been missing."

Anna gave his hand a squeeze. She did miss Rory and her busy life on Brace Street, but she wasn't ready to give up her time alone with Stephen. Her worries were behind her, as was her false marriage to Billy Maguire. She was Mrs. Flynn, with a priest's blessing, entitled to all the pleasures a marriage allowed, and she couldn't seem to get enough of them.

Anna looked out over the sunlit blue waters of the Sound. She'd told Stephen she wanted a porch to sit on, where she could work on her lace and keep an eye on the children splashing in the sandy cove. He'd built her a handsome one that ran around two sides of the place and had sturdy posts from which to swing a hammock. Yesterday they'd spent some time in that hammock. The memory of it made Anna smile.

"The launch will be here soon," she said. "I've yet to pack Catherine's things."

She looked at her rosy pink daughter, bulging with milk, nestled in her da's thick brown arms, fast asleep. It had been a year of blessings, Anna thought, but Catherine's birth last March was more than a blessing; it was a miracle.

Stephen gave the baby a jiggle and smoothed her fine reddish-gold curls. "She's a lucky girl to go on a honeymoon with her mam and her da."

"She's the luckiest girl in the world," Anna said. "Why, she gets so much attention she has barely a moment to herself. If it's not Rory's lap she's bouncing on, it's Gil's knee or Mose's shoulders. And now that Peggy's expecting, she can't keep her hands off Catherine. Even Mrs. Smith-Hampton's got designs on her. She's always after me to bring Catherine up to visit, so she and little Adam can gurgle and stare at each other."

Stephen looked proudly at his daughter. "The sparring room lads fancy she's the prettiest girl in all of New York."

Anna smiled to herself, thinking that Stephen wouldn't be so pleased about that when Catherine was grown.

"An Irishman always has an eye for a pretty girl," Stephen went on. "Why, I recall a red-haired lass on a ship once. She had a way about her that set me afire. Turned out she had some fire in her, too. It's downright shocking sometimes, the things she gets up to."

They exchanged glances that needed no words. The tease in Stephen's eyes faded, replaced by another emotion, breathtakingly familiar. "Nan," he said, his voice gone husky. "I'd say let's stay one more day."

"Why, I wouldn't mind," Anna said, letting him think it was his idea.

He was on his feet so fast his rocker nearly tipped over. He eased Catherine into Anna's arms.

"I'll go over to the dock and tell them to come back special for us tomorrow."

Catherine opened her huge blue eyes. She looked up at Stephen and grabbed at his fingers. He pinched her fat cheek, making her laugh.

"I'll play with you when I get back, darling," he said. "Then I'll be playing with your mam." He bent down and gave Anna a long, thorough kiss.

Anna watched from the side porch as he ran up the hill, his strong legs pumping. At the top he turned to look back. Anna held up the baby, and Stephen waved. She could see his smile, young and eager as a boy's, and she thought what a blessing this man was to her, this man who had given her a new life and taught her how to love.

The steam whistle blasted, signaling the arrival of the launch. Stephen turned and ran again, disappearing over the crest of the hill.

Author's Note

During the nineteenth century many Irish-Americans dreamed of a successful invasion and liberation of their homeland. In 1858 revolutionary groups organized in Ireland and New York. The American branch, named the Fenian Brotherhood by its founder, John O'Mahony, aimed to provide political, financial, and military support to its counterpart in Ireland. Thousands of Irish-American men organized in military companies, preparing for the day of reckoning with the English foe. But before an operation could be mounted, the American Civil War broke out, and the Fenians fought a different war, serving both the Union and the Confederacy.

Emerging from that conflict as hardened veterans, the Fenians sent seven thousand soldiers to invade Canada in 1866. They planned to hold the Dominion hostage until Ireland was free. The invasion failed, as did an 1867 rising in Ireland led by former Confederate officers.

The revolutionary movement on both sides of the Atlantic was rife with informants and weakened by political quarrels. Through it all, the majority of Irish-Americans clung to the hope of a peaceful solution to Ireland's troubles.

449

National Bestselling Author
PAMELA MORSI

"I've read all her books and loved every word."
—Jude Deveraux

WILD OATS

The last person Cora Briggs expects to see at her door is a
fine gentleman like Jedwin Sparrow. After all, her more
"respectable" neighbors in Dead Dog, Oklahoma won't
have much to do with a divorcee. She's even more
surprised when Jed tells her he's just looking to sow a few
wild oats! But instead of getting angry, Cora decides to get
even, and makes Jed a little proposition of her own...one
that's sure to cause a stir in town—and starts an unexpected
commotion in her heart as well.

___0-515-11185-6/$4.99

GARTERS

Miss Esme Crabb knows sweet talk won't put food on the
table—so she's bent on finding a sensible man to marry.
Cleavis Rhy seems like a smart choice...so amidst the
cracker barrels and jam jars in his general store, Esme
makes her move. She doesn't realize that daring to set her
sights on someone like Cleavis Rhy will turn the town—and
her heart—upside down.

___0-515-10895-2/$4.99